The Third Watch

A Novel

Roger Damon

Photographs and cover design by Roger Damon

LIBRARY OF CONGRESS
CATALOGING-IN-PUBLICATION DATA

Damon, Roger.
The Third Watch / Roger Damon

ISBN 9781936711383

Railroad Street Press
394 Railroad St., Ste 2
St. Johnsbury, VT 05819

Acknowledgements

My thanks to the Honorable Madeleine M. **Kunin, Vermont's 77th Governor (1985 – 1991)** and <u>United States Ambassador to Switzerland</u> from 1996 to 1999. That's when WJC was negotiating with the government and Swiss banks about dormant Jewish World War II bank accounts, whose owners did not survive WWII – and for whom there were no death certificates. One must assume these discussions brought up the matter of gold bullion from Nazi Germany that Switzerland had accepted for "safekeeping".

Mrs. Kunin gave me insight on how to conclude the story.

We've tried to set the tale in real places – some of you may recognize familiar haunts – the lake is real, but the chalet is not. Any similarity of my characters to real persons is an aberration of your mind, not mine . . . and any episode that seems familiar to you is in the same category.

The technologies involved in deep diving were patiently explained by Chris Whipple of Colchester, Vermont, a PADI Master SCUBA Diver. Thanks, Chris, I'll just stay with snorkeling. Carl Potter of Essex, Vermont, was my first reader, and I followed his advice on editor selection.

And to my editors – Kay Garrett in Dallas: thank you for releasing me from the entrapment of adjectives, and to Gina Logan of Norwich University for stifling my verbosity. Steve Tuttle of TASER International advised me on the relative safety of the high voltages of Taser projectiles vs. explosive vests worn by people we encounter in the story . . .

Last, thanks to my wife, Doris, for her enduring and long-suffering support, her encouragement and understanding of my long hours at the keyboard.

Roger Damon   St. Johnsbury, Vermont
5/6/2014

Prologue

Vienna, Austria – 1955

Near dusk on a cool February afternoon, a man strolled out of a side door of the American embassy. Clean-shaven, he seemed an ordinary businessman in the mid-forties. He'd thrust his hands into the pockets of his long dark green loden overcoat. His Tyrolean hat sported the whisk-broom of a Gemsebart; the "goat's beard," whipping in the wind, suggested that he was a successful chamois-hunter. He was not. Nor was he an ordinary businessman.

A tan Ford Taunus, with Austrian "W" plates indicating it was registered in Vienna, pulled up as he reached the curb. He got in; the little car accelerated quickly, joining the light flow of traffic on Vienna's *Ringstrasse*. After passing through a number of intersections, the driver picked his way to the Franz Joseph Kai, on the right bank of the Danube River. "Hang on," said the driver as he made a sudden turn onto the Schwedentor bridge, slowed for the Russian checkpoint and was waved through without inspection. The driver turned right and soon pulled into a parking spot overlooking the river and looked in his mirror. "Doesn't look like we've been followed."

"Time for me to hit the road."

"Here's the bike key. Your clothing's in the pilot's cabin. Checked the peat boat earlier, so everything's ready. I'll wait there. You know the signals. Good luck, Andrew, see you Wednesday -- if not, then Friday for sure."

The two men shook hands. The passenger got out of the car, opened a gate and went down a gangplank to where one of the Danube River cruise boats was moored for the winter. He waved at the car's driver and went into the pilot's cabin.

About an hour after dark fell, the same man, now dressed in the worn and threadbare clothing of a typical "DP" – displaced person – left the boat, went back up to the street and unlocked an ancient Puch motorized bicycle leaning against a railing on the top of the wall. A pair of pants clips hung from the handlebars; he folded the cuffs of his pants around his legs, installed the clips, mounted the bike and pedaled it away, gradually coaxing its engine to smoking, sputtering life.

This man was an American named Andrew Henderson. His father had come to America from Scotland in 1904 with his bride. His mother was fluent in English, German, Slovakian and Polish as well as her native Czech. Her only son began talking earlier than most and had inherited her own ear for foreign tongues, so she taught him these languages.

Graduating from Harvard in 1939, he traveled that summer with his mother to Austria and Czechoslovakia, touring crystal and porcelain enterprises while perfecting his language skills. He saw the rising power of National Socialism in Germany. On his return to the United States, Andrew applied to the State Department as a multi-lingual interpreter. Quickly flown to the American Embassy in Berlin, he was assigned as an "assistant to the Under-Secretary." After his recall and the closing of the Embassy in December 1941, he was transferred to the State Department's Office of Special Services, which became the CIA after the war ended. During a 1947 tour of duty in Washington, he married and was posted to Vienna with his new bride. There, two sons were born – first Robert in 1948, then Bruce a year later. They'd lived with him in a small apartment near the Embassy. Accustomed to his frequent absences, his family did not know that the last time they'd ever see him was at Sunday dinner, earlier on this cool February day.

* * * * *

The Puch, its tiny engine popping and moaning, followed the Danube downstream on the left bank. The tan Taunus had departed – a signal to Andrew that he had neither been followed nor observed by anyone interested in his activities. The challenge at this point was avoiding potholes – the motorized bike's headlight was meager.

After about three kilometers of jolting through the dark and rising mist, Andrew saw the Taunus about a hundred meters ahead of him, parked against a wall. Reaching down, he turned his headlight off – then on again. The driver stepped on his brake pedal, flashing the stop lights briefly, telling Andrew that there were no obvious observers. He killed the engine, coasted to a stop, the headlight dimming and going out. Leaning the machine against a tree, he removed the pants clips and hung them back on the handlebar. He looked around, and then walked down a ramp leading to another stone platform just above the water, where a river-boat was moored for the night. It was a small freight-carrying craft, empty, waiting for daylight. In the morning, it was to start another of its twice-weekly trips to take on a load of peat and return with it to Vienna.

Andrew checked the mooring lines – they were secure. He walked across the gangplank and pulled it aboard. Moving around to the river side of the wheelhouse, he saw an ordinary bicycle with a small Czechoslovakian registration plate. Its tires were firm. He opened the single wheel-house door. Above him on the road, he heard a car door slam and the car's engine start. A moment later Andrew heard the motorbike's engine stutter into life.

"Luck to you, chap," he muttered. Entering the wheelhouse, he pulled a small flashlight from his pocket and looked around. Canvas curtains covered the windows. A worn rucksack was under a small chart table. A bunk under a window held a ratty-looking US Army sleeping bag. Engine controls, a cracked wooden stool and the steering wheel were placed before the forward window. A string shopping sack on the table held crusty rolls and a hard sausage wrapped in brown paper and a half-liter bottle of wine. He stepped out the door, closing it behind him. At the end of the short deck, a center gangway led him towards the bow, the empty space for cargo yawning beneath his feet. The day's winds had abated and the river mist was now soupy. He checked the knots in the bow mooring line. The distant streetlights were fuzzy and the warehouses across the street above him were dark and indistinct. While he couldn't see the train that clattered past on the other side of the row of warehouses, the blue flashes from its pantographs lit the sky. He returned to the stern to check the aft line's fastening.

Satisfied, he re-entered the wheel-house. Placing the rucksack on the bunk, he undid its worn fastenings and examined its contents. On top was a Thermos, wrapped in a dirty sweater. He pulled out an Austrian passport bearing his photograph; it was genuine, except that it hadn't been issued by the Austrian government. A pocket in the rucksack contained another passport – also Austrian, not with his picture, but one of a man two-thirds his age. Also in the pocket was a third well-worn Czech passport with his photo. The main cavity of the rucksack contained a Makarov PM – a nice 9mm semi-automatic pistol wrapped in a coarse windbreaker. Wool mittens; peat-stained work gloves; a moth-eaten wool beret. A battered Czech army canteen. A folding corkscrew. A telescoping aluminum cup. A large leather wallet with a modest supply of Czech and Austrian bills and coins. A pocket in the wallet held a photograph of a woman, her Slavic face caught in a worried frown. He held it in the flashlight's beam. Two worn letters of permission – one in German with both a Czech and a Slovakian translation, another in Russian Cyrillic characters – to transit the Czech-Austrian borders as a deckhand.

"Some bed-time communion," he muttered. "No milk and cookies tonight."

He removed the cap from the cup and telescoped it open. The wine bottle's cork popped obligingly and he poured the cup about half full. As he munched the roll, he considered what tomorrow was supposed to bring. First, the skipper – an older Austrian whose boat and business it really was – would appear mid-morning to go down the river. Mostly coasting with the current to save fuel, they'd cruise about forty-six kilometers downstream to where the Morava River joined the Danube. The Morava divided the Russian sector of Austria and Czechoslovakia. A few kilometers further, before they reached the city of Bratislava, they'd tie up next to a large peat field. Then he'd take the bicycle about fifteen kilometers to the north to a farm to meet the agent he controlled. Face-to-face contact like this was infrequent and its planning had taken time. There was little border control activity on the river itself. Patrol craft were few and this modest peat boat was well-known to them.

The uncommon part of this mission was that he'd be escorting the contact out of Czechoslovakia and back to Vienna. The time had come for that individual – a Czech – to disappear. There was work for him to do for – and ultimately in – America.

Andrew was the only person who could positively identify him, as they had met outside Bratislava in 1948, when Andrew had set him up as a source of valuable and reliable information. He fluffed up the sleeping bag. *I've done it before. I know this man. Simple transportation. If the bike gets a flat, I repair it. No real time pressure. If he doesn't show up, I go back to Vienna empty-handed.*

He checked the pistol's magazine; it held eight 9mm rounds and was full. Reinserting the magazine, he pulled back the slide and released it. He felt a satisfying *thump* as a bullet seated in the chamber. Turning the de-cocking lever, which safely lowered the hammer, he slipped the pistol under the belt of his pants, where a sewn-in pocket nestled it against the small of his back.

Andrew – or Nikolai as he thought of himself now – switched off the flashlight and crawled into the sleeping-bag.

Book 1

Zohor, Czechoslovakia

April, 1945

1

April 13, 1945
Zohor, Czechoslovakia

Zohor, a small Czechoslovakian village about twenty-three kilometers north of Bratislava, lies almost due north of the joining of the Danube and the Morava River. A small agricultural center, it lies in a flat plain seven to eight kilometers east of the looping Morava. It is also the home of a small glass factory which had operated for several generations, producing exquisite crystal creations of the glass-blower's art.

A few houses away from the glassworks, a sixteen-year-old boy prepared to leave for work.

"Rudi, did you hear a truck in the night?" his mother called.

"No, *Maminka.*"

"Another load of sand is promised. There's enough for only a few days more. We'll have to stop working if it doesn't come soon."

His father entered the small kitchen.

"Your mother's ears are sixty years old, my son, but I heard a truck about an hour before dawn. They'll probably have to stay until dark again – the American airplanes shoot at the *Ne'mec* (Germans) if they move in daylight. Anyway, it's time for you to get to work. Your *Maminka* and I'll come along shortly. Don't worry, my boy. We won't have to make lens blanks for them much longer."

Rudi hugged his father, saying, "I'll help Sergé with the furnaces this morning. He's teaching me how to use the blowing pipes for when we can make nice things again."

His father sighed as he watched his youngest son leave, and then turned to his wife.

"What a good boy he is, Sarah. We are so lucky to have had him – but this war has made him old and serious. He never got to be a little boy."

"Neither did Georgi, Lukas. We thought he'd be our only

son and then when the *Ne'mec* took him into their army six years ago . . ." She stopped talking. Lukas held her in his arms.

* * *

Rudi reached for his key to the factory office. To his surprise, the door was unlocked. He pushed it open to find two Nazi officers – a colonel and a major, both in combat uniforms and carrying the usual pistols.

The Major snarled, "Come in, boy. What do you want? Why aren't you in the Army? "

He brushed lint from his blouse, and then adjusted the double silver lightning flashes of the SS on the lapels.

"I'm here to help Sergei start up the furnaces, Herr Major."

"Sit down. You won't be starting them up today. Perhaps tonight. What's your name?"

"My name is Rudi Jezocova and they told me to stay here and keep working in the glassworks because it was more important than being in the army."

"Who else is coming to work today?"

"Sergé will be here any minute to start the furnaces, then in about an hour the rest will come - my father and mother and the others."

The major picked up a submachine gun from the table. "When this Sergé comes, you'll say nothing to him. We'll do the talking. What do your father and mother do and who are the others?"

"There should be two more men and three women, Herr Major. My father looks after everything, does what is needed. My mother works here in the office, her health is not good. Then there is my cousin, Anne-Marie and my other cousin, Silvie Jezocova. Melic Tzebik is a glassblower – he has a clubfoot and it's hard for him to walk. And Gustina – Gustina Hûsak - she's also a glass cutter with the diamond wheels. There are others, but they are away or sick."

The major said, "That's enough, *Herr Oberst.*"

"*Ja*, we won't have to drag anyone off the street." The colonel looked over his clipboard, where he had been jotting names. "This Sergé, Rudi – is he a strong man?"

"Yes," answered Rudi

The major slapped Rudi's head from behind. "That's 'Yes,

<u>sir</u>' kid."

Rudi nodded. "Yes, sir."

"We'll wait until everyone's here," said the colonel.

* * *

Rudi's father and mother were the last to arrive. "Rudi, why is there no smoke . . ." His father saw the German officers and stiffened.

"Sit with the others, Herr Jezocova," said the Major. "Effective immediately, you're no longer making lens blanks. We have watched your work for the past three years. You have served the Reich well. Now you'll be rewarded. You'll take part in a very special operation. For a few days, you'll be working at least eighteen hours each day. Nobody is to leave the building. You'll be helping the Reich on a secret mission of extreme importance."

The colonel said, "Frau Jezocova, here is a map of this village. A few families always have more than the rest of you. Isn't that correct?"

She nodded.

"Show me where they live and they'll provide food and blankets. We want you to be well fed and comfortable for this short period."

That afternoon, working under the Major's direction, the workers cleared the operating area of molds and completed lens blanks. The elderly furnace-tenders barred and bolted all the entrances from the inside, except for the door at the truck dock.

"Now, we start over with the new work," said the Major. "In the truck are thirty-two graphite crucibles, tongs to handle them and steel molds with many partitions. Set them up on your work tables. Frau Jezocova, you'll place the scales on a table. Rudi, you'll do the heavy lifting and load our new products into our truck. Sergé, you and Rudi will start the furnaces as soon as it's dark. Then we wait."

* * *

During the next three nights, trucks of every description arrived at the factory. Contained mostly in steel 20-liter pails, their cargos represented every conceivable use of fine gold. There were coins that had been sewn into a refugee's clothing, or hidden behind the lining of a shabby suitcase; coins and bullion from rifled bank vaults and office safes; thousands of wedding rings, tens of thousands of irregularly shaped chunks about the size of a garden pea, whole teeth and jewelry of every description – it did not matter.

This ghastly trove was but a small part of the total yield of the Holocaust – which had made Nazi Germany's SS the world's most successful profit-making military organization. This last stage of the Hitler's "Final Solution" was being carried out in several places throughout the occupied countries of Eastern Europe. Arrangements had been made for the entire shipment of gold to be taken into the heart of Switzerland. From there, it was to provide funding for the birth of the Fourth Reich.

The difference here in Zohor was that these two officers were renegades. They planned to carry out their assigned operation exactly as ordered – up to a point. Then, instead of joining the convoy, they'd take their single truck-load and disappear.

Over the next six days, working almost around the clock, the gold was melted down and cast into bars, using the graphite crucibles and steel molds the Germans provided.

Early in the evening, after the last ingot was weighed, numbered, stamped and loaded, the colonel took Rudi to the truck. The major unbolted and opened the large door; it gave Rudi his first glimpse outdoors in almost a week. It was nearly dark.

"Rudi, you said that you know how to drive."

Rudi nodded. The colonel opened the door on the driver's side. He backed into the seat, keeping his pistol centered on Rudi's chest.

"Slide in behind the wheel and start the engine."

Rudi sat behind the wheel and looked around. He pushed in the clutch pedal, moved the shifting lever through the gears and found neutral.

The colonel reached over and flipped a switch. "There, Rudi. Now you can start the engine. Use that shiny button on the floor."

The engine caught on Rudi's third attempt. Slowly, he let out the clutch pedal and heard the transmission spinning.

"Now, drive the truck out into the yard." He pointed his

pistol at Rudi's chest.

Rudi did as commanded, the truck groaning under its load. "Rudi, stop here. Good. Set the brake – it's there by your left knee. Now, take this uniform, get out and sit down."

Rudi opened the door, took the bundle of clothing and lowered himself to the damp ground, expecting the worst. Over the muttering of the truck's engine, he heard the factory door being slammed shut and bolted.

The colonel continued, "Take off those rags and put on the uniform."

As Rudi unbuttoned his shirt, the colonel opened his mouth to continue. Several short bursts of machine-gun fire and unintelligible screaming came from the building, followed by individual pistol shots. Then, silence. Rudi turned white; he felt a surge of vomit in his throat but choked it back.

"Rudi, we are not going to kill you. You're a bright young man, you speak good German, you know how to drive and you're strong. You'll be our driver - a new Wehrmacht corporal. You'll do exactly what we order. To start, stand up and put on the uniform."

Rudi reached for the heavy wool trousers.

The Major came out, seating a new magazine in his Schmeisser. He said, "They're all dead."

He flipped an open pack of cigarettes to Rudi. "Light one up for me, *Kind*. My hands are full." Numbly, Rudi took the matches from the pack and complied.

"Put on your tunic and cap and get in the truck. We'll see how good a driver you are. *Herr Oberst*, you watch Rudi while I get in the middle seat so I can show our new corporal where to find the steering wheel."

With a last glance at Rudi, the Major took the lighted cigarette, chambered the first round into the machine pistol and climbed into the cab.

* * *

At gunpoint, with the two officers beside him in the cab, Rudi drove the heavily-loaded truck over bad roads. As had been the case for the trucks that brought in the gold, travel during the day was impossible; Allied air power totally precluded it. Luck was with them.

They spent the first day on the outskirts of Vienna. There

was a routine; just before dawn, they simply commandeered a farmhouse, parked the truck in the barn, took Rudi's shoes and handcuffed him to the truck's steering wheel. While the colonel slept on a cot beside the truck, the Major scouted the best route around the damaged city.

Rudi's shock, fear and grief quickly turned to a deep hatred of the Nazi regime and all it represented. Frustrated and conscious of the constant pistol prodding his side, he bit his lip and concentrated on his driving. His thoughts ran in this vein: *"These men are savages. They killed my mother and father and everyone in the glassworks. I'll be watchful. I'll be careful. I'll do exactly what they tell me. I'll watch where they put this gold. Then I'll get it and use it against people like them. The war is over for these pigs. I WILL SURVIVE THIS."* Accordingly, he quickly did everything he was ordered.

As he struggled with the dangerous driving, he considered simply jumping out of the slow-moving truck and running away in the darkness. *But then, they'd still have the gold. If I crash the truck, other people would discover what was going on and that wouldn't work either."*

He concentrated on driving in the near-blackout conditions, with the major directing his every move.

It was midnight before Vienna fell behind them. The two officers talked openly, as if he was not present.

The colonel fretted, "The convoy is only a day behind us."

The Major responded, "They won't be moving any faster than we are. Besides, after Wels we'll be leaving the convoy's route anyway."

At every roadblock – and there were many – the major waved a *dossier* adorned with many stamps, screaming at the guards that they were on a mission ordered personally by *Der Führer.* They were quickly passed through. The SS insignia was more effective than any piece of paper. Each roadblock did offer an advantage, though; they were warned of detours, blockages and advised of the best route to follow to their next waypoint. The ultimate destination was never revealed to these advisors – just the next town.

When the colonel again voiced his concern about being followed, the major reminded him that only the two of them knew their destination.

The colonel asked – for the third time – "Are you sure the barge will be at Wolfgangsee?"

The major exploded, "Will you listen to me? I know the vessel. The captain even let me drive it. If there's no fuel, we have five twenty-liter cans. We don't need that much to get there. If there's no glow plug to start the engine, we'll use cigarettes. If the Americans sunk it, we'll go on to the salt mines in Berchtesgaden or Hallein. Stop your fussing, colonel. I've got enough to worry about keeping this *Kind* out of the ditches."

"Berchtesgaden? You'll take us right into the arms of the Americans! They're half-way down into Bavaria!"

"Don't worry, my dear Herr Oberst; the barge will be there. We'll get this thing unloaded, change our uniforms and become enlisted men, find the Americans and surrender. Remember, this whole thing was your idea."

"*I guess I know who's really in charge here,*" Rudi thought.

Inexorably, the kilometers stretched behind them. After Vienna came St. Pölten, then Melk, where they spent the day near a temporary bridge crossing the Enns River. At dusk, a roadblock officer approached the cab, waving his arms for them to stop. "*Herr Oberst,* there's a five thousand kilogram limit on axle loads," he shouted.

The colonel waved him off. "We are well below that limit. Drive on, corporal."

A guard at the bridge said, "You look too heavy – let me see inside."

Spittle sprayed from the major's lips. "I shall personally shoot you for treason," he screamed. "You're disobeying a direct order from *Der Führer.* You're disobeying orders from a major and a colonel in the Waffen SS." The man snapped to attention and saluted.

As Rudi steered onto the span, he noted a sign with a picture of a tank – "*Panzer verboten*" – 'tanks prohibited."

The Major said sarcastically, "Don't worry, Rudi, we aren't that heavy."

The bridge swayed and creaked. The major muttered, "No problem. Designed by Swiss engineers."

Bypassing Linz on the south, they made fairly good time

as far as Wels, where they again drove into a likely-looking farmyard and demanded shelter and food. The weather improved somewhat the next day. They learned this, shortly after dawn, after hearing an American twin-engine bomber screaming across the field, blasting a small bridge they had crossed an hour earlier.

The major asked Rudi, "Was that your first air raid?"

"No, Herr Major. We heard bombs exploding in Bratislava."

"Well, little soldier, that was your first one in uniform. Herr Oberst will see that you get a combat decoration, I'm sure."

The next night brought the news that heavy air raids had destroyed Route 1 near Lambach, so they took to country roads and made very poor time, stopping at a decrepit farm. The major entered the farmhouse holding the only two laying hens by their feet.

"Cook these for our breakfast." For his meal, Rudi got the neck of one of them – boiled. It tasted like a Hungarian delicacy.

The major had an infinite supply of maps. He pulled out a few and quizzed the farmer on how to proceed southerly, but the old man's knowledge was limited. He had spent his entire life within a few kilometers of his farm. Disgusted, the Major slapped his gloves across the old man's face and stalked out.

He told the colonel, "At least we know exactly where we are. I'll map out the route for tonight. If we start at dusk, we should be on the lake shore well before dawn."

When they reached Ried on the northeast shore of St. Wolfgangsee shortly after one in the morning, they found a powered barge tied to the dock.

"Rudi," said the colonel, "back the truck between those rows of concrete mooring blocks down to the dock. Get as close to the barge as you can."

The barge's fuel tank was half-full. The engine started on the third attempt; it ran quietly.

The major turned it off and stepped back onto the dock. He called quietly, "Rudi, come here. Look carefully at these ropes and remember exactly how they are tied. Untie them and then just wrap them loosely around the bollards. Then, it'll be time for you to do the real work. Herr Oberst, you get up on the road and watch for any vehicles or nosy neighbors."

Rudy did as he was told – as did the colonel, who walked a few paces towards the road.

"Rudi," said the major, "Open the tail-gate and climb up". He checked his Schmeisser's action and then held it loosely in front of him, ready for use. Rudy, stiff from inaction, climbed awkwardly into the back of the truck.

The Major said, "Line up as many ingots as the tailgate will hold, then get out and take them to the barge – one at a time."

As Rudi lifted the first ingot, he thought, *'I must keep my mind busy. I'll count. How many ingots will fit on the tailgate? I think I can get twenty of them lined up.'*

The major watched him closely. When the ingot count reached twenty, he stopped and straightened up.

"Herr Major, why don't I just put them all here? It would be faster than climbing back up several times."

"Too heavy for the tailgate, *Kind.* Just start loading the boat and hurry."

A half-hour later, Rudi, soaking with sweat, was marched aboard.

"Here's a short line, Rudi. Tie yourself to a thwart. We don't want you to go swimming." With the major at the helm, the barge proceeded quietly to the northwest, along a shoreline that appeared uninhabited. Pretending to doze, Rudi watched the mountains looming over the lake in the intermittent moonlight and their relation to the small village of St. Wolfgang, further along on the shore near the head of the lake.

The barge coasted silently to a stop about a hundred meters out from the shore, near the entrance to a shallow cove. The colonel clipped a small weight into the loop of a 50-meter surveyor's tape and let it pull the tape down into the water. When he felt the bottom, he looked at the tape with a shielded flashlight.

He announced, "It's too deep," and guided the boat a few meters toward shore, then let it drift to a stop. Again, he felt for the bottom.

"OK here. Rudi, drop the ingots into the water, carefully,

one at a time."

Then, with the major's ever-present pistol aimed at his chest, Rudi slowly released the ingots over the side. He counted them to himself; number one hundred and eighty was the last one. The colonel was fully occupied in making sketches and writing down compass bearings. The dumping completed, the officers navigated the barge back to its dock.

"Rudi, tie up the battleship. Let me watch you make the knots. It must look just like you found it." Rudi's fingers were swift and sure.

"Close enough," he said. "Get in the truck. It's my turn to drive." He shoved Rudi between them on the front seat.

As they continued along the lake shore, Rudi noticed the onion-domed church in the small village of St. Wolfgang. Turning onto a side road after leaving the village, they came to a small patch of woods.

The major pulled the truck to the side of the road and said to the colonel, "Do it here."
The colonel motioned Rudi out and nudged him with his pistol into the woods.

He said, "Rudi, I'm sorry about this" – and paused. He hadn't actually shot at anyone before.

In panic, the major screamed, "Colonel! What's your problem? Hurry up, get it done before somebody comes!"

Aiming at Rudi, the colonel quickly pulled the trigger twice. Then, instead of simply shooting Rudi in the head, he fired blindly into the air, turned and ran for the open door of the truck, which was already moving.

2

April 22, 1945
Near St. Wolfgang, Austria

The German Luger has characteristics that caused it to be rejected when several countries – including the United States – considering adopting it as a military sidearm. Its trigger mechanism, located on the left side of the barrel housing, can foul with mud. If a sidearm is a soldier's final protection, it must tolerate mud for its owner to survive. Its 9 mm bullets, while fairly high velocity, do not have the "stopping power" of a larger caliber.

Most automatic pistols will raise their barrels from the recoil of each shot; the Luger is no exception.

These characteristics saved Rudi's life. A piece of grit, lodged in the trigger mechanism, caused the weapon to fire before the colonel expected it. As a result, the first bullet missed Rudi completely, snapping past his left ear. The second one knocked him down as it entered his chest between his second and third rib, missing his heart and lungs and broke the third rib as it exited from his back.

Immediately after the colonel shot Rudi in the pre-dawn darkness, the truck went screaming away. Rudi was face down on the forest floor. He was not really aware of much pain. Aside from muscle and soft tissue damage, no major blood vessels were involved. It hurt to breathe deeply, so he didn't. It hurt to cough, so he didn't do that either. He wasn't sure how long he'd been lying there, drifting in and out of semi-consciousness, deafened ears ringing.

When something prodded his leg, he opened his eyes and saw a middle-aged woman holding an empty basket. She asked his name and why he was bleeding. Her accent was difficult to understand. She brushed the twigs and leaves away from his face.

"I'm a Czech. I was kidnapped by two crazy SS officers. They were running away from the Russians and trying to get to the Americans. They dressed me in this uniform and made me drive their car."

Already, Rudi was concealing facts – that it was a car, not a truck; that the SS officers were not trying to get to the Americans – they were trying to avoid everybody, especially other Germans.

"When they got here they knew where they were, so they were done with me and my services. They paid with a bullet."

"The shooting woke us up," she said. "Can you walk? It's only a half kilometer to my house."

She helped him roll over and sit up, then ripped and folded up the bottom of the tunic, pinning it so as to cradle his left arm. With the weight of the bad arm supported by the makeshift sling, he could walk. Her "half kilometer" seemed like half a hundred to Rudi and they stopped frequently to rest.

A talkative woman, she said, "My name's Frau Schäfter; you can call me Aunt Elisabeth. I'm a farmer's widow. My daughter, Elsa, is waiting for me at home. I didn't want her to be near any shooting. Together, we'll do whatever we can do to make you well."

In the kitchen, she said, "I'm sorry it's cold. I brought you home from the forest instead of firewood."

Setting aside the dishes on the table, she helped him to sit up and stripped off his bloody uniform. Going to work with cold water and yellow soap, she clucked in dismay.

"You were shot like one of my husband's roebucks, except the bullet went through you. Your breathing is fine, so your lungs aren't injured. I'm very afraid of deep infection. You might die from it. I must get something."

She left the room. Rudi looked at the young girl – perhaps about ten years old – that had been standing beside her mother. She stared at Rudi silently, her dark eyes large with wonder.

"What's your name?" asked Rudi.

"Elsa," she half-whispered. "Does it hurt?"

"Yes."

"How long were you lying there? Was it from when we heard the shooting?"

"Must have been."

"That was about an hour ago."

Rudi groaned and closed his eyes against a surge of pain washing over him. Tentatively, the girl laid her hand on his. Her fingers were cool.

The door opened and the woman returned with a grey mass the size of a golf ball wound up on a fork.

"Cobwebs," she said. She wiped away blood from the entrance wound. Using her little finger, she pushed some of the cobwebs into the hole. She packed the rest into the torn flesh in his back, poking the larger rib fragments back under his skin.

"This was how my grandmother dealt with deep punctures that don't bleed enough to clean themselves. Most of the blood is from your back. "

Rudi, ground his teeth, squeezed his eyes closed and moaned softly, clenching the table with both hands.

"Elsa, bring the old featherbed case from the barn. We need to rip it up for bandages."

Elsa turned to leave. "Run, child." To Rudi, she seemed to vanish.

"I must keep talking to keep you awake, little man. Most of the German soldiers have already gone north. I think the Americans'll soon be in town. The Germans warned that they are more savage than the Russians. But the Americans dropped messages, telling us to stay inside and lie down on the floor if we heard shooting and to hang out white sheets or towels if there were no Germans inside. Ah, here is my Elsa with what we need. . . . Elsa, start ripping it into strips . . . find me some of the cleanest material to make a pad about ten layers thick."

Elsa wound a strip around her hand and offered it to her mother.

"Here, daughter, hold this in place – gently, now – that's right. Now, hold the end for me . . . we'll pass it over where the bullet went in . . . keep your hand on it, *Liebchen*, while I tie it on this side . . . "

"Mother, I can feel his heart beating. It's ever so fast."

"Good. He's a strong boy . . . aren't you, Rudi?"

He moaned and muttered something they didn't understand

Elsa held a tin cup to his lips. Her hand felt warm and soft.

"There. That's all we can do at the moment, dear boy. Elsa, we must get him to bed. Help me get him up the steps to the top of the tile stove."

Rudi was weakening rapidly. The woman placed his right arm around her shoulders.

"Elsa, support his left arm. Try not to let it move. Come, Rudi, down from the table. Here we go, one step at a time. You're strong, aren't you? I am sorry that there is no fire in this stove. But it's nearly summertime and it won't be too cold up here."

The stove, a large tiled box almost as tall as Rudi, filled one corner of the room. Three steps were built into one side. A rough mattress covered its top. With the women supporting most of his weight, he crawled onto the mattress. Making him lie on his right side, they covered him with a blanket that smelled of horses.

* * *

There followed a two-week blank in Rudi's memory. He remembered thrashing with a burning fever; cold cloths on his head; then long periods of intense cold, with warm bottles placed against his stomach and under his arms. He recalled burning with thirst and being unable to move. During all this time, he had the recurring nightmare that the major was coming back to find him – and he'd wake up, shaking with fright. To wipe it from his mind, he'd focus on how the mountain's outline appeared from the barge. *I must remember this as long as I live,* he said to himself. He remembered Elsa, smiling at him, wiping his face with a cool wet cloth and spooning water or a weak broth into his mouth.

When he tried to throw off the heavy blankets, he was too weak to lift his arms. Above all, he remembered telling himself over and over, *"Don't tell anybody. Don't say anything."*

In this period of time, the war ended. On May 4, 1945, two days before Rudi's fever broke, American tanks clanked into Salzburg. The next day, Linz surrendered without offering any defense. The day after that, Rudi woke up with a clear head and knew that he was going to live. He could sit up and drink water when Elsa supported him and held the mug to his mouth. It tasted like nectar. He lay back down, exhausted and slept soundly until the next day.

The woman, the young girl with her, came in and said, "If you feel good enough to come sit outdoors in the sun, you can have some real beef stew."

He laughed, thinking they were lying. "You're joking with me. Nobody has that any more."

Then he could smell it. His stomach contracted in an exquisite hunger spasm. They helped him to his feet and, leaning on them heavily, he passed the kitchen stove where a pot of stew bubbled. "Did you have to kill your cow?" he asked.

They both laughed and answered, "No, no! This is American beef stew with vegetables!"

They showed him American C-Rations – "Look, Rudi – stew with carrots, potatoes, and green beans; here's real chocolate and American cigarettes; canned fruit and cherries, a tiny can-opener, packets of real powdered coffee, cream and sugar and even fresh bread in a tin!"

"But the bread isn't baked very well," added Elsa. They brought a steaming bowl, telling him "eat slowly, slowly."

Chattering on, they said, "The war is over – the roads are full of people and soldiers – German soldiers trying to get home – Americans sorting out thousands of refugees – but here it's calm. The Germans lied – Americans aren't devils. They pass out food and they love children. A few soldiers spoke some German. They said they weren't supposed to be talking with us but nobody was watching. . ."

* * *

For the rest of his life, Rudi remembered the tranquility of the next three weeks. His left arm in a sling, he sat in the sun, watching the woman and Elsa work in their garden. Occasionally, he'd help them one-handed with light work, stopping to rest frequently, then dozing in the sun for a bit, sitting on the warm granite step with his back against the door, walking with them along the road where he'd been shot and left for dead. While his German was good, the local dialect took some getting used to – and they teased him about his Czech accent.

Every day the widow and Elsa took the string bag and

walked into St. Wolfgang, every day returning with more C-rations and news.

"The Americans brought in soldiers and machines to fix the roads. They put the mayor back in his office and we'll have Austrian policemen again. They're working on the telephone line to Salzburg. They brought in flour and the bakery will open tomorrow. We'll have coal before winter. We must be careful if we find any shells or mines in the fields; we are to tell them right away and not touch them. Every day there is a newsletter on the wall at the Post Office; the postmaster said there were thousands of people killed by the Germans in a labor camp in Mauthausen-Gusen, over north of Vienna – many have survived, but very sick -- do you think that the Germans would have done such a thing?"

Rudi stirred. Remembering the sound of a machine-gun brought instant sobs.

"They shot my parents," he blurted. "They are animals."

* * *

Every day brought new rumors – and demonstrations of progress toward the assurance of survival. Every few days also brought a native son back to his mother's arms.

Each day, Rudi strolled around the farmhouse, pausing at the crest of a slight rise to look through St. Wolfgangsee's valley. He studied the Schafberg on the north shore and thought about what it would look like from . . . *there* . . . on the lake's surface. The day after the widow took off his sling and told him he could try using his arm a little, he had an inspiration.

"Tante Elisabeth!! Are there fish in the lake? Can I go fishing? Do you know where I can get a boat?"

"Yes," she had replied excitedly, "there are good fish in the lake – *Forellen* – fat lake trout. It's the fishing season and the neighbor has a boat. I haven't had *Forellen* for years. There are worms in the garden. You can use my husband's fishing rods; he was *Jägermeister* – the game warden. My husband's journals will locate the best fishing. Elsa can go with you when she finishes her chores and help you with the journal. She can row the boat if you get tired."

Her enthusiasm for the project brought more ideas tumbling forth.

"Rowing would be good for your shoulder but not yet. I'll talk with my cousin about your fishing license-- she is working in the mayor's office. If you would stay with us and be one of the family, perhaps the mayor would appoint you to be *Jägermeister.*"

Rudi recognized an opportunity that would allow him to pin down the gold's location and also put badly-needed food on the table.

"Tante Elisabeth, I'm really interested in fishing, but not in hunting. There are only a few roe deer living now and I don't want to do any shooting." In his mind, he heard the shattering sounds of the Major's machine pistol mindlessly ending the lives of the people that were his world. His lower lip quivered and at last the tears came. Frau Schäfter gathered him to her ample bosom and held him closely until his shaking eased.

"We haven't asked you what really happened, dear boy. Perhaps it'll help if you tell us. It's sort of like confession, because we can share your grief."

Instantly, Rudi's defenses were triggered. He could not put these people in danger by telling them the whole story. It was time for him to tell the story he had concocted – a story he'd use when he returned to Zohor. He hugged Frau Schäfter, sat up and wiped his eyes on his sleeve.

"I worked in our family's glass works. We made pretty things before the war, but the Nazis made us convert the operation. We made blanks for lenses. A few days before you found me, two officers came into the factory and made us destroy everything. We had to melt down the blanks that were finished and burn all the documents – you know, drawings, glass formulas and so forth. Then they took me outside and the Major shot everyone – my mother, father, cousins who worked there – because they didn't want anyone else to learn the processing secrets. They kept me because I could speak German and I knew my way around that part of Czechoslovakia and Austria. They made me wear that uniform so I wouldn't look out of place. When they were done with me, they shot me where you found me."

Frau Schäfter hugged him again. "Dear Rudi, you're one of us now. My husband is dead. My heart tells me that Elsa's brothers will not return." She wiped her tears with her apron.

Rudi said, "I'd really like to be part of the family someday." He glanced at Elsa. Her smile and blush transformed her pinched, wan face.

Then, very seriously, Rudi said, "I must go home to Zohor for a little while. It's just on the other side of Vienna. Most of my family is dead, but my brother was fighting on the Eastern Front. I want to find him and bring him here. You have saved my life, and I promise to come back. I would rather live with you here in Austria than back in Czechoslovakia."

3

July, 1945
Traveling in "liberated" Austria

Rudi left the farmhouse in St. Wolfgang in late July, 1945, three months after being shot. Conditions were improving slowly for the family. Neither of Frau Schäfter's sons had returned. During his last month in the old stone farmhouse, he became a successful fisherman. The Jägermeister's journals were helpful on where to fish; it noted water depths, best time of day, best bait or lure to use, air temperature's effect on the appetites of the larger lake trout and so on. The mayor's secretary was eager to help her cousin's "house guest," and he found himself with a rowboat, fishing equipment and a bona fide license to fish the waters of St. Wolfgangsee. It was the only identification document that Rudi possessed.

Rowing strengthened and loosened his left shoulder. By the time he had caught his first lake trout, it was nearly normal, but he couldn't place his left arm behind him at all. Frequently, Elsa would accompany him to help him understand her father's notes.

Frequently, Rudi "fished" in a cove near the foot of the Schafberg. He was confident that he was close to where the gold ingots went overboard. Also, he walked frequently. His favorite route took him northeasterly along the road, passing the spot where Frau Schäfter had found him, through a little settlement, then followed a rough road along the northeast shore of the lake. The road became a footpath at the cove that he identified from the rowboat. He'd be gone all afternoon on these forays, covering seven to eight kilometers.

Frau Schäfter encouraged him to get this exercise; he also helped with the garden chores and other work. She checked his wounds every evening and was proud of what she had done for him. The entrance hole looked like a flattened rosebud. His back was not a pretty sight; it didn't hurt so much.

* * *

Rudi, walking with a small rucksack Frau Schäfter had given to him, begged an occasional ride to Linz, sometimes riding "second" on ancient motorbikes. He felt like a spawning fish going upstream, as the majority of the refugee traffic was westward, not to the East. People feared the Russians; they were occupying Austria north and east of the Danube.

For several days, he re-traced the same route he had driven in the opposite direction at night. When he came to the temporary bridge over the Enns River, it had been destroyed. Nearby, a new American bridge floated on little boats placed side-by-side.

He watched what was going on and how traffic was handled. Seeing some American soldiers lounging around a small truck – he'd heard Elsa call them "jeeps" – he went over to them. There was a large tall man with totally black skin and dark wooly hair. Rudi was fascinated.

He asked, "Do you come from Africa?"

The man laughed. He said, "No, I'm an original American Indian." The other soldiers laughed. The man asked what sounded like "Go you to Veen?"

Rudi nodded. "Ja."

The American – he had three stripes on his sleeve – turned to his companions. "This kid's walking to Vienna. We better give him something to eat." They rummaged around in the vehicle and brought out several cans of "C" rations and a box of "K" rations, which Rudi had not yet seen. Rudi thanked him and, as he started to move away, the soldiers said, "Hide your food from the Russkies." He took his jacket from the rucksack, placed the rations in it, replaced the jacket and buckled the flap. As he went to the end of the bridge, American trucks and jeeps came across towards him.

Then he saw his first Russian soldier at the far end of the bridge. He had stopped the trucks. A horde of civilians took advantage of the interruption and came across in a double file. They seemed relieved that the Russian paid them no attention. The Russian blew a whistle, pushed the civilians away from his end of the bridge and the two or three waiting American vehicles near Rudi began to pull onto the floating span. Rudi stood there, undecided. The jeep with the friendly Americans pulled up next to him.

As the last American truck headed onto the bobbing span, the black man gave Rudi a friendly pat on the back. "Run behind us, kid."

"Danke," Rudi shouted, staying close behind the jeep. He didn't even look at the Russian soldier on the other side, just scampered up the bank and lost himself in the crowd.

He heard Viennese Austrian, German, Slovakian, Hungarian, Czech, Polish. There were defeated German soldiers, weary, dirty, who never lifted their eyes above their shoes as if trying to be invisible. Four of them stepped aside to let Rudi pass as if he were their commander. Off to the side, several more Russian soldiers surrounded a group of civilians, haranguing them in execrable Czech. When Rudi heard something about identity cards and passports, fear struck him. All he had was a fishing license signed by the Mayor of St. Wolfgang. He put his head down and kept walking – east to Vienna.

4

May, 1947
Zohor, Czechoslovakia

A heavy freight train woke Rudi from a deep sleep. What were the Russians were taking from his country this time? Perhaps the train itself? He smiled at the not-so-funny joke, and then grimaced as pain lanced his left shoulder. It stiffened up while he slept, but loosened after exercise in the morning. The initial care he'd received wasn't the best, but it was better than none at all. *How lucky I am to be alive and to be well. Having a "war wound" kept me out of the new Czechoslovakian army.* Now, just past his eighteenth birthday, he'd told the recruiter that his wound came from a crazy Nazi officer who had killed the rest of his family. After looking at Rudi's chest and back, the recruiter was satisfied. He'd said, "I can get you a good job working for the government. I'll be back."

As the pain brought Rudi fully awake, he remembered that this day would be happier than most. Georgi, his brother, sleeping quietly next to him, was to be married.

Georgi had returned to the family home in Zohor about a year and a half ago. Captured by the Russians as they swept out of the Ukraine and Poland, driving the remnants of the German army before them, he'd avoided being wounded or killed. His luck held even further, as he had been taken deep into the Rodina as a prisoner of war. It was rumored that they were to replace some of the millions of Russian youths killed in the war. But his detention camp had been closed – without warning, without explanation – and the inhabitants turned loose. It had taken him three months to find his way back to Zohor.

Georgi never said much about his experiences. Rudi hadn't told *his* full story either. Georgi hadn't heard about the midnight trip on St. Wolfgangsee. He didn't know about the re-casting of the gold. The assassinations in the glass works were common knowledge, but details were sparse.

* * * * *

The first ray of morning sunshine lit the wall across the room. Rudi scratched a flea bite on his scalp. *Perhaps it's time for another turpentine shampoo,* he thought. Things certainly hadn't worked out as he had planned – at least, not so far.

What a long hike from St. Wolfgang, he thought. *Lucky I lived through it.* He had walked from St. Wolfgang to Zohor. Penniless, he had meager meals using the C-rations given to him by the Americans. He'd supplemented these with vegetables and small potatoes stolen from the fields at night. He'd suffered debilitating diarrhea from bad water; then crippling stomach cramps from little green apples. He had three times encountered soup kitchens operated by small churches for those displaced by the war. He frequently offered to work at a farm for a day for a meal; the work was hard and the meals were meager. His goal was twenty-five kilometers a day. Between illness, or evading people whose looks he didn't like and getting lost on country roads, he'd lost seven travel days. His eighteen-day plan turned out to be 25.

He'd walked through a landscape ravaged by war. Burned-out German vehicles and tanks, destroyed as they fled from the Russian onslaught. Somber former German soldiers assigned to graves registration teams, trying to separate friend from foe, recording data on identity tags and placing the remains in temporary cemeteries. Rudi thought that the dead soldiers were the lucky ones.

Once Rudi left Austria's American zone, however, he encountered roving groups of Russian soldiers stealing everything of value. There were even sporadic fire fights between different Russian ethnic groups – Chechens would assault Ukrainians, or vice versa and the winners took the spoils.

His arrival in Zohor came almost as an anti-climax. He went first to the farmhouse outside the village where his grandparents had lived. When he had left Zohor with the Nazi colonel and his domineering major, his grandmother had been desperately ill with tuberculosis. His grandfather, almost eighty years old and the third generation of glass artisans, had been frail but stubbornly healthy.

He'd arrived late in the day; the farmhouse appeared

undamaged. The war had, in fact, passed it by. His grandfather saw him walking up the narrow cart-track and ran to meet him, hugged him and wept.

"My dearest only grandson – we had a memorial service for you three weeks ago. Are you all right? You're the last of my family – unless, praise God, your brother Georgi is alive somewhere. Come in, come in. I'm still a pretty good cook, though heaven knows there's little enough. I can make soup from nails one more time."

Rudi's boots were in shreds and he hadn't been out of his clothes except for one hot day when he took a swim in a stream. His grandfather stirred up the fire in the old stove; Rudi sat on the floor next to it and wept, his grandfather holding him in his arms as he crooned and rocked him.

Little by little he told his story, leaving out the part about dropping the gold into the lake. He kept that part to himself, because he had plans for the gold. For now, he thought, it would be best if everybody believed that the gold went to a salt mine in Austria and that they got rid of Rudi because they were close enough to where they were going to hide it – and because he had witnessed everything.

* * *

A bit later, a recovering Rudi wolfed down the third bowl of soup.

"My dear boy," said his grandfather, "tomorrow we shall go to the glassworks. We'll start it up in a few days. As soon as those murderers drove away, neighbors went into the shop and found your father and mother and the five others, heaped on the floor by the furnaces, dead. They'd watched the Nazi colonel force you up into the cab to drive the truck.

"Jenna, who makes the beautiful little glass horses, was sick that day, so she was spared. Same for Oskar. Every day, all summer long, they've been cleaning things up, getting ready to start up the operation. No more will we have to make stupid lens blanks – we threw away the molds. I've been helping every day, ever since your grandmother died. The shock of what happened was the last thing for her. She died the next week, after we had a memorial service for everyone. We'll go to our family burying ground on our way home and you can pay your respects there.

"Rudi, I have one question for you – what were my son and his wife doing? Who did what during this melting-down?"

"It was all set up by those SS dogs," said Rudi. "They brought all the tools they needed. We had to melt down everything that came in. The furnace-tenders did the heavy work – lifting the graphite crucibles into the furnaces, and then adding gold to them as the contents melted. Each crucible held enough gold to fill one cavity in the molds. The process was almost continuous. When a crucible was full to the mark, Sergé – the strongest – would take it out of the furnace and place it on a bench. Then any dross, they called it, would be swept off the surface and he'd pour it into a mold. Ann-Marie had the worst job – she and her sister had to remove stones from the rings and pins. The worst part was removing pieces of teeth. My father weighed the ingots. He stamped the serial number and the weight on each ingot. The Herr Oberst stayed right at Father's elbow when he did the weighing. He'd ask, almost every time, 'Are you sure that's correct?' Mother kept the ledger of serial numbers, weights and the sub-total. They were already stamped 'Geld von Zohor CZ'. They kept checking her addition. They were fascinated by the accumulated weight."

"Yes," sighed his grandfather, "there are pails of loose stones – lots of them precious, but we can't tell the diamonds and rubies from imitations. We wondered why they left them behind. Anatole used to be a jeweler – he said that people didn't put cheap stones in gold settings, so that most of it is probably valuable."

"What are you going to do with them?" Rudi asked.

"The Graf thinks we should give them to the Government and ask for part of its value back to rebuild what's left of our lives. Now – there's something you have to see."

Then the old man opened the ancient carved wooden *armoire* that stood against the wall and lifted out a pile of blankets.

"Come, Rudi, I can't pick this up. It's too heavy for these old arms."

When Rudi saw the glimmer of gold, his breath stuck in his throat.

"Where did this come from?"

"Oskar found it under a bench. He hasn't told anyone. He said it belongs to this family."

Rudi dragged it out. The gold had a deathly chill of its own.

"Look, Grandpa," he said. "There's a weight but no serial number. My father hid this one somehow and Mother didn't stamp the serial number. It says '610.09 T' – that means Troy ounces. That weighs a little more than 20 kg, grandpa, and it's worth nearly 500,000 Austrian Schillings."

"How do you know that?"

"The Nazis talked about it. They weigh gold in Troy ounces, Grandpa, not kilograms or anything else. The ingots were around 600 Troy ounces, worth about 21,300 US dollars. That's almost half a million Austrian schillings." This close to the Austrian border, with most of their business coming from the West, both men traditionally thought in terms of Austrian currency rather than Czechoslovakian.

"That's more money than I ever had in my lifetime." The old man shook his head.

"I piled these up as fast as they were cool enough to handle. They made the floor creak and pop. Herr Oberst prodded me down into the cellar with his damn Luger to put a post under the floor. It's probably still there. Maybe that's when my parents hid this ingot. On the last day, I loaded these into their truck. One at a time . . . twenty kilograms each. One hundred and eighty of them. Let's wait a bit before we decide anything. With Russians everywhere, we better find a better hiding place for it."

"How about the family cemetery, next to your mother?" said the old man.

"Good idea, Grandpa."

* * * * *

It was going to be a beautiful day; Rudi had day-dreamed about his journeys for the better part of an hour.

He reached over and punched Georgi, next to him in the bed.

"How can you be sleeping at a time like this? It's your marriage day, brother; you'll do your sleeping with somebody prettier than me the next time you go to bed."

"Prettier for sure, but who's going to be sleeping?"

5

May, 1948
Bratislava, Czechoslovakia

Rudi's palms were sweating as he waited outside the office of the Western District Commissioner for Forests. He wondered if his job – which he had held for only ten months – might be at stake. Though the political situation was in turmoil, he had been careful to do his work thoroughly and enjoyed the freedom that he had.

After a month of training in silviculture, he had received instructions on where to go and to bring his reports every other week to an office downstairs. Three months ago, the Communists had seized power from the government and the new masters were examining each and every arm of the Czechoslovak State. Four days earlier, he'd received a hand-written note from the Commissioner to come to his office for "an interview." It asked him not to discuss his appointment with <u>anyone</u>. At first, he thought it was a joke from a fellow Field Administrator, but the letterhead was genuine. He decided to say nothing and simply appear at the appointed time.

When he arrived at the office on the fourth floor, a pleasant-faced matronly woman smiled at him.

"Good afternoon, Rudi. I'll tell the Commissioner that you're here." She stepped to a closed door, opened it and said a few words to whoever was inside. She closed the door and returned to her desk.

Rudi's stomach tightened in anticipation of being face-to-face with the representative of the new totalitarian regime.

A buzzer sounded and the Commissioner's secretary got up and held the door open for him. He stood and smoothed down his uniform. A voice called, "Come in, Rudi, come in. Will you have tea?"

"Thank you, sir. That would be nice; the roads are dusty this spring."

Rudi had never met – or even seen – the Western District Forest Commissioner; there were others between them in the bureaucracy. The Commissioner was in his middle fifties, with a shock of wavy iron-gray hair going silver at the roots. Rudi relaxed; it didn't look like he wasn't going to get his tail kicked – or anything worse.

The secretary brought a small silver samovar and two glasses in nickel-plated frames. She filled them, offering the tray to Rudi first. He took one.

"You're an observant lad," the Commissioner said, taking the other cup. He said no more until the secretary left the room, closing the door.

"Rudi, please sit with me here at the little table. This is not a formal interview, although I have looked at your work. I have also learned a little bit about you and your family in Zohor. I put on my old clothes and stopped by the glassworks and asked if I could go to work there. You'd be surprised what one can learn about people that way. Your grandfather hopes you'll come back and work for the family again. He praised you and your brother and said your father had brought you up to be responsible men, not afraid of hard work – physical and mental. He is right. You're doing a fine job.

" Now, I have a very direct and personal question. I want to know what you really think about where our country is headed. Speak freely. I'm sure that you know some people are speaking against how the Communists have been helped by the Russians, or are complaining about how the Communists gained the upper hand last February. These dissidents are being examined very closely. I believe their opinions will not be tolerated much longer. Rudi, where do you stand?"

Rudi stirred uncomfortably.

"Before you answer, I want to tell you that I am not recording this conversation. It's off the record. In fact, I am one of those who dislike communism. I thought that our country was headed in the right direction until the last so-called 'elections.' If I speak out, I'll lose my job. Very few people know how I feel. Now, I want to know how *you* feel."

"I saw the result of the Nazi dictatorship," Rudi replied. He paused, his brow furrowed.

"Nazis murdered my parents, and then killed several other

close relatives and friends. They shot me. They were the worst
of their kind. When the wrong people have power, they make
death camps. I think Czechoslovakia is headed for the same
kind of repressive leadership. I don't like it. Already we have a
Czechoslovakian SS – our *Státní bezpeènosti*."

The Commissioner leaned close to Rudi.

He said quietly, "Other people in the world think the
same. They need to know things that you and I can tell them.
They need to know what our government is doing – the
things that don't get into the newspapers. I can do that part
and I have been, for some time. They need to know what the
Russians are doing. Your reports can be an excellent source
for this information, but they need more detail.

"Rudi, do you want to help? Can you keep this
conversation secret? Truly, I would be shot tomorrow if the
wrong people knew these things."
Rudi's heart pounded. The man certainly seemed honest; he
himself was such a small fish that it wouldn't make sense to
trap him.

"I know how to keep a secret," Rudi responded. A vision
of gold bars, vanishing one by one into a dark lake, snapped
into his mind.

"Good man, Rudi. Would you be willing to collect and
pass on, some simple information? I must tell you that the
information is not part of your job; however because of your
job, it would be easy for you to do it."

"If it'll help return our country to where a person has
rights and isn't afraid to speak up . . . yes."

"Excellent." The Commissioner took Rudi's hand in both
of his own and held it. "I want you to meet a man. A friend of
mine. He isn't a Czech, or a Slovak, but he can sound like
either." He jotted an address. "Wednesday – day after
tomorrow – is a holiday. Why don't you go to this little
teahouse at two o'clock? You'll meet my friend. He'll treat you
to tea and cakes. Afterwards, you can stroll by the river and
chat about things. For now, there's very little risk. You'll be
reassured after he describes how we communicate.

"Now, it's time for me to tend to other business. I look
forward to hearing from you, by way of our mutual friend.
He'll have questions for you – questions you can answer very

easily." He rose from his chair and, again taking Rudi's hand in both his own, looked at him intently. He said, "Rudi, please give my regards to your grandfather. Tell him that I admire his judgment very much. Thank you and good luck."

* * *

The teahouse was in an un-named settlement a kilometer or so beyond the outskirts of Bratislava, on the narrow road that led mostly along the Danube. He'd passed it many times; it should take him an hour and a half without breaking into a sweat.

After sleeping late, he told his grandfather that he was going to check his bicycle and take a ride – the State motorcycle was very nice, but he needed some exercise.

"I'll be back for supper, grandfather. I'll see if I can bring some calves' liver – I can cook it for you the way that grandmother always did."

Holiday or not, he knew that the farm to the south always slaughtered calves on Wednesdays. Fresh liver, cooked with garlic, onions and potatoes, would make an excellent supper for the two bachelors.

Other than a little more air in the rear tire, his bicycle was ready. With a gentle north wind helping him, he arrived at the teahouse, parked his bicycle and went in. He noted another bicycle in the rack. He was on time – it was only a few minutes before two o'clock.

Three tables were set up on the rear porch, overlooking the river. Except for one man at the end of the porch, there were no other customers.

The man walked over to Rudi and said, "Here it is, two o'clock in the afternoon of a nice holiday. Most young men would be out walking with their sweethearts, or sitting in front of a cool glass of *Pilsener* with their friends. You're on time, Rudi. Thank you for coming." They shook hands – one firm oscillation, in the Austrian style.

"Help yourself to some tea – they know how to make it here; and bring some cakes along as well. You must need some sugar after your bicycle ride from Zohor."

As Rudi filled his glass cup from the samovar on the sideboard, he tried to place the man's accent. He'd switched between Czech and Slovakian smoothly, as many of Rudi's family did; yet, one or two of his words had a different accent. *Strange. Must be my imagination.* He returned to the table. He sat facing the man, who was about his own height. *He's the sort of chap who wouldn't be noticed in a crowd. Sandy hair, blue eyes, rough clothing of a working man. About thirty-five.*

"I know what you're thinking, Rudi. Neither Czech nor Slovakian is my native tongue. My name is Nikolai. Not my real name, either. I'm not Russian, Czech, or Slovak, but I can pass for any of them when I have to. I know lots about glassmaking; in fact, I visited your parent's glass works in nineteen thirty-six when you were about seven years old.

"Rudi, we're here to talk about you working for me, supplying me with information that I really need to do my job, which is managing espionage. We aren't looking for secret formulas or plans for new airplanes or anything like that. My job is to watch what the Russians do. We know that they are building up their military and political power in Czechoslovakia, in Poland and Hungary, everywhere in every country they occupy in the eastern part of Europe. Why? Are they going to invade Western Europe? Start World War Three? How much influence, or direction, or even control, are they going to apply to the government of Czechoslovakia?

"Rudi, the answers to these questions can be developed by people far smarter than either one of us. If they have information they'll turn it into intelligence. It isn't hard to get. Anybody who's free to move about – as *you* are – and free to use their eyes, can get answers to simple questions, some of which may seem silly and trivial. But please understand that a question about an insignificant matter may be the key to a complex situation.

"Rudi, you're in an excellent situation to see or hear answers to our questions – without even asking anyone. You're free to travel about the country. You're uneasy and worried about what is happening in Czechoslovakia. These are some of the reasons why we thought you would be the ideal person for this work. Let me give you some examples. For instance, you know the reports you submit about the condition and number of the varieties of saplings in a given area?"

Rudi nodded, in awe of what they already knew. Then he

remembered that it was the Commissioner who was responsible for his duties.

"Here's an example of how you can tell us what's happening." Nikolai pulled out a piece of paper, unfolded it and handed it to Rudi.

Saplings less than 20 mm diameter – Area Nr. *413 793*		
Tree family	Quantity/hectare	*Code for:*
Pine, long needle	165	*T-34 tanks*
Lime (Linden)	35	*200mm mortars*

Rudi recognized the first and second columns as part of a report he had submitted two weeks ago. The "area number" looked like map coordinates; the right-hand column was self-explanatory. He said, "This looks like child's play, Nikolai," and handed the paper back to Nikolai.

"It is, Rudi. You'll be able to answer our questions very easily. You won't have to ask anybody anything. It's what you see and hear that will reveal the answers. The secrecy involved has to do with what things mean. The codes that we'll get to you must be guarded carefully. You'll need a safe place for them and destroy them when you've answered that set of questions. You shouldn't ever have to hurry, or change your normal schedule. We'll know where you're going and if there are answers we need, you'll get the questions in plenty of time. There'll be different code sets, as there are many more areas of interest than there are types of trees. What I mean is: while a 'long needle pine' today represents Russian T-34 tanks, next week it might mean ten pallets of 75mm ammunition in an ammunition dump."

"How accurate do I have to be?" Rudi asked.

"When we need numbers, if your reports are within plus or minus fifteen percent, it'll be very good. You can always add little phrases to clarify – 'more hidden in the underbrush in likely places' or 'more have sprouted since I was last in this area' and so forth. The important thing is that if anyone picks up your report, it'll appear to be exactly what it is – one of your 'field notes' that you'll consolidate into your normal periodic reports. The difference is, of course, that it'll disappear when you pass it along."

"Sounds simple."

"Rudi, even though I know this tea-house is secure, we'll discuss how we pass information along as we walk along the river a little bit. Would you like another cup of tea, or shall we go now?"

"Let's get outdoors and enjoy the afternoon."

* * *

They sauntered along the remains of an old tow-path that followed the Danube.

"What sort of things will you need to know, Nikolai?"

"Mostly stuff like unit identification and location."

"I learned some Russian. Had to in order to understand temporary road signs they put up and unit identifications on their trucks and tanks. They do a lot of damage in the forests."

Nikolai swatted at a fly. "Here's the easy part – we'll need to get the same sort of information on the Czechoslovakian army. Typical questions will be: what new units have appeared? What type – artillery, infantry, mechanized, or supporting units? Have new storage areas for ammunition and fuel been created? Are they building up these supplies? Are there complaints about shortages? Simple phrases like 'the soil is poor and needs fertilizing' can describe troops that are discouraged or rebellious. Or hungry. We'll develop these phrases as we go along.

"You'll leave your report with Jonas in the mapping department in your headquarters building. He'll give you the new assignments, coordinated with the areas where you'll be within the next couple of weeks."

"How often do I do this?"

"You deliver your regular reports to Jonas every other Friday, right?"

Rudi nodded.

"If there's more for you to do, Jonas'll pass it along. If there's something new in the meantime, he'll get a note to you that the replacement map you needed has arrived."

"Sounds pretty simple."

"In this business, the simplest things are the best," answered Nikolai. "Now there are three more things I need to know. First, do you have any particular scars or features that can prove who you are to anyone else? We don't use photographs because they can be altered too easily."

Rudi peeled up his shirt and turned around.

"Take a good look, Nikolai. This is one reason I don't like oppression."

"Looks like a bullet might have come out there."

"You're right. It was a Nazi bullet. I'll tell you all about it sometime. What's next?"

"Your grandfather's house is a nice, large one. Was it once a farm?"

"Yes, it did. In recent years, though, we've had only a cow for milk and cheese and chickens for eggs. My brother's wife looks after them, does the milking."

"Do your brother and his wife live there?"

"No. They live in a little house on the road towards Zohor."

"I'd like to meet you at the farmhouse the next time I return. It'll be our 'safe house,' where comings and goings will not be noticed. It's close to the Danube, which is important to us."

"I see no problem with that. What's the third question?"

"You're holding me to my word, aren't you? The third question is how much we'll pay you for the extra work and how you want the money."

"Pay me?" Rudi's retort was a bit heated. "For doing what you ask, I want no pay at all. Call it my way of fighting back, of getting even. Keep your money, Nikolai. Besides, if I suddenly had more money than I should, I'd be tempted to spend it and people would accuse me of robbing my grandfather – or worse."

"You sure?"

"Yes – I'm sure." Rudi stopped walking and faced Nikolai. "However," he continued, "I may want you to deposit some of our family assets in a bank in Austria, because someday we'll find a way to live there. Is that something that you can do, when the time comes?"

"No problem. We can set up a bank account anywhere – Vienna, Salzburg, Geneva, wherever you want it to be. We'll need to decide what the assets must be. Moving currency across this 'iron curtain' isn't worth the effort unless it's US dollars or English pounds."

Rudi's eyes lighted. "Tell you what. Two things. Maybe I can convert some of our assets to gold – will that work? And, when I am ready to leave Czechoslovakia, can you give me an Austrian passport?"

Nikolai smiled and laid his hand on Rudi's arm.

"That'll be easy, Rudi. But remember, the time may come when you feel threatened by discovery. If that happens, ask *me* to come to the farm. I'll take you into Austria. The rest of the time, I'll be telling *you* when I'll be coming – usually overnight. But – bear in mind – we are counting on you to do a vital job and we want you to stay here as long as you can."

6

February, 1955
Zohor, Czechoslovakia

Rudi paced the floor of the empty farmhouse. Frequently, he went to the front door, opened it and looked down the road. He was expecting a lone cyclist to pay him a visit. It had happened several times before – always on a Monday, always shortly before supper. His guest, Nikolai, had always established the time of the visit. This time, however, Rudi had asked Nikolai to come – just as soon as possible. In almost seven years of information-gathering, he had never felt the need for urgency as he did now.

After February 1948's *coup d'etat*, Czechoslovakia's situation deteriorated. Communism displaced the peaceful democratic rebuilding underway for the preceding three years. "Class Enemies," initially defined as those who operated large farms or factories, became people who openly opposed Communism. Food and materials shortages developed. The populace despaired, saying, "Under Communism, we have shortages of everything except jails." If an informer heard it, the speaker most likely would be seriously interrogated.

So far, the little glassworks in Zohor had not come to the attention of the authorities. Georgi, the "working manager," divided his time between keeping the equipment operating and running a modest machine shop. Georgi had concentrated on making parts for machine and equipment repair. There were two glass artisans, one furnace and sand specialist, two apprentices and two machinists. They were all more or less related, either by blood or by marriage. Including Rudi, the nine people represented five households.

Rudi hadn't told Georgi the full story of the gold. As a factory manager, he could be arrested, just on general principles. Earlier, Rudi suggested that the entire group prepare for escaping to Austria. The plan was for him to go first, with Georgi, Hilda and their son Peter, joining him there.

The others would follow.

Georgi made small steel molds. One Sunday, they re-cast the ingot their grandfather had hidden. The little molds produced ingots about one inch wide, two inches long and a quarter inch thick, weighing a bit more than five and a half ounces.

Rudi told Georgi and Hilda, "Trust me on this. I have a way to get this gold to Austria, where it'll assure our future. I don't want to tell you how, so you won't be implicated. That's all I can say. Someday, when it's safe, I'll tell you everything. We've heard the stories about torture and drugs – Czechs doing that to Czechs! This is why we have to leave our country!"

Hilda sewed hidden pockets into an old jacket. It held forty ingots.

Nikolai carried the first fourteen-pound load to Austria. On his next visit, he'd handed back the empty jacket, saying, "Here's a deposit slip for one hundred and fifty-two thousand Austrian schillings, in the name of Eduard Holder. That'll be your Austrian name after I give you your passport, Rudi. Don't ask how I converted the gold to cash. The first time was hardest; the next will be easy. The price of gold is going up. The next deposit should be about twenty-five percent more."

Rudi had told no one about the additional work he'd been doing for Nikolai, which had turned out to be simple. He was a diligent Forest Supervisor, concerned with assessing the value of the State Forests as a natural resource. He'd become fluent in Russian and worked closely with the political representatives of the Czechoslovakian Army and the occupying Russian troops. As he roamed his jurisdiction, he saw – and reported – more and more building up of military capability. More tanks. More ammunition dumps hidden in the forests. More and more artillery; mostly self-propelled, with every caliber represented. More "Stalin organs" – the trucks bearing forty rocket launchers. He'd seen construction of crude wooden barracks, surrounded by multiple fences of razor wire with guard towers in every corner. He'd signed many forms permitting cutting hundreds of trees for the lumber consumed by these concentration camps – *that's what they are, just like Mauthausen and the others we heard about, except these are full of our own people.*

Four weeks previously, when he'd turned in his reports to Jonas, there was a dark, sharp-eyed man behind the counter with Jonas.

The stranger had asked, "Who is this man and what does he want?"

"This is Rudi, the Chief Forester for the Western Region," Jonas replied. "He turns in his reports here every other Friday. I match them up with new maps and send them all upstairs." Jonas rubbed his nose as he spoke and Rudi quietly shifted the stack of envelopes in his hand, placing the special one at the bottom. They had agreed on this signal only two months before – it meant "things aren't right here."

"Give them to me," commanded the stranger. Rudi handed over all but the bottom one.

"I said give them to me . . . *all of them*."

Struggling to appear casual, Rudi handed over the last envelope. "This one isn't complete. I have to check some map coordinates before I turn it in. I'm taking it home with me, because there's about two or three hours of work involved."

"Well, let's just take a look at it," the stranger had said, "and I'll be on my way . . . if I like the looks of it."

The stranger ripped it open and raised reptilian eyes to Rudi.

"If your work is unfinished, why'd you seal the envelope, Comrade?"

"A mistake. I was sealing the others and automatically licked this one too."

The dark man's eyes bored into Rudi's for what seemed a full minute. Rudi held firm until the man shifted his gaze to the envelope in his hand. He ripped it open, pulled out the documents and tossed them on the desk. Turning the envelope over, he examined it closely, running his fingers over Rudi's handwriting. Then, he picked up the documents.

There were several pages, all reporting on different sections of forest and all dated within the past week. The dark man perused it, his eyes glinting.

"Hmm – birch trees, Norway spruce, lime, ash, stunted saplings, damage by Russian vehicles not staying on roads – is *this* what you do?"

"Every day, Comrade."

The man placed his hand on the pile of envelopes and smiled. "I think I'll just compare this with one of these."

Selecting an envelope from the middle of the pile, he tore off the end and pulled out the report. He laid the documents alongside those from the special envelope and compared them. Then, he carefully smoothed each page of Rudi's "unfinished" report on the counter and lightly ran his fingertips along each sentence as if he were "reading" a Braille document.

Abruptly, he straightened, his coat swinging open, revealing a shoulder holster. Leaving all of Rudi's reports on the table, he looked at his watch.

"I'll be on my way," he said. "I didn't know so many different trees are so important to our leaders. Keep up your good work, Comrades. I may want copies of my own, next time. I'll let you know."

He went around the counter and left, letting the door slam behind him.

Rudi said, "So now it begins for us, Jonas. What was he doing, feeling the envelope and the paper of the special report?

"He was feeling for microdots. We are not that sophisticated, so he saw nothing amiss – your special reports look like all the others. Words can say more than they appear."

"I can finish up that last report in a few minutes, Jonas." Swiftly, he penned in *"Get me out of here as fast as you can."*

Ever since the encounter with the ferret-faced man from the Secret Police – Státní *bezpeènosti* (or "StB" for short) Rudi, Georgi and his family and every worker in the glass works and their families had been preparing to leave Czechoslovakia.

In his travels south, Rudi had found people arranging border crossings from Czechoslovakia to Hungary. A night crossing of the Danube at the right place was not too difficult. Guides took their groups to the Austrian border, where friendly Hungarian guards would close their eyes at the right time. Many were successfully reaching Austria, freedom and a chance for a new life.

The plan was for the glassworks group and family members – twelve people, all told – to travel together. Georgi had been south once with Rudi to meet their "travel agent" and make the initial payment for the group. Rudi was to go with Nikolai and meet the group in Austria where they were to slip through the rip in the Iron Curtain.

The next alarm had come late that very afternoon. Jonas had cycled out to the farmhouse and left a note for Rudi. The note said "Rudi – the WDC (Western District Commissioner) didn't come to the office today." This most likely meant that the Commissioner himself had been arrested, or at least, brought in for questioning. *"If the WDC is forced to tell all, I'll be next. Then Jonas. Then Georgi and the rest of the family. It's time to leave,"* Rudi thought

After reading the note from Jonas, Rudi went to George's house. Hilda and little Peter were there alone, as Georgi was still at the glassworks.

"Hilda, I have very little time. Go to the shop and tell everyone the time has come to leave. *Now.* Tonight."

"What's happening, Rudi?"

"I leave tomorrow morning. Wait for me in Oberpullendorf. I should be there in six days, maybe quicker. It'll take you at least four or five. If I don't make it by a week from today, you and Georgi know what to do. But I *will* be there. Trust me and God bless you all."

On the way home, he stopped the family cemetery. Kneeling at the graves, hands clasped, he composed his mind. *Farewell, my dear parents. So many of you were murdered. I shall do my best to follow the commandment that says an eye for an eye, a tooth for a tooth. You shall not have died for nothing; your souls shall be the power that helps to make this a world free of terror and oppression.*

Now, it was near dusk. Nikolai would be appearing at any moment – if he was coming today. Rudi placed the cold stew on the stove and added a few sticks of wood to the fire. A knock sounded on the rear door. Lost in thought, he jumped in alarm. He calmed as the door opened and Nikolai came in.

"Man, I thought you'd never come. Come sit by the stove."

"What's all the excitement?"

"I'm pretty sure our operation is over," answered Rudi:

"Four weeks ago, we had a visitor in the map room. He went over my reports – including the special one – very carefully. He even checked for microdots. And today, the WDC didn't come in – and he's always at the office on Mondays. Jonas thinks he's been arrested. That'll lead directly to us. When the StB arrests people 'on suspicion,' they don't come back."

"You're right, Rudi. I called his office Friday and he wouldn't talk to me. That means he's sure his telephone line's tapped. I've been around Bratislava all weekend and things are coming to a head. Same in Hungary.

"Now – I have a question for you. You told me that you had very important information to pass on. Ready to tell me?"

Rudi sighed and checked the stew. It would soon be piping hot. He uncapped two bottles of Pilsener and passed one to Nikolai.

"This is the last of the beer; does that tell you something?" They touched bottle-necks together and each took a swallow. Rudi sat down, took a deep breath and faced Nikolai squarely. "When we first met, I said someday I'd tell you how I got my scars. I guess this is the day."

Rudi told the story of the deserting major and colonel, melting down the gold in the glass furnaces, the murders, his trip to St. Wolfgangsee and depositing of the gold in the lake and finally being shot.

"By then, I was pretty hardened and didn't miss a trick. Four weeks later, I confirmed where I'd dropped the gold in the lake. The people in St. Wolfgang who saved my life write chatty letters and they want me to come back there. If anyone was looking for the gold, they'd have said something."

"How much gold's there, Rudi?"

"One hundred and eighty ingots went down. About twenty kilograms each. The water's about thirty meters deep – at least that's what the damned Oberst said. *Forty meters – too deep. Go in a little further.*' I can hear his words as if it were yesterday. I hope his measurements were better than his marksmanship."

The smell of hot stew broke their silent contemplations and Rudi ladled out generous portions into two large bowls.

"I'm going to miss this old table," said Rudi. "My great-great-grandfather made it for a wedding present to his bride five generations ago." Rudi broke some bread and passed the loaf to Nikolai.

"I didn't tell you about the gemstones. My cousins, Anne-Marie and her sister had the job of separating the stones from their settings. There's everything – diamonds, rubies, emeralds – about five kilos. More than half of it was glass. Anatole used to be a jeweler – it took him four years to sort it. My grandfather talked to the old Graf about whether it should go to the Government. He never said anything to anyone, or we'd have heard about it, because the Graf died soon after I returned.

"Now, the plan is for the glassworks group to divide it up and take it along. That will give them resources in Austria if I don't make it. We've come to consider it as something we were paid for the loss of our family members and for the loss of our homes and the glassworks. We know where the gems came from, but there's no way to return them to the dead owners."

Nikolai shook his head. "I don't know how you've held on this long."

"So where do we go, Nikolai? And how do we get there?"

"It's quite simple. Very early tomorrow morning, we take our rucksacks and bicycle to the peat fields beyond where the Morava River joins the Danube. You know the place – it's about three kilometers this side of the teahouse where we first met."

"There's a dock there, right?"

"Yes. We have to be there early to help load peat on the boat. Then we get aboard with our bicycles and ride the boat upstream to Vienna. The boat goes every Tuesday and Friday, about mid-morning. The fare is a thousand schillings. I'll pay for both of us. Strange; if you don't help load peat, you don't ride. Not even for ten thousand schillings. I've got your Austrian passport and letters allowing you to work as a deck hand on the boat. In Vienna, we'll get cleaned up and into new clothes, then to my house and we eat. Next day we'll go to the American Embassy where we'll talk about what comes next. Recovery of the gold is going to be a ticklish issue, considering where it came from."

"Sounds good," said Rudi "I need to be in Oberpullendorf

a week from now to meet the glassworks group."

"I can help with that. More and more people are coming across – soon the Russians'll replace the Hungarian border guards with their own soldiers. Rudi, how come you didn't go back to work in the glass works?"

"I couldn't, not after what had happened there. I'd come home and go to bed and it would be nightmares over and over – our family working until they dropped, constantly goaded by those rotten Nazis. When the recruiter offered to arrange an interview with the Forestry people, I accepted. But I drop by the glass works from time to time. They are all friends and relatives. They understand why I can't stay very long."

"Who else here knows about the gold?"

"I'm the only living eyewitness. The Nazis locked all the doors and didn't let anyone in. Their trucks came before dawn and stayed under cover all day. The colonel went out for food just once, telling the nearest neighbor that he wanted three meals a day for eleven people, delivered to the office door and if they didn't, he'd come back to the house and start killing people.

"As soon as we left in the Nazi truck, neighbors went into the building and found everyone dead. They took the bodies into the Church and had a service as soon as coffins were built.

"Early the next morning, a heavily guarded German convoy came with a general leading it. They stopped outside town while the general came into the village. When he heard we'd left, he got excited and wanted to know which way we went. The trucks spread out, driving into barns and sheds. They were afraid of American bombers. Soldiers went into every house, taking food. They left that evening right after dark."

"Rudi, I understand. I was afraid that there might be hard feelings in the family or something. Now, I've got to get some sleep. What time do we leave?"

"Wake me as soon as it's light."

7

February 7, 1955
Zohor, Czechoslovakia

The morning dawned warmly – in contrast to the previous days. Rudi shook Nikolai and said, "Stew's hot."

"I don't know how your grandfather slept on such a soft mattress," Nikolai said. "My back feels broken. I'll be there in a minute after I go to the outhouse."

A steaming bowl of stew greeted Nikolai as he returned. He rubbed his face and hands roughly on a towel and sat down. "Smells good enough to eat," he said.

Rudi said, "I ate earlier. Couldn't sleep very well. Been up for about an hour. Nikolai, I have a serious question for you."

"Go ahead."

"Who exactly are you? How do I know you're not working for the *Státní bezpeènosti?*"

"You've had a bad night. I was going to tell you once we got on the boat. I'm an American."

"You lie. Say something in American."

"Ok, Rudi, we speak English, not American. It sounds like this: *'Our favorite game is baseball. You'll have to learn the game and also teach it to your nephew Peter. Our best food is hot dogs and we always eat in restaurants.'* There – does that satisfy you? "

"Who do you work for?"

Nikolai sighed and said "OK. Nikolai is not my real name. I told you years ago. My real name is Andrew Henderson and I work for the CIA. I'm married to a Czech woman and we have two sons in Vienna. I'm very good with languages. *Wie findest Du mein Deutsch – spreche ich wie Dein Herr Oberst?* There. Now, if we're both arrested on our way to the boat, they'll drive toothpicks under our fingernails to make both of us tell separate stories and the stories will be the same. I just broke every rule in the book. You'll have to believe me and understand why I don't have any identification with me that proves what I told you."

Rudi shook his head. "Sorry. Last night was full of nightmares and unanswered questions."

"You'll never know how much you have done for the side of freedom, Rudi. Hey, time to go. You all packed?"

"Been packed for two weeks, my friend; we won't even close the door. We'll leave the farm to the Gypsies."

They swung their rucksacks onto their shoulders and mounted their bicycles.

"What a strange winter," Rudi said. "The ground hasn't frozen at all. I'm not even going to look back." They turned south and picked up a brisk pace, traveling side by side.

"I never knew that bicycling could be so much fun," Nikolai said

"Great until it rains."

After two or three kilometers of easy pedaling, they came to a rise, gaining perhaps fifty meters of elevation before they reached the crest, where they paused briefly. The rising sun made them squint and shadowed the descending road ahead..

Nikolai pedaled quickly downhill, looking back, laughing. Rudi was about to shout a warning, when Nikolai's front wheel smashed into a pothole. Flung over the handlebars, he crashed head-first on the road, his head resting at a strange angle.

Rudi ran to him and felt for a pulse. There was none. He laid his head on Nikolai's chest and listened for a heartbeat – none. Nor did Nikolai's chest rise and fall with normal breathing.

Rudi looked both ways – nobody in sight. Dragging the limp body by the shoulders, he headed into the dark woods, Nikolai's head flopping uncontrollably. He made two more trips and brought both bicycles to where they couldn't be seen and laid them down. He opened Nikolai's rucksack, found a poncho on top, unfolded it and spread it over the body.

He knelt next to Nikolai. He folded his hands and bent his head to Nikolai's chest. *"Dear God, please tell me what I should do now."*

Book 2

Explanations

Washington, DC

1

November 4, 1968
Washington National Airport

A group of unkempt youths, some carrying crude "Stop the War!" and "Peace Now" signs, milled about the terminal's main entrance. Their strident chanting of anti-war slogans drew little attention from people hurrying in and out of the building. A tall young man, emerging from a taxi some distance from the group, handed several bills to the driver.

The cabby said, "Good thing you ain't in uniform, sailor. Those hippies'll spit on you and the cops'll just watch. Take it easy, now and don't let them bother you."

"Thanks, man, keep the change. Guess my chief was right about not wearing my uniform in public. Some homecoming! Keep the faith. Semper Fi!" and the two bumped fists.

The sailor was a member of Navy Seal Team 2, having just returned from fourteen months in the Mekong Delta with the "Brown Water Navy." He quickly passed by the demonstrators un-noticed, as they were concentrating their fury on a young soldier with the bad luck to be in uniform. Shaking his head, he scanned the "arrivals" screen for his brother's flight from Augusta. It was listed as "on time."

With time to spare, he ducked into a coffee shop, got a cup of black with sugar and sat down. Jet-lagged from traveling half-way around the world, he'd slept for hours on his mother's couch.

He hadn't seen his younger brother, Bruce, for two and a half years, but they worked hard at staying in touch. Very close, the brothers had decided to stay in the military for a few more years. Shaking his head and smiling, he recalled their escapades. In spite of his being a year older, he usually looked to Bruce for guidance – which was usually pretty good. Bruce had decided on the Army for himself, after suggesting that the Navy would be a good start for him. "Hey, Rob, it'll give us broader experience in whatever we decide to do together after we get out," Bruce had said.

The Vietnam conflict had loomed over their middle teens and they decided that by enlisting they'd get to choose what they'd be doing.

So, here he was. Their mother and step-father had seen the opportunity for a family reunion. Robert had passed up the opportunity for "R&R" in Hawaii by responding to his mother's telephoned plea when he laid over in Honolulu.

"Please come home, Rob," she'd said. "Bruce has leave before he goes to some kind of advanced schooling and Stephen and I need to talk to the both of you. It's very important." Her familiar voice, with its European shadings, made him catch his breath.

"OK, Mom," he replied, "I'll get to LA on my next flight."

"Robbie, Stephen will get you a reservation to DC. You know he loves pulling a few strings. Let me know as soon as you have a confirmed flight."

After that, things had gone smoothly. He'd bought a small suitcase and enough civilian clothes to get him to Washington and made arrangements to store his sea-bag.

Checking his watch, he crumpled up the empty cup, tossed it into a trash can and walked along the concourse to gate A14, where a gleaming Boeing 727 "three-holer" was nosing in to its berth. Within minutes, passengers began streaming into the corridor.

Bruce appeared and loped over to him. They embraced, then drew back and looked at each other. They had similar features, hair color and buzz cuts. Bruce was slightly shorter and chunkier.

"God, Rob, where did you get that awful Hawaiian shirt? Haven't you been eating?" A punch on the arm. A returned feint to the belly.

"No, you little twit, I've been leading my team through the jungle while you've been playing soldier in Georgia swamps. Let's get home. Check a bag?"

"Nope. What you see is what I've got. Clothes enough at home for a while."

Heading for the cab line, Robert said, "Finally the cops

are moving these hippies along. They've got no idea of the harm they are doing. If it keeps up, America is going to be split down the middle."

"Watch your words, brother. How's your Slovakian?"

"Pretty good," answered Bruce in Slovakian. He continued in that language – a practice that hadn't endeared them to their teachers or coaches. Their mother, realizing the value of foreign language skills, had drilled them in Czech, Slovakian and German from the time they began talking. This allowed them to soar through foreign-language courses in high school. Coincidentally, their father had also been raised in a multi-lingual environment.

"Not as good as yours, though."

"How's Mom?" Bruce asked.

"Her health is not all that great. Says Washington winter is going to get to her this year. But she's only fifty-four."

"Looks frail, but she's tough. Good thing she's had Steve all these years. Hey, what's your next assignment?"

"Got what I put in for – teaching at the Army Language School in Monterrey. Steve must have pulled some strings."

2

November 4, 1968
Bethesda, Maryland

Robert gave the cabby an address in Maryland. "No need to expose you to the rigors of rush hour public transportation in DC," he said. "Told Mom we'd take a taxi."

"How's her health?"

"That's something we need to talk about. Pretty soon, the Bethesda house will be too big for her. They'll need to get into something smaller. When we get out we won't be living at home anyway."

There was a long silence, as the cabby cursed the traffic, the cold weather and the world in general.

Bruce finally sighed, "Ok, big brother; so whadda you want to be when you grow up?" They'd spent many hours at this old game. They'd fantasized about being fighter pilots, railroad engineers and all the other aspirations of childhood. Their maturation came quickly in their respective military services and they believed only two things – first, they'd be together and second, that they'd be successful in whatever "it" was.

Robert replied, "You first. Your ideas are better."

Bruce took a deep breath. "Here it comes, Rob. LBJ isn't running. Humphrey didn't win. I think Nixon has the horsepower to bring Vietnam to a conclusion. Then I think he'll turn our foreign policies around. This country is going to prosper as soon as this stupid war winds down. There's going to be outfits willing to spend lots of money to protect their property and persons. I think we can be the guys to offer the highest possible levels of that kind of protection."

"Sounds interesting, keep talking."

"OK, so let's look at skills. First, dogs."

"Dogs?"

"Yes, dogs. You've seen how Seeing Eye dogs work. They recognize threats to their owners. Look how some police departments have success with K-9 departments. Our MP's use them in guarding sensitive installations. I spent my first tour at the Bell Labs in New Jersey. They were working on communications crypto stuff. Their contract required the premises to be fenced, with foot patrols accompanied by dogs trained to assault intruders."

"Remember Tasso, the police dog next door to us in Austria?"

"He was a pussycat as soon as we learned he hadn't been trained to accept food from strangers."

They chuckled together, but thoughts of Vienna sobered them. It had not been a happy time at the end.

"Yeah," said Robert, "Mom said we needed to talk about Vienna."

3

November 4, 1968
Bethesda, Maryland – 5 PM

The taxi pulled up in front of a medium-sized house in the northwest section of Bethesda. Contrasting with its white-painted Colonial neighbors, its brick exterior glowed warmly in the setting sun.

Bruce muttered, "Steve's sticking with GM, I see." He'd spotted a '66 Pontiac parked in front of an older Buick.

"Guess he's waiting for this Iranian oil crisis to settle down. You saw gas prices back on Wisconsin."

Robert paid the driver and, as they turned up the walk, the door flew open and there stood a tiny woman, squinting in the late afternoon sun. She stepped briskly onto the small porch, wrapped her arms around Bruce and said, "Can't call you 'my baby boy' much longer, can I? C'mon in, boys. Steven just got home. He'll be right down. He said, 'They'll be here just as soon as I go upstairs.' And here you are."

Holding Bruce's arm, she turned and led him inside, Robert following, carrying Bruce's bag.

"I've some Pilsner in the fridge," she said. "Sit down and I'll bring it. You boys must be exhausted, all this traveling on short notice. Was Steven successful in smoothing the way for you both?"

"Hey, travel arrangements are what we do best!" their step-father said. He entered the living room as their mother headed for the kitchen. "Glad everything worked out for you both. Girls in the office can do wonders, even if the Iranians have stirred the pot. We've got people going and coming like you wouldn't believe." He and Bruce wrapped each other in a bear-hug.

"Here's your mom – thanks, Lattie, this looks great – Czech beer and appetizers," said Steven. He reached over to his wife and took a tray of crackers, cheeses and four brimming Pilsner glasses. He set it on a low table and each of them took a glass.

Steve toasted, "Here's to safe journeys and happy days for us all." Glasses clinked. They sat.

"I'm always the impatient one," said Bruce. "In the taxi I told Rob that I thought we were going to hear about Vienna. You always said we'd hear the whole story when the time was right. Is this the right time?"

"Yes, and it's long overdue," said Steven. "You boys were seven and eight when your father disappeared. I was Chief of Station in Vienna at the time. Andy worked for me. Your dad ran three Czech agents; one in Bratislava, another in Prague and the third was a rover. We called the first one 'The Third Man' because of that 1949 movie. By the way, this conversation can't leave this room, but you boys know that. It's a long story, but let me get it all out.

"Andy got a message from The Third Man. He wanted out, promising information that 'would explode the top off the world.' Your dad pushed him for several weeks, saying that it would be easiest and safest for him to get the information to us without coming out; use double blind drops, whatever could be worked out. No go. Third Man insisted there was someplace he had to take us. 'Not far from Salzburg, in the American zone, perfectly safe.' Andy'd met him several times. He'd picked a face out of a book of mug shots, said would be good enough for an Austrian passport. We'd made one up, had it ready.

"Your dad convinced me that he could safely re-enter Czechoslovakia, try to talk the guy into staying, that the stuff he was giving to us was working out really well and so forth. Also, he'd try to figure what Third Man had to offer – value versus risk – same BS we went through all the time. But – and this was a big but – if there was no way Third Man would stay, he'd bring him home.

"We talked over all the possible angles. What could Third Man have that was so valuable? Or, was his cover about to be blown? We knew about everything the Russians were doing. Czechoslovakia had turned into a repressive state. We had two informants high up in the Czech secret police. They didn't know about each other's activities or Third Man's. The Bratislava agent disappeared in 1958 – he'd been in the Czech

Forest Service – he'd recruited Third Man.

"STASI – East Germany's secret police – couldn't turn up anything for our guy who ran their mail room in East Berlin. Third Man was a stand-alone; his data covered what the Russians were doing – StB training camp activities, Russian order of battle data and maneuver evaluations. Most useful was his data on Czech and Russian ammunition stockpiling. We figured that one of the indicators of a put-down of a Czech uprising would be increased Russian security of pre-positioned ordnance and a surge in building it up or moving it around. However – and this was important for us – preparations for invading the West in force would see the same activity, but many times greater. There'd been no signs of this.

"Also, the Third Man once told your dad that thwarting Communism was payment enough. He wasn't in it for the money. Strange in itself. "

Steven sipped his beer. Sighing, he rubbed his head. A quaver thickened his voice.

"So – I cleared him to go for five days of exposure; hopefully, four nights would be in safe houses. We had protective surveillance until his little freighter went downstream the next morning. A pickup detail, in two cars, was to be at the dock the following Tuesday and Friday evenings, when Andy would return on the same boat – with or without Third Man. He didn't show up on Tuesday.

"The call came from the pickup detail about six pm on Friday. I was waiting for it and beginning to worry. Andy wasn't on the boat."

Steven shook his head, cleared his throat. His voice shook. He said, "Only the skipper and a deckhand were aboard. We'd expected another deckhand – Third Man. The deckhand looked like Andy in the dark, but he walked right past the pickup, went between the buildings and crossed the tracks. We lost him."

Stephen tugged out a handkerchief and blew his nose. Lattie patted his back. "By the time we realized there was a problem, both the deckhand and the skipper were long gone. The skipper wasn't one of us – he only took folks back and forth on the river between Czechoslovakia and Vienna. He never asked questions so he never knew anything. If somebody was waiting at his boat at either end, they were expected to work their passage by helping load peat. Andy had used him several times. Your dad was so good with languages that he could easily be taken for a Czech, a Viennese Austrian, a Slovak, or a German. All he needed was identity papers and a passport.

"We'd had the skipper under continuous surveillance for four months. He'd started the business right after the war. The boat belonged to his father, who'd died in 1941. All his phone calls were about peat orders or pickups. We never saw him use a phone booth. A one-hour tape reel was enough to record a week's conversations.

"We thought about drops and watched his apartment for a long time – nobody touched his bike, only the postman – one of ours – put mail in his box. We checked his mail many times. No personal letters, only checks, bank statements, bills and advertisements. He never sat in a park. Never went to the movies, opera or theater. He didn't sit around in a coffee shop – not once in all the time we were working him. He used his bike to get around and it's pretty hard to work a drop from a bicycle. It's also pretty hard to tail a subject on a bike, but our guys were good at it. We searched his apartment thoroughly – no hidden transmitter, no documents tucked under the drawers.

"There was a definite pattern to his life – he'd leave early Monday mornings, return on Tuesday evenings. Rode his bicycle home. Checked his mailbox. Went to the bank Wednesday mornings, then to the boat to watch unloading. Bought groceries, went home. Left again Thursday mornings, returned Friday evenings. Saturday mornings, he'd be back at the boat, watching the unloading. He slept on the boat every Monday and Thursday night and had a watchman on it Tuesday and Friday nights if he didn't sleep on it himself."

Stephen sipped his beer. Lattie handed him a piece of cheese; he popped it into his mouth.

"We had two Austrians make the round trip with him. Sometimes a Czech patrol boat would check him out, but it was cursory. He always had beer for them. There was no meaningful conversation. He spoke only Austrian.

"We even tried to tempt him with a nice-looking lady, but he said he was too old to try anything new. We finally decided he was just an old man whose entire life was a tiny business.

"He did everything in Austrian schillings. Didn't care that his passengers weren't all they appeared to be. Never asked names. Never seemed to recognize people the second or third time – he just held out his hand for a thousand-schilling note. Your dad said that even on his fourth trip, the old guy simply said *'Thousand schillings, please.'* If someone showed up, the old man would say "If you want a boat ride, help us load." He wouldn't take Czech currency.

"You boys know the rest. I was around quite a bit, as I was assigned to duty at Langley and kept close tabs on all of you – at first, out of a sense of duty. Well, duty turned to affection and you know the rest."

Lattie hugged him. "Is that the end of the story, Stephen?"

"Almost, dear. We followed up on every possible lead – not that we had very much. Whenever a body was discovered in Czechoslovakia, it was a war casualty. Many were Russian. Never had a clue who the Third Man might have been. Don't know if your dad even met him as planned. All we have is the mug shot that your dad picked out, saying, 'This one is pretty close.' Like quite a few others, boys, your dad's file remains open."

After a long silence, Lattie spoke. "The hardest day of my life was that February day in 1962, when you, Stephen, took us to the Arlington National Cemetery. You pointed at a star that had just been chiseled into the CIA's Memorial to Unknown Soldiers and said 'This one is for your father, boys. He was a soldier as heroic as anyone buried here.' Bruce, you went up and touched the star and asked, 'Uncle Steve, will you be my dad now?' You looked at me, Stephen, and we both knew that it was right and it was time."

She wiped her eyes, sighed deeply and hugged her husband. "It's time for all of us to think about supper. Then we can talk some more about the future and put the past behind us. I'll go get it started – the roast has been in the oven long enough. Robbie, you can smash the potatoes, if you promise to keep your fingers out of the pot."

4

November 4, 1968
Bethesda, MD

Robert pushed his chair back from the table, keeping his glass of sherry in one hand. Picking at crumbs of lemon meringue pie, he said, "Mom, that was a meal and a half. First time I haven't been hungry in months. Steve, does she feed you like this all the time?"

"I'd look like a walrus if she did."

"Rob, I've been sitting on my butt for three weeks," said Bruce. "Want to take a hike up Little Stony Man tomorrow? We might even see a little snow in the shady places."

Rob looked over at his mother and lifted his eyebrows. Lattie smiled and nodded.

"Go ahead, boys. I never could keep you home anyway. Besides, that mountain has always been one of our favorite short hikes. Wish I could go, too. You can be home by mid-afternoon. Stephen has to work tomorrow – can you come early, dear?"

"Yes," he said. "I have a few things to check out, but I'll be home by three-thirty. What are the long-term plans? You guys still talking about staying in for a while?"

Eyes flashed between Bruce and Robert.

"You first, Bruce."

"Yep," said Bruce." We talked about some possibilities in the taxi. I'm headed for Army Language School in Monterey . . . thanks to you, Steve, for the help on that." Stephen lifted a hand and nodded.

"Then," continued Bruce, "as soon as I have three years under my belt, I'll apply for OCS. Then I want to get into the Signal Center at Ft. Monmouth. Communications and electronics fascinate me. I want to be involved in it when I get out. I'll be a civilian looking for work in 1973."

Robert picked up the thread. "I've been in since '65 and am the new guy in SEAL Team 2. I'm due for a re-enlistment decision a year from now; I'll have had a year and a half in Nam and want to try for an instructor's slot in Coronado. Another four-year hitch would have me out about the same time as Bruce."

"We talked about starting a personal and facility security service," said Bruce. "I told Rob that there's going to be people and facilities that will need all kinds of protection – from would-be kidnappers, or from some of these crazy kids we saw at the airport, from plain old thieves – you name it. We could furnish site security when a Senator makes a speech and do a better job than the FBI or Secret Service. Rob has a great understanding of combat strategy and tactics.

"We have to improve the protection of our public figures," Bruce said. "They're targets for any nut. That's where Robbie comes in. I've seen him hang by his knees and nail the eye of a squirrel at a hundred meters. He can be a trainer and consultant for any law enforcement agency – federal or civilian. We learned from Kennedy. It'll be a long time before another president rides around in an open convertible."

"Another thing – physical protection of facilities. Remember my tour at the Bell Labs?" He repeated his earlier conversation with Robert. "I'm convinced that we can train dogs to do any kind of protective work. Also, the sensors used to set the focus in Polaroid cameras is a technology that somebody will expand into motion detectors. We're in a period of technical transition, leading to an explosion in miniaturization and capabilities of electronics. We'll give things – say, until 1973 or so – to settle down, let science fiction become reality, then we'll go to work together."

Stephen said, "You have been doing some thinking, haven't you?"

"Bruce has," said Robert. "I listen. Haven't heard anything yet that I don't like."

"Neither have I," agreed Stephen, "and in 1974 I'll be sixty-three and probably ready for retirement. If I don't mess up anything more than I already have, I may be an Assistant Deputy Director – hopefully still in Operations. The CIA will be ready for good technical consultants by then. We're learning that there's a lot of talent out there, far better than we can develop in-house. You might consider locating right here in the DC area."

"Since you brought up retirement, Stephen, what do you and Mom have in mind? Gonna go to Florida and desiccate away?"

"Never, never!" sputtered Lattie – "we'll NOT go to live in Florida and watch our skins turn to leather!"

"Wow!" Bruce chuckled; "see how quickly our dear mother turns into a Czech harridan, just at the thought of her pretty face turning to wood like on a ship's figurehead!"

"What is this *harridan* – something you made up just to torment this poor old lady who doesn't understand these new American words?" Lattie asked, laughing.

"This lady of culture reads, writes and speaks better than the head of the English department at James Mason." Stephen said, "along with Czech, Slovakian, German, French – and now she's studying Arabic! When I take her to a reception, she has to smile, be gracious and listen to three conversations at once to tell me afterwards what the others were saying! No, boys, to answer your question, we plan to stay right here. We might look around Warrenton. Good roads, a good medical center. Maybe find a little three-bedroom ranch where we can watch the sunset over the Blue Ridge Mountains. It should have a big yard for the grandchildren to play in."

With the last sentence, he cast his eyes at Robert. "This is what they call a meaningful look, Rob. Since we knew you'd be here for only a couple of days, we didn't tell Elaine that you were coming."

"I didn't call her, either," responded Robert. "I'm going to, in a little bit."

"Hey," said Bruce, "ask her if she wants to go hiking with us tomorrow. Maybe we could bring the minister and you could get married on the summit of Stony Man."

"You've had better ideas than that one, Bruce."

"What's wrong with it?"

"My hazardous occupation, bro. We'll get married after I get out. I'll call her in a minute and see if she can cut classes and come with us."

Lattie rose from the table. "Call her right now, Robbie," she said. "You did the potatoes; Bruce can help me clean up the kitchen."

5

November 5, 1968
Bethesda, MD

Bruce didn't try to enter his brother's bedroom quietly. He banged the window closed and looked at Robert lying there. He raised the shade and the bright sun played on Robert's face. Still, no response. Bruce yanked his brother's hair . . . and instantly found himself on the floor, face down, both arms doubled behind his back.

"Don't mess with a SEAL, little brother," said Robert, speaking quietly into Bruce's available ear. "Seals read minds. Even when you KNOW they're asleep."

Robert released his prisoner. "Didn't they teach you that at Fort Benning?"

"Thought you'd be totally wasted. How long were you at Elaine's, anyway?"

"Never long enough, but she needed her beauty sleep if she's hiking with us today."

"Wish she had a sister."

The three had been close friends ever since Lattie, Stephen and the boys moved to his house in Bethesda. Two years younger than Robert and a total tomboy, Elaine was the only girl in a family of three older brothers. She hiked, she ran, she hunted birds with the boys. Like them, she was skilled in Aikido.

She liked Bruce and he liked her. She loved Robert and he loved her. They understood the difference. Marriage was only a question of when.

At twenty, she was attending George Mason University, pursuing a degree in criminology. The previous evening, she was totally surprised to hear Robert's voice. He'd come right over to her house.

She'd decided to cut her second class and go hiking with the boys. Already wearing hiking boots, she came in the back door, directly into the kitchen where Bruce was just starting to clear the breakfast table.

"Morning, sweetie," Robert said, rising and folding her in his arms. "Sleep well?"

"Mmmmm, yes, what there was of it."

"There they go again," Bruce muttered. "Raging hormones screaming in anguish."

"Just you wait, Brucie – your turn will come!" said Elaine, finishing the coffee that remained in Robert's cup.

"Not me, Laney. Haven't found a girl that could walk a straight line and chew gum at the same time. Are we using your car this morning?"

"Sure, if you guys will gas it up on the way home. I've packed the lunch. Hey, it's nine-thirty – are we hiking or are we hanging around here all morning? First, I gotta go." She disappeared into the lavatory.

"I wonder what she made for lunch," said Robert. He slid his feet into his boots.

The boys picked up their day packs and they headed for Elaine's car. With Robert driving, Elaine in the front passenger seat and Bruce sprawled in the rear, they crossed into Virginia and diagonalled southwest through Vienna.

"Remember our first home here?" Bruce asked. "What a coincidence – leaving Vienna and moving half-way around the world to Vienna. Laney, you should have known us then – obnoxious ten-year-olds playing cowboys and Indians, watching high schoolers practice football, then playing tackle with our friends."

"Mom wasn't too happy when I came home with new cords full of red mud," said Robert. He eased into the westbound entrance to Interstate 66.

"I don't blame her," said Elaine; "and you better not try it more than once with me, either."

"The Navy has an easy solution for that," observed Robert; "when we get back from a turkey shoot, we rinse 'em out in the river. – want them to smell bad. That way we blend in with the jungle." "What kind of turkey shoots you been having, Rob?" Bruce asked.

"You name it. The last go, they had four of us kidnap the groom on his way to a VC wedding. Snatched him right off his bicycle. Tied the best man to both bicycles and left him in the road. Took their weapons. Nobody got hurt and nobody fired a shot. Took the groom to the Delta and gave him to an ARVN officer. Intel was good on that one. The chief just yelled out the guy's name from the edge of the jungle, they both stopped and we had them. Talk about two excited Charlies – they didn't have a clue who we were, because my buddy and I chattered away in Czech the whole time." Rob paused. "Pretty heavy traffic for this time of day on a Friday."

The smooth switch of subject told them that was all he'd say about what went on in the "Brown Water Navy."

"Take exit to 211 " said Elaine; "through Warrenton."

"I wouldn't mind being stationed here after OCS," said Bruce.

"What's here?" Robert asked.

"Army's got a facility – Vint Hill Farms – this side of Warrenton. It's a Signal Corps operation – used to train radio intercept operators, but now it's more for SIGINT – signal intelligence gathering and analysis. Also, they do a lot of cryptanalysis there. There's a big antenna site – they must have more than four hundred acres of them."

"'Why would you want to go here, then?" Elaine asked.

"I want to get back into Europe after Language School and OCS. Training here in electronic security and intelligence-gathering would be a natural, I think. It's fit into some of the things Rob and I might do when we get out."

"Oh," said Elaine, "Are you guys going to be spooks like Steve?"

"Well, sweetie," said Robert, "I don't plan on living on a disability allowance. I'll support you in the style to which you're accustomed. Isn't that part of the marriage contract?" She punched him in the thigh.

"Hey," said Bruce, "let's keep our eyes open today. Last night, Steve said we oughta consider locating more or less in the DC area; we know we want to be somewhat in the country and we're in it now. How 'bout that farm right there?"

"Farm?" Elaine asked. "I can't picture you guys milking, shearing sheep and spreading manure."

"Oh, we do lots of that!" Robert said.
Elaine punched him in the thigh again.

"We're thinking about raising and training dogs as part of

providing both an overall personal and site security service... Let's keep our eyes open today, anyway – be looking for places that have capabilities for physical security and accessibility to places like CIA's Langley and perhaps even Vint Hill Farms. It'll give us something to begin planning. Remember what Steve said about a place to visit his grandchildren." He rolled his eyes at Elaine.

"Better cut that out," she said, "or we'll get the raging hormones lecture from the back seat."

They left 211 at the top of the pass separating the Shenandoah Valley from the Potomac. Robert stopped at the park entrance to pay the fee.

The park ranger said, "You kids have a nice day for it. There hasn't been enough snow to close the Parkway, although you'll see some patches in the shady areas that face north. It's good to see short hair, guys. Military?"

Robert nodded. Then he asked, "We're headed down to the Little Stony Man trailhead. Many people using the park today?"

"A van full of grade-schoolers and a couple teachers – but they'll probably go all the way down to Skyland and take the short trail."

Leaving the entrance, Robert headed the car south. The road began a gentle climb. Within a few minutes they were above the haze layer. They looked at the glacier-polished bedrock reflecting the sun from Old Rag Mountain.

"Best time of year to be up here," said Elaine. "Leaves are off the trees, air is clear and we can see forever."

"And no bugs and no snakes either, Rob."

After another three miles, their trailhead appeared on their right, large enough for a dozen cars. It was empty. Rob parked the car; they got out and stretched.

"Just eleven o'clock," said Bruce; "we'll make the summit for lunch easily. Ready?"

The Little Stony Man trail quickly joined and followed the Appalachian Trail as they proceeded to the south. It was nicely graded and worn smooth by the thousands of feet that pass over it every year. They walked along at a steady rhythm, each enjoying the tranquility of the forest. As the trail began a series of gentle switchbacks, the grade increased perceptibly and their pace slowed slightly to accommodate the change.

"Guess this is what they call culture shock," said Robert.

"Hard not to be looking for trouble every minute. Better not get too used to it."

"I can't imagine how you have to live," said Elaine.

"Don't even think about it, sweetie," said Robert. "We're always looking out for each other."

"That's what we have been doing for the past six years," said Bruce. "Hey, there's the trail junction."

They swung to the north, joining a trail that showed much eavier use than the one they had been following.

"Isn't this the trail up from Skyland?" Elaine asked.

"Yup – haven't you heard the chatter of kids coming up the short way?" Robert said. "We'll hang to the right, head for the north summit."

Leaving the AT, the trail bent around to the north and terminated on a ledgy summit which offered superb views in nearly all directions. Taking off their packs, Robert asked,

"Laney, what's lunch? My stomach thinks my throat's been cut."

"Hey, Lane, did Rob eat anything at your house last night? Said he was stuffed, ten minutes before he left for your place."

"He seemed to be more interested in other things."

"Yeah. I bet he was."

"Enough already, said Rob. "Let's eat."

Laughing, they settled into natural seats in the rocks. The November sun was almost strong enough to dispel the chill in the north wind and they soon put on their light windbreakers They attacked their peanut butter and jelly sandwiches.

Bruce said, around a mouthful, "You know, Elaine, you could start house-hunting. There must be an old farm down there." He pointed his thumb back over his shoulder to the east.

"We could fix it up – maybe a couple hundred acres or so, mixed fields and woods. Maybe a nice house nearby for you guys. Maybe a barn on the farm that would do for kennels. Not on a main road. Perhaps this side of Warrenton, where the rolling hills begin."

"I'd love to do that," said Elaine. "What are we planning to use for money?"

"Rob, after you left last night, Steve and Mom sat me down and we talked. They'd hoped you could be there, also, but that they felt it more important that you see Laney, because your time here is so very short. They knew I'd tell you everything.

"In a nutshell, Steve said to me 'Find the place that's right. Don't worry about the money – it'll be there.' Seems Dad was the son of a canny Scot. He knew how to invest the inheritance that came from our grandparents in 1953. Steve followed the guidance he left and Lattie has been – and will be – taken care of, as we'll be also. Also, Steve and Mom want to buy into our business. After we're established, we'll be pretty much on our own. So that answers the questions about start-up costs."

Robert's mouth dropped open. "How much are we talking, little brother? Millions?"

"A few. More than enough to get things going."

Robert buried his face in his hands. After a few moments, he said, "Wow. Mom and Steve sure kept this quiet, didn't they? You'd never know that they weren't ordinary folks. Never anything fancy or extravagant. Always encouraged us to earn our spending money – paper routes, packing bags at Shop 'n Save."

Elaine said, "Somehow I knew this was going to be quite a day." She turned to Robert and hugged him tightly. Stroking her hair, he stared at the Massanutten ridge. Tears streaked his face. Several minutes passed in silence.

Rob rose, stretched, wiped his face on the sleeve of his windbreaker. "Never told you about my genetic dysfunction, Laney. My eyes are too close to my kidneys."

Bruce looked at his wristwatch. "As long as you're up, Rob, let's get moving. Steve will be getting home about the time we get there." He zipped his pack closed and swung it to his shoulder and offered a hand to Elaine. The three impulsively huddled and hugged for a moment.

"Elaine, do start looking for a place that will make us a good base of operations in this area," Bruce said. "Mom and Steve will help you and we'll talk to them tonight – and tell them that we've made up our minds about what we are going to do when we grow up."

Elaine said, "I've always thought of Steve as being your real father."

"You're right, sweetie. I don't know about you, Bruce, but I can hardly remember Dad. I was nine when he didn't come back; we were both born in Vienna; Dad was posted there in 1949."

"That's about right," Bruce said. "Mom took care of us pretty much by herself. Steve was around a lot after we came back to the States, but they waited out the legalities that follow an MIA."

"When were they married?" Elaine asked.

"In 1963. Rob was best man and I gave away the bride."

"That sure kept it in the family," she said.

"Right. We all went on the honeymoon – took a June vacation trip to Montana and learned to shoot and ride horses."

"Remember the night at the ranch? Must have been the third or fourth night there; we were starting an overnight trail ride the next day. Steve said he knew that we were wondering if we should call him Dad, or what."

"Right," said Bruce; "that's when they told us what they had decided about adoption. Steve said that we could drop the 'uncle' part and call him 'Steve.' He was concerned about security. Said that because they never heard anything about Dad's disappearance, they had to assume that whoever had him learned everything – real name, family, other agents, whatever. No question about his defecting – they'd have heard that right away. But since there was never anything subsequently – no accidents, no other people missing, after four or five years --they assumed there were no repercussions. Steve was glad when mom took his name. The move to Bethesda meant a new school for us and new last names would not be noticed. Mom said that our last names – Henderson – were the last part of Dad that she had and that she didn't want to lose it."

"Laney needs to know what she's getting into," said Robert, "We'll chat about it tonight. Can you stay for supper with us, Laney?"

"You bet," she answered, "but if we don't get moving we'll be late." They turned and headed back down the way they had come up.

Book 3

Gold

1

November, 1973
St. Wolfgang in the Salzkammergut, Austria

Rudi and his older brother Georgi had purchased land on the lake shore in 1960, extended the road to their new property and built a chalet facing a shallow cove. They worked diligently building up business for the machine shop they had established shortly after their arrival in Austria. Then they had waited patiently while they learned the art of scuba diving.

On this still, clear Friday night, shortly after ten, a rebuilt US Army three-quarter-ton truck stopped inside the cedar hedge that screened the isolated chalet from the road. Rudi, the driver, extinguished the headlights and backed down the sloping gravel driveway. The three men in the cab sat for a moment, enjoying the last of the warmth.

They had used their machine shop to alter the vehicle. Originally a US Army three-quarter ton truck, the cargo bed and tailgate were lower. The original canvas and bows were gone – insulated aluminum panels created a van-type cab and body. A pair of aluminum ramps hung from one side. The ramps contained rollers, allowing pallets to be winched into the cargo space. Two heaters – one under the dash, another heater in the rear of the truck – were adequate for all but subzero weather. To all appearances, it was an all-purpose work vehicle.

What didn't show was the reconstruction of the suspension system. Wheels, axles, springs and shock absorbers accommodated loads five times its original capacity. A powerful electric winch, mounted behind the front seats, pulled pallets into the bed. Next to it sat an air compressor for scuba tanks. A second battery powered either the winch or compressor.

In the chalet, a larger compressor was in its own small basement room, lined with sound-absorbing panels.

"Time to suit up," Rudi said. The two other men went

into the chalet. Rudi, who would be the winch operator and security observer, backed the truck to the water's edge. The truck's lights were neither desired nor needed – he'd done it many times. He turned off the engine and got out. Hooking the tailgate's chains to level it, he opened the truck's double rear doors, took out a heavy wooden step and climbed up. Grunting, he moved three sets of double air tank packs and weight belts onto the tailgate.

The three men – Rudi, Georgi and Peter, his nephew – twenty-five – were expert scuba divers. They'd completed hundreds of previous dives, all at night. Diving in darkness was always hazardous, especially when they needed to remain undetected. It took many dives to find and arrange what they were looking for – the gold ingots Rudi had dropped into the lake twenty-five years earlier, only a few days before the Russian army swept into Czechoslovakia.

This was the night they'd remove the gold from the lake. They had completed their preparations during the previous two dives.

On the first night, following a light guide rope and dragging a doubled haul rope behind them, Georgi and Peter descended ninety-eight feet below the water's surface to their objective. Placing two double-cam anchors in a rocky outcrop close to the pile of gold ingots, they'd inserted a bridle with a pulley. Rudi had wrapped the haul rope around the truck's capstan, and checked the anchoring of the fixed end of the haul rope to its clevis on the truck's frame. Two jerks on the rope signaled him to take up any slack.

Rudi acknowledged with two jerks. Then, he applied tension to the free end of the rope, as the capstan turned slowly, firmly seating the anchors. The tension was enough to cause the truck, its wheels chocked, to dig itself firmly into the ground. This was the objective of the night's dive. The entire operation took just six minutes.

The night of the final preparatory dive – Rudi again operated the winch – they guided their aluminum sled down to the pulley. Three feet wide and five feet long, it slid on wooden runners allowing it to be pulled in either direction. Side and end boards prevented any of its load from sliding off. Swiveling headlamps at both ends let the divers avoid underwater obstacles. The sled carried extra air tanks, short steel pry bars with safety leashes and spare headlamps. This dive was to be hard work; dropping air tanks at predetermined depths, guiding the sled along the rocky bottom; removing the cam anchors, transferring the pulley and haul rope to the uphill end of the sled and unloading the remaining air tanks. Only then could the divers return to shore, following the guide rope and stopping periodically to decompress. The night's work went as planned and rehearsed – only eight minutes at depth. The sled was ready to receive its load – one hundred and eighty gold ingots. They were heaped in a low pile on the lake's sloping floor.

The retrieval equipment was selected by trial and re-trial. They tried rock pitons for anchors, but pounding them in wasn't possible underwater. American double-cam anchors purchased in a Salzburg mountaineering store worked well and were easily removed.

Trials showed that ordinary nylon climbing rope stretched too much. In the same store, Peter found a Swiss-made nylon rope, developed for cavers, who found it ideal for rappels and load-hauling. This eleven millimeter rope looked like a climbing rope, but had very little elongation at high loads. They'd bought a 300-meter spool directly from the Swiss factory.

Georgi calculated that using a single rope for the haul line would stress the system at 84% of its capacity, if they had to start it moving at the steepest point with the sled resting on rock. This left little reserve, so they decided to use a pulley on the sled to halve the load. This also enabled the sled to be pulled down along the lake floor until it reached the anchored pulley.

They tested the entire process by loading the sled with steel bars. They rigged the rope from the sled down to an underwater pulley anchored a few meters out. It started smoothly; however, the steel runners made horrendous screeching noises underwater, as it rode over rocks. Immediately, they stopped the trial, because they couldn't chance a midnight swimmer or, worse, another diver, investigating the strange noises.

Taking the sled back to the shop, they changed the

runners from steel to wood. While it took a beating, it was silent. It took seven trials and one on-shore rehearsal before they were satisfied the reliability of the equipment and with the dive tables they calculated for each phase.

Once they had verified the gold's location, being discovered became a major concern. Divers were looking for gold in every lake in the Salzkammergut. Rumors abounded about gold having been dumped in a certain lake, or hidden in this or that salt mine. Obviously, they couldn't use their boat. They kept their actions concealed by maintaining legitimate activities. Business thrived in the machine shop. While they were well-known divers, their underwater operations at the site were conducted only at night from the shore in front of the chalet. They made many weekend dives, like other divers who were also looking – but only at other Salzkammergut lakes on the pretext of having fun.

After they mastered the basics of scuba diving, they went individually "on vacation" from the machine shop to Mediterranean schools for deep diving. They learned to calculate "dive tables" – the planning for the slow staged ascents necessary after spending time at depth. Each stop, called a decompression stop – a "deco" – allowed nitrogen dissolved in their blood to come out of solution and be expelled through their lungs. Below a certain depth, if a diver made a non-stop ascent, nitrogen would form actual bubbles in veins and arteries, causing disabling pain – "the bends"-- in the joints. Nitrogen bubbles in the brain could be fatal.

They'd learned how to use "dry suits" necessary in St. Wolfgangsee's cold water. Tight rubber cuffs on the wrists and a seal around the hood kept the water out.

Finally, they were ready to pinpoint their treasure. While pretending to fish from their rowboat, they submerged markers to define a rectangular area, reasonably sure that the gold was more or less in the middle. Their diving operations commenced by sweeping across the near edge, parallel to the shore, close to the bottom. They marked each traverse with a two-hundred meter length of string. Leaving the far end of the string tied down with another weight, they moved about two meters out and repeated the process. The lake floor sloped abruptly at first and then became less steep. They were operating at depths requiring deco stops after their sixteenth sweep.

They found the pile of ingots scattered on the bottom about 110 meters out and 30 meters deep. They left a last guiding string on the bottom as they made for the shore.

That night, two bottles of fine champagne wasn't enough for the three of them. They returned to the gold two nights later and concealed it under weighted and camouflaged canvas. Then they planned the retrieval operation, procured equipment, then designed and built what they couldn't purchase.

One day in mid-September of 1969, Georgi arrived at the chalet with lunch, saying, "Two men are down the road getting ready to dive. I pretended I didn't see them."

Rudi grabbed his arm, visibly shaken.

"What did they look like? Young? Old?"

" I didn't want to stare. One was younger."

"What were they doing?"

"Pulling on their wet suits behind a Volkswagen van. It had a Bavarian license plate."

"Georgi, bring our gear along the road. I'll grab the binoculars and see what they're doing. If they're in the water when you reach the crest of the hill, go to their van as fast as you can. But don't let them see you."

Rudi ran out the front door and along the road towards St. Wolfgang. As the road began to rise, he slowed to a walk. When the lake shore came into view, he stopped. Raising the binoculars, he saw the divers standing waist-deep in the water, talking and pointing. He watched them put on their fins and paddle for about 20 meters, where they dove.

He ran to the van. All the doors were locked. He pounded on the side in frustration and anger.

Georgi ran up, red-faced. "I brought a pry bar," he panted.

Rudi eased the bar under the rear hatch and popped it open.

"Hey, the keys are right under the mat. Let's find out who these people are."

They quickly searched the van. The key unlocked the glove compartment. A Luger lay atop two wallets. The first wallet had a German passport showing a young man with a Bad Tolz address. When Rudi opened the second wallet, his face went white and his hands trembled.

"This is the major, Georgi! I'd recognize these snake eyes anywhere. This man was the real brains of the operation."

Taking the passport, Georgi examined the pages. "Gunther Schmidt. From Bad Tolz."

Looking at the other passport, he said, "This younger one must be his son."

"Georgi, good thing the colonel shot me, because if it had been this one, we wouldn't be here. We won't worry about Nazis finding us any more. They're here in the lake. The colonel must be dead, because if he could stand up and breathe, he'd be here too. This guy's the only other person who knew exactly where to look. Thank heaven he was wrong by half a kilometer. "

Hastily, they continued searching. The wallets contained credit cards and drivers' licenses and Austrian and German currency. They found a yellowed sketch of the Schafberg as seen from the lake and a compass bearing to St. Wolfgang. Below it was a written description; *65 meters out from shore; small rocky cove; 30 meters deep.*

"They're in the wrong cove, Rudi," said his brother. "All that's missing from the sketch is our chalet. Good thing it wasn't here then. Wonder what took them so long."

"The major must have been too busy watching me and counting ingots as they went over the side. It was dark when clouds covered the moon. As for how long it's taken them, look how long it's taken us! Maybe the major had to wait for *Herr Oberst* to die."

They placed the wallets and the Luger under a nearby brush pile.

"Now what?" asked Georgi.

"Remember how we learned to use a baton against the Adam's apple from behind?

"Rudi, do you – "

"There's no choice. You can use the pry bar. What else do we have here?" Rudi opened a side compartment. "Here's a jack handle. I'll use it. We'll snorkel on the surface - where did they go?"

Georgi picked up the binoculars and scanned the lake. After a moment, he pointed. "I see bubbles about a hundred meters . . . back towards the chalet."

"They know where to look. We'll snorkel out, get above and behind them. Sun's in front of them – won't see our shadows. Dive, get behind them, rip off their masks, pull out their mouthpieces... Do that with one hand - bang, bang – then immobilize them with the baton choke."

Quickly, they stripped to their shorts, put on their BC vests and tank packs and checked each other's equipment.

"No time for dry suits today, brother."

"Water's warm as it ever gets. Won't be in it for very long," said Georgi.

"No other way. You take the one on the left, I'll get the other. Let's go."

Quietly, they snorkeled to a spot above and behind the intruders. Nodding to each other, they put in their mouthpieces and kicked down about eight meters to where the unsuspecting searchers – about fifteen feet apart – were scanning the bottom. Simultaneously, they ripped away the intruders' face masks, yanked out their mouthpieces and applied cross-arm chokes with the tools.

The struggles were ineffective and short. The bodies went limp. They deflated the victims' buoyancy vests; the bodies sank to the bottom.

After surfacing, Rudi said, "Take a good look, brother; we'll have to find this spot in the dark." They agreed on landmarks and directions, then returned to the van and drove it back to the chalet.

They draped camouflage netting over the van so that it couldn't be identified by some boater. Then, they examined everything in the van.

"This equipment is new. But no dry suits. Really weren't ready to spend any time at depth, were they?"

"Stupid – they should have done a lot of reconnaissance from the lake and along the shore first. Typical Nazi; just push right in. Strange that they had no safety person with them – lucky for us that they didn't."

"No, they wanted to keep this to themselves," said Georgi. "Eventually, they'd have needed a third person,

Rudi."

"You forget they are specimens of the Master Race."

"Let's hope that they don't stay well preserved. Good food for *Forellen,*" answered Georgi, referring to the large lake trout that inhabited the lakes in the Salzkammergut. "We'll take them to Traunsee and sink them where it's deepest," said Rudi.

After scrubbing the van's interior to remove fingerprints, they took the pistol, notebook and the wallets with the passports into the chalet, Everything else in the van – maps, clothing in suitcases, receipts, dark glasses, cigarettes, cameras -- was set aside in a cardboard box, destined for piecemeal disposal.

As soon as it was dark, they put on wet suits and SCUBA gear.

Snorkeling to where they thought the bodies were, they dove.

Ten minutes of increasing panic followed when they couldn't locate them, but finally their headlamps picked up the reflection from a regulator. The second victim was nearby. Tying each corpse's ankles together, they re-inflated the buoyancy vests and let them slowly float the corpses to the surface.

"I'll tie the tow rope to the back of your weight belt," said Georgi when they surfaced.

"That'll work. I'll do the same to yours."

They began kicking. The bodies came into alignment behind them, masks and regulators dangling. Progress was slow. An hour of effort brought them to the chalet's beach where they left them grounded close to shore. They went into the chalet and got out of their diving gear.

"This part won't be easy," muttered Georgi, as they returned to the water's edge.

"Take the Herr Major first," said Rudi. "He's the biggest. We'll drag him up to the truck; his wet suit should slide easily on the grass;"

Rudi was correct; getting the corpse to the truck was not difficult; wrestling it up and into the truck was a different matter. The other body was easier.

After closing the tailgate and the rear doors, they turned

on the interior light and examined the corpses. The first was the younger man – perhaps in his early twenties. They examined the other body. Rudi said, "The major here has put on weight."

They cut the wet suits from the bodies, leaving them clad in swim trunks.

"Save the pieces of the suits," said Rudi, "We'll use them to line the bottom and sides of the sled to protect the ingots."

"I'll check for name tags or identification on their equipment," said Rudi.

"While you're doing that, I'll take the serial number plates off the tanks and regulators," said Georgi, "They are only thin aluminum – no problem."

Rudi began a careful examination. He removed a second van key from the Major's wrist. There were no rings or necklace ID's. He took the watches from the divers' wrists. He tried to put the BC vests back on the corpses, but it was too much of a single-handed struggle – especially when he saw the Major's black eyes staring at him.

Georgi returned with the regulators and tanks. "The serial numbers came off easily," he said. "I emptied the tanks."

"Good. Help me get these dear friends ready for their final dive," said Rudi. "I couldn't do it by myself. They're starting to stiffen up."

Grunting and heaving, together they were able to get the BC vests and tank packs back on the near-naked bodies. They took extra weights from the German's van and filled up the weight belts. Then, after stuffing the regulators underneath the BC vests, they inflated the vests to their limit.

They arranged the bodies, side by side, face up, ready for head-first extraction. Then Rudi tied tow ropes around each neck. "They'll tow easier from the head," he said, "and it'll save us time when we get there."

Rudi drove their truck, followed by Georgi in the German van, along the road towards Schwarzenbach, then turned towards Traunsee on the main road. Both men were dressed in their wetsuits.

Reaching Ebensee on the Traunsee, they drove directly through town.

Rudi had said, "There's an isolated bit of beach, out

beyond the water treatment plant by the Sports Platz. Even though it's practically in the middle of town, there won't be anyone there this time of night. Remember when we repaired the treatment plant's precipitator?"

It was as he recalled it; the Sports Platz was deserted; he drove past it, turned onto the beach, turned off his lights and backed up until the rear wheels were in the water. Georgi parked the German's van in a grove of trees at the north end of the beach, killed his lights, and jogged over to Rudi, who already had opened the rear door of the truck.

"I'm glad there's no moon," said Rudi. "Let's get these into the water and I'll move the truck over to the van."

The bodies slid easily into the lake. Rudi parked the truck and, after picking up his snorkel, mask and swim fins, locked it and joined Georgi, who was by the bodies, putting on his fins.

"These guys are floating very well," Georgi said.

"Good. Let's this over with," said Rudi. "I think if we swim about 45 minutes, we'll be over the deepest part of the Traunsee."

They knew the lake well; it was by far the deepest in the Salzkammergut. They towed the corpses out to where the depth was more than 180 meters. Removing the tow ropes, they rolled the corpses face down, and then unbuckled the buoyancy vests. Wearing nothing but swim trunks and weight belts, the corpses sank quickly.

"Drahý Maminka, Otec," – "Dear Mother, Father," said Rudi, *"Jsem se držel první část mého slibu pro vás"* – "I have kept the first part of my promise to you."

"Bon appetit, Forellen," said Georgi. "Those weights will ensure they will sink below the depth where our bodies lose their buoyancy, and gravity alone will keep them on the bottom."

Venting the buoyancy vests, they made bundles from them and the tow ropes, tying them around their waists to minimize their drag in the water. They made good time returning to the little beach, which remained deserted. They took the time to obliterate the vehicle tracks in the sand, using garden rakes they'd brought along in the truck. As they worked, Georgi said, "Tomorrow morning'll be soon enough to scrub out the truck bed, just like we did to their van yesterday afternoon. There's bound to be hair and debris from the bodies, and we'll burn the BC vests. I wore my neoprene diving gloves. I'm certain that if fingerprints are found, they'll belong to our departed friends."

Rudi agreed, saying, "I tied a knot in the ends of the ropes, where they were tied around their necks. I'll cut off those ends with a hot knife and burn them along with the vests."

To confuse searchers that were certain to be looking for the missing men, Georgi drove the van, followed by Rudi in their truck, back the way they had come, then turned right on Ischlerstrasse to Attersee – another lake, thirty-five kilometers away – leaving it parked and locked, at a popular dive site.

Exhausted, Rudi drove their truck back to the chalet, reviewing the situation. "We never saw another vehicle on the road, Georgi, did you notice that?"

Georgi said, "It seemed like we were the only people alive on the earth."

"It'll be only a short time before the owner is identified."

Days later, there was an extended uproar from Bavaria about missing divers – a father and son – but the bodies were not discovered during several subsequent searches – in the wrong lake, of course.

Rudi and Georgi's wives and children were never told about this episode. Elsa, however, looked at Rudi with knowing eyes when she read the newspaper accounts.

2

November, 1973
St. Wolfgang im Salzkammergut, Austria

During a dive several weeks before Rudi and Georgi planned to extract the gold, they sketched the disposition of the ingots. Laying out the pattern on the chalet floor, they decided where to place the sled to transfer the ingots. During earlier dives to count, to evaluate and practice handling the ingots and to organize the pile, they learned that swimming with an ingot was dangerous. Even picking up an ingot was demanding. After trials, they decided there was too much complexity involved with tools – plus the danger of dropping one. They found it best to form a "bucket brigade." One man picked up an ingot and handed it to his partner, who would turn and place it on the sled. It looked like a slow-motion ballet.

They learned that fins had to come off to maintain agility and to minimize stirring up silt, reducing visibility. They rehearsed each task to minimize time at depth, averaging nine seconds per ingot, or twenty-seven minutes total. Adding the time needed to change tanks and secure empties, removing and securing their fins and a bit more for contingencies, they planned thirty-nine minutes at depth. That brought them dangerously close to having oxygen narcosis, delaying thought processes and slowing reactions.

They memorized rock formations and drew up the recovery route profile, pinpointing deco stop locations. Each dive's timetable was recorded on charts strapped to their forearms as well as in Rudi's hands.

The divers were responsible for signaling each decompression stop – and when to re-start the withdrawal. Two double taps on an air tank signaled both starting and stopping the winch. Their charts had each decompression depth recorded, when they ascended to the desired depth and signaled "stop". Rudi would release the tension on the haul rope and start timing the duration of the decompression stop. By having the divers do the signaling, Rudi could verify narcosis wasn't affecting their mental condition. They had learned that divers sometimes dozed off during a long "deco" – and if the deco ran over more than a few minutes, Rudi planned to start the winch. "That'll wake you up."

Prior to each dive, they pre-placed air tanks at deco stops. Their problem: the longer the time spent at depth, the longer the delay periods were needed on return. They prepared for any eventuality, including building a hyperbaric chamber in the basement of the chalet. In the event of a run-away ascent, a diver would be placed in it and the compressor would pressurize the chamber, eliminating the crippling pain of the "bends." Then, the pressure would be bled off slowly, in accordance with the dive table that had been violated.

The electric winch had a capstan – a steel drum with flared sides. Two or three turns of rope, when pulled tight on the constantly-rotating capstan, provided the pull. It was easy for Rudi to maintain moderate tension on the rope, letting the capstan do the work of reeling in the sled. They planned the operation to take under three hours.

Rudi set a pair of chocks behind the rear wheels. He lowered the tailgate and attached the ramps to the rear of the truck bed. He placed his dive chart on a clipboard. Fastening a hydrophone to an underwater stake about a meter from the shore, he unreeled its wire as he returned to the truck. The hydrophone arrangement worked perfectly; tapping on an air tank with a pry bar could be easily heard, even from two hundred meters distant.

Now, shivering from the cold and tension, Rudi donned his dry suit. As the leader, he'd stay on shore – and also because his left shoulder was not completely functional. As he completed an equipment check, his brother and nephew helped each other don their air tank packs and weight belts and make final checks. Then Rudi placed his dive equipment on the truck bed, ready in case of an underwater emergency.

The divers walked into the water carrying their fins. Not a word was necessary.

"Good luck, Georgi, you too, Peter," said Rudi as they shook hands. As they paused to put on their fins, Rudi picked up the end of the haul rope, took in the slack, passed three turns around the winch capstan and tied the end loosely to the tailgate.

Rudi turned to watch for a quick flash from a headlamp which meant *"Alles in Ordnung"* – "all's OK." When the signal came, he started the stopwatch. *"They should be there in four minutes, fifteen seconds."*

Inserting the hydrophone's earpiece, he heard air bubbling as they exhaled. Now all he had to do was wait for the rope signal, or the two double taps of a pry bar against an air tank and the final stage would begin. It was half an hour before midnight.

* * *

The layer of fine silt initially covering the ingots was gone – fanned away during each visit. Their camouflaged canvas minimized subsequent accumulation and the ingots flashed in the beams of the divers' headlamps as they pulled off the covering.

Each ingot scattered on the floor of Wolfgangsee weighed forty-two pounds. Only a couple of pounds lighter in water, if a diver dropped one he might shoot upwards uncontrollably before he could respond by venting air from his suit. The total weight of gold on the sled – 7,530 pounds – had a value of four million US dollars. By the end of the century, its value would be more than \$32 million US dollars – if it stayed hidden that long.

* * *

Five pings. Rudi felt several light jerks on the haul rope. He responded with a few tugs of his own – they meant "I understand – go to work!" The divers were ready to load the sled. He reset the timer. Almost immediately he clearly heard *thump . . . thump . . . thump* from the hydrophone, the sound as accurate as a metronome's. To Rudi, it was music of ecstasy. He could not help himself – he shook with excitement, and then forced himself to calm down and listen. He realized that he'd been counting the thumps and was already at twenty-one. Transfixed, he continued to count – now twenty-six; the sled's neoprene-surfaced floor should soon be half-covered. The depth timer read one minute forty-five seconds; the divers were averaging four seconds per ingot. The rate would slow down as the divers worked further from the sled.

Rudi raised his head, looked around, pulled out binoculars and scanned the surface of the lake. Nothing moved. Nothing ever did at this time of night, but this was the crucial hour. In concentrating on scanning the lake surface, he'd lost count. No problem; he'd listen for the double thump which meant the last ingot was going onto the sled.

Swinging to the left, he inspected the shoreline of the cove, panned across to the road that led to St. Wolfgang. Everything was dark, nothing moved. The thumps were definitely slower now; he counted to himself; *tausend eins, tausend zwei, tausend drei* . . . and was at 'tausend zehn' before the next thump came. Ten seconds apart, now. *Very close to covering the floor,* he thought.

Then it came – *thump THUMP!* There! The sound of eager joy in a "thump!" Now, the noise of loading would change. Gold striking gold would be almost inaudible. He might be able to hear the start of each new row as the ingots contacted the sled's side. He could picture Georgi building the next layer, starting at the lower left-hand corner of the sled, where gravity helped the process. Orderly stacking was mandatory so they'd fit in the available space.

One-third done, six minutes elapsed. On schedule. Now, the process would be silent. And slower. *This suspense is stressful – maybe we should have a way to signal "everything OK". But no, they are very busy. I just have to wait.*

He picked up the binoculars again and strained to see something – anything – out on the dark water. *Maybe we should have picked a night with some moonlight,* he thought. *No, that would make it easier for anyone with binoculars to spot us.* He doused the dim red light over the dive chart. No sense advertising, even though testing proved it was invisible at a hundred meters. *Maybe it would be better if some fog developed – no, that would hide anyone sneaking up on us.* He checked the revolver – it was in the special holster next to the binocular case; its retaining strap was unsnapped, its silencer protruding. *Relax, Rudi, it's not even time to hold the rope. Watch for intruders; listen for the next double thump, except it'll be five taps on an air tank, followed by a tug on the rope.*

I'll respond with an answering pull on the rope – I heard, I know that you're starting the last layer. All's OK up here."

It seemed an eternity – but the stopwatch said the next signal came only nine minutes after they began loading the second layer. Total time at depth: fifteen minutes and a few seconds. *So far, so good.* The divers had begun loading the third and final layer. The transfer rate would be slowing now.

Each man was taking a few slow-motion steps. They had started at the edge of the pile closest to the sled and worked their way inwards. Most of the first layer required only a step or two. While one was picking up an ingot, turning and walking toward the sled, the second man took similar slow-motion steps towards him. The first man handed off the ingot and returned to the shrinking pile.

Rudi's wristwatch indicated 1:30 AM. Across the lake, headlights flashed briefly in his direction. The vehicle was not a concern. Orion was well above the horizon; mirrored in the glassy water. Twenty minutes at depth, now, Rudi was as cold as if he'd been in the water. No matter; he'd warm quickly enough when he begin to maintain tension on the rope around the capstan and keep his eye on the timing for the decompression stops. They had already experienced the way that time seemed to stand still during the deco stages. Rudi jogged in place and swung his arms around – then scanned all quadrants. Still quiet.

The clink of a pry bar on an air tank startled him. Two hits – they were changing air tanks. Time at depth: twenty-one minutes. The hard work underwater caused breathing rates to increase drastically, but air consumption was only a little above what they had predicted. The loading was nearly complete. He listened to the faint sounds coming from his earphone. He scanned the adjacent woods and shoreline. Two more clinks. Tank changes were complete and they were continuing to load. Twenty-six minutes. .

Then silence again. Four minutes crawled past.

Then, definite metallic thumps: *There go the empty tanks on the sled.* Five clangs. He took the rope in his hand and felt two strong pulls. Thirty-one and a half minutes – perfect! He answered with two pulls of his own and switched on the winch motor.

Bracing himself, he pulled the rope tight against the

capstan. The truck's springs squeaked as the rope came taut and quivered.

Slowly, slowly, the rope came to full tension and stopped slipping around the capstan. The sled was moving after 32 minutes at depth. Rudi started a second stopwatch – this one had a chart of time versus depth, based on the rate of extraction.

He could hear muffled grinding noises as the runners complained; things were moving smoothly. He could picture Georgi and Peter fastened to the haul line by a short rope. They didn't have to work to keep up with the sled as they used their pry bars to stay on the path of least resistance.

The gold was now only eighty meters away. Rudi kept a constant strain on the rope; the winch growled as the sled came scraping and creaking up the floor of the lake.

Rudi was sweating heavily now. As the second-hand approached its sixth circuit of the dial, he heard the signal – tap, tap – tap, tap. He relaxed his strain and the haul rope went slack. He started the second stop-watch, turned off the winch and verified the deco time – three minutes for deco halt #1.

He picked up the rope that had been accumulating around his feet and coiled it on the ground. A minute and a half to go on the stop; he picked up the binoculars and scanned the surface. Bubbles at the right place. A half-minute to go.

Two double taps. The divers were right on. He stopped the deco timer, started the haul timer and pulled the rope tight around the capstan. He glanced at the profile sketch – *six meters to haul, but the slope's steep.* The winch growled.

Forty seconds. Two double taps. Rudy let up the tension but the rope didn't slacken. The sled was sliding back on the rock. Two urgent double taps sounded and he pulled hard. It was if he and the divers were reading each other's minds – *take it up a little more, over the crest of this rock face* – he knew the spot, he visualized the problem. He pulled in two more meters.

Again, two double taps – the sled was over the crest. He relaxed the strain; this time the rope slackened. He turned off the winch and started the deco timer. Deco halt # 2 would be seven minutes.

* * *

The agony was in the waiting. *Are you watching me from Hell, Major Gunther Schmidt? How many thousand souls are on that sled, dear Major? What were you going to do with the gold? Send it to Argentina to keep some tottering madman alive a little longer? Didn't you understand that oppressed people will strike back eventually? Didn't you learn anything from the trials at Nuremburg? How many others like you have avoided that fate? I am not a murderer, dear Major; I just carried out the sentence you would have received for murdering my family. I wonder if you passed a similar sentence on your own Herr Oberst – is that why he was not with you on your last dive?"*

3

November, 1973
On the northeast shore of St. Wolfgangsee – 1:30 AM

What I should do with the gold, Rudi wondered. *My father taught me not to spend money I don't have and don't plan to buy anything with money I think I'm going to get. First, set the goal of getting the money, and then achieve the goal. But who do I talk to? If only I could talk to Nikolai.*

Rudi wanted desperately to free his homeland, which was suffering under a yoke of oppression as bad as anything the Nazis imposed. People who spoke their minds in Czechoslovakia simply disappeared.

Watch the deco timer; wait for the seven minutes to pass. Smiling, he rotated the egg timer given him as a joke by his daughter Lisa. *"Watching the sand will keep your mind off worrying about what's happening down there. Just don't lose count of the number of times you turn it over."*

When he'd come back to Austria the first time, in 1955, he'd gone straight to the old stone farmhouse outside of St. Wolfgang. Rudi had maintained contact with the Schäfter family by mail. After 1946, most letters got through.

Some years earlier, Elizabeth had told him in a letter she preferred to be called Elsa, because Wagner's "Elizabeth" seemed tragic. Within seven months of his return, he and Elsa were married in St. Wolfgang's onion-steepled church. At twenty-one, she was a pretty bride. Their only child, Lisa, was born in 1958.

Now he was officially Eduard Holder, who preferred to be called Rudi. Georgi and his wife, accepted as new Austrian citizens, took the same family name.

Rudi realized the sand had stopped flowing – some time ago. *Needs an audible signal, h*e thought. Deco timer said two minutes to go. He picked up the binoculars, swept the lake surface and the adjacent shorelines.

Again, two double taps interrupted his scanning of the

area. He put down the binoculars and checked the deco timer. Turning on the haul timer, he took up the strain. The rope came in easily. The double tap sounded; he relaxed the strain and the haul rope slackened. He started the deco timer running. This was deco stop #3 and it required fifteen minutes. Every stop doubled the wait time of the previous one and, without keeping careful track, it would be easy to make a mistake. He gave four slow tugs: *"I'm going to look around. I'll signal when I'm back."* Four answering tugs said *"OK."*

Pulling out the earpiece, he rubbed his ear. Putting the revolver's lanyard around his neck, he walked up the driveway to the road. He scanned in both directions. *Nothing.* He cupped his hands to his ears and slowly made a full circle. *Nothing to see, nothing to hear.* An owl hooted in agreement.

Returning to the truck, he put the revolver back in its holster, replaced the mini-speaker in his ear and listened. Bursts of bubbles, rhythmically burbling. *All's well.* To check, he tugged lightly on the haul rope. . . *I'm back.* It tugged back . . . *"Good."*

Attaching the divers to the haul line was working well. They could feel rope signals without having to hold a line all the time. *It's lonely down there – dark, headlamps turned off to save batteries. Hope they are warm enough.* He looked at the dive profile. Deco stop #3 was 12.3 meters below the surface. If he had to go to their aid for any reason, he wouldn't need to be in his dry suit – a wet suit would be more than adequate.

Their planning considered the need for emergency response by Rudi. The simplest scenario would probably be a problem with an air tank. There were extras on the sled, more at the next deco stop. *I'll get a folding chair from the chalet during the next pause.*

Two pings – he answered with two tugs, turned on the winch and took up the strain. Again, the line snapped taut, spraying water. *Pulling harder now . . . the slope to the fourth stop is steeper . . . forty seconds to go.* He relaxed his hands on the wet haul rope as the next pings sounded. Re-starting the deco timer, he the circled <u>Stop #4</u> on the chart. *26 minutes. Check. They've been in the water one hour, eight minutes and fifty seconds. Hard part of the waiting is yet to come.*

Rudi turned out the dim red light, tugged four times on the rope and felt the answer. He took out his earpiece, picked up the revolver and binoculars and headed for the chalet. He knew Elsa would be sleeping lightly, if at all.

He dialed the number; the phone burred twice, then twice more.

"*Ja.*"

Rudi took a breath, overcome with emotion at the sound of her voice. His throat swelled and he couldn't speak.

"What's wrong, dear?" asked the tinny voice in his ear.

He swallowed and said, "Nothing, pussycat. We're on schedule. I'll call you in another two and a half hours. Get some sleep."

He replaced the handset. Picking up a thermos of coffee and a folding chair, he left them in the driveway and went up to the road. *I hear nothing.* He headed back down the driveway, picked up the chair and the thermos, went down to the truck and signaled with the rope that he was back on station.

Ten minutes to go. He opened the chair and sat, suddenly realizing how fatigued he was. He lifted the binoculars to his eyes; the lake's surface was still. He thought about coffee. *I'll wait until the next deco stop.*

After a few minutes, he got up heavily; the dry suit was awkward to move around in. He holstered the revolver, swinging out the cylinder and feeling the back end of the cartridges as he did so. He turned on the light over the timers; and checked the chart again. He put the hydrophone's earpiece back in.The second hand needed two more revolutions to make and it would be time. He tugged lightly on the rope – no response. He yanked it harder, several times and finally felt a steady pull – "*Yes, we're awake down here.*"

He waited a bit, finger on the switch that started the winch. The time ran to its end; as he watched it go past the vertical, he waited before starting the next leg.

How accurate is their timing? Are they alert?

Two vigorous yanks came on the rope and two pings from an air tank.

Good. Ten seconds over – close enough. He started up the haul timer and took the strain one more time.

As the rope tautened, again snapping water in all

directions, he realized that the sled's sound was different — more muffled. *It's firm mud between deco stops #4 and #5. Must be getting tired.* Hand over hand, he pulled the rope in, watching the timer. Finally, two quick pings — he relaxed his strain, watching the haul rope go slack. He started up the deco timer and circled deco stop # 5 — a 51-minute halt, where they'd change air tanks.

At least, they'll have something to do for a bit, helping each other with tank changes. He looked at his watch — one-twenty AM. *Time for me to have some coffee.* He sat, opened the thermos and filled the cup. He heard four separate *clunks* as a depleted air tanks were stacked on the sled.

No sign of anyone on the lake or onshore.

Abruptly, Rudi jerked fully alert. His eyes had closed. He reached for the thermos, unscrewed the top and sniffed the steam that came out. Pouring the cup half full, he looked at the deco timer; he'd dozed for ten minutes. They had agreed that dozing was fine on the bottom, but that Rudi should maintain a security watch. It was probably not necessary. In all their night-time operations on the lake, they had rarely seen or heard anything, once the summer traffic stopped.

The night sky was so clear that the stars on the horizon were as bright as those directly overhead. He turned to the deco timer — three minutes to go. One more stop. Now, the gold was only 25 meters away. He heard activity from six meters below the surface; they were checking the straps on the sled. The haul rope stirred lazily in the water. Time for one last look across the lake; still nothing.

He took the rope in his hand and held slight tension. There! Two firm yanks!

He switched on the winch, took the strain and the sled and the truck springs groaned a duet that only he could hear. Fifteen, thirty, forty-five seconds — and two hits on an air tank. He relaxed the strain, turned off the winch and reset the deco timer. Now the gold was only three meters below the surface, thirteen meters from the shore. He pulled out his earpiece, verified that the haul rope was slack, grabbed his mask and put it on as he ran into the water.

Flopping onto his belly, he dove down to Georgi and Peter, pounded their shoulders and looked at the sled.

Just as he'd envisioned – a shimmering flat plane of bright yellow. He needed air – he turned to Georgi and motioned to his mouth. Georgi handed him his regulator; he took a couple of deep breaths and reached out with both arms. The three embraced. He turned to the sled, slid his hand across the gold ingots, felt the depressions of the swastikas. He pointed at his watch and surfaced. A few strokes brought him to shore; he stood up, light-headed from the sudden effort. It was 2:15 AM. *Two more hours of darkness,* he thought. *Enough time to get the sled into the truck and lock up everything.*

Now began the longest deco stop of all – an hour and forty-three minutes. It would be 4 AM when the gold surfaced for the first time in twenty-eight years.

Another long look around. *Nothing.* Rudi gave four tugs on the rope and felt the response. Again, he took the revolver and headed for the chalet. Inside, he stripped out of the dry suit and donned the torso section of a wet suit.

His brother had prepared heavily sweetened milk and cocoa. He filled two insulated plastic bottles with the hot liquid. He jogged back to the truck, holstered the revolver, put on his face mask and headlamp and splashed in. He dove down and handed a bottle to each of them. Not replacing liquid and calories could get to be a problem on a long dive, unless they dealt with it.

He popped back to the surface and returned to the truck. When they'd emptied the bottles, they'd just let go and they'd bob to the surface. He'd swim out and get them and, about three-quarters of the way through the deco stop, he'd refill them.

4

November, 1973
On the shore below the Chalet on Wolfgangsee

Another owl called in the darkness. Three o'clock in the morning. Less than an hour to go. Rudi was sure his watch had stopped – was the battery dead? No, the second hand twitched. Five quiet clinks came from the lake floor; Rudi watched where the bubbles continued to break the surface. He saw two yellow bottles bob up. He paddled out to where they floated lazily.

Looking down, he saw his brother and nephew flash their headlamps at him as they lay on their sides. The sled remained in darkness. He waved; they were only three meters below him . . . a vital three meters. Even now, if they came to the surface, there was a very good chance of bubbles forming in their blood. They had the time; they had acquired the discipline to maintain the schedule for the procedures that would keep them out of trouble.

Collecting the bottles, he kicked easily in to the shore. He pulled the rope four times, then scanned the lake shore and the surroundings. *When is the best time for an intruder to launch an attack? Right about now?* he thought grimly. *When I'm dog-tired and my guard's down?* He picked up the binoculars and scanned again. *This time, I'm looking for somebody looking at me. Is that a reflection of starlight from his binoculars? Do I hear a muffled cough? Was that a click of a Mauser's bolt closing on a bullet that will find me?*

All was as still as a cemetery. He strapped the holstered revolver around his waist, then walked up to the chalet and circled it.

He paused at the lower level door and again scanned a semi-circle. *This time, I'll leave by the front door upstairs.* After refilling the two bottles with the still-hot chocolate, he eased up the stairs and released the dead-bolt on the front door. It opened quietly on oiled hinges; he scanned the front yard and the cedar hedgerow. Nothing moved. No sounds. Vapor from his breath drifted away.

He took a key from a hook and inserted it in the lock from the outside. Stepping out, he turned, quietly closed the door as he held the key against its return spring. Then he released the key and the bolt seated quietly. *That would have sounded like a gunshot if I hadn't used the key.* He walked quietly up the path and passed through the screen of cedars to the road.

If one turned right towards the village of St. Wolfgang, it quickly became a footpath and only bicycles were permitted. If one turned left, the road led past the driveway into the chalet. He walked a short distance along the road, climbing steadily. Pausing at an old memorial – Falkenstein – he looked back at the chalet with his binoculars. He could barely see the outline of the truck at the lake shore through the cedars.

He followed the road's trace through the glasses, aware that it had grown perceptibly lighter. Three new chalets were under construction – the builders' cranes marking their locations. *We couldn't have waited any longer,* he thought. *In another year, this place will be swarming with more people, even in November.* A hundred meters away, a fox ran across the road toward the lake. *Thank you, my good friend. You're a good watchman. If anyone was within a half kilometer, you wouldn't be there.*

He turned, walked briskly downhill and entered the chalet. Picking up the insulated bottles, he went to the truck and checked the deco timer. Fifteen minutes to go. Exhalations sounded clearly in the earphone. He jerked the haul rope four times and it responded with four answering tugs, seeming to ask *what took so damn long?*

Holding the bottles, he waded in to his thighs and relaxed, letting the water cradle his weight. He pulled his dive mask into place and bit down on his snorkel's mouthpiece. After a few strokes he switched on his headlamp – its brilliance startled him. A flash guided him to the others. Jacknifing down to them, he handed over the bottles. He took a breath from the proffered regulator, held out his hand and opened his fingers three times – fifteen minutes to go. Thumbs up from them.

He allowed himself to rise to the surface, where he stopped. It was darker than ever – he'd spoiled his dark-adapted eyes by turning on his headlamp. Floating quietly, he could gradually make out his surroundings. He bobbed there, listening; the silence brought back his confidence. He stroked for the shore, stood up and waded in to the truck. Six minutes. Only six minutes and he could begin to plan what to do with the gold.

The deco timer said one minute to go – *close enough for government work* – as his American friend said.

He turned on the winch motor and pulled the rope. The winch's whine seemed terribly loud and the haul rope vibrated like the strings on a bass viol.

Thirteen meters . . . now twelve – eleven – he wondered how loud it was and he realized he hadn't put the hydrophone speaker in his ear. *No time for that now, just keep it coming.* He glanced over his shoulder, just in time to see the two men stand up in the water.

They stumbled towards land, one on each side of the sled, each with a hand on the front rail. As Rudi maintained tension, the sled's skids slid over a half-meter of dry ground and touched the end of the ramps. Rudi dropped the rope, switched off the winch motor and went to them. He took his brother's tank pack and swung it out of the way. Then he did the same for Peter, who was shaking violently.

"Cold, Peter?" He nodded, his teeth chattering.

"Run up to the house and get dry clothes on. There's also more hot chocolate."

Georgi said, "Me, too, Rudi – that last decostop went on forever. We'll be back in a few minutes."

"Best you don't turn on lights upstairs. The curtains are all in place downstairs so it'll be OK – just make sure the door is closed before you turn them on."

"Ja, ja." Georgi ran off, lifting his legs high to get the blood flowing and unzipping his dry suit as he went.

Rudi busied himself, trying not to look at the gold. His wristwatch indicated five minutes after four A.M. The sky over the Schafberg was brightening perceptibly. It would soon be dawn. Finally, he looked at the gold.

It lay neatly on the sled, shining brightly. Drops of water beaded each ingot. He leaned over, flattening his hands on the top layer. *Cold as ice.* He bowed his head and wept, thinking of all the pain that this little pile represented.

Book 4

May, 1998

The Ranch

1

May 1, 1998
the Ranch – Sperryville, VA

If you were able to proceed westerly from the nation's Capital for 58 miles, you'd be on a hilltop, eleven hundred and sixty feet above sea level – the highest point of The Ranch. The view to the east revealed lower hills descending to the Potomac River valley. To the west, the Blue Ridge hid the final stages of sunsets. The sparsely populated area contained homes whose owners respected each other's privacy

Bruce and his brother Robert called it "The Ranch" as a private joke, because the CIA called their facility in Langley, Virginia, "the Farm." Several clearings, scattered in four hundred acres of trees and scrub, were connected by woods roads. The main building crowned the hilltop where Bruce lived alone. A path led north to a knoll, where another slightly smaller home housed Robert, Elaine and their two sons, both in their twenties.

An obstacle course for dogs was in one clearing; another was the site of a 200-meter target range. They fired through ports in an air-conditioned building lined with sound-absorbent foam.

Bruce and Robert had installed chain-link fencing around the property. They needed to keep errant dogs inside while keeping out white-tail deer and hunters. Seismic sensors covered three-quarters of a mile of the fence. When they'd installed the first trial equipment, Bruce had said, "Rob, if these things work as advertised, they'll detect human footsteps or running dogs. A half-dozen of these can be placed around a very large building to control lighting and the lights will come on and go off, illuminating only the area where the intruder is. Also, Rob, at the main gate, we'll install similar sensors with the capability for vehicle count and type – automobile, small truck, or larger vehicles. Three of these can tell us if visitors are in trucks or cars and how many of each, from a distance of more than a hundred meters. This will be our demo installation for customers. A central solar panel will keep the entire system fully charged.

"I'm not concerned about actual infiltration. We need to get first-hand experience with what works and what doesn't and develop a demonstration site for clients to observe the relative effectiveness of various devices. "

Four-wheel RV's made it simple to move people and material quickly around the complex of internal roads and paths. To their great delight, each nephew had received his own RV on his thirteenth birthday.

The horse barn looked its age, but it was sound and weather-proof. They'd moved it onto new footings, walls and concrete floors. The barn now sat down the hill, about a hundred yards from the main house.

Four separate areas on the main floor, each with a series of box kennels, opened to large outside fenced areas. Dogs had full-time access to their kennels, the indoor area and outdoors. The smallest area was reserved for females in heat, or as the maternity ward. Each area had its own microphone and two TV cameras – one for normal light and one infra-red. Loudspeakers and monitors were in the control center on the house, adjacent to the consoles for the intrusion system.

The barn basement served three purposes. It was a garage for the ATV's, a workshop – Robert's empire-- and an armory.

The temperature and humidity-controlled armory occupied the last section of the building. It held an array of weapons in five cabinets designed for storing large drawings – one cabinet for each family member. Each cabinet contained pistols, revolvers and accessories for each, ranging from .45 caliber Glocks to little Colt .380s with a selection of holsters. Most revolvers had silencers.

An Israeli 9mm Uzi occupied another drawer, along with a German MP-50 .45 caliber machine pistol. A commercial gun safe housed long weapons; a fifty-caliber sniper's rifle, with its suppressor and day and night telescopic sights; two Springfield 30-06 rifles equipped with a choice of telescopic sights, for either day or night use; a launcher for M79 grenades, two .22 caliber Remington NRA match rifles and a

Savage Model 99 250-3000 rifle. A separate custom-made gun safe stored a dozen Russian rocket-propelled grenades in their launch tubes.

Robert maintained this array of lethal weapons. He was the weapons coach for the family.

In contrast to this array of firepower were two dart-firing CO_2-powered rifles. The projectiles held a variety of medications – all non-lethal-- that would produce short-term incapacitation or extended unconsciousness. Robert, Bruce or Tom could routinely put a dart into a person's thigh or calf from forty meters away. The torso itself was assumed to be protected with body armor.

The newest addition to this array of firepower was five Tasers, non-lethal weapons that immobilized an individual in a half-second. Carried and fired like a pistol, its twin darts trailed thin insulated wires. Even through several layers of clothing, the high voltage discharged into the target's body scrambled the individual's nervous system, creating an instant loss of muscle control. The effect lasted several minutes, providing enough time to disarm and secure a perpetrator.

Several hundred rounds of ammunition for all weapons were kept in the armory, along with five sets of night vision goggles. Kevlar body armor for each family member was stored in wall lockers, along with clothing suitable for any climate or camouflage pattern.

Light-weight body armor was included for the dogs. Covering the dog's flanks and chest, Bruce understood this protection was minimal and that he was at best reducing the lethal target area. A dog hit by any of the higher-powered handguns would experience a tremendous impact, perhaps breaking a few ribs – but would not kill him. But the sight of an animal in body armor could distract a perpetrator.

Daily life at the Ranch was routine – at least for the dogs. Five to nine adults and two or three pups between three months and a year old were enough to create a significant amount of work. Hank often sighed, "I wish I had a dog's life."

Every morning, the older dogs took a long run inside the perimeter fence, usually with all the family members. The humans jogged about two and a half miles while the dogs simply ran and ran, enjoying the freedom to simply tear around, harass squirrels, chase rabbits and only occasionally sweep by their slow human companions. Then, back to the kennels for a quick physical check for thorns in paws, removing the morning's burdocks, a quick but enjoyable grooming with a wire brush, a look in the eyes, ears and mouth and a slap on the rump and off they went. If there was an accumulation of snow, the morning run was an extra delight. The dogs loved to dive into snowbanks and snap at ski poles whenever the humans used cross-country skis.

Each dog had some training each day – walking exercises, a session in the confined space or a section of woods to find an explosive device or a concealed person, or a monitored perimeter sweep.

As dogs advanced in training, they were taken one at a time into the outside world. New distractions challenged concentration on what the trainer was trying to achieve. They walked with one of the family in cities, in parks and supermarkets, to apartments, learning how to be docile and obedient. Several weeks of training would find a dog keeping his head by the trainer's left knee, always with slack in the leash – through crowded sidewalks, across busy streets, paying no notice to strange dogs – loose or leashed. They were simply above all that.

By then, their vocabulary contained up to twenty words and ten hand signals – single-syllable commands spoken with varying degrees of urgency and intensity. Words used by the average person attempting to control a dog – "stop" – "down" – "no" – "here, boy" – were simply not in the vocabulary.

Physical discipline was never used. The word "shame!" stopped misbehavior. As the dog's skills developed, he was happy to hear praise and have a quick rub on his head for a task done well.

2

May 1, 1998 – Dog days

On this bright Friday – unusually crisp for May – Bruce and Robert were each working a dog in separate areas. Bruce had Toby in a "final review" session; they had done a series of short repetitions of heeling, bracing, staying and coming. They were on their way to the edge of a clearing where Tom, Robert's oldest son, waited in concealment, wearing a padded suit.

The scenario: Toby, unleashed, would be told to search – "Toby, BUMP" – "find somebody hiding and bark when you do." Toby took off on a circling run and quickly spotted Tom, crouching behind a fallen log at the clearing's edge. The dog backed away, his eyes on Tom and barked.

As Bruce approached the dog, Tom rose and produced a dummy pistol, hanging loosely in his hand. Because Toby had not been wearing a bungee lead, he would not attack Tom – he'd keep perhaps ten to fifteen feet of separation, dividing his attention between the two men. The dog did not think that an attack was imminent either because Tom had a gun, or because he was wearing the suit. To reinforce this, half the time, the two trainers would go hug each other and the exercise would be over. The dogs loved the suit, because they could demonstrate their capability of subduing a potential enemy. This time, the dog could not differentiate friend from foe.

Following the plan for this morning's exercise, Bruce came closer and said: "Toby, DONT." The dog stood still and waited for the next command. He looked at Bruce when he heard the command, saw Bruce's right arm bend upward to the vertical and he lay down, facing Bruce. He kept rolling his eyes towards Tom, as Tom was still an unknown quantity. Taking two steps, Tom leveled the pistol.

Bruce yelled "Toby, BITE."

The big dog launched at Tom, clamped his jaws on the

gun arm, the force of his impact knocking Tom down. Toby quickly shifted his attack to Tom's throat and Bruce called "Toby, BACK." The dog backed away from Tom, who rolled to his belly and began to get up.

"Toby, SPOT" called Bruce and the dog bounded to Bruce, looking up expectantly. Bruce bent down, scratched behind Toby's ears and said "Good Booooy, Toby, Good Boooy. Toby, STICK." The dog bounded up and raced around the two men. He found a tree branch and proceeded to thrash it. Carrying the stick's remains in his mouth, he trotted over to Tom, who grabbed it and they had a brief tug-of-war.

"This pup's a winner, Bruce. Does he go to the prospect for an interview this afternoon?"

"That's the plan, Tom. Want to go along?"

"No, I need to work with Pete. He took off after a rabbit yesterday while we were on SPOT with no leash. About five minutes later, he came back looking disgusted. I don't know if it was because the rabbit got away, or if he was feeling guilty."

Bruce helped his brother remove the heavy Kevlar-reinforced suit.

"I'd bet on the rabbit angle. How did you handle it?"

"I said SHAME and he got mournful, so we went to STICK for a few minutes and he seemed okay, so we jogged back to the barn. Who's the prospect today, by the way?"

"We're going to see Duncan Firney," Bruce answered; "Dunc was a classmate of mine in OCS at Fort Benning. After he got out, he finished up at Harvard, and then joined the Diplomatic Corps. Did OK there – was in Bonn for a tour, then to Saudi Arabia all through the Gulf war. He's keeping tabs on some of those Saudi princes as well as on Saddam. Don't know if his diplomatic job is cover for CIA or NSA or something. He's a good guy. Said he's in exposed positions from time to time. I think he'll seriously consider taking Toby here. So – we'll go see him and Toby will strut his stuff. I dated Marie – his wife – a few times before he came into the picture. We're pretty good friends."

"Yeah. I remember her. The flighty one." Tom finished rolling up the suit and lashed it to his back pack.

"All set? Let's get moving'."

The two men settled in to a steady jog for the half-mile back to the barn, with Toby bouncing at an easy trot at Bruce's left knee.

3

May 1, 1988.
The Ranch House

The group gathered for lunch at the ranch house; Elaine brought sandwiches and two fresh strawberry pies from her kitchen garden.

"I didn't see your four-wheeler today, Laney," said Bruce. "Did you walk over?"

"Yep. Too nice a day to spoil it with exhaust fumes."

"You're all duded up, Bruce. Heading into town this afternoon?" Hank asked.

"Yup – Toby is going for an interview. Anybody need anything?"

"You could drop a book at the library for me, Bruce," said Hank. "It's due in a couple of days."

"No problem. Put it in a paper bag and I'll let Toby carry it to the desk – the girls love to see one of the dogs."

Warrenton's County Public Library and the Jail Museum each had posted signs – "Service Animals Only" so Bruce had procured bright red vests labeled "Service Dog in Training." The dogs were so well-behaved that there was never a problem.

"While I'm away, review the training schedule and see if we need to make any adjustments," said Bruce. "Tomorrow – Saturday – it looks like Tom and Hank will be working all of the Stage I dogs, I'll have the Stage II's and Rob, you have the Stage III's. Laney, could you ask Karen if she'd ride over with one of her horses on Sunday. We'll see if it goes better than last time."

Karen, a good neighbor who boarded horses, was always eager for off-road riding. During a previous visit, a Stage I yearling was so excited by being around a horse for the first time that he broke commands and had to be taken away. Since then, he'd been exercised several times near the horses in Karen's paddocks and had settled down somewhat.

"It's time to get going," said Bruce, pushing back his chair "Toby, SPOT."

The big dog had been sprawled on his side all through lunch. Only Stage III dogs were allowed in the house; it was a privilege that they loved.

Toby got up, yawned, stretched and walked over to Bruce.

Bruce said, "See you folks at supper. Let's hope I bring good news."

"It's good and bad news, Bruce; I'll miss ol' Tobe," said Elaine.

"Gotta put dog food on the table somehow," laughed Bruce. "Hey, before I go, I had a call from Sid, asking asked if we'd run a security mission for them on Friday, week after next. A foreign politico is speaking at the National Press Club. Sounds like it'll take all five of us with Tuck and maybe Riggs – he's good on search. I'll tell him we're good to go. They'll no doubt have a briefing next week at 14th and F."

A chorus of "OK" sounded around the table. Bruce waved and went out the door with Toby, looking expectant, at heel.

* * *

Toby needed no invitation or command – he knew a ride in the car when it was offered. The driver's door opened. He jumped in and sat on the passenger seat. As the engine warmed, Bruce picked up his cell phone and dialed his contact in the Secret Service. A call from Sid usually meant that the Service was again slightly short on manpower and needed assistance with site and VIP security and interdiction, if necessary.

The Hendersons all had security clearances just short of nuclear data. Their talents for observation, communication monitoring, close-in protection and assault interdiction were frequently called on. It meant that the Ranch would receive photos of individuals who might provoke an incident, or to harass a public figure. Like most assignments, this one would require a site visit in company with federal officers to discuss possible scenarios to create a VIP protection plan.

Sid answered his phone on the second ring: "Hi, Bruce, thanks for getting back promptly. Can we meet at the Poppa Charlie next Wednesday, eight AM?"

"We'll be there. You want coverage from the street to the podium and back to the car again? Or is your party coming in through the basement?"

"Tell you when we see you. Still discussing it."

"OK. See you Wednesday."

He punched the *end* button on the cell phone, touched Memory 1. Elaine answered on the first ring: "Henderson Enterprises."

"Next Wednesday morning – 0800 briefing. The three of us."

"Got it, Bruce."

"Tell Hank somebody'll have to stay home to work the dogs."

He broke the connection, put the car in gear and headed down the driveway, mentally reviewing the layout of the "Poppa Charlie" – standing for the National Press Club. Calls from cellular phones had been intercepted. Users discussing sensitive issues kept their calls brief and non-specific.

* * *

Forty-five minutes later, Bruce stopped by a row of large homes in Chevy Chase, not far from Westmoreland Circle. He got out, went around the car and opened the door.

"Fella, we're almost there. Break time. Toby, STICK."

Toby looked at Bruce, wandered over to a tree, sniffed and urinated copiously.

"Should have let you do that before we left, huh? Good boooy, Toby." His tail wagged.

"OK, Toby, SPOT." The dog came to heel and they returned to the car. They drove a few more blocks, turned onto Grafton Street and parked in front of an older Victorian house.

"Wouldn't do to have Duncan see you peeing all over his shrubbery before you'd been introduced, Tobe. Come on out, fella." He patted his thigh; the dog jumped out and looked at Bruce. "Toby, SPOT." They went up the front walk and Bruce rang the doorbell.

4

May 1, 1988
Chevy Chase, MD 3:30 PM

Duncan answered almost immediately. "Right on time, Bruce, come on in. The dog, too."

Duncan led the way through the way into a living room overlooking the rear gardens.

"I see Marie's still into gardening. Toby'll love it."

"Yeah, she has help – man comes in two days a week. Drink?"

"Thanks, maybe later. Toby, PLATZ." Toby dropped to the floor and lay there quietly, watching.

"I must say that I've never seen a dog so well-behaved and comfortable in a strange environment," Duncan said. "You said that you trained them for different purposes. Like what? Finding drugs?"

"Not quite that," said Bruce, "Some are trained to sniff out explosives and we train others as protectors."

"Like Seeing Eye dogs?"

"More as bodyguards. Toby, here, can make you a difficult target if you're attacked. He's trained to deal with direct assaults. Looks like just a well-trained and obedient companion; what doesn't show is that he remains aware of possible hazards to you from unexpected, close-in sources."

Duncan contemplated Bruce's answer, obviously considering the possibilities.

"Yeah, the Company wants me to beef up my personal security when I'm off-duty. What all did you teach him?"

"In the beginning, Dunc, it's similar to teaching avalanche dogs to search for people buried under the snow. First, they learn to find the trainer by playing hide-and-seek and then they learn to find the trainer, who may be partially buried and then fully buried – under controlled circumstances, of course. The breakthrough comes when the dog realizes that they are to find <u>somebody else</u> who is under the snow.

121

"We work essentially the same way. Done as a game, it's fun for the dog, but the transfer from finding the trainer to finding a stranger isn't easy. I have the same problem; I can train the dog to protect me. Training the dog to protect somebody else is harder. I have found a way and I can tell the minute the dog recognizes that his mission in life is to protect – not just me, but whoever holds the leash."

"Interesting. Are they trained to be attack dogs?"

Bruce went to the sideboard and helped himself a glass of water. Toby, who appeared to be dozing on the rug, opened his eyes. His head remained between his paws while his eyes rolled to watch Bruce.

"Yes, but only against a person that they don't know, or a person who smells wrong, or a person holding a weapon. I had an embarrassing demonstration one time, when my client's bodyguard went down with my dog on his arm. He'd pulled out his gun when my pretended assailant made his move from behind a parked car. Dog didn't realize he'd gone for the wrong person. Problem was, I hadn't introduced the dog to the bodyguard."

"You gotta be kidding!"

Bruce pulled a short leash from his briefcase. "I'm serious. Already Toby thinks something's up." Toby, watching, thumped his tail on the floor.

"Dunc, if you want a demonstration right now, we can do it. But not unless you make a decision for more training – not for the dog, but for yourself. You'll learn his vocabulary and you'll accept the fact that Toby is trying to teach you how to behave."

Duncan opened a box on the table and took out a cigarette.

"By the way," said Bruce, "Toby is a non-smoker. You'll have to be one too. You told me you were trying to quit, anyway – so that's another commitment you'll have to make." Duncan put the cigarette back in the box.

Bruce continued, "A dog's nose is a complex organ. Toby can detect and remember hundreds of odors that we can't even perceive. Second-hand smoke can destroy much of his capability. In the moments before a strike, a professional hit man isn't as cool as he pretends to be. His metabolism is really pumping. You want him to smell that fear and excitement. Toby recognizes that and will focus on him."

"Wow," said Duncan, frowning, "how long can he live in a constant start of alert like that?"

"It's this leash." Bruce waved it, Toby's eyes following. "It's the principal control element. He's only on 'full alert' when it's on him. It's very short – just long enough to reach from your hand to Toby's collar, with a little slack. Two elements make it different – it's made from a bungee cord so it can stretch and this link" – pointing – "releases with about a five pound pull. Toby will never pull on this leash unless he perceives a problem. Then he'll break away and deal with it. Normally, he'll be on your left, just far enough ahead to have clear vision on both sides. The really important part of this leash is something that can't be seen; it's that Toby knows that when it's on, he is to protect me." The room was silent. Toby thumped back down onto the floor and sighed deeply, his eyes fixed on the leash in Bruce's hand.

"One other thing," said Bruce, "A large dog like this has to run nearly every day for an hour or so. You can turn him loose and he'll keep you in sight. You hike two miles in the woods, he'll do ten. Or fifteen. Anyone can do this, but it's gotta happen."

After a pause, Duncan nodded. "Gotta do it, I guess!"

Bruce said, "OK – here we go. Toby's been waiting for this ever since I took out the leash. Toby, QUICK!!"

The dog leaped to his feet, took two bounds and sat in front of Bruce. Their eyes locked. There was a *click* as Bruce snapped the leash on Toby's collar; the dog, quivering slightly. Bruce took the leash and offered it to Toby, who took the end in his mouth.

"Get up, Dunc, ya bum. This is a formal occasion!" Bruce said.

"You see, Dunc, Toby knows that 'quick' really means 'come and sit down and stay there until I tell you to do something else.' Because he has the short leash in his mouth, he's in control of himself , but he can't give himself any orders so he'll stay there until hell freezes over. So I'll resolve it by calling him by name and telling him to come. Toby, QUICK!" The dog again took a couple of bounds, sat, with his eyes locked on Bruce's as before. Bruce took the leash from Toby's mouth and placed it in Duncan's left hand. The dog stood up, looked quietly from one man to the other and back again. Then, he moved to Duncan's left and sat down, eyes on Bruce.

"There,'" said Bruce, "you're now in the family, chum. Let's take a walk outside."

Bruce went to the bottom of the front stairs. "Marie, Duncan and I are going out for a short walk. We'll be back in fifteen minutes."

"Okay, but we have to leave at four and he has to get out of those awful clothes."

"Women," muttered Duncan.

"Before we start, Dunc, you're now in charge of ninety pounds of dynamite, waiting for the fuse to be lit. Because we don't want him excessively defensive, you can switch him to a standby mode with the command – I spell, we don't want him to hear me say it – C-H-E-C-K. Say it to him now, say his name first, make it a sharp, incisive command, in a conversational tone – don't shout – ever. Now."

Duncan drew a deep breath and said, "Toby, CHECK." The tension dropped out of the dog. "We are going to walk to the front door. He'll stay on your left side. Because he's on the short leash, he's anticipating trouble. If Marie threatened you with her rolling pin, she'd be down and he'd be on her throat – not biting, but she'd feel teeth.

"Now, Dunc, he's waiting for a command. He's in limbo, but because he's on the short lead, he's expecting to either go defensive, or to stay on standby. If you start to walk, he'll go with you. Walk to the front door with me. Open the door, say 'Toby, B-R-A-C-E' and he'll be back on the defense, a head-length ahead of you. Give him a moment to see if it's safe. Then just walk out. I'll repeat these important commands in a sentence and he probably won't pick up on it – you'll say 'brace' when you want him ready for an attack and 'check' when you want him to standby with the short leash. Ready?"

Duncan nodded assent and opened the front door, Toby at his side. He said "Toby, BRACE." Toby took a step, his head swiveling, his nose wrinkling furiously.

"OK, Dunc, step out and walk down to the sidewalk

normally." Toby led, the short leash staying snug, his head continuing to scan in a half-circle. "Stop at the end of the walk, Dunc."

He did so; Toby looked back at Bruce, waiting to see who was boss.

"Duncan, say 'Toby, CHECK' and unclip the leash." He did so. The dog sat, looking at Bruce.

"Here's what's happening, Duncan. Toby hasn't developed allegiance to you; he kept looking back at me. It's the first time that he's worked with a possible owner. We do this only when we're pretty sure there's going to be mutual acceptance. For safety's sake, I'll take over Toby's leash now. You follow on behind and watch. I'll explain what we are going to do. We'll walk around the block; I'll turn his defensive mode on and off a few times. He's having fun!" They walked along together, Toby keeping his eyes even with Bruce's left knee. "Toby, BRACE."

The dog moved forward about eight inches; his walk stiffened up and his head and eyes constantly scanned the semi-circle in front, with a frequent check on Duncan at the rear.

"What if you simply unhooked him from his leash?"

"He'll relax and stay right here at heel."

"What about the neighbor's Golden? It's always running loose and is quite a barker."

"Don't worry about it, Dunc. He'll want to show his dedication to me."

They walked on, with Bruce alternating the commands – "BRACE" and "CHECK" a few times, while they both noted and commented on, the change in the dog's attitude, alertness and position.

"He'd really like to tangle with somebody," said Bruce, "but we'll wait for that until we can have one of the kids put on the protective suit out at the Ranch and come at you with a knife or a handgun."

While Toby was in the "check" mode, Bruce reached down and unclipped the short lead and put it in his pocket. Toby sat down. Bruce gave Toby's head a rub. Toby's tail wagged.

As they turned a corner, a large Golden launched at them,

barking. Toby looked up, first at Bruce, then at Duncan. The Golden went to Toby and sniffed his muzzle. Toby blinked and turned his head away. The Golden crouched, yipped like a puppy, feinted a rush and backed away, tail waving. Toby yawned.

"How long will this go on?" Duncan asked.

"As long as you're willing to stand there and watch," said Bruce; "or until the dog's owner calls him back inside. He's ten or fifteen pounds overweight, obviously well cared for. Tried working with the breed, but couldn't develop the aggressiveness we need."

"What if a dog attacks him?"

"Toby, BRACE." Instantly, Toby faced the Golden; his lips drew back in a snarl and he rumbled a deep growl. The Golden raced for his porch, where he turned around and watched Toby silently.

"Toby, CHECK!" Bruce said; the big dog sat down and licked his lips. Duncan unclipped the lead and they resumed walking. Toby took up his position and never looked back.

"Quite a performance, Bruce."

"Tell the dog, Dunc, don't tell me. Say 'goood boy.'"

Duncan rubbed Toby's head and didn't dodge the face-lick.

"If I'd said 'bite,' that Golden would be in dog heaven right now – same with any other attacker. Or if I'd unclipped the leash and said 'stick' – the command for play – they'd be friends for life."

They turned the last corner and approached Duncan's front walk. Bruce asked, "Think he's the dog for you, or do you want to interview another one?"

"I'd say yes right now, Bruce, except Marie's afraid of dogs."

"Not a problem. She can handle Toby as easily as you just did. I'll set up a meeting for the three of us without the dog, then as many sessions at the Ranch as we need. She'll learn that he'll be a wonderful, affectionate creature to have around the house."

They found Marie in the front hall. "Too warm for a coat, Duncan?" she asked. "And did you tell Bruce about Lisa?"

Bruce was instantly alert. Marie was an inveterate matchmaker, especially since she and Bruce had decided to remain "just friends."

"Who is Lisa?" Bruce asked.

"Lisa Holder. She's a fairly new under-secretary at the Austrian Embassy. I think the two of you would get on ever so well."

"How's her English?"

"Her legs are ever so pretty, not at all dumpy like so many Austrian girls, Bruce." Marie chattered on, ignoring Bruce's question.

"Nice boobs, too," put in Duncan.

"Oh, you men!"

"What do you mean, 'you men', Mrs. Firney, I only asked you if her English was good. The last date you got for me was a linguistic challenge. She spoke half Swedish, half Finn."

"Well, anyway, Duncan has to be at the Austrian Embassy Tuesday afternoon and he's going to bring her here for supper. Why don't you come and perhaps take her home? Duncan has an early flight Wednesday and needs his sleep."

Bruce thought for a moment. *Austria... I wonder if she's from Vienna. My German is rusty. Why not?* He pulled his calendar out of his shirt pocket and flicked it open.

"That'll work," he said; "What time?"

5

May 5, 1998

The Ranch – Sperryville, VA

"I think I've spent the whole morning on the phone." Bruce pulled off a light rain-jacket and rubbed his face, as the family gathered for the noon meal. They were at Robert and Elaine's house, in her kitchen with its panorama of the Blue Ridge. Today, however, the mountains were hidden in mist.

Nobody needed an invitation to dig into the pile of sandwiches on a platter. Elaine ladled soup into bowls and started them down each side of the table. Finishing his soup, Robert asked, "How was training this morning?"

Tom said, "I think the dogs are depressed by the weather. I worked the fence with Victor, Snow and Abbie. Abbie was easily distracted and seemed content to watch the others."

"Think she's cut out for this?" Bruce asked

"She'd be a great guide dog. We'll keep an eye on her and decide in another month. Remember, she was on the small side for what we wanted to breed."

"Glad we stopped doing our own breeding. It's a lot easier for us to look over what our breeders have. Also, we had the danger of creating a limited gene pool."

"Speaking of gene pools," put in Hank, "Don't you have a date tonight, Bruce?"

Hoots of amusement erupted.

"Yes, Hank. Since us three grown-ups have an early meeting with Sid and his crew tomorrow at the Press Club and since I've been inveigled into taking my date home from Duncan's after supper, I'll stay at the Central Holiday. That's close enough to the Press Club. Laney, why don't you and Rob join me there for breakfast? It's a fifteen-minute walk to the Press Club. That'll save us from the usual parking problems."

"I wouldn't mind a break from preparing breakfast for four guys who eat like wolfhounds," Elaine answered. "But listen, guys, I've been thinking."

"Got an idea, Laney?" Robert asked.

"Yes, I have. There's been another suicide bombing in the Middle East – he was wearing explosives, walked into a crowded restaurant, set it off and killed himself and a bunch of innocent people. Aren't these events often followed by an imitator? And is this a situation that could apply to the Press Club, if the speaker is from an eastern Mediterranean country? I seem to remember hearing that he was. And shouldn't we have our best explosives sniffer there? Riggs? Or maybe Tuck?"

The table was silent as each visualized various scenarios of the Press Club.

"Elaine, that's an angle that hadn't occurred to me," Bruce said. "I've been thinking of defending against a more overt action. Who is the speaker?"

"I'll call Bess."

"OK, find out what you can, Laney." Bruce continued: "Your angle is a good one. We haven't dealt with a suicide attack in the USA. There's always a first time. Let's all of us think over that idea and we'll talk about it at breakfast. In the meantime, Elaine, could you please set up sessions for Riggs and Tuck with the Warrenton police? Need to have a stranger wearing the explosives vest for Riggs to isolate in a crowd. The supermarket would be ideal. Hey, time to get back to work – gotta leave about four, so you guys have a good afternoon and I'll see you at breakfast."

"Have a good time, Bruce. Hope she's a pretty lady."

"Thanks, Hank. You got out of telling what you did this morning, but I assume it was productive."

6

May 5, 1998
Wisconsin Avenue, District of Columbia

Bruce yawned and stretched, looking at his watch. Four-thirty. It seemed as if he'd been sitting in stop-and-go traffic forever. His plan had been to take Wisconsin Avenue to Massachusetts Avenue, then follow Massachusetts north to Westmoreland Circle

Worked well last week, he thought. *But it was an hour and a half earlier. Marie said cocktails at five; if I'm indecently late I'll call her. Got a half-hour yet.*

He was stuck in a parcel of traffic that stayed out-of-sequence with the lights. *I wonder what her last name is. How does a single Austrian girl get to be an Under-Secretary? If I could have found a girl like Elaine, I'd have been married long ago. What a mind — "how about a suicide bomber?" Wonder if the CIA thinks about that. How would we take down a guy wearing explosives? Can't shoot him — could set off his load. Robbie could — he's so quick with his hands and feet. Have to keep a perp's hands immobilized. Riggs would follow, his tail wagging like he smelled steak. Wonder what a perp would think if he saw a happy dog looking up at him, grinning? Would he understand he was being fingered? Never thought about a dog taking down a walking bomb. One of us'll have to do it. If Rob was wearing a waiter's outfit and carrying an empty tray as a shield for a Taser while I worked Riggs . . . when a perpetrator has explosives around his belly, a hit from a Taser would work if the dart struck anywhere on his body — in the legs, in the ass, in the arms. . . we'd take him from behind. . .*

Bombers have used pull-wire igniters, or they close a circuit from a battery to a blasting cap. We'd get the battery out of the circuit right away. . . Pull-wire igniters and conventional fuses give a perp the chance to change his mind about going to Paradise. Rob could move against traffic, I can tell him to look left, central, or right. Riggs would be tagging right along beside him and the perp probably won't even notice.

Rob'll let the perp pass by, then turn and nail him in the butt at very close range. We'll talk about that scenario at breakfast.

Bruce finally got a break in the traffic and turned north onto Massachusetts Avenue. A few minutes later, Bruce swung the Blazer onto Grafton and spotted Duncan's car in the driveway. He pulled in behind it and parked. He got out and headed for the front door. *Wish I was a dog. Could use one of those bushes right now.* He rang the doorbell and Marie opened it.

"Come in, Bruce. Right on time – always so reliable."

"Thanks, Marie, been looking forward to this all weekend." *Cross my fingers, that's a lie.*

She took him by the arm and led him to the living room. "Duncan's in the kitchen, doing something about drinks. I'm no good at that sort of thing."

"Marie, you said that if we ever got serious, you'd learn to cook and be a real domestic jewel," said Bruce, laughing.

"Hush, you goose; Duncan doesn't think along those lines. We have a nice Puerto Rican gal – she truly does have a green card – I'm not going to get Duncan into trouble like some women here in Washington – and she's a great cook."

They turned the corner and entered the large living room. "Lisa," said Marie, "here's Bruce Henderson. I bet he hasn't slept a wink wondering what you'd be like."

A tall woman with long tawny hair rose and turned towards Bruce. He felt cool fingers curl around his. She shook his hand once, and then released it.

"I'm Lisa Holder," she said. "Marie said you work with dogs. Must be very interesting work."

Eyes are the bluest I've ever seen. Handshake was Austrian. Just a hint of a "v" when she said "work" . . .

"Lisa, it's Bruce. Where in Austria do you call home?"

"In the Salzkammergut, a dozen or so miles east of Salzburg. Do you know Austria, Bruce?"

"Not very well. My older brother and I lived in Vienna when we were young. We played with the local kids and spoke the language. Mom made sure we kept it up into our teens. Both of us speak in what we think is German every now and then, just for fun." *Why am I babbling like this?*

Marie interjected, "Why don't you two stop staring at each other and sit down there on the couch?"

"Do you remember what a *Heiratsvermittlinerin* is, Bruce?" Lisa asked, smiling.

"Yes, Lisa; please sit there in the chair so I can look at you and where Marie can't pick up my arm and drape it casually on your shoulder."

They laughed and sat in chairs facing each other. Lisa stretched out her legs and crossed them at the ankles, her dress swirling around her knees. *Marie was right. She does have pretty legs.*

Marie, a frown wrinkling her eyebrows, said, "Whatever are you two talking about?"

Lisa answered, "Marie, do you remember the musical, 'Fiddler on the Roof,' and the song that the oldest daughter, sings: 'Matchmaker, Matchmaker, make me a match?'" Lisa sang the words as wistfully as any Tzeitel had ever sung.

Bruce said, "A *Heiratsvermittlinerin* is a match-maker, Marie."

"Well, it certainly sounds nicer in English – especially the way Lisa sings it."

Bruce quickly changed the subject. "Do you sing, Lisa? Professionally, or for fun, or anything?"

"Of course, Bruce. I'm an Austrian country girl, just like Julie Andrews in 'The Sound of Music.' My father had me learn English and other languages, when I was very young. That's when he got television. There were stations from other countries – he asked me to tell him what was happening in London, in France, in Prague, in America – all in the languages I heard. It was a challenge . . . and fun. He insisted I become multi-lingual and I'm very glad that he did. It has opened many, many doors for me."

"C'initi vy mluviti C'esky?" Bruce asked, picking up on her mention of Czechoslovakia's capital.

"Yes, Czech and Slovakian - fluently," she replied in English. "Dad was a Czech. But we shouldn't talk strange languages in front of Marie. She'll think we are talking about her."

Bruce said, "You're right. We'll stick to American English. I'm somewhat of a language nut myself and my brother is also. Your accent is purely American, perhaps like a girl from Ohio."

Duncan appeared with a tray of drinks. "Lisa, here's a nice Austrian white wine for you; I made you your favorite,

Bruce – simple Scotch with a touch of water and ice. Marie likes Singapore Slings, so I've outdone myself."

Lisa said, "Thanks, Duncan. I've been avoiding Austrian wines here, because American wines aren't common at home and it's fun to have something different."

"Thanks, Dunc. I'm ready for this," said Bruce.

Duncan handed Marie her concoction, saying "Here's your vitamin C, dear," and took his drink – a duplicate of Bruce's – and sat beside Marie on the sofa. "Here's to happy days," he said.

Bruce asked, "Lisa, what brings you to America? You're in the Austrian Embassy?"

"Yes," she responded. She shaded her eyes – the late afternoon sun shot its rays through the window. Duncan got up hastily and lowered a window-shade, but not before Bruce saw that Lisa's tawny hair turned golden in the sun – *all the way to the roots*, he noted. *A natural girl. I wonder how old she is.*

"I'm an Undersecretary to an Undersecretary in the American Law Division. I'm studying the intricacies of how Americans do business – both with each other and with other countries, so I can advise my countrymen how to better present themselves and their products, to America and the rest of the world."

"Are you a lawyer at home?" Marie asked.

"Yes, in government and business law. Being a lawyer is a respected profession and there aren't as many female lawyers in Austria."

"There aren't as many lawsuits anywhere else in the world as we have here, are there?" queried Bruce.

"No. Sometimes I think that America is bent on self-destruction. It's terrible that courts can award these astronomical judgments for frivolous – oh, what's the word – situations or episodes. And to see lawyers appearing on TV advertising that they can 'make them pay' for alleged accidents or alleged product deficiencies – this pervasive attitude is going to destroy your economy. Please excuse me; I am sermonizing and as a recently arrived guest in your beautiful country, I apologize."

"No apologies needed, Lisa, you speak the truth," said Duncan gravely. "It's a big problem. We complain to each other about it, but it's going to take years to repair what it has already destroyed."

"Bruce, Lisa would be interested to hear about your work. She loves dogs. Tell her about Toby," Marie commanded.

"Bruce, who is Toby?" Lisa asked.

"One of the dogs that I've trained. He'll be joining this household soon. In England, he would be called an Alsatian, but here in the USA, his breed is called a 'German shepherd.' You would know him as a *Schäferhund.* His two brothers are also in training."

A woman wearing a small apron had quietly entered. "Mrs. Firney," she said, "dinner will be ready in just a few minutes. Perhaps you would enjoy the appetizers now?"

"Thank you, Delores. We'll be right in." Marie rose from the sofa reached out, took Duncan's hand and pulled him to his feet.

Bruce held out his hand to help Lisa rise from the deep chair. She took it willingly.

They followed Duncan and Marie into the dining room. Bruce pulled out a chair for Lisa. As they sat, Bruce had the feeling that Lisa let go of his hand reluctantly. She smiled at him as she sat. A whiff of fragrance – *cloves and roses – something?* – teased his nose. A frisson swept through him – and he almost rested his hand on her shoulder for a moment. *Must have been a hunger pang,* he thought. He went around the table and concentrated on the appetizers.

"What are these, Marie? I've never seen anything like them," asked Lisa, indicating her appetizer.

"Soft-shell crabs from the Chesapeake Bay. Ordinarily, they are a little messy to eat. Delores prepares them so they aren't intimidating for anyone who hasn't had them before. Hope you'll like them as much as I do. Delores makes a lemon sauce that is really nice."

Bruce noticed that the crabs' heads had been removed, along with the legs and feelers. The remainder had been separated into golden brown pieces, arranged on a bed of rice, garnished with fresh fennel fronds. A clear glass dish containing a yellow sauce was next to each plate.

"Ordinarily, these are cooked and served whole," continued Marie, "but since this is probably the first time you've had a chance to have soft-shells, I didn't want to scare you off. " She took up her small fork, speared a piece, swirled it in her sauce, popped it into her mouth, closed her eyes and chewed blissfully. "Mmmmm. Now I know spring is really here."

"Most of the fish we had when we growing up came right from the lake we lived near," said Lisa. "My father and uncle were both fishermen and we had *Forellen* – lake trout – a couple times each week. After we got a freezer, we had fish all year. Father always knew where the best places and times were for fishing. Before the war, my grandfather had kept a journal where he recorded the places and conditions when the fishing would be best." She took piece of crab.

"Marie, I understand why you have that look on your face. This is delicious."

Bruce asked Lisa, "Do I recall that there are quite a few lakes in the area that you mentioned – which one do you call home?"

"It's called St. Wolfgangsee, Bruce. I was brought up just outside St. Wolfgang, at the northeast end, closer to Salzburg. I have an apartment in Salzburg, close to my office. It's nice to go home on the weekends – summer or winter. Tell me about your dogs, Bruce. I've always wanted one"

"My brother and I have built up a rather nice business training dogs to be unusual companions – actually, they are more of a protector for people who may feel they are at risk when they appear in public, or they want protect their homes. We also train them to detect any kind of contraband the owner may want to identify."

"Drugs?"

"No. We're more focused. We train them to find explosives, or identify people who have handled them recently."

Bruce was thinking of Riggs as he spoke. Riggs would alert on a firecracker buried two inches deep. He didn't mention suicide bombers, thinking it best to down-play the other part of the business, at least for a while.

"How many dogs do you have and where do you do this?"

Bruce poised a small piece of crab leg on the little fork as he responded.

"We've fixed up an old farm about an hour's drive to the southwest. Right now, we have sixteen dogs in various stages of training. We learn about aptitudes and higher training proceeds accordingly."

Lisa said, "That was very nice, Marie. Very rich. Bruce, do you ever have guests at the dog academy?"

Marie cut in, "I think Lisa is asking for a show-and-tell, Bruce."

Duncan kicked her leg under the table.

"Ow, Duncan." They all laughed.

Duncan asked, "Bruce, how is your mother doing?"

"Very well, Dunc. She's an unusual combination of frail and strong. We found a nice assisted-living place in Warrenton for her and Stephen. She's fiercely independent, as you know; 'I can do it' is her whole approach to life. I stop by several times every week and so do Robert and the boys. She and Stephen come to the ranch frequently – they enjoy getting out. He no longer drives."

"How old are they, Bruce?" asked Marie.

"Mom is eighty-two and Stephen is eighty-seven and sharp as a tack. He was seventy-five when he retired – and he's as knowledgeable about what's happening in Central Europe today as he was when he had the chair. He still talks with people he mentored."

"Stephen is your step-father, Bruce?" asked Lisa.

"Yes. They were married back in nineteen sixty-two. I gave the bride away and my brother was the best man."

Silence followed Bruce's answer.

"I'm sorry," Lisa murmured. "Didn't mean to throw cold water on the party?"

"Not at all, Lisa. Someday I'll tell you all about it." Bruce surprised himself with his own words.

Duncan gave Marie a look that said *"don't say a thing."*

Dolores appeared and collected the plates.

Lisa said, "Marie, those were certainly delicious. Where can I find them? I'd love to cook them, if Delores could tell me how to make that sauce."

Delores glanced at Marie, who nodded.

"Yes, ma'am, I'll write it out for you. One of our family

secrets."

Bruce said, "Family secrets are sometimes the best kind. Are there secrets in your family, Lisa, besides your grandfather's fishing journal?"

Her face contorted. Quickly, she regained her composure.

Quickly, Bruce said, "I didn't mean to pry."

"That's all right. As you said, I'll tell you about them someday."

Duncan said; "Hey, we all have hidden scars and disappointment. Let's move on."

"Father Duncan saves the party," Bruce said, laughing. "It was headed for 'True Confessions' for a few moments!"

"Anyway, here's Delores with our supper," said Marie. "It's one of my favorites and I know you'll enjoy it." Delores placed a platter of broiled salmon in front of Duncan.

"She smears the salmon with mayonnaise and seasoning and then broils it. Very simple; even I can do it. Please, Duncan, start the serving dishes around, but you can hand your plates to Duncan – he'll dish out the salmon. That's a heavy platter."

Delores returned with a marble wine holder. She placed it in front of Duncan and lifted out the bottle part way. He glanced at the label. She inserted a cork extractor, pulled the cork and poured a small amount in Duncan's glass.

"Just want to be sure," he said. He sipped it and nodded.

Delores moved around the table, filling their glasses.

Bruce said, "I've never seen a cork come out of a bottle that easily."

Marie answered, "Brute strength, Bruce; you should feel her biceps. She's a black belt in Tai Kwon Do." Delores smiled.

Bruce answered, "Think I'll pass on feeling her biceps – or perhaps I should offer her a day job, except that sometimes it's not a day job."

Lisa looked at Bruce and asked, "Why do you need people with black belts to train dogs and what is this Tie Can Doo thing?"

"Good questions, Lisa. Tai Kwon Do is one of the martial arts. Originated in Korea. You've seen those people on television – whirling around, kicking each other?"

Lisa nodded, her nose wrinkling.

"It has nothing to do with training dogs – sometimes we assist government agencies in providing physical protection of key people – either to discourage physical attacks, or prevent them from taking place. The dogs are extremely valuable in these situations and we all have capabilities of protecting ourselves and our clients. Site security and VIP protection is an integral part of our business." Bruce stopped himself from describing the purpose of the next morning's meeting.

"How many people do you have working at the dog ranch, Bruce?" came from Marie.

"It's still just the family – my brother Rob, Lisa; his wife, Elaine; their two sons. We have part-time help – a local man comes in most days – maintenance, mostly. He was with my brother in the Navy before he retired. He feeds and waters the pups when we all have to be away. His wife usually keeps him company when he stays over."

"Does he help with the training also?" Lisa asked.

"Sometimes he'll hide and a dog has to find him. If we are all away, he'll exercise the dogs. They haven't bonded to him, but they'll obey him pretty well on the simple things. He always has dog biscuits in his pockets; they know that and will hang around just in case."

Lisa asked, "Bruce, what if somebody tosses a raw steak to a guard dog and then does whatever they want to do while the dog is eating it?"

"Our dogs would probably do the same thing. Difference is, we train them to work with a handler. Hopefully, they'd ignore it if their handler told them to search an area. They might go back to it when the job's done. If they are distracted by something like that, a single word from the handler would put them back on track. We have to remember that they are dogs and have all the instincts of a dog. However, a basic instinct of every dog is to please the humans with whom they are closely associated; we build on that characteristic."

"Is there training every day?"

"Yes, Lisa. We are pretty busy. Elaine's our scheduler. She says, 'eighteen dogs divided by four men is four and a half hours. That's what you guys will spend with the dogs today, if you want them to have an hour a day.' The dogs look forward to it; we all have fun working with them. But – eighteen pups is the maximum. We can work more than one at a time, as they sometimes are called upon to do that. One could be looking for a threat, while another is providing area security. Same as with sheep dogs – a handler will work two dogs; both herding, or one with the handler to be dispatched when he's needed."

"How do you punish a dog that misbehaves?"

"We never use physical punishment, Lisa. We merely tell them how bad they are. The tone of voice does it all. . scornful, loathing. We're pretty good actors. You should see how quickly their tails go down between their legs. They know when they've been bad and will come groveling. Sometimes, when they are feeling frisky, they'll test us to see how close to being a bad dog they can be. They really develop quite a vocabulary. I've even said, 'C'mon, whoever, you don't want me to call you a bad dog, do you?' and he'll snap right out of it and go to work. Their favorite time is when they hear 'good boy' and get petted behind the ears."

"I'd really love to see it, Bruce. I mean it."

"We can work it out, I'm sure. Marie, this has been an excellent supper and I bet I know what dessert will be," said Bruce.

Marie said, "How much do you want to bet, smarty?"

"A dollar says it'll be crispy meringues with vanilla ice cream and fresh strawberries."

"Ha! Gotcha! I'll take your dollar! It's meringues with fresh strawberries, but with frozen vanilla yoghurt – I'm watching Duncan's waistline!"

As Delores cleared the dishes, Bruce pulled out his wallet from his jacket pocket, found a dollar bill and passed it over to Marie. She folded it neatly and tucked it in her bra, grinning wickedly.

Duncan shook his head. "Lisa, I'm married to a compulsive gambler. Trouble is, she wins a lot. Some nights I'll see her take ten or fifteen dollar bills out of her brassiere. I tell her I'll cut her allowance, but she doesn't change her ways."

Delores brought in a silver coffee pot.

Duncan said, "I'll pass tonight. I'm up early tomorrow to

catch my flight."

Bruce glanced at his wristwatch; two hours had flown by. "I have a meeting early tomorrow morning, downtown, so I'm staying in the city overnight. The gang is meeting me for breakfast so we can discuss our agenda for the meeting."

Lisa turned to Bruce. "Marie said you'll take me home? That would be so nice – I haven't really figured out how the bus system works here in Washington."

"It remains a mystery to many people, Lisa," Bruce said. "Now, if you had a dog…" They all laughed.

"Ever the salesman," Duncan said. "From what I saw last week, the products pretty much sell themselves." He checked his wristwatch. "You know how to get to the Austrian Embassy, off Van Ness Northwest? Follow Reno Road south?"

Bruce nodded. "I can find it."

"I keep forgetting that you used to live around here, Bruce."

Lisa glanced at Bruce; he missed the look.

They all pushed back from the table. "I won't ask if you want to take a doggie bag," said Marie. They all groaned at her humor. In the hallway, the men shook hands and the girls hugged.

A chorus of "goodbyes" resounded as Bruce and Lisa headed towards his car.

7

May 5, 1998 8 PM
Chevy Chase, MD, to Georgetown, DC

"Oh – a Blazer. Nice. What's the grillwork for?"

"We often travel with more than one dog. Older dogs have learned to stay in place in a car. Younger ones may be more excitable. We need to be sure that he doesn't wind up helping to steer."

She laughed and as he swung into the seat, he again smelled *roses and... Cloves?* teasing him with a subtle fragrance. *I wonder if she's ever been married. Certainly is pretty. Got a good head on her shoulders, too.*

Lisa laughed. "I like a man with a sense of humor, one who can tell a funny story." She turned serious as she added, "My father hardly ever laughs. He's had some sad times and has tried to make up for it in different ways, but I've never heard him tell a funny story."

"How old is he, Lisa?"

"He's almost seventy. He's in excellent health, still goes to the machine shop that he and my uncle started up right after the war. Uncle Georgi's a couple years older than my father and is pretty much retired. He was the best machinist in the business – my father was more of a coordinator, designer and salesman. They're both fishermen."

"How many people work there?" Bruce asked. He turned on to Cedar Parkway and began looking for the next turn.

"It's small – last I knew, there were four machine operators and a couple of apprentices and a driver. My cousin Peter's been the boss for the past few years. I've never seen three men as close as they are – never an argument, they talk things over, come to decisions and work together to achieve whatever's needed."

"How come a small manufacturing operation is successful located away from large population centers?"

"My father always said that quality and being on time

would create success. He was right."

"What a wonderful, simple philosophy."

"The word spread around and they always had plenty of work."

"Is your cousin your age?"

"No, Peter's a mathematical genius about ten years older. He got Father into modern computer-controlled equipment. He used to help me with my algebra homework. I had a schoolgirl's crush on him. Mother said, 'You have to learn to love him like a brother, Lisa. He's your cousin – he can't be your sweetheart.' I finally outgrew that love. It was hard for me to accept his wife, but I knew I couldn't ever let that show. Peter knows, of course, but he never teased me about it. Now, you know one of my secrets."

There was a few minutes of silence as Bruce thought about what he had heard as he concentrated on the traffic.

"We have funny ideas when we are young." Bruce made a turn onto Van Ness. *Wonder what she's trying to tell me about being in love with her cousin. That she has no love interest?* "Lisa, your facility with English took a lot of work."

"It did, Bruce. One of my father's firm requirements. "You must be able to speak American English as if you were a native. It's the only way we can be part of the only country that can bring freedom from tyranny to the world."

"But how did you perfect your accent?"

"Father got American video tapes. We'd listen to a sentence of conversation and repeat it into a tape recorder to compare the way I said it to how the actor talked. 'Frankly, my dear, I don't give a damn!' – What movie is that from, Bruce?"

Bruce laughed. "That was Rhett Butler in "Gone with the Wind.' I wondered why you were quick to use examples from movies – 'Fiddler on the Roof.'

"Mama said 'Don't listen to Tevya's wife – she's an American trying to sound like a Jewish mother.' Father said 'never mind – we owe a great debt to the Jews,' and he'd lapse into one of his brooding silences."

Switching to Czech, she asked, *'What kind of an accent do you hear now?'*

"A country girl from the western part. Talk to me some more and maybe I can tell you."

"Oh, you're good. A little rusty. My father always said 'if you don't use it, you lose it.' My uncle Peter and Aunt Hilda, like my father, came from near — guess where?"

Bruce laughed as he said; "You mix in some Slovakian so you must be from near the Danube River. My mother came from there and she drilled us in Slovakian, Czech and German. My brother and I drove our teachers crazy. But you're right, I am a little rusty."

"Yes, you are, Bruce. We can spend the rest of the evening talking in any language you want."

"Let's stick to English — not that you need the practice. Hey, here's Van Ness. Not far now."

"Next right turn. Third building on the right, the light gray one . . . turn in this side, drive around to the back."

Bruce complied.

"The open spot this side of the green BMW is for guests," she said. "Like to come up for a bit?"

"Nothing I'd like better." His heart pounded.

They got out of the car; Lisa turned to the BMW and popped the locks. She took a paper bag from the trunk and waved it. "Didn't have time to get this into the refrigerator — Duncan picked me up at the Embassy. Needs a little chilling. Shouldn't take long."

Perfect English, perfectly spoken. What a melodious voice she has. "What is it?" Bruce asked.

"An after-dinner wine from home. Thought it might taste good, now that Marie's salmon has settled down." She handed him the wine and keyed the door. Bruce followed her through the foyer to an elevator, where the door stood open.

"What's your floor?"

"Twelve." He pressed the button. The door purred closed and the elevator rose. She stood close to him.

"How did you find an apartment so near to your work?" asked Bruce. Again, he sensed the delicate scent of . . . *roses and . . . what is it?*

She held his gaze. "It's an apartment the Embassy keeps. It goes with my job."

The elevator stopped. When the door opened, she said, "It's down at this end." She keyed the door and Bruce followed her in. "Welcome to my little home, Bruce." She closed the door and engaged the safety lock. "They told me to always be careful here in the city," she said. "There's never been a problem here. Security man watches the doors on his TV."

"Lisa, can I use your phone to check if Elaine got me a reservation in town?"

"Phone's right there." She pointed at a couch where a telephone sat on a side table. "I'll put the wine in the freezer, then freshen up. Make yourself comfortable, Bruce, I'll be out in a few minutes. There's a bathroom in the guest bedroom there if you'd like." She went through another door.

Never pass up a chance to use a bathroom. Should have gone at Duncan's. Marie seemed anxious to get us off together, I guess. He found himself in a bedroom that shrieked *AUSTRIA!* An eiderdown puff covered the bed; an ancient wooden *armoire* stood against one wall, white Dotted Swiss curtained the corner windows and the walls held paintings of Salzburg's fortress, Vienna's *Ringstrasse* and an old *Schloss* framed by snow-capped peaks. One door led to a small closet – empty. *Wrong door.* The other door was the bathroom. He chuckled to himself; the toilet was Austrian.

Relieved, he pulled the knob. *Sounds American.*

He dried his hands and returned to the living room. Picking up the phone, he sat down and dialed.

Elaine answered on the second ring.

"Been waiting for your call. You're all set at the Central Holiday. So are we. We're leaving shortly."

"Thanks, Laney. Things got a little rushed; Marie practically pushed us out the door. Can you note this number from Caller ID?"

"Already did. Dogs are set for the night – we're working the sniffers tomorrow with the PD at the supermarket. Speaker's from Tel Aviv. See you in the AM, Bruce."

"Thanks, Elaine, see you."

She's talking in alphabets like the rest of us. Bruce noted the number on the phone was blank; only the area code was displayed. *Somebody knows how to be very careful. Bugs here? Oh boy. Laney said 'Speaker's from Tel Aviv.' My sweeper's in the Blazer.* He checked the Southwestern Bell handset; it was factory sealed – *or apparently so. When I leave, I'll see if there's a terminal box in the basement. Why am I so paranoid?* He replaced the handset on the cradle.

The door to the other bedroom swung open and Lisa said, "How do you like my 'Welcome to Austria' guest room, Bruce?" "

"The crowning touch is the imported toilet tank top. Somebody saw an easy way to avoid a lot of plumbing."

As she crossed the room towards him, she passed through the last rays of the setting sun. She had changed into a blue blouse that matched her eyes; her white slacks emphasized the slimness of her waist.

"I'd been in that dress all day, Bruce, and felt like I had to really freshen up." She headed for the refrigerator. Bruce followed.

"That was a pretty dress on a very lovely lady. In her sales pitch, the match-maker said that you had very nice legs. She was right."

Lisa smiled. "Thank you. Want to open the bottle?" She handed it to Bruce. "I'll get the glasses."

Bruce looked at the label.

"You brought this over when you came?"

"No," she replied. "You should see the wine cellar at the Embassy. This one comes from Vienna's Grinzing. They call it 'Last Harvest Wine.'" She leaned back against the counter, arms crossed against her chest, and studied him as he pulled the cork. He poured a little of the wine into one of the small crystal glasses and handed it to her.

She tasted it, letting the wine linger in her mouth, swallowed, then said, "Mmm. I think you'll like this."

Putting her glass down, she faced him. "Bruce, why have you never married?" Her voice shook.

"Guess because I've never met anyone quite like you." The silence that followed his answer lasted for what seemed an eternity. "Sorry, Lisa. That sounded like I was trying to make a joke. I wasn't – it just came out."

She reached for his hand. "Sometimes this happens between very lucky people," she murmured. "I am very lucky to have found - no, wrong word – to have met you."

She stood in front of him, her eyes boring into his. Instinctively, Bruce reached out and they hugged.

Their bodies molded tightly together; Bruce felt his

emotions washing over him. Time froze. They drew apart slightly; eyes locked. Lisa's face was flushed. Her eyes held him in thrall. She took a step backwards, breaking the physical contact and the burst of emotion that had pulled them together.

She took a deep breath, passed both hands through her hair and quavered, "Maybe you'd better pour a little more wine, Bruce."

He turned to the counter and filled the glasses.

She said, "Thanks . . . and not just for the wine."

Puzzled, he remained silent. *This might be part of learning to understand women.*

She took his hand; their fingers interlocked. "Bruce, I have something very serious to talk about. What happened just now is part of it."

They walked into the living room. She raised her glass to him; he touched his to hers. Each took a sip; each remained silent. Lisa placed her palm against Bruce's cheek; no longer cool, it was warm – as was his face.

"Oh, Bruce. Let's sit down." She placed her glass on the low table in front of the couch.

Words tumbled out of Bruce's mouth. "What just happened is still happening, Lisa."

"I know. What we are going to talk about was supposed to wait. Until later. Oh, dear."

They sat facing each other. She reached out and took his hand between both of hers.

"Bruce, please tell me about your father."

"My father? He died when I was seven – in an accident. We had to come home."

"From where, Bruce?"

"Vienna."

"What kind of an accident?"

Bruce stared blankly at her, his mouth open. "We have no idea. Stephen told us the story, years ago, before Laney and Rob were married. They could never find out. They really don't know where, or when, or even if, he died. He just . . . disappeared." His lips quivered.

Lisa placed her hands on his shoulders. "Bruce, we haven't met by chance. I'm here in America to find you."

Tears streamed down her face. "I have known about you and your family for years. Bruce, my father was with yours when the accident happened."

8

May 5, 1998
Lisa's Apartment; dusk

Bruce was stunned. "I could hardly remember my father's face when Stephen told us. Made me feel guilty, but I could remember his smile." He felt his throat constrict and tears flowed; he realized that they were mixing with Lisa's. She was cradling him in her arms, her head against his cheek as sobs shook her body.

Bruce couldn't speak. *Who is this woman? Is it possible to love a person in a few hours?*

Lisa drew back and met Bruce's eyes.

"Oh, Bruce, I'm so sorry. I've done this all wrong. I was supposed to wait until my father came . . . he wanted to tell you himself."

She sat up and wiped her eyes with the back of her hand. Bruce reached into a pocket, pulled out a handkerchief and gently wiped her eyes and face. *She feels this pain as much as I do.* She took the handkerchief from his hand, blew her nose vigorously and held it in her hand as she snuggled back against him.

"Don't say anything, Bruce. Let me tell you some of it. Oh, I'm so sorry. I was supposed to simply make friends with you and be very sure who you were and then my father was to come over and tell everything to your whole family – to your mother and Robert, to Elaine and to your nephews. But the moment I saw you, I knew that you were the right person – not only for our family, but in other ways. It crystallized for me when we held each other in the kitchen." She wiped her eyes again.

"Bruce, my father was raised in Czechoslovakia, in a little town near Bratislava. As a young man, after the war, he worked as a forester for the government. But – he was also a spy for the Americans and he passed information to your father."

"Oh, God," said Bruce, "your father was – is – the Third Man."

"The third man?"

"When Stephen told us what they knew, he said that Dad was to bring a man out to the West, because he was in danger. They'd called him 'The Third Man' because of a movie – the one with the zither music. Dad didn't get off the boat in Vienna when he was supposed to, but there was another man that disappeared."

"That was my father. Please trust me, Bruce. He'll tell you why he couldn't go to the Americans right away. He didn't know anyone in Vienna, he couldn't trust anybody. Our fathers were riding bicycles --"

"Bicycles?"

"They were on their way to a boat landing on the Danube early one morning to get a ride to Vienna. Going down a hill, your father hit a pothole and fell very hard. He died instantly. My father was very worried about being discovered, so he hid your father's body in the woods. Later that day, he came back and gave him a proper burial. He was alone; the rest of his family had left for Hungary to get into Austria. Our fathers were to meet them when they came across, because your father could make sure that everything went smoothly in Austria.

"After Communism collapsed and the Czechs and Slovaks made their own Republics, my father had your dad's remains reburied in our family cemetery. I've been there. A cross over his grave says 'A True Soldier for Freedom' in Latin and I cried for you then as I do tonight." Lisa sighed deeply and looked at her watch. "It's only two in the morning in Austria." She sat up and wiped her eyes and nose again. "I must look a sight."

"Lisa. Sweetheart. How nice that word sounds. I've never used it before to any woman. You look adorable to me and you always will."

She threw herself into his arms. "Bruce. How I have loved that name all these years. You must have so many questions. I'll call my father after midnight and he'll be here in a couple of days."

"How long have you known about this?"

"Since I was fifteen. My father kept this terrible secret from all of us for so long – and for good reason, as you'll learn. After he came to Austria in 1955, it took some time for him to make the right connections. He found people in Vienna that had worked in the American Embassy as clerks and so forth. One of these people had packed up your personal belongings and sent them to a house in Manassas, Virginia."

"That's where I got my Teddy Bear back," Bruce said.

"Fortunately, he kept that Manassas address. He gave the address to his wife, who used to take care of you. She wanted to contact your mother."

"That was Anna. A very kind lady."

"Your Dad was the only person in the entire world that my father trusted – except for our own family, of course. Father had information that he believed would alter the future of the world if it got into the wrong hands and the only people he could trust were Americans, but had to be through the Henderson family."

"Incredible. Please go on, Lisa."

"In a couple of years, my father traveled to Washington, found a lawyer and explained that he wanted his will to provide for an American family. He told the lawyer that he did not want them to know about it. The lawyer agreed to give him periodic reports and to keep him informed of any changes. That's all my father wanted to do. The lawyer hired a surveillance agency and they did a good job. They should have – they were being paid very well."

Bruce shook his head. "Can't wait to see Stephen's face when he learns that for years, he's been watched by his former spy."

"That wasn't quite what it was, Bruce; it was just knowing where your mother could be reached. My father still thinks of her as a Henderson and a Czech. And of course, you and Robert bear the name. You and Robert are both fighters for freedom like our own fathers." She sighed and ran her hand up his neck and stroked the soft hair there.

When he bent his head to kiss her, she placed a forefinger across his lips. "Have to tell you one more thing, Bruce. On my sixteenth birthday, father gave me your high school yearbook and graduation photographs. The smallest one is still in my wallet. I was sixteen, you were twenty-six. You're just as handsome today as you were then, Bruce. I've loved you ever since."

She reached up for him and their lips met. Bruce was shaken by the passion and yearning that moved between them. She hugged him. "I love you so, Bruce." She pulled back and wiped her eyes with both hands.

"Shortly after you graduated from high school, when you went into the Army, my father had a few years of agony because he lost track of you until you were commissioned. He was greatly relieved when you settled down in Virginia and got telephones. Thank heaven you didn't pick Alaska. For years, I prayed every night, 'Dear God, please keep him safe until I can be with him.' I would have died if *Vati* ever told me that you'd married. Did you ever go to Europe?"

"I was stationed in Munich, for two years, where we could listen to Czechoslovakian and Russian radio communications. I was part of an intelligence-gathering organization, very hush-hush. Now, it all seems wasted. Ridiculous."

"If I'd have known you were in Munich, I would have thrown myself at your feet. Probably why *Vati* didn't tell me."

He hugged her, amazed at the feelings that warmed him. "You feel as if you could purr," he said, stroking her back.

She wriggled. "I am. Can't you hear it? I'm just where I want to be."

"So am I, Lisa." Bruce lay back against the sofa, his eyes closed as his mind flashed from question to question.

"Lisa," he asked, "what do you know about what Robert and I do?"

"Until tonight, just that you raised dogs. I didn't know what kind of dogs, or what they do until tonight. We didn't think it was much of a challenge, but now I understand."

"Did the surveillance team ever come to the ranch to look around?" Bruce thought about the gates, the fences, the alarm systems; their establishment was not exactly inviting.

"Once you and Robert were settled in, it was assumed that you were there to stay and that's all that my dad wanted to know. We know that your mother and Stephen moved to Warrenton a few years ago. Most of the checking was done by telephone books. My father thought it was strange that you didn't advertise under 'dogs' in the newspapers. 'How can they sell dogs if they don't advertise? I should go over there and show those boys how to run a business.' He'd shake his head."

"Lisa, if your watchers had looked under 'Security Assets" in certain publications, they'd have found us. The dogs are only part of what we do."

"What do you mean? There's more?"

Bruce looked at his watch. "Yes, sweetheart. In less than ten hours, we're meeting with a government agency to plan how to protect a foreigner who'll be appearing in Washington. It's not just the dogs, although at least one dog will be part of the team. We have to consider that someone might either interrupt the proceedings or even attack the speaker – who, by the way, is Israeli. I just learned that. Lisa, is your phone secure?"

She sat up, eyes large. "Oh, dear. I think so. You're talking about *Nachrichten-übermittlung* – bugging, I think you call it, aren't you? The security officer at the embassy never said anything about it . . . they've no reason to check on me. I have a legitimate job and they know nothing about why I am really here, which is a family matter."

"If you're going to call your father tonight. . ."

"I am, Bruce."

"Then let me check the phone, just to be sure. Can you come down to my car with me, so I can get back in easily?"

They rose from the couch; Lisa picked up her keys and they went into the hall. Bruce touched the "down" arrow. As they waited, Lisa leaned against him, her arm around his waist. "Hope I haven't caused you any problem."

He hugged her, laughing. "You've fired up longings I didn't know I had and taught me to believe in love at first sight." The elevator door rumbled open and they stepped in. As the door closed, they turned to each other, embraced and their lips met. They were not aware of the elevator starting until it slowed and they stepped apart. Lisa's cheeks glowed.

Bruce said, "I wish your apartment had been on floor number two hundred – things were getting interesting."

She squeezed his hand. "Later, *Liebchen*."

The door opened. Bruce stepped out. Lisa held the door open and watched Bruce as he walked toward the car, key-ring in his hand. He opened the tailgate and pulled out a briefcase.

Closing the tailgate, he turned and looked upwards. "No lights in the apartment next to yours. Know if they're home?"

"Never see them." They made for the elevator. Bruce pushed the button labeled "12." Lisa held Bruce's free hand.

"Bet your security watcher thinks I'm an insurance salesman," Bruce said.

"Don't care what he thinks," Lisa murmured. She hugged him fiercely. "You'll never know how long I've waited for this."

As before, the elevator lurched a warning. The door opened and they stepped into the hall. It was empty.

Bruce looked around. "Don't see any security cameras, Lisa. Is this entire building occupied by Embassy people?"

"Just a few other apartments. . . I'm the only one on this floor. Ordinary working people here, mostly."

"Know who's in the apartments next to yours?"

"Haven't met them. I think there's a man in one and a woman in the other. Never hear anything."

"I need to check the common walls – they'll be the bathrooms and closets in each bedroom. Ever hear water running on the other side of the wall?"

"Haven't noticed, Bruce." She unlocked her door and went in. Bruce followed, turned and swung the security latch over its knob. He set his briefcase on the table. "Somehow, Lisa, we never got back to our wine."

He popped the latches on the briefcase and swung it open.

Lisa gasped a quiet "Oh" when she saw the little .380 Colt automatic nestled into its ankle holster atop equipment. Three laminated photo ID's were clipped to the partition in the lid – FBI, National Press Club and Secret Service. Bruce took out an instrument in a leather case. He reached for the telephone, pressed the latch and pulled out its line. He clicked the phone line into the instrument and clicked another lead into the phone. They heard a dial tone. A small message window read *IN TOLERANCE*. Bruce re-connected the telephone.

"Lisa, do you have another phone?"

"In my bedroom. It's on the same line."

"Let's check it too."

Bruce followed her. "We'll do the same thing." He switched the connections. "Look – same results. Wonder why there's no number on your phones."

"Security man from the embassy took them off."

"Makes sense. Okay, we'll get out the heavy stuff."

"Phones okay, Bruce?"

"As far as I can tell, the lines and the phones themselves are clear. Now we'll check for bugs." He closed the leather box and returned to the living room and replaced it in his briefcase. He took out another unit and unwound two small headsets.

"This is a scanner, Lisa." He plugged in the headset cords and switched it on. Lisa leaned close, watching

"What does it do?"

"It's called 'sweeping.' If there's an active microphone – a 'bug' – in your apartment, no matter how small, this'll find it. Hidden mikes transmit weak signals to a receiver that's near. Or, if it's connected by wires to another apartment and if there's an operator listening right now, he'll turn it off and we won't find it. Think the chances of that are pretty low. More likely, it would record conversations. Follow me around and hear what I hear. First, though, I have to unplug your TV. It's the kind that's always on, even though you think it's off. It's transmitting enough energy to mask anything we want to hear."

Bruce lay on the floor and reached behind the unit. Finding the outlet, he unplugged a power cord. He got up and pressed a button on the TV's remote controller. Nothing happened.

"Good," said Bruce, "it's dead."

Picking up the sweeper, he pulled a small round device from a clip and plugged its leads into a panel.

"This is the antenna," he said. Then he attached the device to a telescoping rod and extended it. "This handle lets me sweep the walls from the floor to the ceiling."

With Lisa following, he went to the panel of light switches in the hall.

"Here's a headset. You can listen." She put it on while he

plugged both headsets into the scanner. Then, he swept around the switches. They heard only a low hum.

"Good so far, sweetheart. That's what we want to hear – nothing."

Bruce continued by checking every light switch and interior wall in the apartment, ending in Lisa's bedroom.

"OK if I go in the bathroom? I need to get on the common walls." She nodded assent.

Following him into the bathroom, she watched him sweep the tub shower stall.

"People who think someone's listening go into a bathroom and run the water. So, we put a sensitive microphone in the bathroom wall from the other side, then run the water. Then we filter out the sound of water running and conversations will be recorded pretty well."

They left the bathroom and returned to her bedroom.

Bruce continued, "I'm going to change the sensor now, to detect a different type of microphone." He replaced the sensor on the rod with another. "Nice painting," he said, pointing to a city scene above the headboard. "Nice large frame, too. It could conceal enough double-A batteries to run a transmitter for a year."

"That's the footbridge over the river in Salzburg," Lisa said. "I walk across it every day."

Bruce slowly swept the sensor around the frame, chanting "Testing, testing, one, two three" several times in a soft voice. The earphones remained silent.

"You have no idea what kind of information can be collected from a painting above a bed." He waggled his eyebrows; she giggled.

Bruce moved to the windows, humming as he ran the sensor along the curtain rods. "We'll just look at your interior walls, Lisa. Easier to use eyeballs than equipment. We'll finish up by sweeping the curtains in the living room and in the guest room. Then, a look in the kitchen and the closets and we're done."

They completed the search quickly and Bruce returned the equipment to his briefcase. He picked up a small flashlight.

"Now for the closets. Got anything in them you don't

want me to see?"

"Not a thing." She waggled her eyebrows.

"Business first, sweetheart."

Opening the sliding doors on the kitchen side of the hall, he pushed aside clothes and boxes and examined the walls next to the kitchen, guest bedroom and bathroom.

"Nothing." He spent a few more moments in the closets, then backed out.

"Lisa, this apartment is clean as a whistle. So now you can speak freely to your father."

They returned to the couch and Bruce stowed the equipment in his briefcase. Lisa went to the kitchen and returned with the wine glasses.

"Now, they're too cold," she said; "I forgot about the wine while I was watching you work. Fascinating, Bruce – do you do it often?"

"Maybe two or three times a month."

She placed the wine glasses on the table. She slid onto the sofa; he reached his right arm around her shoulders as she leaned against him. He glanced at his wristwatch.

"What an evening," he said. "Told Elaine and Rob to keep their evening open in case I decided to bail out of this first date. Fat chance."

"What time is it, Bruce?"

"Almost eleven."

"Do you need a clear head in the morning?"

"Yes. What you've told me tonight has turned my world upside down. But concentrating on working kind of leveled me out. Then, too, what is happening to my heart is new for me. Here you are – a highly intelligent, beautiful woman, who feels she has known me since she was sixteen. Me? I feel drawn to you like steel to a magnet. I know that you're going to teach me the joy of loving you."

"Bruce, it's new to me as well. We'll have to feel our way, slowly, carefully. I know I can be impulsive – I scared myself in the elevator. I never knew that I could want you as badly as I did right then."

"The feeling is mutual – I think you could feel that."

"Mmmmm. I could." She reached forward and picked up both glasses of wine and handed him one. As before, she touched the rim of her glass to his and said, "To you, Bruce. I do love you."

He was amazed to hear himself say, "And I love you, Lisa. This comes from my heart – my brain has overloaded tonight."

"I have my mother's genes. She was only ten when she met my father. He was badly hurt and she helped nurse him back to health, knowing that one day he'd come back and marry her. She waited twelve years with only occasional letters giving her hope and confidence. I've been waiting for almost twenty-four years. The only assurances I had were from *Vati* – my father. He always said, 'Bruce will be there for you, *Schatzi*. He'll have the answers to my questions also. I have strong feelings about these things.' I would go to bed and cry my eyes out, afraid he'd be wrong."

Bruce pulled her close. "That part's behind us, sweetheart. I'm here for you now. But only for a few more minutes. Gotta be sharp in the morning and I really should go."

Lisa pulled open a drawer, took out a small pad and pencil and wrote.

"I understand, love. This is the phone number here. The second one is my Embassy number and extension. Will you call me when you wake up in the morning, so I know I didn't dream tonight?" She handed him the note.

"I will, Lisa. I have much to dream about tonight as well. Don't know what to say to the family – perhaps I'll tell some of it tomorrow afternoon. We're going to be busy the rest of the week and I need you there when we tell them everything. Can you come out to the ranch this Saturday? I can pick you up early Saturday morning."

"I'll be ready. I'm sure that my father will come to America very soon – perhaps I'll know when you call me in the morning. You can stay while I talk to him – it'll be only another couple of hours."

"Love to, but I'd really better go now. Going to be difficult to leave you anyway."

Lisa smiled and finished her wine. "How long will you be staying in town?"

"Most of the day."

"Could you have supper with me? Men usually want to

know if their girlfriends can cook."

"I'll be here tomorrow, as close to five as I can."

They rose from the couch, arms around each other and headed towards the hall. Lisa said, "I make a wonderful Hungarian goulash – does that sound good?"

"Sounds wonderful." He set down the briefcase and opened his arms. She flew into them, squirmed closer and buried her head on his shoulder.

"Mmmm – you're just the right size for me," he said. They drew slightly apart and looked into each other's eyes. Bruce said, "I can't believe what today has brought. I'm going to have a hard time being all business in the morning." Pulled her close again, they brought their lips together; hers met his with willingness and urgency. Breathing deeply, they pulled apart slightly.

Together, they said, "I can taste your wine." Laughing, they went to the door, fingers entwined.

"Bruce, please call me to say goodnight and call me again in the morning to wake me up. I am in a dream." He cupped her cheeks between his hands saying, "Sleep well, Lisa. What a pretty name." She placed two fingers against her lips, then against his. He kissed them back, opened the door and stepped out. Halfway to the elevator, he turned saw her framed in the doorway. He blew a kiss, saw it caught and returned. Her fingers waggled and she closed the door.

The elevator started down with its usual thump. Setting his briefcase on the floor, he took out a small key and a flashlight. After placing a bottle of nail polish in his pocket, he tore a piece of masking tape off a roll and stuck it loosely on the flashlight. Closing the briefcase, he stood up and waited for the elevator to stop. He thought: *I walked away . . . am I a stupid fool? It's much more than just physical attraction. . . .*

The elevator stopped and the door slid open. Instead of stepping out, he placed his foot against the door, reached out and standing on the up-ended briefcase, placed the masking tape over the small black orb of the tiny TV camera. *Sorry, fellas, you have a technical problem for a few moments. Do not adjust your set.* After placing the briefcase so it held the elevator door open, he turned to a Chesapeake Bell panel set into the wall. The key made quick work of the tamper-proof fasteners; he set the panel against the wall and surveyed the wiring. A scan showed no alligator clips or jumpers that were the usual sign of meddling; everything was neat and in order. Neat rows of terminal strips bore numbers, starting with 1, followed by four digits and a letter. *OK – that's one row for each floor.*

He quickly found 1212, followed by the four digits that Lisa had written on the pad. The next pair held the same numbers, followed by the letter *A*. "*That's the bedroom extension. Apartment 12.*" He daubed around each of the eight terminal screws with dark red nail polish.

They can't connect into that without being obvious.

Replacing the panel, he pulled a hair from his head. Kneeling, he made a small dab with the nail polish brush where the bottom of the panel met the case and laid the hair into it. He returned his implements to the briefcase, closed it and stood it up. Stepping up on it, he reached up and lifted the masking tape off the lens and balled it between his fingers. After waiting a few moments, he stepped briskly out of the elevator and left the building – flipping the tape ball under a bush.

9

0600 Wednesday May 6, 1998
Holiday Central – Washington, DC

Bruce reached for the telephone. He tapped in the ten numbers – *How did I memorize them so quickly?* – and the phone burred once. There was a click and he heard Lisa say, "Good morning, my love. I wish you were next to me."

Desire shot through him.

"So do I. Were you sleeping with your hand on the phone?"

"Practically. Just lying here, thinking of you and of my father. Talked to him after your call last night. Thought he'd be angry because of what I told you, but he just laughed and said 'I knew that Bruce was right for you and you'd know right away and you'd tell him about Nikolai.' Felt better right away. Haven't heard him laugh for so long. Bruce, he's getting on a flight this Friday from Salzburg to Zurich, then on to Dulles, arriving mid-afternoon. I'll pick him up and bring him here and he can go out with us to the dog farm Saturday morning, as we talked about."

"That will work, Lisa. We'll talk more about it tonight. Sleep well?"

"Yes, sweetheart. I've been keyed up for the past few days – now I'm peaceful and comfortable. And you?"

"I dreamt all night. I don't remember much, except that you were there and I kept reaching out for you. I love you and I can't wait to see you for supper."

"Don't worry about being late – supper will stay warm without hurting it at all. Do you have to go home tonight?"

"I don't want to, but I think that I should. We'll have to rearrange some things and Elaine needs time getting ready for Saturday."

"Goodbye, Bruce. If I was there I'd scrub your back for you. Call me if you're free earlier."

"I will. Bye, Lisa. I love you."

* * *

Twenty minutes later, he stepped out of the elevator just in time to see Rob and Elaine emerge from the elevator next to his.

"Hey, that's perfect timing. Are we a team, or what?" Like himself, they were carrying their briefcases and overnight bags. "Let's leave our stuff with the bell captain and pick it up later."

They followed the breakfast room hostess. A waitress appeared at their table almost immediately, saying, "I'll be right back for your orders, folks," as she filled their water glasses.

"We're ready right now," said Elaine. "We'll each have a large OJ, the New England with eggs poached on wheat, sausage and three coffees."

"I'll be right back with your coffee. Nice to see folks who know what they want."

Turning to Bruce, Elaine said, "You haven't said a word about your date. We stopped calling your room at ten-thirty. We won't ask what time you finally dragged yourself in – we can tell by the look on your face. What was that talk about bailing out early?"

"I'll be having dinner with her tonight before I go home. She's a very nice lady and I like her very much. In spite of Marie's active mouth, she doesn't have a clue about what we do for a living."

Robert grinned at Elaine. "Laney, you always said that when he fell, it would be fast and hard. Supper with her tonight? My little brother's had it."

Elaine smiled and laid her hand on Bruce's. "I'm happy for you, Bruce. It's been too long. When do we get to meet her?"

"Saturday. Along with her father. He's flying in from Austria day after tomorrow. I'll bring them out to the Ranch. They'll be staying for at least Saturday night. I'll probably pick up Mom and Stephen on the way through – they'll probably want to stay over. Let's talk about arrangements later – I've got a couple of ideas. In the meantime, we've got a job on our hands this morning."

Elaine looked at Robert, her eyebrows raised.

Robert said, "Something big is coming down."

Bruce said, after looking around, "Laney, you're superb. Interesting to see if our friends have considered a suicidal attack. Let them talk first and if they don't suggest a defense against it, we'll drop the concept on them. It'd be great if you do the suggesting, Elaine.

"Taking down a walking bomb'll be scary. Rob, how about this – I'll work Riggs in the foyer. You'd work near the ballroom entrance. If he alerts, I'll tell you while I follow the perp and Riggs, hoping for a clear shot. You can start moving against traffic flow. If I haven't had a chance for a close-in shot, you can pass by the perp and tag him with the Taser from behind. Then the two of us'll inactivate whatever device he was wearing. That's a general outline."

"Sounds good, Bruce," answered Rob. "Riggs would alert on the perp's hands, because he would have handled the charges quite recently. How about air flow?"

"We can arrange with the PC's maintenance crew to have a couple of large fans set up to move air in any desired direction."

"We'll need our own backup. Hank and Elaine can do the TV thing. The perp could be spooked by the TV in his face, so I don't want you close to him. If he panics, he'd either run, or discharge it then and there. His motivation is to get to the speaker."

"Glad we have bone conduction communicators," said Robert. "I want to check with Scottsdale on the reaction between Tasers and blasting caps – voltages might be too high and the power too low for there to be a problem, but I want to be sure. I'll call them this afternoon. No firearms except for backups. Don't want hard rounds into a Semtex vest. We'll make sure that everyone understands that.

"Now," continued Robert, "there's another thing. I'll ask if anyone has reported the loss of a Press Club ID in the past couple of weeks. If the answer is 'yes' I'm going to make a point." He produced two photo ID's and handed them to Bruce. Bruce glanced at them, raised his eyebrows and passed the ID's to Elaine, who grinned and passed them back to Robert.

"Cute trick, Rob," said Bruce. "Do it. Now, how's this for

initial assignments? The line will be forming just outside the ballroom at the last checkpoint. Rob on standby, close to where the line forms, looking like a waiter, Taser hidden behind the tray against his chest. Tom's on standby, also dressed as a waiter, ready to keep people away from the perp when he goes down. Elaine and Hank will remain upstream with the TV. You'll be the primaries for any visual ID's you get from mug shots. You'll be ready to get an intercept if the perp turns and runs and gets by me. We'll assume that Riggs and I will follow the perp. The perp's hands are the principal targets in any event. Worst case: assume he's run wires down under his sleeve and is holding a switch."

"Bruce," said Elaine, "you might stick a 'Service Dog' vest on Riggs and stand where they leave the elevators. Folks tend not to look at disabled people."

"You're remarkable. Any other ideas? No? Meeting's adjourned. Let's check out and hit the bricks. I need a brisk walk."

10

Tuesday, May 6, 1998
National Press Club – Washington, DC

Quickly falling in with Bruce's "brisk" pace, they turned onto Massachusetts Avenue. They were part of an early-morning throng of people – all of whom seemed late to work. As they waited for the "walk" light near Thomas Circle, a tour bus discharged its load of Asian tourists. A pair of pretty young girls – obviously identical twins – left the group and swung towards them, shiny black hair glistening in the sun.

Elaine stopped short in the middle of the street and grabbed Bruce by the arm. "What if there are two of them?" she asked.

"Two of what, Laney?"

"Two perps!" she exclaimed; "A primary and a backup!"

"Good grief, Laney. Hang on to that thought!" He pulled her the rest of the way across 14th Street, oncoming vehicles honking at them.

As they ran, she blurted, "Those cute twins made me think of it."

"It's a scary concept."

"What was that all about?" Rob asked, as they came up to where they waited for them.

"Laney had a traffic-stopper of an idea. Said, 'What if there is a walking bomb with a back-up – a duplicate?' She's got me nervous."

"Yeah. We'd focus on the first one and the second one would slip by in the melee. Let's not spring that on our Service friends and see if they come up with it. I bet they don't."

"No bet. Means two sniffing dogs, Bruce."

"Better do some training with two perps," Bruce muttered as pedestrians flowed around them.

"Interesting," said Rob. "We've never thought to have one sniffer on standby, pass a target by the active dog, let him go into trail and tell the standby to SNIFF – and hope he alerts on a second target. I'll make up a second perp vest for the *plastique* – we just have the one. No problem – the pattern's in Laney's sewing basket."

They continued along as Massachusetts Avenue transitioned into 14th Street NW. They could see the National Press Club's building in the distance.

Bruce glanced at his watch; "We might be the first to arrive this morning." They continued on in silence, each mulling over various options they could pull together for the scenario that had come from Elaine.

At the National Press Club, Rob held the door for Elaine and a man holding a clipboard turned to meet them. They placed their brief cases on a table and, taking out their Press Club ID's, they clipped them on.

Mr. Clipboard examined them, looked at his data and said, "I take it you know where to go." They went to the elevators; one had its door open. Bruce's mind flashed to the elevator rides he'd had the previous evening. He thought, *Gotta put her out of my mind for a bit.* Even so, there was a warm spot glowing in his heart. His finger paused in mid-air next to the buttons.

"Bruce, you look like the proverbial cat that ate the canary with cream sauce," said Elaine. "Better get rid of that silly grin or our friends will think you're not taking this affair seriously enough."

"Sorry, didn't even realize I was smiling."

"She must be quite a gal, little brother."

"OK, OK, people. I was just thinking --"

"We know," cut in Elaine, laughing.

"No," said Bruce, "not about last night. Maybe we should probably take a quick look in the basement, but our hosts will no doubt have the usual familiarization tour. Might as well go upstairs." He pushed the button for the thirteenth floor.

"Not many public buildings have a floor labeled 'thirteen,' do they?" he said, stepping back. The door slid closed and the elevator accelerated smoothly.

"Guys, every time either one of you says 'perp,' I'm thinking of twins. I still have a funny feeling about this one."

The elevator slid to a stop and the door opened. They

headed towards the ballroom. Workers were re-arranging tables. The adjacent bar was shuttered. The first entrance into the ballroom stood open; a man they knew stood inside.

"Hi, Jack," said Robert. "How's the building maintenance business these days?"

"It would be free of problems if we didn't have VIP's that require people like you to be on hand," answered the man. "I remember this pretty lady, who pretends to be with CBS." They shook hands all around.

Jack said, "You're the first to arrive. Grab some coffee and Danish."

"Anybody special coming this morning, Jack?"

"If a pair of Israelis from Mossad are special, yes," answered Jack. "Advance party for the speaker's protection team. Roaming the building. Gave them a master key an hour ago."

In a corner, a table was set for fourteen. Placards listed names and affiliations. Elaine's seat was between Bruce and Robert.

Elaine said, "The last time we were here, I told Jack about my problem with the man from London. I finally had to say, *That's my husband sitting next to me. Do you want him to break your roaming hand, or shall I do it myself?*' He got the message, the old letch." She called, "Thanks, Jack; you know what for."

Jack smiled and waved.

Robert and Bruce returned with their coffee. In the next few minutes, groups of men arrived. Bruce and his companions recognized most of them – from either the Secret Service or the DC Metro Police. Sam was the last to arrive, coming straight to the table and placing his briefcase next to Bruce's. They shook hands.

Sam turned towards the coffee service. "Move it along, gentlemen," he called. "We've a lot to cover and we need to be out of this room in an hour and a half. You folks know each other, so there's no need for introductions. The two empty seats are for the Mossad reps – I saw them on my way up and they'll be here directly."

As if on cue, two men appeared in the doorway and made their way to the table. Sam said, "Welcome, gentlemen. Folks, here's Ari and Richard. This is their first visit to the USA;

make them part of the family. You can chat with them during the break."

Sam sat. "Folks," he said, "you all know who the VIP is. We'll be providing security that's gotta be as good as for the Chief."

"There's three threat possibilities. First, at the building entrances. Second, a shooter or pre-placed device along the internal route or in this room. Third, a device or an individual with proper credentials in this room becoming a shooter at any time – probably before the VIP's speech. The faction he belongs to won't like what he has to say, so they see a chance to stifle it.

"This meeting is to test these options. So, we'll start at the White House. Henry?"

A ruddy-faced man said, "We're making it simple. The VIP arrives at the back alley in an unmarked vehicle, while the limo arriving out front has a look-alike decoy behind the dark glass. It'll wait out front until the VIP is inside the building via the alley door, then it'll just leave. The alley to the rear of the building will be cordoned, with DC police enforcing the 'no-drive' zone. We like Mr. Henderson's earlier suggestion – use the service elevator from the basement to this floor. The timing of this will be such that the VIP will enter this room through the connecting door from East 'A', when everyone is seated. We'll reverse the route for his exit. It's customary for guests to remain seated until the speaker has departed. That's our initial plan – comments?"

"Will he be wearing body armor?" came from a man near Bruce.

Ari spoke up immediately, "No, sir. We're trying to convince him that it's not a sign of weakness."

Elaine nudged Bruce's leg. He knew she was thinking: *"Knowing this, a perp would choose an explosive weapon."*

"Now," said Sam, "building security. Jack?"

This was routine for Jack; as Operations Manager for the building that housed the National Press Club, his security preparations and procedures were well prepared. Many Press Club luncheons featured speakers ranging from off-shore presidents to Nobel Prize winners. His own security detachment had sixteen former Marines or Navy Seals with extensive combat experience.

"I'll have twelve people for this operation," Jack began. "The evening before the luncheon, we'll sweep the basement, the route, this room, adjacent rooms, library and balconies. Following clearance of each section, it'll be locked. The door from the lobby to East 'B' will be unlocked when the VIP is in the elevator and two of my men will remain in the room. They'll immediately re-lock the door, stay in the room and unlock it when it's time to for the VIP to exit. There will be two security people in West, which will be the primary entrance and exit for the service staff. Those people know the service staff by their first, middle and last names. I would welcome- in fact, urge – anyone to accompany our people for all or any part of our preparations."

Ari raised his hand, as did his companion.

"I was sure you folks would. Anyone else? OK." said Sam. "Now – the crucial part. Who gets in? Or, who gets into the building? Let me answer my own questions." He pulled a sheaf of papers out of his briefcase, as did Jack. "The invitation list is mostly journalists who've registered for the luncheon. Jack's list is the CV's of the service staff, with mug shots, each of whom have been cleared previously. It'll be a capacity crowd – about three hundred and eighty people. Jack advises that they won't – repeat won't – be using the balconies. Only this midsection – neither the East nor West Rooms. "Many of these people are not cleared for 1600 Pennsylvania Avenue and we have begun background checks on those that we don't know. It's a constantly changing cast and it's challenging when a Press Club member from Podunk decides to exercise his membership rights. Let me pause for questions at this point."

Elaine raised her hand. "Yes, Mrs. Henderson?"

"Are there assigned seats for the people who'll be here" Sam raised his eyebrows and looked at Jack; who answered.

"Not for this many people. First in, first closest. Also, they'll want to sit with their friends or future employers. Good question, though."

"I have a follow-up question, Sam," continued Elaine. "What'll be going on in the meeting rooms on the other side of the atrium, on or below this floor?"

Again, Sam cast his eyes at Jack, who picked up his pocket calendar, opening it to a paper-clip marker. "Zenger room has a Wilderness Society lunch meeting, with a press conference to follow. It's been scheduled for couple months, while we've known about the VIP for three weeks. I don't have a clue about who's coming to the Wilderness thing. We'll do ID checks across from the Holman Lounge and that'll keep out anyone without a lunch pass."

Robert raised his hand; Sam nodded at him.

"A question for Jack. Anyone reported loss or theft of their Press Club ID?"

"Yep - last week, a correspondent from one of the New York papers said his PC card was missing. Ellie handed it to him, told him to be more careful. Somebody'd turned it in a half hour earlier – said they'd found it in the men's room."

Robert tossed two photo ID's to Jack. "Can you tell which one's fake? Don't point. Just say yes or no."

Jack glanced at the passes. "Sure. Easy to tell which one's fake."

"Harry, do you see any difference?" Jack asked the man on his left, a Secret Service representative. He looked at both sides, felt their stiffness.

"This one's the fake," he said, waving the one. "Doesn't have your picture on it, but has your name and affiliation." Chuckles resounded around the table.

Jack said, "Rob, I don't want to think about how you did this."

"I copied my Press Club pass in the Services Room. Did both sides. Paid the gal for two copies. Stuck my son's passport photo over mine, glued the front side to the back and went to a hole-in-the-wall copy shop and asked the guy to laminate it. Gave me a funny look, charged me twenty bucks. Said he charges teen-agers fifty.

" Guys, here's the point. You're trained to look at pictures first. If the photo matches, he gets in. Especially if you've got three hundred and eighty people to clear in about twenty minutes. Point I'm making is that if there is a perp, we have to ID him before he gets to the last checkpoint."

Bruce said, "Your turn, Sis." She raised her hand. Sam nodded.

Elaine cleared her throat. "I'd like to pose a couple questions. Who think handguns are a perp's first choice?" Hands went up. "Thought maybe, myself, but then I had a disturbing thought. Has anyone considered a suicide bomber?" The table went silent. "Or a suicide bomber, unaware <u>another</u> suicide bomber has the same mission? A back-up orchestrated by a higher-ranking terrorist?"

"Guys rigged like that would waltz right through the metal detectors," said an acetic man from the DC Metro Police.

"In light of what Elaine has brought up," said Bruce, "Perhaps you could best use us to ID, isolate and neutralize a perp – or perps – who've handled explosives recently. We don't care what the explosives are; any variety of nitrates or plastic – putty or briquettes. Our dogs will alert if anyone's carrying it.

"We'll clear the ballroom and the lobby for the dogs before anyone arrives. Then we'll be at the north end of the lobby and wait for a dog to go right to the perp. Whoever's handling the pup will take down the perp with a Taser, or we'd pass the word to another person ahead of him, who'd take him down as he passes by. In the confusion and uproar we'll disarm whatever he's carrying. I think he'd use a very short fuse and a pull-wire igniter – he'll keep it simple – no wires, no batteries and, as Brick observed, he'd waltz through a metal detector.

"Our second handler and the back-up dog will be on standby. If there's a second perp, they'll follow the same routine. It'd be highly unlikely that they'd arrive on the thirteenth floor at the same time."

Bruce returned to his seat. "Mrs. Henderson here and one of her sons will run their usual TV scam. Her son's camera shows the mug shots you'll be giving us and she'll move right in on any of these people for an 'interview'. That's the signal for your guys to take him away, Jack. Worked before."

"What's your team packing?" asked a DC Metro representative.

"Brick, we're afraid of hard rounds hitting an explosive vest," said Bruce. Murmurs of agreement echoed. "We'll all be carrying Tasers. We strongly suggest that you do likewise. If a dog fingers a perp – that's what he'll be, not a suspect – it's imperative that he can't use his hands."

All eyes were on Bruce. He looked around, "If we make a mistake, which in my opinion is highly unlikely, I don't need to remind you that Tasers are non-lethal. After a half hour of recovery, a 'mistake' can walk away. None of us in this room would want to take a hit from what most of you carry. Ari, that's an interesting smile on your face. Must have something special."

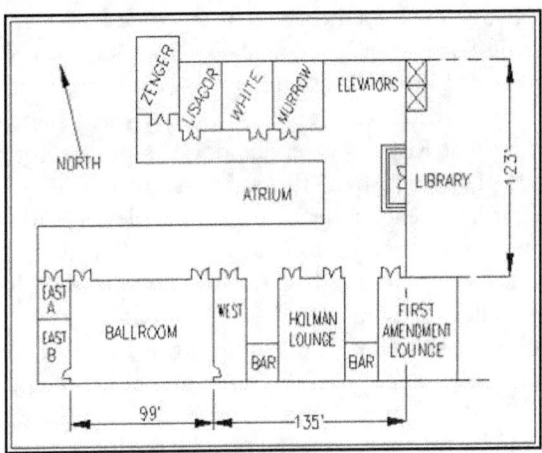

"We're not special, Bruce," said Ari. "Israelis just stay away from fair fights."

Sam, speaking above the laughter, said "Coffee break, guys. Reconvene in twenty minutes. No problem with open discussions - we've cleared these servers."

Chairs rustled on the rug as most people headed for the coffee service. Ari and Richard approached the three Hendersons.

"Could we go to the blueprint on the wall?" Ari asked. "Sure," responded Bruce. They gathered in front of the floor plan.

"Mrs. Henderson," said Richard, "We've dealt with suicide bombers for years. Problem is, we can't identify – let alone track – one before he dies along with his targets. Your concept – a back-up bomber – is brilliant. We'll take home that idea. That and how you'd use your dogs. Tell us about it."

Bruce answered, "We'll know the thirteenth floor is clear"

– he swept his hand over the drawing – "because Jack's crew'll cover the service stairways on a personal recognition basis. Everyone else'll be coming off the elevators. Jack'll put a couple of floor fans here to establish air flow that'll help the dogs. We'll have one dog downwind from where people step out of the elevators and start towards the Ballroom. We've got two dogs highly trained to alert on any organic or plastic explosive – I mean anything. Their noses are hundreds of times more sensitive than yours or mine and we know they've got a phenomenal memory when it comes to scents. For example, if Tom – that's my nephew, Ari – and a pup named Riggs station themselves about here" – he pointed to the letter "A" in the word "elevators" – "they'd just stand there, pretending that Riggs is a service dog. As people got off the elevators, Tommy'd tell Riggs to 'sniff.' He'd sit, nose working; if he smelled a perp carrying any device, or had even handled it earlier, he'd go to that person, follow him, wagging his tail furiously, looking back at Tom frequently. He might even try to lick the perp's hand.

"At that point, Tom'll take him down from the rear with his Taser. Or he could pass the word to Rob. If the perp is in the middle of the crowd, Rob, looking like a waiter, would be working his way upstream. He'd pass by the perp – it's hard to miss a dog – turn and take him down from behind at real short range. It'd take no more than half a minute to get the perp defused and out. We can do this by the time he's at the library stairs. Laney, please make a note – if this plan is adopted, ask Jack to stash a gurney in the White room."

Elaine added, "Ari, the dog wears a 'Service Dog' vest – which will essentially make his handler invisible. Strange, but true."

"What about a second perp? How would you handle that?" Richard asked.

"We've talked about that. I'd be in the hallway, down by the Margaret White room. As soon as Tom followed an alerting dog, I'd go to Tom's station. Regardless of what went on, I wouldn't tell Tuck – the other really good sniffer – to go to work until the situation resolved. As soon as they were off the floor, I'd tell Tuck to sniff and we'd repeat the scenario. My gamble? It's that if there are two perps, they won't arrive within a couple minutes of each other."

"How do you people communicate?" Ari asked.

"Bone conduction earbuds," answered Robert. "A custom mike/speaker/transceiver combo that fits in the ear of our choice. No wires. Small, short-range transceivers with integral voice-actuated switching go onto our belts. If we say anything – even quietly – it gets transmitted. We're all on the same freq and can communicate by coughing if we need to. Sounds weird, but they really work. We're the 'Beta test' for the folks developing them. Got all the frequencies we need."

"Bruce, how'd the Hendersons like to move to Israel?" Richard was smiling.

"Thanks for the compliment, Richard. However, I don't think there's enough money in all of Israel to convince us to do that," answered Bruce.

"You should see what we could add to your armory."

"Really?"

"Down, boy," said Elaine. "Ari, I guess you've checked us out."

"Mmmm," was Ari's non-committal response.

Sam had strolled over during this last exchange. He said, "No recruiting, guys. We need these people."

"I'm impressed. Maybe if they were government employees, the dogs would have pay scales," Ari responded, grinning. "We all know about bureaucratic empire-building."

They all chuckled. "Seriously, Ari and Richard, what do you think about the overall plan?" asked Sam. "You're the folks who call the shots."

"I'd like the Hendersons' concepts put into the overall action plan and implemented," said Ari. "Their proposal's a good one and it's aimed at a threat that you guys haven't had to deal with yet. We'd be derelict if we didn't add the Hendersons' capabilities to whatever else you folks have in mind. At our end, we never get any warnings that a walking bomb is on the street. When it does happen, there are usually at least two groups who claim credit. A couple of times, we've picked up the person who made the claim and got him to expand on the subject – after we made him fully cooperative. Both times, turned out he was lying and was trying to build up the image of his own party. Same with car bombs and IED's.

By the way, the White House detail didn't mention those possibilities. I'll want to talk to them about it."

Sam said, "Car bomb's the real reason for the decoy, Ari. There's several alternate routes and the route selection is made at the last minute. The look-alike understands that he may in harm's way and we assure him the limo offers excellent protection – as does his helmet and body armor. Believe me, we haven't forgotten about the Dallas Schoolbook Depository. Countermeasures placements are standard and we'll review them during the balance of this meeting."

Turning to Bruce, he said, "Well, it looks like you have another job with us." A quick handshake and then he hugged Elaine. "Nice work, lady."

Sam turned to the group and said, "Listen up, folks. First, I want action plans with personnel assignments on my desk not later than 1100 on Tuesday the twelfth. We'll be utilizing about two hundred and fifty people and we must have total understanding and agreement about individual and group missions.

"Second – and last – I want the communication plan, with network frequencies, distributed to all participants on Monday afternoon the eleventh. This will be for review by all of you, as you represent every agency involved. Chuck, check with the Hendersons – they may have a new frequency. Brick, I don't think there are any unusual aspects of this mission for the Metro Police – Henry'll have the route alternates selected and in your hands – by Monday, Henry?"

The White House representative said, "No problem."

"Richard and Ari, you're the umpires. Make the calls on anything you don't like, or want to do different." They nodded assent.

"Bruce, any other activity you think appropriate? You folks are breaking new ground for us."

Bruce leaned toward his brother. "Rehearsal, Rob?"

"Yup."

"Sam, we think that a rehearsal right here would be in order. I'd need half-dozen volunteers for the incoming crowd and a couple more to wear our exploding vests. They have everything except fuses." Chuckles echoed.

"This'd be to check procedures, communications and get

the dogs cool with this environment. Jack, got a free morning when this floor would be available? An hour would be plenty of time."

Jack had his pocket calendar open. "Wednesday the thirteenth, same as today – 0800?"

Bruce raised an eyebrow at Elaine. She nodded. "That'll work, Sam."

Ari said, "Count us in. Want to see it."

Bruce said, "More the merrier. Here's a blanket invitation to all of you and to your people. Jack, if a couple of your people can attend, we'll work on getting perps out of sight quickly. We've rehearsed situations many times and will be doing it again in the Warrenton supermarket with two dogs active against two perps."

"No problem, Bruce. Want to have the floor fans in place for air flow?"

"That would be ideal. Doesn't take much, but dogs can't work as well downwind."

"Sounds like a plan," said Sam. "Gentlemen and lady, there's two rooms on this floor available until three PM for those needing to confer with associates. Other than that, this part of the meeting is over. Lunch is ready in the First Amendment Lounge. Resume in the lobby outside here at one PM for a walk-through of this floor and the basement."

11

Bruce glanced at his wristwatch. "Eleven-thirty already –
where'd the time go? Sure didn't seem that long," he said to
Elaine.

"My butt says it was."

Sam said, "I've reserved a table for six. Want the three of
you, with Ari and Richard, to join me."

"OK, Sam; I'll get the others before they vanish,"
answered Bruce.

* * *

Robert and Elaine sat between the two Mossad agents.
Elaine turned to Ari. "What's 'Mossad' mean?"

"It's the popular part of our name, like when you call the
CIA 'the Agency.' In Hebrew, it's *ha-Mossad le-Modiin
ule-Tafkidim Meyuhadim* – The Institute for Intelligence and
Special Tasks. We're here for a special task."

"How long have you been here?"

"Me? A week. Richard – a couple of years. He's assigned
to the Embassy. Our mission is to protect our own VIP –
same as your Secret Service does for your President. On your
ground, you're supplying the manpower."

Sam sat across from Elaine. "What were you folks saying
about Mossad?"

"I gave Mrs. Henderson a quick run-down on our
organization," Ari said. "I'd like to hear more about what Mrs.
Henderson does with a TV camera."

"Our son, Hank, uses a regular studio camera," Elaine
explained. "It has the '9 News' logo of the local CBS affiliate
clearly visible. The viewfinder is rigged to show him mug
shots. If he spots a suspect, he cues me on possible ID's. I ask
for an interview. If they are reluctant, I get insistent while he
blocks their passage and I back them to a wall. Jack's guys
step in and ask the suspect to come with them to continue the

conversation elsewhere."

"Did you ever get an interception?"

"One, so far, out of about twelve jobs. Hank spotted a man looking like one of the mug shots. He turned on his light, verified the suspect to me through my headset, all of which steered me to the individual, who didn't want to do an interview. I insisted and asked him to move back to the wall; he cut and ran, right into the arms of two agents. He was carrying two loaded pistols. Hank switched the camera over to real-time and taped the arrest and search. The camera mike picked up everything quite well. The hand mike's transmitter's on my shoulder holster."

"What else's in it?"

"My little .380 Colt loaded with Geer's 90 grain Gold Dots. I've put several thousand rounds through it in practice. My husband made walnut grips to fit my hands. I love it."

"We all have the same back-up weapon, usually in ankle holsters," said Robert "We've standardized on Geer rounds for our other nine's. We use 90 grain loads in the shorts and 115 grains in the regulars. Since Elaine can't wear an ankle holster in this assignment, her hands and feet are her back-up."

"Rob, what if I start interviewing, move a guy to the wall and Riggs alerts on him?"

"No problem. Riggs would have picked up on him before he gets near you. Safe to assume he's clean – at least from the walking bomb standpoint. He could still be a perp, but with a different agenda. We'll walk through it quickly with Jack right after lunch, before the tour."

"Ari, were you here in time to see the cherry blossoms?" queried Elaine. "Will you be able to visit anywhere else in our country, Ari?

"I'd love to visit your place. Perhaps after this operation."

"No problem. You can even bring any of your toys along. We're nicely isolated and have ranges for anything up to six hundred meters – we use portable tunnels lined with sound absorbing foam. The range uses a firing house, shooting through slits."

"How often do you practice?" asked Richard, who had joined the conversation.

"Weekly and if we aren't up to Elaine's standards, we go back and shoot some more."

"You folks must go through a lot of ammunition," Sam said.

"We do," said Bruce. "Mostly nine millimeter. Hank's our armorer. He puts out several hundred rounds at a time and we recycle our brass – a real production set-up. Ninety-nine point nine percent of the time, deficiencies are in the shooter, not the ammunition and we all know it. I heard last week, 'Hey, sport, I had a vertical pattern, an inch wide, but five inches high. The whole darn clip.' Hank said, 'What were you doing? Lying on your side?'" The entire table erupted in laughter.

Sam said, "Richard and Ari, this team that has joined us today from 'outside' has phenomenal skills, techniques, habits and experience. They provide security assessment, intrusion detection, covert site safety, communication interception and utilization, as well as individual self-defense skills. They say things like 'the dogs do most of the work' or 'we've learned to look out for each other'. I was a platoon leader in Vietnam after a 1959 battlefield promotion. In recent years, there've been times I know I would have been better off with the five of them instead of my entire platoon."

He looked at his watch and pushed back his chair. "Back to work, guys and gal."

Ari stood, reached for Elaine's chair, then withdrew his arm. She looked at him with a grin. "You could have done it, Ari. I wouldn't have broken your arm or anything."

"Mind-reader, too?"

"No, I can tell when a man's deciding if he wants to play gentleman, or if he thinks that women are truly liberated. Some gals get insulted when a man offers to hold a door for them – and they let him know it. That's dumb. I appreciate a little chivalry."

Hearing the conversation, Bruce's mind flashed to Lisa. *When I'd helped her up from the wing chair, pushed in her chair at supper and held doors for her, she'd gracefully accepted it and was pleased by my attention. Perhaps it's the physical contact. Certainly, something very powerful passed between us with every touch. I can still feel her last kiss on my lips. . . Bruce, clear your mind.* He shook his head and followed the others into the lobby.

12

1500 Tuesday May 6, 1988
The Henderson van – Holiday Inn Central
Parking Garage

"Let's grab the Metro," Bruce said. "It'll save us a few blocks and besides, I need to talk to you before we go our separate ways." They headed southeast on "F" Street to 13th, where they descended into the coolness of the Metro Center complex.

Bruce needed a few minutes without conversation to shift his focus and decide what Rob and Laney needed to hear.

They entered the nearest subway car. Bruce sat behind Rob and Elaine, closed his eyes and thought, *what if Rob learned something about our dad and didn't tell me right away? How would I feel? I'd be angry and resentful. I can't let that happen. When we get to the garage, I'll tell them everything.*

Leaving the Metro at Farragut North., they entered Holiday Central's parking garage.

"Where's the van? I didn't see it when I parked last night." Footsteps echoing hollowly, they turned a corner and Bruce saw he had parked opposite the van. "Hey," he laughed, "guess I missed it."

"You were looking but not seeing, or the love-light wasn't bright enough."

"Guess that's the answer," Bruce muttered. He slid the rear door open and hopped in. Turning the front seats, they faced each other.

"I really had quite an evening," Bruce began. "This has been a tough day for me. Here's why. First of all, Lisa is a wonderful woman. Second, I believe she's totally honest, but she hasn't told me everything. You both raised your eyebrows this morning when I said her father would also be joining us this weekend – he's flying in to Dulles this Friday."

"Quick decision?" Robert asked.

"Yes. Lisa called him last night after I'd left and told him

179

she'd found me." Comprehension darkened Rob's face. After a moment, he grabbed Bruce's leg. "It's about Dad, isn't it?"

"Yes."

"I bet her father's 'The Third Man.'"

"Right, Rob. He was there when Dad took a spill off a bicycle and died instantly. They were leaving Czechoslovakia and her dad was about to be compromised. After communism collapsed, he returned and had Dad's remains re-buried in their family cemetery. From what Stephen told us it was her dad that slipped by the pick-up people."

"He's got a lot of explaining to do," said Elaine, anger sharpening her tone.

"You're right on that, Laney. Bruce, how'd she find you? Us?"

"Through Anna, whose husband was the janitor at the Embassy. Simple, low profile, obviously effective."

"Why the secrecy? Why not just go to Mom or Stephen?"

"Lisa said the problem with her father is that Dad was the only one in the world that he trusted and he's got information that'll alter the future of the world if it gets into the wrong hands and the only people he'd trust was the Henderson family. She has our high school yearbooks, photos of us when we graduated and carries a wallet-size one of yours truly."

Elaine asked, "Brucie, what do you make of all this?"

Bruce sighed. "I think I'm in love . . . we cried together last night."

There was silence. Elaine laid her hand on Bruce's.

"She said there's much more and her father will have the whole story."

"Are you planning on your mom and Stephen hearing this for the first time from these people?" Elaine asked, quietly. "Or are you going to prepare them? That'll be an awful shock for your Mom — especially after all these years. Another thing — can we meet Lisa this afternoon? I want to get a woman-to-woman feel here."

Bruce reached forward and pulled the cell phone from its holder and quickly tapped in seven numbers.

"He's in love, Rob," Elaine said. "Only thing that makes a man remember a phone number after one date."

Bruce said, "Lisa! I'm glad you're there. Can Rob and

Elaine stop by to say hello, before they head home?" Silence hung; Bruce frowned in concentration. Then, he smiled.

"Sounds good. We'll be there in half an hour." A pause. "And the same back to you, Lisa." He replaced the phone. He turned to them and chuckled. "Said she thought this would happen, which is why she's made Hungarian goulash. You kids have a supper invitation."

13

1630 Tuesday May 6, 1988
Lisa's apartment

The two vehicles, with Bruce in the lead, pulled up to the apartment on Van Ness. Bruce pushed the button marked 1212. They heard Lisa say, "Come on up!"

"On our way, Lisa."

A buzzer resounded. Bruce pulled open the door. "Elevator's over here."

Bruce punched the button for the twelfth floor and the door rumbled closed.

"This is going to be interesting," Elaine muttered. The others remained silent; Robert caught Bruce's glance and lifted his eyebrows in a look that said "Oh, boy." He fisted his left hand and punched Bruce lightly on the shoulder. The elevator stopped; the door opened.

"It's to the left, Laney," Bruce said. They took a few steps and the door at the end of the hall opened. Lisa was silhouetted. Bruce felt his shoulders relax; he felt that she was going to create the same acceptance and trust in Robert and Elaine as she had in himself.

"Come in, come in, I'm so glad that you could come," Lisa said. She hugged Bruce quickly. They walked together behind the others into her living room.

Bruce said, "Lisa, this is my brother Robert and his wife, Elaine."

Lisa went to Elaine, both hands extended in greeting. The two women's eyes and hands met and locked; something the men could not detect flashed between them and they hugged and held each other, saying nothing. When they separated, each woman was crying. Lisa turned to Robert.

He opened his arms, saying, "I never pass up an opportunity to hug a beautiful woman."

And they all laughed.

The late afternoon sun streamed in through the window

and fell on Lisa. She wore blue slacks, a white blouse with a blue scarf that matched her eyes. A small silver pin kept the scarf in place. Her eyes continued to brim with tears.

"I am so sorry. This is not at all like it was supposed to be," said Lisa, wiping her eyes with the back of her hand. "What a burden I have put on you. There is so much that you have to hear. Please come and sit down."

Bruce handed her his handkerchief. "This is getting to be a habit, Bruce. Thank you."

A bottle of Riesling sparkled with condensation. Four crystal wine-glasses waited in an adjacent tray surrounding an assortment of cheese and Danish *flatbröt*.

"Elaine, Bruce, perhaps you'd all like a glass of wine? And would you pour it, Bruce? My hands seem a little shaky."

"We'd love a glass of wine," said Robert. "Today turned into a real pressure-cooker. We knew that Bruce had some kind of an epiphany last night. He told us most of it just now. You know a lot more about us than we do about you."

"Yes and no," Lisa answered. "Please sit down." Sitting on the sofa, she took her wine from Bruce's hand. Elaine sat across from Lisa. Bruce handed one to Elaine and Robert and they all sat.

Lisa held up her glass.

"Here's to the past, the present and whatever the future may have in store for us." They reached out to each other, touched glass rims and drank.

"What a nice wine and what lovely wine-glasses," said Elaine.

"I brought ten of them with me," said Lisa, holding hers up to the sun. Fragments of rainbows flashed from the facets. "There's more that'll stay in Austria. They've their own story; my father'll tell it. Fourteen were made for when we could all be together. There's seven Americans – six Hendersons and Mr. Oakes – my father considers your mother still a Henderson. There's five Austrian Holders – myself, my father Rudi, my mother Elsa, uncle Georgi and cousin Peter. The thirteenth person was my aunt Hilda, who died in 1990." Lisa sipped her wine and handed Bruce's handkerchief back to him.

"The fourteenth person was your father, Robert. My

father knew him as Nikolai. His wine glass is in a little niche in our chalet – a place of honor. But let me tell you a little more of the story, because you'll want to talk to your mother and to Mr. Oakes before my father does. He called later this morning, Bruce. He's arriving at Dulles Friday afternoon. I'll meet him and he'll stay here Friday night."

"Rob," said Bruce, "I'll get the Chief to bring me here Saturday morning and I'll bring Lisa and her father out to the ranch in her car." Lisa's brow furrowed.

Bruce caught her expression. "The 'Chief' is a retired Navy man who works out at the Ranch," he said. "We call him that because that was his Navy rank."

"Oh, yes, you mentioned him at Duncan's. I'd forgotten."

Elaine added, "His name is Fred – Fred Schutt. His wife, Martha, helps me. They stay at the Ranch when we're away overnight. They're good people. They've been married about forty years – he was away from home in the Navy so much that Martha says she'll never sleep without him again."

Robert said, "I knew Fred from Vietnam. He was a SEAL – that's one of our special military tactical outfits, Lisa. We stayed in touch and it worked out for everyone."

Lisa asked, "Will it be all right if my father and I stay at the ranch?"

"Yes, Lisa," Bruce answered, "we've got four bedrooms in the main house. One's mine and the three others are for guests. It's a big old farmhouse – it's comfortable."

"That's the old bachelor talking, Lisa," said Elaine. She laughed. "It needs a woman. It's needed one for years."

Robert refilled the wine glasses. "Sounds to me like the ice is broken at this party," he said. "Lisa, let me see if I've got the story right. OK?" She nodded.

"Your father was a spy for America in what was then Czechoslovakia. Our father was his controller. Your father was near to being discovered and arrested. Our father was bringing him out but Dad died in a bicycle accident. Your father buried him and got into Austria. Right so far?"

"Yes," answered Lisa. "My father'll fill in the details."

"Why didn't he go to the Americans in Vienna?"

"Remember, that was a time of subterfuge and double agents. My father was a stranger in Austria. He felt compelled to safeguard the information until he could contact your mother. He regards the Hendersons – and Mr. Oakes – as the only people who can deal with it. I won't tell you what it is – he will. It's his life. His guilt is a terrible burden for us all." Visions of gold bars flashed through her mind. She shuddered.

"OK. Let me go on," said Robert. "After he arrived in Vienna, he looked up the people who knew how to find us."

"Yes. That part was easy. He went to the Embassy and asked an Austrian clerk where Mrs. Henderson was, because he had something that he wanted to send to her. There was an Austrian man who had the address, because his wife worked for your mother. She helped your mother with her two mischievous sons and they were corresponding."

"That was Anna," Robert said. "I bet Stephen never knew that Mom was sending letters and pictures to Anna. They were good friends. But to go on – then your father came to America to see us for himself?"

"Not really, Robert," said Lisa. "He had a lawyer just keep track of you. There was no – what's your word – surveillance?" They nodded. "Just reporting the new address in Bethesda, your mother's marriage to Mr. Oakes – *Vati* approved of that and felt very happy. He didn't understand, however, that Mr. Oakes was your father's superior and might have known what happened on the American side when your father didn't return to Vienna. I just learned that from Bruce last night. *Vati* had a limited view of how espionage operates – he understood the compartmentalizing necessary to limit damage after an agent's compromised, but that's about all."

Bruce said, "Something bothers me. Stephen'll want to bring in someone from the Agency. Dad's case is still open – it's never been closed."

"Please don't do this right away, for my father's sake. He's counting on all of you to advise him. And, Bruce, what is this Agency?"

"It's the Central Intelligence Agency, Lisa. Stephen was a deputy director. It was his entire life. He's highly regarded. He trained, supervised and mentored many people. He's a little feeble, but his mind is needle-sharp and he's still called on for his opinions."

"Ooooh. Oh, my." Her brow furrowed. "*Vati* didn't know that. Mr. Oakes will be very interested in what he has to say."

"Lisa, can you tell us a bit more about where Dad's body is buried now?" Robert asked. His voice turned husky.

"Yes. *Vati* showed us exactly where the accident happened. After the Wall came down he took us to Zohor. It's a little town – let me get a map." She went to a table, opened a drawer, took out a folded map and an envelope. She leaned against Bruce's shoulder as she unfolded the map.

"Here's Vienna; follow along the Danube River to where the Morava River comes in. Go northeast a little way, here, and there's Zohor. Now, of course, it's in the Czech Republic. It's still a small rural village. The war wasn't kind to Zohor. My grandfather's old farmhouse was outside the village, about a kilometer and a half to the west. They abandoned everything in 1956. The family burial ground's on the old farm. Your father's accident happened about here" – pointing – "and my father came back later that day and buried him in the woods, marking it so he could find it again.

"After the Communists were thrown over, Father went back and had your father's remains transferred into a new coffin and re-buried in our family plot. Your father's cross says 'A True Soldier for Freedom' in Latin."

Lisa opened the envelope she'd been holding. "I didn't show you these photos last night, Bruce – guess we'd had enough emotion. Here's our family burial ground – you can see the old farmhouse in the background" – pointing at one photo – "and here's my grandparents' graves" – she held the last photo and her voice broke. "And here's your father's, Bruce." He put his arm around her shoulders as he held the photo. Their fingers touched and he hugged her.

The photo showed a smooth stone marker which read *E VERITAS PRELIATOR LIBERTAS* and the dates 1929 - 1956. An Eastern cross, with its double bar, was cut above the lettering.

"My father will explain why he chose these words."

Bruce handed the photo to Robert and Elaine. Robert cleared his throat . "A true fighter for freedom. Your father thought very highly of ours." His voice was strained.

She cleared her throat and continued in a low voice. "My father still thinks of him as Nikolai, not as Andrew Henderson. He said that your father had actually visited the family glassworks in the mid-thirties."

"Lisa, that would have been with our Grandmother Henderson. Wish we knew more about her and our grandfather. He was a Scot, she was Czech. She was an artist in glass and crystal. Perhaps Mom can tell us more. She hasn't talked much about Dad for years."

"*Vati* said that your father sounded like a native of Brno."

"Lisa," asked Robert, "did you know that our mother is Czech? She always said that her husband's mother had the right idea – teaching children as many languages as they could learn when they were young. She did that with us. Lisa, if I didn't speak Czech, I wouldn't be alive. It saved me and my close friends in Vietnam. Tell you about it sometime."

He handed the photos back to Lisa. She said, "No. You keep them. I have extra copies for your mother." She stood up and stretched. "Anybody hungry?"

14

1800 Tuesday May 8, 1988
Lisa's apartment

The Hungarian Goulash was served with a bottle of
Merlot. Lisa said, "It's Hungarian because I use a lot of
Hungarian paprika in it. Otherwise, you can call it beef stew.
My father said the best meal he ever had was American beef
stew from United States Army field rations."

Bruce looked at Robert and grinned. "C-rations, I bet.
That beef stew always reminded me of home."

"Right. Back in the sixties we augmented it with field
food."

Lisa followed the conversation between the brothers.
"Robert, what's field food?" she asked.

He chuckled. "Field food is anything that you can catch
and eat. It's a challenge of innovation and tolerance. Now, this
Hungarian goulash is no challenge at all. If there's more in the
pot, I'll take it off your hands."

Lisa reached for his bowl and looked around. She asked,
"Does anyone else want more?" Bruce handed his bowl to her
and she pushed back her chair and stood up. "There's enough
left for both of you and then no more. I'm glad you liked it."

"Remember what you said last night, Lisa?" asked Bruce.
"About finding if my new girlfriend can cook? You pass with
flying colors."

She bent over and kissed his cheek as she went into the
kitchen. "Thank, you, Bruce."

Conversation during the meal had been animated and
revealing. Lisa had told them about her life as a young girl,
how her father insisted on developing language skills and her
acceptance into a private school, then five years at the
University of Vienna, working summers in the American
Embassy, meeting and assisting tourists. Then, how
completing law school and passing the Austrian bar led to a
full-time appointment in the Austrian Diplomatic Corps,

specializing in international law.

She'd ended by saying, "My father's objective was achieved when I was assigned to the DC embassy, allowing me to find a way to meet Bruce."

"So how did you manage that?" Elaine had asked.

"That was the hard part," Lisa had responded. "I went to the State Security Specialists in the Embassy. I told one young man – Kurt – I think he had romantic notions – I needed to meet a woman with a wide circle of American friends. Pure luck; he knew Marie Firney, whom he'd met at a Christmas party. She'd introduced him to an American girl. He did a little research and learned that Marie's husband and you, Bruce, were friends and saw each other every now and then. So – I arranged for the Firneys to be invited to a reception for a new Saudi under-Secretary. It was an appropriate invitation, no eyebrows were raised, Austria buys Saudi oil and so forth. I introduced myself to Marie and we became great friends. Told her that I might be interested in meeting an American who was somewhere near my age. Your name was at the top of her list. When she said, 'Bruce Henderson. You'll like Bruce, he's such a dear!' I thought my heart would stop."

Bruce had shaken his head. "Good grief," he'd said, "So Marie was manipulated. I didn't think it was possible. What if it hadn't worked? What'd you've done?

"I'd been in DC for six months and was making no progress. I was going to knock on your door and introduce myself, but what if you had a woman living there? I'd looked up the address from the phone number on the Internet, but I hadn't dared to go. Marie'd said you raised dogs and I thought I'd ask about buying one."

"You'd have had a surprise, Lisa," Bruce had said. "We get visitors, but they don't arrive un-announced. Hey, gang, Marie can't ever learn she was set up. Surprised she hasn't already called to learn what happened last night."

"What did happen last night, Bruce?" said Elaine.

Bruce turned to Lisa. "Two people who were put on this earth to be together found each other."

Lisa's voice was low and husky, "I fell in love with a boy's picture when I was fifteen years old. There has been no other love in my life since then. Last night, I learned that the man I've been waiting for is this one. *Vati* always promised me, 'He'll be there for you, Lisa.' I always knew in my heart that it would happen."

"Just like you and me, Laney," said Robert, reaching his hand out to ruffle her hair

"Yes, you big bum," said Elaine, turning to Lisa in the kitchen. "Never asked me to marry him. Formally. On his knees, with a ring in his hand. Or with my father's permission. It was me that said, "How 'bout we get married on the twenty-first?' He said 'OK by me. Tell your folks, will ya?' Lisa, don't say 'yes' until he produces a great big diamond ring."

"Wonder if she'd settle for a dog collar. . ." Bruce mused. "A big rhinestone one."

"That does it," said Elaine. "You brutes get to clean up Lisa's kitchen. She and I need girl talk."

"What'll we do about Mom and Stephen?" said Robert. "They can't get this cold turkey."

"Laney, what's set up tomorrow with Riggs and Tuck?" said Bruce. "Did you schedule working in the supermarket or wherever?"

"Wait a minute, let me get my planner." She shot a grin at Lisa. "The Boss has no patience. He expects me to remember EVERYTHING." She opened her journal and plucked at the ribbon.

"OK, Bruce. Tomorrow morning, 0900, you're with Tuck at City Hall and Tom's with Riggs at the Giant store. You'll swap locations at 1030. Everything you need is all set. Afternoon's clear."

"Sounds good. Robbie, where will you be?"

"At Laney's sewing machine, making another dynamite vest."

"Can you and Laney come into Mom's? We can do a Chinese takeout lunch for them."

"That'll work."

"What time's it?" He muttered, looking at his watch. "Almost eight PM." He pulled his cell phone from its holster.

"Hey, Elaine," said Lisa, "is this how they get out of doing dishes? Business, business?" She carried some dishes into the kitchen.

"You've got it, Lisa – want me to wash or dry?"

Bruce sat alertly, phone at his ear. "*Dobrý vecer, Maminka,* it's me. Would it be OK if we brought in Chinese lunch tomorrow for you and Steve? Something important has come up." Another pause. "No, more important than that. We'll be working in town and thought it would be a good chance to see you...Sounds good. See you a little after noon tomorrow. Hi to Stephen...Bye, Mom."

He hung up the phone. "We're on. What're you writing, Elaine?"

She looked up from her journal.

"Moo Goo Gai Pan and Cashew Chicken. You get no choice. That'll be lunch tomorrow. I get to eat high on the hog on field trips in this outfit."

"At least you had tonight, Laney," Robert said contritely. He stood.

"So what did you contribute to it, big boy? It was all Lisa's work and now I get to thank her by helping in the kitchen."

Grinning at her husband, she closed her journal. Placing it in her carry-all, she patted his rump on her way to the kitchen.

Robert and Bruce sat on the other side of the living room. "Wonder how they'll take this, Bruce."

"Don't know. Dad disappeared in 1946 . . . 42 years ago...wondering, no closure, no clues, thinking maybe she's a bigamist and he'll pop up."

"I think she believed he was dead," Robert said. "For her, closure was probably the day that Stephen took us to Arlington and showed us the new star in the CIA memorial. Only time I ever saw her cry. Hope what we learned'll reinforce that closure. Lisa's news'll bring her a feeling of peace. And, little brother, it'll be closure for Steven as well. He'll have hard questions for Lisa's father."

"Yes," Bruce answered, "Hope his answers'll be straightforward. It'll be a test of his courage to face Mom. Why has he been silent so long?"

As he said the last few words, Lisa and Elaine, who had been following the conversation, joined them. Lisa sat on the floor, leaning her head on Bruce's thigh. He dropped his hand to her shoulders and stroked her back gently.

"When you hear what he has to tell, you'll understand why he has been silent until now," said Lisa. "It has to do with a problem that doesn't involve any of you . . . yet. Everything we ever did was pointed towards its solution. But since I've learned of Mr. Oakes' associations, with his understanding and assistance, it should be possible to solve it. It's an extremely sensitive matter that has international consequences."

Her voice quavered. "In the meantime, please, you have to trust me." She turned her face up to Bruce. Her tear-filled eyes turned brilliant blue with the intensity of her emotions. She picked up his hand and laid it against her cheek.

Bruce heaved a deep sigh. "Here's what we'll do, Lisa. Tomorrow, after lunch, we'll tell Mom and Stephen that the Third Man has been found and will be coming to visit us all on Saturday at the Ranch. I'll tell them that he was with Dad when there was a fatal accident and that he was afraid of being discovered by the Czech Secret Police, and he did what he had to do at the instant. I'll tell them that in later years he arranged for a proper burial and that you have photos."

"Knowing my father," said Lisa, "he'll be weeping at your mother's feet. He can be very emotional."

"*Maminka* will do her crying between tomorrow and Saturday," said Robert. "She's a tough old bird. Bet she'll greet him with a hug, saying 'Hush, my dear friend. I understand.'"

Lisa said, "Probably after we've all had a good cry, he'll settle down and talk about the next part. It's what's given him the courage to come."

"Rob's right," Bruce said. "Got a busy day tomorrow. We'd better hit the road, sweetheart. Been quite an evening for all of us. Hope we're doing the right thing the right way. Lisa, you are something." She rose from the floor, took his hand and they embraced.

"Thank you, Bruce," she murmured into his ear. "When I can sleep with you in my arms, there'll be no more nightmares. Want you so badly that you'd better go before I embarrass myself in front of Rob and Laney."

Elaine chuckled, "No secrets in our family, Lisa. There'll

be plenty of time later on for you to try to embarrass us. But it won't be easy!"

"I'll call you at bedtime, Lisa," said Bruce, "to tell you how it went with Mom and Stephen."

They moved to the doorway. Bruce felt Lisa mold to him. Her closeness and urgency left him breathless.

"Mmmmm – this is habit-forming," Lisa whispered as they separated. "Night, my love."

15

0730 Saturday, May 12, 1998
Route 211 east of Warrenton, Virginia

Bruce rolled up the passenger-side window of the Blazer.

Fred said, "Finally got cooled down, huh? How long did you guys run the dogs?"

"About an hour, Freddie. It'll be a rest day for them with all that we've got going on. Probably the dogs did three times what we did. You should have seen Toby. He had two pups hanging from each end of a big old stick and he started to shake his head. If the stick hadn't broken, he'd have flung 'em over the fence."

"Yeah, he's about the strongest dog I've ever seen."

"He'll be in a good home with Duncan and Marie."

"Is he going to get in on the action next Friday?"

"Nope – we'll be using just Riggs and Tuck. First time that we've used two sniffers on one job."

"I don't understand why we don't keep a handle on who we let into this country. Who came up with this suicide bomber idea, anyway?"

"Elaine did, Freddie. Bet if we had fifty cents for every illegal alien we could buy the White House."

"Right. And how many of them got an agenda? Scary picture."

Bruce yawned and stretched. "Wake me up by Chain Bridge if I don't do it before then. Gotta catch some z's, Fred." He released the seat back and reclined.

"Right. You Army brats got that down to a science."

* * *

The Blazer swung off Nebraska Avenue onto Van Ness.

Bruce said, "The apartment building's in the fourth block after we cross Wisconsin."

"I'll go back the same way, Bruce. Shall I call your mother when I'm about ten minutes from their place?"

"Good idea."

Bruce fell silent, remembering how his mother and Stephen had acted when he had told them about his father's disappearance. He'd said, "We can close the circle on Dad. He died in a bicycle accident. It was instantaneous."

Lattie had answered, "Son, I've known he was dead ever since Stephen brought us home. I'd felt it."

The five of them had sat in silence for several moments. Finally, Stephen cleared his throat "How'd you find out?" he asked.

"The Third Man's daughter told me," Bruce answered. "And that leads me to the second thing I have to tell you. The Third Man will be here on Friday. Why don't you folks to come out Saturday morning to hear what he has to say?

Lattie said, "Poor man. He's carried that burden all these years."

"His name is Holder," said Stephen. "Eduard Holder. That's the passport we made up. We had flags on it. He never came to America."

"You're right on the name, Stephen. He did come to America, though – for a short visit back in fifty-seven or eight."

Stephen had stirred uncomfortably. "Must have missed him. But I'll never forget the name. Damned important to us. Wonder why he waited so long to come."

"I think that we'll hear the answers to that, Stephen."

"What about his daughter?" Lattie said. "How'd you find her?"

"It was the other way around, Mom." said Bruce. "She found me. Her name's Lisa Holder. She's an Austrian lawyer in the Austrian Embassy."

"She's a kind and gracious lady," Elaine said.

Lattie straightened up in her chair, her eyes sparkling. "Well, then – that's settled. Can't wait to meet her. Are we all going to be staying at the Ranch? Poor Mr. Holder – we'll need a lot of time to catch up."

"Yes, as long as you want. Lisa says there is some problem they've been struggling with and she hopes that you, Stephen, can advise on it. Lisa didn't know that you'd been in the CIA, or that you're still connected there. She thinks that they'll want to be involved but not right away."

As the Blazer crossed Connecticut Avenue, Bruce brought his mind back to the present.

"There, Freddie. Third building on the right, the light gray one. Pull right in to the front and you can be on your way. Tell Mom that we'll be about twenty minutes or so behind them. It'll take me longer here than you'll need picking them up."

"OK, Bruce. Good luck."

Bruce turned to the front door. Thinking of what was about to happen, his heart pounded. As he pushed the button labeled 1212, he thought, *"At least I can reassure him that he's not going into a lion's den when he meets my mother."*

Entering the foyer, he went to the elevators. Entering, he punched Lisa's floor button; the door closed and acceleration tugged at him. *"Wonder if she looks like her mother."*

Stopping, the elevator gave its familiar shuddering lurch. Bruce stepped out and saw Lisa waiting for him. She pulled him into her arms and hugged him fiercely. *"Mein Gott,* how I've missed you," she said. Cupping his head with both hands, she kissed him. He wrapped his arms around her waist and pulled her against him. Her aroma teased his senses. "Mmmm – tastes like honey," he said, coming up for air.

"Silly; I just had a muffin with honey on it." Releasing him, she looked at her fingers. Deftly, he caught her hand and put the ends of her fingers in his mouth.

"Yup – definitely you've been in the honey pot," he mumbled around her fingers.

Laughing, she snatched her hand away and said, "I'm glad I pulled the door closed behind me. *Vati* might not have understood that."

Stepping apart, they looked at each other. Their hands reached out, their fingers latched. Lisa's sapphire pendant nestled tantalizingly in her cleavage. Bruce stared, his heart pounding.

"God, you're so beautiful," and he swept her into his arms again.

She clung to him. "I'm glad I wore this dress today. It won't wrinkle. Oh, Bruce. We better go in." She took his hand and they entered the living room.

"Father, here's Bruce Henderson. Bruce, this is my father,

Rudi Holder."

Bruce saw a tall, somber man, with piercing black eyes. His jet black hair was streaked with white. Both men extended their right hand, grasping the other's firmly. In a flash, Bruce thought, *"An Austrian handshake would make him feel welcome"* so he raised the hand he clasped, made one firm oscillation and released it. "I am very happy to meet you, Mr. Holder. Lisa's told me much about you."

"You'll excuse my English, Mr. Henderson, it's not as easy for me as for Lisa. I must say that I would know you anywhere. You – umm – resemble? " He looked at Lisa; she nodded. "Yes. Resemble your father very well. Except you're older than he was when I knew him." Rudi's voice was deep and resonant.

"Herr Holder," said Bruce in German, "If you would be more comfortable speaking in German, please do. We speak that reasonably well. Except we are also out of practice. Please feel free to say anything in German or in Czech if it'll help you find the right word."

"Czech? You speak Czech?" Rudi said eagerly. Instantly switching to Czech, he asked, "But why do you speak such a difficult language?"

"My mother is Czech, Herr Holder."

"I knew that she was a Czech, but thought that she'd have given up that language since many years. Please, your mother, she's well?"

"Yes, Herr Holder. She's very excited today . . . very anxious to meet you and hear what you have tell us."

"Please, call me Rudi so I can call you Bruce? Your mother, she's angry for me not telling everything many years ago?"

"No, Rudi. Just sorry that you've had to keep this to yourself for so long. She'll say that it'd been easier for if you had told her earlier. She knows those were difficult times for many people. Don't worry. She'll be a good friend."

"And Mr. Oakes? Lisa told me about him. Does he know your President well?"

Bruce thought, *now there's a question that caught me flat-footed.* "Not at all. But he has friends where he worked.""

Lisa interjected, *"Vati,* we'll talk about that later, when you and Mr. Oakes have gotten to know each other."

"*Jawohl*," said Rudi, sighing. "She runs my life like a jail-keeper. *Ja Ja*. Always has. Don't let her do it to you also."

"Now, *Vati*, don't go giving Bruce bad ideas. He'll be running my life, not the other way. Bruce, shouldn't we be getting along?"

Bruce glanced at his watch. "Yes. We'll get there about eleven, shortly after Fred brings Mom and Stephen to the Ranch. Can I carry your bags to your car?"

16

Bruce parked Lisa's BMW in the driveway next to the Blazer. "Welcome to the Ranch," he said.

"It's lovely, Bruce," said Lisa.

A single quiet "woof" came from the front porch, as the front door opened and Elaine stood in the doorway.

"Come on in, folks. We just settled Lattie and Stephen into their room." Suzie stood next to Elaine, her head against her knee, her tail waving lazily.

"Bruce, please, can you bring my bag?" Rudi asked. "There's some things I want to have with me."

His mother and Stephen were standing in the spacious living room. Stephen's arm was around Lattie's shoulders. *"How frail Mother looks,"* thought Bruce.

"Mom, Stephen, this is Lisa Holder and Rudi, her father."

Rudi stood stiffly, his face working.

Lattie took two steps, reached out and pulled him into her arms. Her head barely reached his chest; it looked as if he was hugging a child. His shoulders heaved with sobs.

Lattie spoke softly, but clearly, in Czech. "Dear man, it's over, I understand. You must cry so you'll be cleansed. You only did what you had to do. We'll go and sit on the porch together for a little while." Lattie and Rudi went out the front door together.

Lisa hugged Bruce, her eyes streaming tears. "What a wonderful woman!"

Bruce handed his handkerchief to her; she wiped her eyes and blew her nose.

Hank stepped into the hall, with Tom right behind him. They both smiled at Lisa. Elaine said, "Lisa, this young scamp is our son Hank; and this tall man is Hank's older brother, Tom."

Taking her hand, Tom said "Welcome, Lisa. We are happy to meet you."

"I always wanted a pretty aunt," Hank said. "I was going to mention something about the way you blow your nose, but we'll get used to it." He gave her a quick hug. Elaine rolled her eyes at Lisa and shook her head.

"Lisa, this is Stephen Oakes, my step-father," Bruce said. "He's the rock this family rests on."

"I apologize for my father," Lisa said. She went to Stephen, hugged him and kissed his cheek.

"She'll bring him back when they're ready, Lisa," said Stephen. "Lattie is a strong and compassionate woman. He'll be a different man when they return."

"Well, folks, let's sit down and relax," said Elaine. "We'll be having lunch in a little while, but in the meantime, I've got a pitcher of iced tea. Lisa, would you like some?"

Lisa nodded. "That would be very nice."

"OK, Hank, payback time," said Elaine. "The green pitcher's in the fridge. The matching glasses are on the kitchen table. Do it." He curtsied, grinning and left.

"Is he really your son?" Lisa asked. "Looks as if he was your younger brother. You people are so fit."

"Thanks, Lisa," answered Elaine. "You're very kind. We all run every day. This morning we saw the sun rise over the District. Looks like you're in good shape, too – do you work out?"

"Yes," answered Lisa. "I wanted to be a dancer, but I just kept growing. Finally realized there's not many ballerinas my height, weighing sixty kilograms, I just hiked, skied and ran. Still do. Run in Rock Creek Park instead of eating lunch."

Elaine placed her left foot next to Lisa's. "Close enough to the same size. I've a brand new pair of Nikes – still in the box. Want to use them tomorrow morning?"

"Thanks, Elaine. Told Bruce I had enough clothes for a week, so I have my own and a sweat-suit." She gave Elaine a quick hug.

"Looks as if you've got a new girlfriend, Mom," said Hank, placing a tray on a table. Lisa picked two of the glasses. "Let me take these out to the porch, Hank."

Hank watched her go across the room. He said, "Nice

walk. Pretty legs, Bruce."

Elaine rolled her eyes at Robert.

Lisa came back in. "All's OK out there," she said. "The dog's lying between them, getting the petting of her life. They're talking quietly. Don't think they even know who brought the iced tea."

Elaine said, "There's something therapeutic about animals. Especially females, I think. I've seen it before; they sense emotional distress and seem to know that their presence is soothing. Suzie has been a mother several times – perhaps that helps. She also knows that she shouldn't be on that sofa and that she'll get away with it."

"I think that there are two very brave people out there," said Bruce. Lisa placed her hand on his thigh. It held the coolness of her glass.

Stephen cleared his throat. "Wonder how Rudi will prove what he's going to tell us. Not that I doubt him, but he seemed on the verge of panic, shaking like an aspen."

Lisa said, "I truly understand your thinking, Mr. Oakes. You'll be totally satisfied. His little bag contains Nikolai's – Mr. Henderson's – original passports – one Austrian, one Czechoslovakian. They're extremely good forgeries, probably made in America by your former associates. In 1959, he had to turn in the passport that Mr. Henderson had for him before it expired. He was afraid to ask for it back when the passport officer was ready to toss it into a wastebasket, but he did. It's because of that passport that my last name is Holder. The only document with his real family name is a fishing license issued in July, 1945, by the mayor of St. Wolfgang. It hangs on the wall, in a little frame. He's never uttered that name in our presence. He left that identity behind when he left Czechoslovakia – as did my uncle Georgi and Aunt Hilda – and their son, my cousin Peter. I was born in Austria in 1958 and have an Austrian birth certificate. We've always had fun with the fact that I am the only family member whose origins and parentage will stand up to close examination – and, being a lawyer, it *has* been examined."

Stephen said, "Lisa, thank you for your patience. I've been a slave to detail all of my professional life. Check, check and check again. I'm sure those passports passed through my own hands. We had them prepared in 1950. The work was done here in Washington. We were – and still are – quite proud of the quality of our products. The Austrian government was very cooperative in these matters – they gave us blank pre-numbered passports, asking only that we furnish them with the names, birth-dates and place of birth that would be applied. They told us that local records – primarily, church records – wouldn't agree, but that was a chance we'd have to take."

Robert said, "Also, Stephen, he has photos of Dad's grave. We had them with us last Wednesday, but under the circumstances, we didn't feel that they were necessary."

"Lattie will want to see them," said Stephen. "She may want to travel there."

Lisa said, "After hearing my father's next story, going to Austria and the Czech Republic might be a very good idea."

A squeak from the screen door signaled the return of Lattie and Rudi, who stood erect, shoulders back; his smile beamed at them all; his eyes sparkled. Lattie held his arm; he appeared to be escorting a princess. Lisa left her seat, went to him and hugged him.

"We told you that this woman is wonderful, *Vati*." She kissed Lattie's cheek, saying, "Thank you, Lattie."

Lattie turned to Stephen. "This gentleman has discovered that he's hungry."

17

Elaine's lunch, served under the awning, was totally enjoyable. Rudi, free of the stress preceding his time with Lattie, entered eagerly into the casual banter that flowed around the table during the meal.

Rudi wanted to retell every word and experience he and Andrew had shared. But when he described the bicycle accident, his cheerfulness evaporated.

He said, "I was just going to call to him to 'slow down, watch where you're going, Nikolai' when so fast it happened. He was having such a good time. He was still smiling when I reached him but no life was in the smile. I moved him into the woods, and then went back for both bicycles. I was very afraid of being discovered."

After a long silence, Stephen asked, "Rudi, how did you get into Austria? The borders were watched very closely then, weren't they?"

"Yes, they were. Also, I was certain that the *Státní bezpeènosti* were looking for me. The night before we were to leave, Nikolai told me how the peat boat operated. I couldn't take the Tuesday boat, it was too late. I had to take care of Nikolai.

"After the accident, I went back to the farm. There was wide boards there, so I cut twelve to exactly two meters and six to a half meter. It was several trips *vor und rückwärts*" – he looked at Lisa.

"Back and forth, *Vati*," she said.

"*Ja*, back and forth, carrying the boards on the bicycle, then get nails and a hammer and shovel and build a proper coffin right there in the woods. It was two kilometers to the nearest house so I didn't worry about the noise of hammering – it sounded like gunshots. God was with me because there was nobody on the road all that morning. I put Nikolai's extra

clothes in with him and made sure there was no identification.
I said goodbye, dear friend and closed up the coffin and put it
gently into the ground. I took the license tag off Nikolai's
broken bicycle, which I left in the barn for the gypsies.

"Then I hid in the woods near the grave, watching the
road. There was money in his rucksack and his passport, there
was two more passports sewed into a slot – one for me and
another for him and the letters that he told me about. Also a
nice pistol. His rucksack was bigger than mine, so I put
everything together in his."

"You must have felt terribly," said Stephen.

"Yes," answered Rudi. "It was the worst day of my life –
worse than when my parents were killed." Looks were
exchanged around the table.

"But that is a part of another story," Rudi continued. "I
slept in the woods by his grave that night. In the morning, I
found I had a flat tire on my bicycle. It was cut and I couldn't
fix it. I walked back to the house through the woods and
fields – I didn't want to be seen on the road – and watched
the house to make sure it was still without people. I went into
the barn, left the shovel on its hook and took from the broken
bicycle the tires - new Austrian ones.

"I am sorry about my English, I have practiced this story
in my mind since many years, but now I forget little things
and don't know the words."

"Rudi, you're telling the story very well," said Lattie,
laying her hand on his. "It's bringing me peace and comfort to
learn how kind you were to my husband."

"Thank you, Mrs. Henderson." Lattie didn't correct the
mistake.

"What did you do next?" she asked.

"I wanted to make sure of the peat boat. I had a good
bicycle with good tires. It had the license tag from Nikolai's.
There'd been nobody on the road. So I hid my rucksack in the
woods, took my bicycle and a little money and went towards
Bratislava. When I got beyond where the Morava River joins
the Danube, there were the peat fields on both sides of the
road. There were piles already dried, waiting for the boat. I
didn't stop, just kept going. I went to the coffee house where
I first met Nikolai. I used to stop there when I went to the

office. They joked with me, saying that I was getting like the Communists, getting somebody else to count trees for me while I took the credit. I had a large supper – sausages and dumpling soup and I ate myself full. At sunset there was enough light to find my way back to the grave where I spent the second night.

"Thursday morning, I walked back to the farmhouse, staying off the road – still nobody around. I had to keep myself busy, so I cut pieces of wood – one about a meter long, the others less than half. I took a *meissel* -"

"Chisel, Rudi," said Lattie. "I think I know what you're going to do."

Rudi sighed. "You'll for sure be correct, dearest lady. I should be telling you this in German or Czech, *ja*? I went back to the grave and made a cross. I used the – chisel?" – Lattie nodded – "to notch the wood for a proper fit, so tight that nails might not have been needed. With my knife I carved the edges of the arms, carved a crown in the top of the post and cut the letters *V E I L B*. Then I made a little roof and nailed its peak on the top. I'd brought a tin of oil and soaked the cross in it so it would last longer than plain wood. I pushed it into the ground at Nikolai's head and piled many large stones over the mound of the grave and around the base of the cross."

"What do those letters mean, Rudi?" Tom asked.

"It's Latin," Rudi said. "Lisa, *Liebchen*, help me with the English."

"Tom, the Latin words are '*VERA ENIM IN LIBERTATEM BELLO*' – they mean 'A true fighter for freedom' which we know your grandfather to have been."

Stephen asked, "And how did the boat trip go, Rudi?"

"Friday morning," he said. "It was cold. Much frost, but I'd slept warm in Nikolai's sleeping bag. I woke at first light. Everything was packed except the sleeping bag and I pushed it into the rucksack. When the sun rose I was waiting at the peat dock. The boat was already there. Pretty soon, a man came out of the cabin and said he'd be back after breakfast. I asked him if I could ride the boat, he said 'if you help load the peat' and pedaled off. An hour and a half later, he came back and the boat was loaded. The head field man gave him a piece of paper. He pulled schillings from his wallet and counted them out. They shook hands. He looked at me, all covered with peat and said, *'Tausend Schilling, bitte.'* I had it ready. He put his bicycle on board, I did the same and we were on our way. After an hour, he said to me, 'Austria on both sides, you know.' That was all he said the whole day. We didn't reach Vienna until after dark.

"He said *'Auf wiedersehen.'* I told him that I'd get my bicycle in the morning because the dynamo was broken and I had no headlamp. He just nodded. I lied - the dynamo, it had no problem – I needed the excuse.

'I went across the street. There was a car parked there with two men in it. I went in back of it and hurried between two buildings. I ran across the railroad tracks – nobody followed. So I walked along the tracks a little way, then went back to the street. The car was still there. It was getting misty.

"The captain came out of the cabin and left on his bicycle. A man got out of the car, went up on the boat and looked in the cabin with a flashlight. He came back quickly and left in the car and it drove away. I waited for another ten minutes; there was another car down the street; it started up and drove away also.

"I waited a little longer, then got my bicycle and pedaled through the city towards Linz. Stopped in a *Gasthaus* and ate a large supper. The streets were well lit, I had a good dynamo on the bicycle, so I rode for an hour. Then I left the road, went into the woods, took out the sleeping bag and slept until dawn. In Pressbaum, I had breakfast in the station, and then took the train to Linz with the bicycle in the baggage car. In Linz, I got the local train to Vöcklabruck and pedaled south along the lakes there and walked with the bicycle up over the pass to St. Wolfgang, where my friends were.

"The further I went from Czechoslovakia the less afraid I was. After all, I was an Austrian named Eduard Holder, in a free neutral country."

Stephen said, "Rudi, you couldn't have done that better if you had planned it. We had people watching train and bus stations, but it was hopeless. We were looking for Eduard Holder, we never thought that Eduard Holder might be carrying a rucksack that was once Andrew's, but that was all.

Many men were questioned by the Viennese police during the next seventy-two hours, but of course, none were you. We didn't know if the man who ran across the tracks in the dark even had any connection with Andrew or was just another border-crosser. Waiting out of sight, then going back for your bicycle was brilliant. Absolutely brilliant. We had two cars there, but our people didn't wait long enough."

"The rest of our family actually left Czechoslovakia two days before I did," said Rudi. "It took them two days to be in Hungary and another three days to cross into Austria. This was another thing that bothered me very much – Nikolai and I planned to be in Oberpullendorf when they came across the dangerous Hungarian border. I lost three days in leaving – and I was in Austria, St. Wolfgang, Saturday evening. The rest of the group could be in Oberpullendorf as early as the next Monday.

"I spent Sunday with my friends in St. Wolfgang; they got some clothing for me. So, early Monday morning I went, first by bus back to Vöcklabruck, then by train through Vienna south to Oberpullendorf.

"It was the middle of the afternoon when I came to the reception center and waited. They said new refugees appeared early in the morning, after crossing the border at night. So I went to a *Gasthaus* for supper and sleeping and was back at the Center at first light. The first trucks that came carried my family and friends. I stayed with them through their reception. The Austrians said new people without *cestovní pas* – umm, passports? – was normal. So, my brother and his family also became Holders. The next day – Wednesday – my family received new identity cards and we were able to leave as long as they stayed in Austria. I took them all to St. Wolfgang. I never told them of my difficulties until much years later."

Lisa stood and stretched. She patted her father's back. "I have something in the car that you might all enjoy. Bruce, there is a cooler in the trunk. In it are the special wine glasses and I have four bottles of the Riesling that we enjoyed the other night."

Elaine said, "You beat me to the punch, Lisa. I've cheese and crackers ready. I'd love to have some more of that Riesling."

"You mean she beat you to the wine, Mom," said Hank. "Who wants punch when there's Riesling?"

Lisa and Elaine laughed.

"My little brother was born to be a quick-witted stand-up comic," Tom said. "Please don't laugh, Lisa, it only encourages him."

"I think he's funny," she responded.

Hank got up and came to her with a hug. "Stay on my side, Lisa – you'll have the first chance at the laughs. Bruce, hand me those keys and I'll get the cooler."

Bruce tossed the keys to him.

"Thanks, dad." He looked at the insignia on the ignition key. "A Beemer. This may take a while."

"Watch my lips, son. You'll – be – right – back," said Robert.

"OK, Dad. Wanna go for a ride later, Lisa?" he asked, passing her chair. "I can show you what your Beemer can really do." He winked.

"Maybe I should show _you_ what it can do," Lisa responded. "At home, speed limits are much higher than you allow. In Bavaria, close to where I live, there's _no_ speed limit. High-speed driving isn't something you do safely without a lot of practice. Get any speeding tickets in the past month?"

"Nope."

"Then you're out of practice, Hank. I'll drive."

He gave an exaggerated sigh. "I just got sand-bagged." Rudi looked puzzled; everyone else laughed. Lisa leaned close to her father and there was a rapid exchange in German. Rudi laughed and said to Hank, "Better just you bring the wine, Hank. Lisa gets speeding tickets where there is no speed limit!"

Elaine rose from her chair, saying, "I'll get the munchies. We'll have supper about six-thirty."

Lisa said to Rudi, "How are you doing, _Vati?_ Your body thinks it's bedtime. Would you like a little sleep this afternoon? I'm sure everyone would understand."

"No, no," He replied, "I must tell them about the – you know. But perhaps a little wine first. Then, maybe I take a little walk before dinner."

"Rudi, you can do anything you want here." said Bruce

"We understand that you have another story; if you want to tell it now, it'll be fine."

"Perhaps while we have our wine," said Rudi.

Hank came up on the deck, carrying a large cooler. "Party time," he said, placing it next to Lisa.

"I've got Salzburg beer, too," said Lisa. "Nice and cold."

Elaine returned and placed a variety of crackers, cheeses and cold vegetables on the table. Lisa placed a wine cooler on the table. "Anyone want beer?" she asked. There was no response. "Wonderful. We'll all share in these special wine-glasses."

She placed a wicker basket on the table and removed nine crystal glasses.

"I almost raised my hand for beer," Hank said. "Glad I didn't."

"I won't take the beer home with me, Hank," said Lisa. "If you like, I'll give Bruce a case for you. One of the perks at the Embassy. There's a walk-in cooler filled with Austrian beer and wine. From the smile on your face, *Vati*, you've already looked in my refrigerator." Rudi nodded, grinning.

Lattie picked up two of the glasses. She moved out of the shade over to the edge of the deck and held them in the sunlight, examining each one closely. "These are exquisite," she exclaimed. "Lisa, where did you ever find them?"

Her question stopped the other conversations. All eyes turned to Lisa.

"They were made in Austria by people who worked in my grandfather's family glassworks in Zohor, Czechoslovakia," Lisa said. "That's where my father's second story begins. Bruce, Robert and Elaine know a little about these glasses and I'll tell the rest of you. Bruce, please pour the wine now?"

Bruce finished pulling the cork on the first bottle, poured a bit into a glass and tasted it.

"This is excellent," he said.

His mother held out one of the glasses and he filled it. She handed the extra glass to him; he filled it for Lisa. After filling the remaining glasses, he held up the last bottle.

"One glass left. We'll save it for you, Rudi," he said.

"Thanks, Bruce. I'll need it. Lisa, *schatzi*, tell about the glasses."

Lisa took the nearly-empty bottle and placed in the wine cooler. "I'd like to offer the same toast I did the other night," she said. "So" – raising her glass – "here's to the past, the present and whatever the future may have in store for us." She turned to Bruce and touched her glass to his, leaned forward and kissed his lips.

"Rudi told you about leaving Czechoslovakia in 1955," said Lisa. "At the time, my mother, Elsa Schäfter, was only twenty. She and her mother, Elizabeth, were the friends in St. Wolfgang that *Vati* mentioned. He's already told about meeting his family after they came over the border. That 'family' was three true relatives – his brother, Georgi, his wife, Hilda and their son – my cousin, Peter – who was seven. The others were cousins or workers at the glass works in Zohor – twelve in all. They'd worked there since before the war. Otto and his wife Zelda made a wonderful team – he blew these glasses, she cut the designs freehand. They still do this; they have a place up in Lambach, similar to what our family did in Zohor."

Lattie said, "Do I remember something about Zohor? Andrew's mother was in the glass business; she wanted Andrew to continue in it, but he was having too much fun with languages. She was Czech like myself."

Rudi leaned forward, his eyes bright. "Nikolai once said he'd visited our glass factory with his mother before the war. But please go on, Lisa. I am ready now."

"My father's story begins in the glassworks when he was sixteen. Things had changed during the war – the Nazis made them to stop making 'useless things' and had them producing high-quality lens blanks. Highly repetitive work and boring, but enough to 'keep their heads on their shoulders' as the Czechs say. On a particular April day, in 1945, something very unusual happened. This is where *Vati's* story begins. *Vati?*"

Rudi swallowed the last of his wine, took a deep breath, then took them through the arrival of the Nazi officers, everyone being confined to the shop during the creation of gold ingots, separation of precious stones from jewelry and cleaning of tooth residue and cement from crowns. As tears rolled down his face, he described the massacre of everyone except himself, the harrowing night drives across Austria, when he learned about the two Nazi officers and how they hid the gold for themselves.

He told how he was shot and left for dead, then found by Frau Schäfter and her daughter. "This morning, I said that my friends in St. Wolfgang were the only people I knew in Austria. It was Lisa's mother and little Elsa who saved my life in 1945 – they took me in and cared for my injury. I didn't tell you that Elsa, who came in dreams as an angel, was the beautiful woman I married when she was twenty. After we married, I told her about the gold and that I had to save it from the Nazis or from whoever else would use it for equally terrible purposes."

Bruce filled Rudi's glass.

"You know where the gold is, Rudi," said Stephen, "and this is the secret that you told Andrew and why you had to get out of Czechoslovakia."

"That's right, Stephen. I couldn't trust anyone. Told Nikolai and he was dead within hours. My heart told me to stay quiet until I could trust someone. Now my heart tells me it's you."

"But you say you know where the gold is, Rudi," persisted Stephen, "we've all heard the rumors about this lake, that salt mine, people have written stories about it. How do you know it's still there?"

"Because we got it out! All of it!" His fists pounded the table. "It's all in a vault we built in the cellar floor in our chalet! God forgive me, *we killed two Nazis who came looking for it!"*

Lisa paled and said, *"Vater, was sagt du? Ermordet?* Killed?" She put her hand on Bruce's arm.

Rudi covered his face with his hands. "Georgi and I never tell you. Or our wives. Or Peter. Yes. It was the Herr Major and his son, after we knew exactly where it was, after we'd built the chalet. In open daylight, they came with their wetsuits and they entered the water. Georgi and I, we opened their van, find their passports. I see Herr Oberst's sketches and his Luger. I see the Herr Major's black snake eyes staring from his passport. We follow them into the water. They'd have found the canvas over the gold, held in place by stones. Now, they stay underwater. When they went under, I told my mother and father I've kept the promise I made on their graves."

Shocked silence followed his startling, emotional outburst. Lisa put her arms around his shoulders and said, "You did what was right, *Vati*. You did what had to be done."

Lattie went to Rudi and took his hand, saying, "Dear Rudi, men die in war. Those men were double traitors – to their own Nazi party and to the whole human race. They knew where the gold came from and deserved what they got. You've kept this bottled up inside for too many years. Now, we're going to forget we heard this. It was nothing but a bad dream."

Elaine, noting the look on her husband's face, felt that he was about to say something about killing people. She said, "It's my turn, people. This conversation is about to turn into True Confessions. Bruce, let's open more wine and toast to forgetting the past. Let's salute the present and whatever the future may hold."

"Sounds good, Elaine," said Stephen.

Rudi raised his head. "Please. . . I'm sorry. Still have bad dreams . . . wake up feeling as if I'm drowning."

Lisa hugged her father. "*Vati, Vati* – why didn't you tell us? That was the same as stepping on a cockroach."

Rudi patted the hands that were comforting him – first Lisa's, then Lattie's. "

"I'm sorry," he said. "But what for? I'm not sorry for what I did – I'm sorry I upset everybody. Georgi and I didn't promise never to tell – we just didn't talk about it."

"It's best forgotten, Rudi," said Lattie. "Now the bad dreams are over."

Lisa said, "Mother Oakes, you're truly a remarkable woman."

Rudi nodded. He sighed deeply and said "*Ja ja*. Lattie is right, of course. I should have thought of it since years. Bruce, why is it taking you so long with the wine?"

Laughter broke the tension.

"How much gold is there?" Stephen asked

"On today's market, its value is more than thirty-two million US dollars," Lisa said. "Its moral value is incomprehensible and therein lies the problem."

"There's more," said Rudi. He seemed totally recovered

from his near-breakdown. "One of our workers discovered an ingot a few days after the Nazi convoy came through Zohor. We kept it hidden, especially from the Russians. Later, we recast it into smaller ingots. Nikolai carried them back to Austria before the last trip. He sold them somehow and deposited the money against the name on the Austrian passport he had for me. He carried forty little ingots each time, except for the last trip, where he carried thirty-nine. I have the last one in my bag. Hank, please get it, as there's some things I want to give to Lattie and to Stephen."

Hank hurried into the house, returning moments later and handed the bag to Rudi.

"Thank you, Hank," said Rudi. He opened it and took out a small tissue-wrapped packet. He placed on the table. Next came a large manila envelope.

"Now," he said, "first, the little souvenir."

As he unwrapped the tissue paper, gold gleamed. He handed it to Lattie, who had taken the chair next to him. "Careful," he warned, "it's heavier than it looks."

The weight surprised Lattie. "Your husband carried these from Zohor to Vienna, three times," said Rudy. "How dangerous that must have been for him. Hilda, my sister-in-law, made a vest with forty little pockets. When it was loaded, it weighed about seven kilos. He said the first time was difficult converting the gold to money, but got easy after that. After the last deposit, there was one and a half million Austrian schillings in a Salzburg bank in my name – not my real name, but in the name of Eduard Holder."

"Glad he never told me *exactly* what he was doing. He only told me he was helping the Third Man move assets from Czechoslovakia to Austria, against the day he'd come in," said Stephen.

"We – Georgi and I – never used any of it for anything personal. It paid for things that would help us find the gold and get it out. It paid for diving equipment and deep diving school and for our special vehicle – winches and so forth. We did the work ourselves. It paid for some of Lisa's education."

Rudi sipped from his glass. "It paid for anything that would prevent the rest of the gold being used for another Reich, where rule is maintained by terror and murder. . . and that was just from the one ingot that my father and mother hid from their murderers. And what we have is only a small part of what went to Switzerland.

"It can't ever be returned to the rightful owners, or their descendants. When entire families are murdered – thousands and thousands of families, millions and millions of people – how many descendants can there be?"

Rudi became agitated. "When Georgi and I, in 1990, see a man like this Saddam, how could we, by ourselves, have offered this gold to any country to pay for striking him down? He, who kills his own people? So, dear friends, that's the first thing I have to tell you. The gold has remained untouched since that day."

"*Vati*'s last dive ended a very stressful period," said Lisa. When I was twelve, *Vati* told us why he was in Austria in nineteen forty-five and why he had been shot. That's when we learned about the gold and that we were going to get it out and keep it safe until it could be handed over to the right people. And that's why he and Georgi built a chalet on the other side of the lake.

"All six of us Holders went to the chalet that Saturday morning. *Vati* backed the dive truck to the lower door and we lined up to pass ingots from the truck into the basement. Uncle Georgi pulled the rug back and opened a steel door set into the floor. 'This is really more than just a sump,' *Vati* told us. It was almost a meter square and deep enough to take the ingots, so that the top layer'd be eight or ten centimeters below the pump. They'd already removed the pump and the float switches that made the pump start and stop. We cleaned each ingot, sorted them by serial number and weighed them."

"We had to weigh them all over again, because the journal that my mother made for the Nazis was never found," said Rudi.

Lisa continued, "We had pieces of clean linen cloth to go between each layer. *Vati* had each of us feel the weight and coldness of the gold. 'That is the coldness of the death of millions of people,' he told us. I was sixteen years old and can remember just like it was yesterday, holding those heavy ingots and weeping."

"Ja, that was a day," said Rudi. "I'd checked dimensions

carefully before designing the sump. Contractors didn't even raise an eyebrow – perfectly normal, deep enough so that the motor wouldn't start and stop too frequently, but also deep enough to take all the ingots underneath the pump. We stacked them in ten rows across, three rows the long way. The pit was bone dry and always had been. As soon as the sixth layer was completed, we had all one hundred and eighty ingots in a safe place. We'd put lifting eyes into a square nine millimeter aluminum plate, painted it with several coats of epoxy paint, then fastened neoprene strips from an old diving suit around the edges."

Rudi's mind flashed back to cutting the neoprene suit from Herr Major's clammy body and he shivered. He reached for his wine glass and took a sip. "Somebody just walked over my grave," he said.

"We pushed this piece of aluminum on top of the ingots, hammered the neoprene to make a good seal and covered the aluminum plate with a couple centimeters of new concrete. We put the pump and switches back in place. A few days later, we checked the concrete and poured in some water to cover the new concrete but not enough to start the pump and closed the door. If it ever smelled a little stale, we'd add water and run the pump and put clean water in. Never added much, so I think the gold is still dry."

"You planned this to perfection, Rudi. You're a perceptive and careful man," Stephen said. "Take any photographs?"

Rudi smiled. "I did. Never printed the negatives till this week." He opened the manila envelope, pulled out several black-and-white photographs and handed them to Stephen, who spread them out on the table. "Impressive," he said. "Shows everything you told us."

Rudi removed two passports from a smaller envelope. "I think you've seen these before, Mr. Oakes. They were sewn in the rucksack. Austrian one's for Nikolai Wenk; the other – it's Czech – is for Nikolai Hodonin. Never told me his real name until our last night together. His Austrian passport was in his pocket with my new Austrian passport – Eduard Holder. Passport number was same as on the deposit slips."

Lattie looked at each of them. "That's Andrew," she said.

"I also have one of these little passport photos." She flipped through the pages. "Andrew traveled a lot."

"We probably did most of those stamps," said Stephen, taking the passports from Lattie.

"Here's his wedding ring and his wristwatch." He opened another envelope and gently handed the contents to Lattie. She wiped her eyes. "Once," she said, "He came back after he had been away for several days and his wedding ring was on his right hand. When I asked him why, he was angry with himself. 'A mistake like that could have gotten me killed,' he said."

Lisa said, "Bruce, sometimes I would ask *Vati* to see the wedding ring again. I would hold it in my hand and dream about what I would do with it some day."

Lattie handed the ring to Lisa. "It's yours now, Lisa."

"Thank you so very much, Lattie." She blew a kiss to Bruce.

"There are two more things to tell you and then there is nothing more," said Rudi. "First, the German passports from the diver's van. One was for Gunther Schmidt. He was the major with the eyes of a snake – the man who murdered my parents, Lukas and Sarah Jezocova; along with the others in the glassworks. They're all buried in our family cemetery in Zohor.

"The other was for a younger man also named Schmidt. Same address in Bad Tolz. Newspapers said the missing divers were father and son. When we learned their names from the newspapers, I burned their passports.

"The very last thing. Here's a list of the gold ingots, by serial number, with their weight and the total weight in Troy ounces." Rudi handed a handwritten document to Stephen. "Lisa told you the total weight and its value. The facts are detailed here. It's thirty-two million dollars. Now, what do we do with the gold?"

18

Rudi's question hung in the air, unanswered. Bruce got to his feet and said, "We'll all have to think about that and perhaps we'll need some outside help. Let's talk about it a little more after supper. Now, who else needs to stretch their legs?"

Stephen said, "I think that Lattie and I'll take a short stroll – all right, dear?"

She nodded and rose to her feet – a bit unsteadily, Bruce noted...*and it's not from the wine, either,* he thought.

Lattie said, "Stephen and I'll take short walk with Suzie. She's getting as old as we are and we don't have to go far to get our circulation excited."

Hank said, "It's close to feeding time; that'd be fun to watch." He and Tom hopped down the stairs, three at a time and headed for the barn.

"Lisa and Rudi, let's start down towards the barn," Bruce suggested. They rose from the table and followed him as he headed for the stairs.

Robert said, "I'll open up the armory. After they take a look at that, it'll be feeding time." He jogged down the stairs.

Bruce said, "We feed the dogs about five in the afternoon. It's the highlight of their day and they're pretty frisky.."

Lisa asked, "Do they all take training together?"

"No, sweetheart. They're separated into stages. Stage I pups are beginning obedience training, learning verbal commands and hand signals. At the end of Stage I, we decide on promotion or rejection. Rejection isn't bad – they're dogs that'll make a fine companion, or a Seeing Eye prospect. So that's where they go. Pups that go into Stage II have had about a year in Stage I and are beginning to specialize in one of three categories – personal protection, or site sweeping – looking for people who shouldn't be there. The third specialty are those that can find explosives. A Stage III dog is proficient in his specialty. We call explosives dogs 'sniffers.' They stay here and go with us on assignments, like the one we have next Friday."

"How can you tell which specialty to train them for?" asked Rudi.

"By which attitudes they display. If a yearling is trying to be an Alpha early on, he's headed for a career in protection."

As Bruce was talking, they had walked behind the barn, then entered the vehicle parking and workshop area in the basement.

Bruce explained, "Another part of our contract work is providing security for critical personnel in high risk situations. To do that, we have to be able to neutralize a subject – that means somebody like your Herr Major, Rudi – an assassin. Accordingly, we have a variety of weapons and we maintain our own proficiency with each weapon. We've very rarely found it necessary to use them, thank heavens, but it has happened."

When they passed through the vault door; Rudi whistled at its size. Bruce pulled open a flat file drawer open to display its contents. "We each have our own weapons cabinet," he said. "This one's mine. Weapons we select for an assignment are based on how close we'll be to a perpetrator, the density of other people and the probable actions that we'll defeat. We always look out for each other as we identify and neutralize a perpetrator. 'Neutralize' doesn't mean kill him, Lisa – it means perhaps just identifying him to our employers, or make him realize that he can't accomplish his objective. Sometimes that's when a dog is used; they're an effective deterrent. We work closely with our employers, who usually are the DC Police, FBI, Secret Service, CIA, or some combination of them." Bruce looked at this watch. He said, "It's about time for the pups get supper."

Robert had been standing quietly off to one side. He said, "Go on up, folks, I'll close up down here."

"Thanks, Rob," Bruce said. He turned back to Lisa and Rudi.

"Robbie here is probably the best marksman and hand-to-hand combat person in the United States. He trains and tutors specialists in all three agencies I mentioned – and mentors their own trainers."

"Keep talking, Bruce can't make me blush," Robert said.

They went to the outdoor cages where Tom was pulling a plastic cart. A shovel handle protruded. "Everybody's healthy, as far as I can see," he called.

"A clean environment is vital," said Bruce. "We don't leave droppings around – twice a day we rake up. If anything's abnormal, we see it and deal with it right away. Each pup develops his own place to go and we learn who has the problem. Not a pretty subject, but it's one that we pay close attention to."

Bruce led them to a spot behind the cages, which were about eight feet high.

"This corral is for the Stage Threes," he said. "They know Stage Ones and Twos eat first and they like to watch." The dogs disregarded the visitors; they sat, concentrating on the other enclosures.

They continued to the next cage, where the dogs sat along the fence that adjoined the next. "Here's the stage II's," said Bruce. "They're waiting for Hank to try to get the Stage I's to obey a couple of basic commands. There, Hank's in the doorway. He's already put their food in front of each kennel and they know it."

Hank came out of the barn and into the Stage I enclosure, gave a sharp whistle and raised his right arm, palm outwards. The Stage Ones paid no attention; they danced around him, yipping.

"Look at the other dogs!" Lisa said. "They're lying down!"

"Yes, they know what that hand signal means. They're probably disgusted with the Stage I's tomfoolery."

Hank said, "Platz!" in a firm voice.

Rudi chuckled. He said, "You teach them in German!"

"Just when a single syllable word is more effective." said Bruce.

"PLATZ!" Hank raised his arm again. He went to the dogs, pushing rumps down and finally they were on their bellies, eyes rolling, panting. Again, he went to them, passing his hand over their eyes, saying, "STAY." He backed towards the door, paused for about five seconds and said "STICK" as he opened the door. The dogs launched at once; Hank dodged out of their way and ducked inside.

Shortly, the door opened in the middle cage. Hank stepped out, his forearm raised. Each dog dropped to its belly. Again, he passed his hand across each pair of eyes; when he was done, he sauntered around the cage and called out, "Pretty good kids tonight, huh?" "Abbie, STICK!" One dog launched for the door; the others watched, quivering. "Snook, STICK!" He went. "Victor, STICK!" Victor trotted to the door, looking back and grinning.

In the Stage III enclosure, the seven dogs turned their heads to the door. "Let's see if we can distract them," said Bruce; he gave a sharp whistle and slapped his left thigh. Instantly, they were at the fence. Bruce reached both hands through the openings and stroked heads, rubbed ears, scratched chins as tails waved. "Go ahead, Lisa, you can help with this part," he said.

She came up next to him and offered both hands through the fence. One after another, the dogs smelled her hands, then backed off. "They don't like me," she said, concern in her voice.

"You haven't been introduced yet, my love. They're wary of strangers. Get them one on one, at first with me and afterward they'll be your friends for life. We'll take Toby for a walk with us after supper. Stick, boys, Stick."

The dogs looked at Hank. Bruce called, "OK, Hank, Thanks."

Hank whistled and slapped his left thigh and the dogs ran to him and sat expectantly. He began the litany: "Bert, STICK. Goood Boooy...Jack, STICK. Goood Boooy...

He continued until each dog ran past through the door and out of sight. Hank followed them.

"They were behaving very well tonight," Bruce said. "Let's go see where they live." He led them through a small door and they were in the kennel area. The dogs had emptied their bowls and were on their pads, licking their lips. Tom was filling water dishes.

"We've continued class separation in the kennels," Bruce explained. "Let's go into the Class III kennel. They'll be gentlemen, except for Snow and she's a good lady."

"Will she ever have pups?" said Lisa, smiling.

"No, Lisa; she doesn't have the necessary parts – our vet took care of that. But she'll make a great sniffer."

Entering the kennel area, Lisa saw seven open-front spaces, separated by wooden partitions, each with a low threshold. A hinged top covered each space

"Each dog has his own pad," Bruce said. "As you can see, they're spread around. Dogs drag them wherever they want. They'll pick a favorite spot – usually against a side wall. They respect each other's pads. When we are deployed, we take the pads with the dog. There's cedar chips for bedding in the kennels – they smell great, helps keep their coats glossy and they absolutely discourage fleas. Let me show you something."

He pointed up to where a little red light glowed on the wall. "That's a TV camera. Each kennel area has one, as well as one directly over our heads" – pointing – "that looks from where we are to the outside wall. A third camera looks at the outside area; there's three monitors in the house – we can see where the dogs are supposed to be. There's another camera next to these – they're infra-red cameras that see heat. We can see what they're doing without turning on lights. That makes it easy to check each dog during a storm, or whatever. When Hank leaves tonight, the doors from the kennels to the runs will be left open. We can take Toby with us now."

Bruce opened the gate and said, "Toby! SPOT!" The big dog bounded to Bruce, who rubbed his head and said, "Gooood Boooy, Toby." He took Lisa's hand and they walked towards the entrance. "Over there" – he pointed – "we do daily checks after exercise –baths, nails, pads and teeth checks. We've got bath tubs, exam tables and grooming equipment."

They walked through the front door of the barn and looked up at the house. Toby nudged Bruce's left knee. "Toby was responsible for me going to supper at Duncan's," he said, squeezing Lisa's hand. "It's time for you to meet formally."

He said "Toby, RUG." Toby sat, his eyes on Bruce. He brought Lisa's hand to Toby's nose. "Toby, FRIEND. FRIEND, Toby." The dog sniffed her hand. "Toby, STICK." The dog picked up a stick, dropped it in front of Lisa and looked up expectantly.

"He wants to play tug-of-war, sweetie. Be ready – he's strong."

She bent over and picked up the stick. Instantly, Toby pulled the free end and she was yanked off balance.

"Wow, you pull like a horse, Toby."

"Give up, Lisa," said Bruce. She let go and Toby trotted away, waving the stick.

Rudi observed, "You're right, Lisa, he's strong like two horses. Bruce, we have many of this breed in Austria. Usually they're trained to attack anyone coming inside their fence."

"They can be very dangerous, Rudi. We train these to respect everyone unless we tell them otherwise."

Rudi said, "Bruce, I'd like to see more of your gun shop. Could Hank do that?"

Hank said, "Sure. Dad set it up. He's teaching me about weapons and their capabilities. We'll use the inside stairs – Dad's still down there." They returned to the barn together.

Bruce called "Toby! QUICK!" The dog dropped the stick, came to Bruce and sat, eyes on Bruce, who said, "Toby, PLATZ." The big dog dropped to his belly. "Goood Boooy, Toby."

"I never thought that in America, I'd hear dogs being told what to do in German," said Lisa. "We use single-syllable words, Lisa. Not the every-day ones that others would use. Toby, STAY. Let's you and I take a short walk away from here and we'll do a little test." Hand-in-hand, they walked towards the house. Bruce stopped and turned Lisa around so she faced Toby. He said, very quietly in her ear, "I love you, sweetheart. Now, say, TOBY! QUICK!"

She did; the dog bounded to her side and sat. "Give his head a rub and say 'Goood Booooy, Toby."

As she did, Bruce said, "Now, pass your hand across his eyes. That's telling him to stay and we'll walk along a little further." She did as he instructed; Toby kept his eyes on her.

"Bruce, is there a command that'll make you rub my back?" She looked up at him.

"How about 'Want to rub my back, Bruce?' – that should work pretty well," he answered.

"Mmmm. I'll remember that," she said.

"Let's get Toby off the hook. He's done well. Look at him and slap your left thigh with your hand. If you can whistle, do that first." Lisa put her tongue behind her teeth and emitted a piercing blast; as Toby looked at her, she slapped her thigh and he ran to her side, his head against her left knee. She rubbed his head. "Goood boooy, Toby."

"Where did you learn to whistle like that?"

"From my cousin Peter," she said. "Comes in handy – especially getting a taxi."

"Surprised me. Let's go along towards the house – Toby should keep his head close to your left knee." They walked along, hand-in-hand.

"Don't I remember that Toby's going to Duncan?" Lisa said.

"We'll be seeing lots of Duncan, as there'll be transition sessions for Toby."

As they walked along, Toby transferred his "heel" position from Lisa to Bruce, pushing his head gently between them.

"Is he jealous, or what?" asked Lisa.

"No," Bruce said, "just has more allegiance to me. We overcome that with transfer training. We won't correct it now, because he's not going to be your dog."

Bruce opened the front door and Lisa went in. Bruce rubbed Toby's head and gave him several firm pats. "Goood boooy, Toby. STICK." The dog wandered into the living room and lay down in front of Lattie, who was sitting on the couch with Elaine. Stephen was quietly using a phone in the corner of the room.

"Well, Lisa, what do you think of my boys' operation?" Lattie said.

"I never imagined this," she said, "and the dogs are so quiet. Thought there'd be continuous barking."

Elaine said, "When Hank was ten, he convinced Warrenton's police chief to give him a 'NO PARKING' sign. He changed the 'P' into a 'B' -- he'd heard us saying 'no barking' so often that he thought it'd help. Now he claims the Stage Ones'll stop barking if he points at the sign. He breaks me up."

Elaine looked at her watch. "I hope people will be

coming along pretty quickly for supper," she said. "Maybe I'd better give them a hoot on the intercom." She got up and headed for the kitchen. Lisa took Elaine's place on the couch.

"Stephen is making arrangements with George for a couple of key people from the Company to come out whenever Rudi's ready to talk to people that we trust," Lattie said,.

"I believe that, for *Vati*, the first time was the hardest. I don't think that it's necessary for any of us to ever mention those – ummm – other people who might have gotten involved in the search. If he wants to tell us more about it, he will, but I won't ask any questions. You certainly calmed him down, Lattie. Thank you. And please – who might 'George' be?"

"The Director of Operations – and he has access to the President and to the Secretary of State but we hope that the situation can be resolved to Rudi's satisfaction without getting them involved. They want to talk about some ideas first. It'll take a little time. Does Rudi have plans to go back to Austria soon?"

"Not till the situation is 'under control' – his words. He can stay with me as long as he wants."

"You both can stay here as long as you want."

"Great – I may be commuting from here after a few days."

"Stephen will want to spend some time with Rudi. Stephen wants to show him how valuable his information has turned out to be. It saved U.S. millions in resource deployment – while the Russians were breaking the bank on military expenditures."

"And Elaine and I have lots to talk about, Lattie. Also, Bruce and I have some decisions to make."

Elaine nodded and said, "You'll see the entire family under a great deal of stress, Lisa. We have a very important job next Friday . . . rehearsals, meetings and so forth. The four of us'll be spending lots of time together while they practice with the pups here in town. Maybe we'll be meeting with George next week – Stephen will tell us when he gets off the phone."

"Do they dare talk about it on the telephone?" asked Lisa.

"Yes," said Lattie. "Stephen's plugged his phone into that little box on the table. It's called a scrambler – converts voices into squeaks and chirps – Bruce helped to design it a few years ago. Friends started a business making them and Bruce is one of their directors. The government's their best customer. Stephen talks to George and others so often that they gave him one and we brought it along."

Elaine said, "Lisa, the guys are on their way up. If you want to freshen up, turn right at the top of the stairs. You'll find your room at the end of the hall. Bruce's room is at the other end. Feel free to look around. Dinner in about a half hour."

"Thanks, Elaine, but can't I help you in the kitchen?"

"No, Lisa, thank you, but I'm all set. I put the beer into the frig for Hank and dried out your cooler. One of the boys'll put it in your car." She disappeared into the kitchen.

"I thought we might be eating out on the deck, Lattie," Lisa said. "It's so nice out there."

"The sun sets behind the mountains about an hour before it does in Washington, dear," Lattie said, getting to her feet. "It's okay on a hot summer evening, but on a cool afternoon like today, it becomes quite chilly and discourages sitting around the table – at least for these old bones. And I think I'll take a short lie-down before supper. But first, I'm so happy I am for you and my Brucie. It shows right away when two people are made for each other. He's truly smitten, my dear. I know that true love can happen very quickly. Robert told me that you fell in love with his picture when you were a young girl. When I was not much more than a young girl, I fell in love with a man when he walked into the room. And he with me. Couldn't keep our eyes off each other and when his business was concluded, he came to my desk and asked if we could have supper together. And we did. It was the boys' father – Andrew."

"Where did this happen?"

"I was an interpreter here at the Czechoslovakian Embassy. My uncle was a diplomat and was sent over here right after the war. My family was in the glass business and my uncle thought that it would be helpful to have me learn the American market and return home with the knowledge and the contacts that would help the business. I married Andrew instead and never regretted it. His mother was a Czech, too and had a very good business sense importing glass from Czechoslovakia and porcelain from Germany and England. She passed away in 1949, never seeing her grandsons."

"How strange that glass-making and artistry is a common thread in our families."

"Your tongue slipped on you earlier today – you called me 'Mother Oakes.' That was very nice and it tells me how deep your love and affection is for my son. Now – I'm going to lie down. Please wake me in time for supper – Stephen will stay on that phone till we drag him away."

19

2030 Saturday, May 12, 1998
The Ranch – dining room

"Good thing we run every morning," Hank said, wiping away traces of Boston cream pie.

Robert chuckled. "Tomorrow morning'll be no exception, son. Saw that you helped yourself to seconds."

"Yep – leaves two for breakfast. Wonder who the lucky early risers'll be. Tom, I'll race you home."

"No, you won't. Remember Sergeant Beano." The Hendersons laughed. Rudi and Lisa looked puzzled.

"Tom's talking about when Hank was old enough to get his first all-terrain vehicle," Robert said. "The boys got one when they turned thirteen. With two vehicles driven by teenagers, I made a rule – 'There Will Be No Racing.' The boys called me Sergeant Beano, after an old story about a Sergeant Jones, who said 'There'll Be No cigarette butts on the ground. There'll Be No dirty rifles.' And so forth. His men called him Sergeant Beano Jones."

Hank pulled on a hurt look. "I meant running, Dad."

"Sure you did, son."

Elaine picked up her clipboard. She glanced at Bruce, who had been sitting quietly for several minutes. The group's hilarity hadn't stirred him; it looked like he didn't know what was so funny.

Bruce said, "We have an extremely full week coming up. Lisa, can you and Rudi stay all week? There's ways you can help out. Friday, we have a very important assignment. There'll be a prominent Israeli leader speaking at a National Press Club luncheon. We're assigned to identify anyone carrying explosives. We haven't yet had a suicide bomber in America, but it's a definite possibility, considering the speaker. We all have to go and we have to do several things before then. We'll focus on two dogs – Riggs and Tuck. Done some training with them working together, looking for two suspects

— but we have to do more. Rudi, I'm breaking rules by telling you all this, but I know you can keep a secret." Lisa and Rudi nodded in understanding.

"Second, our action plan's gotta be on Sam's desk Tuesday morning by 1100. Laney?"

"The draft's in my computer," she said. "I'll have copies for everyone at breakfast, when we can decide on changes. The Chief'll take the final version into town Monday afternoon."

"Thanks, Laney. Tomorrow," continued Bruce, "will be a regular Sunday, with no training scheduled except for our usual run before breakfast. Mission-specific training begins on Monday. Tom, you'll work Riggs and I'll work Tuck. The library opens at nine on Monday; we'll start by sweeping it then – and the same on Tuesday, with our actors from the P.D. in sequence a few minutes apart."

Elaine's pencil flew across her clipboard. She said, "Fred'll plant the explosives before they open. The only contaminators will be Fred and the Pee Dee officers. The library's busy – the pups'll have plenty of people to check out."

Bruce said, "What needs to be done for Wednesday?"

"I need to sew up another explosives vest," said Robert. "Material's all cut – no problem. Just haven't had time to do it."

Lisa said, "I can sew. Is that something I could do?"

"It's just a one-size fits all vest with a couple of different size pockets. You can copy what I've done."

"I can do that."

Bruce said, "Now, communications. We'll use the bone conduction headsets. Channel One'll be for us, Channel Two'll be the floor frequency. Like before, I'll set Channel One on all the odd channels and the floor frequency on the evens. That way, if things get intense, you're one click in either direction to the other channel. Next, weapons. . . Rob?"

"Tasers. Our Israeli friends'll want to see them. We all need some dry firing – full silhouette, fifteen foot range, aim point's mid-thigh. Then change to the Woodsman twenty-twos, same target setup. Point and shoot. Remove batteries when you put the gear away. Bruce, Scottsdale said OK on Tasers versus explosives.

"I told everyone 'no hard rounds' – don't want bullets hitting an explosive. Besides, it'll likely be in a crowd. For back-ups, your three-eighty Colts. That's it on weapons, Bruce."

"Sounds good, Rob. Last, target characteristics. Ari described suicide bombers they've encountered – they're in two categories; the first just wants to take out lots of people. The second tries to get as close as possible to his target. They mostly use pull-wire igniters, a short fuse and a plastic blasting cap."

"Any other questions?" Bruce took a sip of water and set his glass down. "We go to work on the thirteenth floor. It's possible for a person using a pull-wire igniter to get through the metal detectors; our responsibility's to identify and neutralize him. We'll remain on station until the speaker leaves at 1400. Pups'll stand down at 1200 after everyone's off the elevators.

"Using Elaine and Hank's TV scam, we'll try to identify and isolate any perp whose picture's in Ari's file. These might be people with pre-planted weapons, not necessarily explosives.

"The action plan: Tom'll work Riggs by the elevators; I'll be on standby in the Murrow room with Tuck. If Riggs alerts, Tom will follow for a Taser takedown. Rob will back up Tom and will be primary for disarming the perp and defusing the explosives. A Metro Police gurney team will move the disabled perp to the Murrow room. Another Metro team will engage anyone identified by Elaine and Hank. We'll sweep the rooms that are open and the people that are in them, between 1100 and 1115. Last, we'll plan on a quick break outside for the pups at 1115 and back inside to be on station in fifteen minutes. Elaine?"

"OK, that's the plan," she said, closing the cover on her clipboard. "Hank, Tom and I'll take the station wagon; you and Rob'll take both pups in the Blazer. Plan on departing at 0600. We'll park in the alley by the basement entrance of the NPC."

Rudi said, "A few years ago, I was allowed to listen to a briefing of our Austrian military people during the Olympic Games. My nephew, a reserve officer, was called up for an assignment there. He thought it would be something I would like to observe. Bruce and Robert, what you're doing here is like what I heard in Innsbruck. You have planned this as a military operation."

"Thanks, Rudi. It is essentially a military operation – we have a possible threat, we consider the enemy capabilities, his probable – and most likely – courses of action and we plan and provide part of the defense. Hopefully, there'll be nothing for us to do except go through the plan and remain pretty much in the background."

Robert pushed his chair back and got up, saying, "Got an early day tomorrow. I'll take a look at the monitors on my way out – the kennels should be quiet. See you folks at seven."

Tom said, "Comin' with ya, Dad."

"Grab those dessert plates and silverware, Hank," said Elaine. "Breakfast'll be at eight. You folks might enjoy watching the entire pack of dogs run by at about quarter after seven. It's quite a sight."

"Lisa," said Bruce, "you're off the hook in the kitchen. Let's sit on the front porch – there's a nice view to the east. The moon was full last night and it'll be rising again in about a half hour." Lisa took his hand; followed by Rudi, Stephen and Lattie, they made for the porch.

Bruce said, "I think this is too big to be called a porch. Deserves to be called a veranda – it was the focal point of everyone who ever lived here. First thing we rebuilt. We all gathered here at the end of the day -- watched the shadows of the mountains move east."

Wicker sofas and chairs were clustered in a corner. They settled down, looking east, where distant lights twinkled.

"How'd you ever find this place, Bruce?" Lisa asked, after several minutes of peaceful silence.

"Elaine and Lattie found it. We told them to buy it. Spent years fixing things up and building Rob and Elaine's house, all while we were in the service. Rob and Elaine were married while he was still in the Navy and she moved into their new home while he was stationed in California."

"How far away were you?"

"In Munich, about as far as you could get, being a Cold Warrior. We were out of the services within a month of each other – Rob moved in and went to work getting things ready and I came along and settled here in this house. Our first contract was with a military operation on the other side of Warrenton. It's been job after job since that first one. After that we just fell in to the routine that you've seen a little bit of today."

Stephen said, "Our security agencies can't do everything by themselves – although God knows that some'll die trying before learning that 'outsiders' can do it better and more economically. Allows for reduced staffing. These boys are always at the peak of training; it'd be wasteful for any agency to maintain high-level skills the boys have for occasional employment. Also, we've worked on coordination and cooperation between agencies – specifically, the FBI, CIA and the Secret Service. There's always been professional jealousy between these agencies; critical information gets lost and a mix-up ends with agencies pointing fingers at each other."

Bruce said, "Our rehearsal next Wednesday is a good example, Lisa. Overall control is in the hands of the Secret Service; they're coordinating everything with the Metro Police." He lapsed into silence.

Lisa leaned over, tucked her hand through his arm and said quietly, "A penny for your thoughts, Bruce."

"This assignment is complex and I've been playing 'what if' in my head."

The light evening breeze brought a hint of apple and cinnamon. He inhaled deeply and said quietly, "Your perfume has made me forget all about Wednesday, Lisa." She leaned against him and he put an arm around her shoulders, drawing her closer.

"I could stay like this forever," she said.

"It was the same way with your father and me, Bruce," said Lattie; "it was almost instant. You must marry this beautiful girl while we old folks are still around to see it. Come, Stephen. You too, Rudi. We must leave these two young people to enjoy each other. It's been a very full and busy day. The age of our collective bones is approaching two centuries and it's time we took them to bed."

Rudi stood up and yawned. He said, "I'll sleep very well tonight – better than I have for a very long time." He bent and kissed Lisa's shining hair, squeezing Bruce's unoccupied shoulder and said *"Schlaf gut, mein Kind."*

Lisa put her hand against her father's cheek and said, "Thank you, *Vati* dear, we'll sleep well. Please put us all in your prayers."

As the three returned inside, Lattie hugged Rudi and said, "I hope you do sleep well tonight, Rudi, and every night from now on. Thank you for carrying my Andrew – your Nikolai – in your heart as such a heavy burden for all these years. Somehow, I knew his soul was at rest."

Wordlessly, Rudi held her close for a moment, then stepped back, shook Stephen's hand, turned away and went up the stairs, tears silently streaming from his eyes.

Lisa and Bruce, unaware of the emotional outpouring in the front hall, sat in silent communion. Bruce sighed and said, "I'm going to wait a bit before I ask you to marry me."

"How long, Bruce?" Lisa asked. She lifted her face to his, then nibbled at his earlobe.

"Until we can see the moon," he answered. "It should be rising in a few minutes." She brought her lips to his. Their kiss started sedately, but quickly they were overwhelmed and strained against each other.

"Are you going to wait until we can see all of it, or just the first little bit?" Lisa asked, breathing a bit unevenly, when they separated.

"I don't know, but I'll decide when I can see the first little bit of it." A few clouds on the horizon began to glow bright silver, indicating that the gibbous moon was about to appear in all its glory.

20

1000 Friday, May 18, 1998
The National Press Club
– Murrow Room – thirteenth floor

"It's a good thing we have this room available," said Sam to the assembly. Tuck lay at Bruce's feet; Riggs lay next to Tom's chair; Sam and Jack – the building's maintenance and security chief, as well as Ari and Richard, along with the Secret Service personnel assigned to the floor, were seated around the large conference table. Hank and Elaine's places were empty for the moment; they were in a corner of the room, unpacking the TV camera. Robert wore the waiter's whites that Jack had furnished.

"Thank you all for being here on time," said Sam. The table quieted. "First, I was very pleased with Wednesday's rehearsal. There are no changes to the plans that you don't already know about. You folks all did very well and so did your dogs, Bruce.

"A very quick review: we are going to use the dogs to clear the rest of the floor, then return here, do a comm and weapons check, and wait until it's time to go on station at 11:20. Our entry team down in the lobby has been on station all morning; some of you'll join them at eleven. Bruce, your show."

Bruce rose and quietly said, "Tuck, SPOT." He went to the head of the table, Tuck following. "We have already cleared the Holman and First Amendment Lounges as a warm-up for both dogs. Robert and Riggs will now clear the two bar areas and the ballroom and its adjacent rooms. Tuck and I'll clear the library, the lobby and the three other conference rooms adjacent to this one. Give us a minute to leave this room with the dogs and you're all invited to step into the room or area being swept to observe. The dogs will check you over if you're in the room. If anyone has food or a doggie treat in your pockets, please leave it here." Laughter followed his last remark.

"Ready, Bruce?" Robert asked. Robert rose and moved away from the table. He said, "Riggs, SPOT" – and they left the room. Bruce followed; Tuck, still under the SPOT command, kept station at his left knee.

About half the group of eighteen agents followed Robert down the hall; the other half went into the library with Bruce. "Everyone inside that wants to be?" Bruce called. "Please close the door, then. Tuck, QUICK." The dog sat, eyes on Bruce, yawned deeply and licked his lips.

"Tuck will probably go to you folks first, then he'll make a pass through the entire room. When he's satisfied, he'll come back to me. Please try to stay more or less in place. Normal conversation is fine. Please hold any questions until we are done, as I have to keep my full attention on the dog. As the man said, this is no drill. Tuck, SNIFF."

The big dog, his coat glistening in the brightly-lighted room, leaped to his feet and trotted to the group of observers. He wound his way in and around their feet, nose wrinkling furiously. He ignored the occasional hand that touched his head or fondled an ear, came out of the crowd, looked at Bruce and went to the nearest table. Apparently at random, he examined the underside of every table, gave each chair seat a "visual," and occasionally rose on his hind feet as he circulated through the stacks and along the walls. Finally, he walked to Bruce, head low, eyes up and sat in front of him. "Goood Boooy, Tuck, Goood Boooy," said Bruce, rubbing his head and scratching his throat. Tuck lifted his head, grinned and wagged his tail energetically. He leaned against Bruce's leg, savoring the rewards of doing a job well. He flopped onto his side and rolled onto his back, all four paws waving in every direction as Bruce scratched his belly.

"Tuck, STICK," said Bruce and Tuck leaped to his feet and ran from person to person, getting more head scratches while getting in a few hand licks of his own.

"Gentlemen, there are no explosives either in this room or on your persons. Robert should be inside the Ballroom by now. Please leave; Tuck and I'll follow and we'll do the lobby. Tuck, SPOT."

The group that had decided to watch Tuck's performance

went quietly through the door and stood at the north end of the lobby. Bruce looked toward the other end, he saw no activity.

Assuming that Robert and his observers were already in the ballroom, he said, "Tuck, SNIFF." Again, the big dog headed first for the observers and went through the group – more quickly this time, it appeared. He then loped halfway down the lobby, turned to the right and disappeared from sight. He returned within a few seconds and moved at a trot along the low wall which opened onto the atrium. He stopped once, put his paws on the top of the wall and strained to see over it. He ran back and forth a few times along the wall and finally went into the north corridor where the doors to the Murrow, White, Lisador and Zenger rooms were closed. He stopped at the door to the White room and sniffed at the crack where the door almost met the rug. He backed away, shook his head as if it was soaking wet and went back to the crack at the bottom of the door. His tail gave a feeble wag, but then he stopped, looked at Bruce and stood with his tail down. "Tuck, QUICK." The dog bounded to Bruce and sat facing him, wearing a grin that everyone could see. Bruce repeated the "Gooood Booooy" routine, then said, "Tuck, STICK" as he took a small chewie out of his pocket. The dog lay down, the chewie held in his paws and went to work on it.

"Here is a demonstration, hopefully, of how a well-trained pup behaves," said Bruce. "His chewie is about half gone; let's see if he'll give it up. This is a really tough obedience test. Tuck, DONT." The dog stopped crunching the brittle rawhide and looked at Bruce.

"He looks like he just went into mourning," somebody said.

"Perhaps he has," said Bruce as he picked up the remains of the chewie and put it in a plastic bag. "But he followed the command. How should we reward him?"

"Give him his chewie back!" several men said; Bruce said, "Tuck, STICK," and took the chewie out of the bag and flipped it to the dog. Tuck caught it in mid-air and, holding it between his teeth, with his nose high in the air, trotted in a triumphant circle in front of the observers, tail waving. "Please don't applaud, guys, it'll only encourage him to show off even more. He knows he's done a good job. Gooood Booooy, Tuck, your day has just begun."

They heard laughter coming from the direction of the ballroom. The first thing they saw was Riggs, also with a chewie in his mouth, racing up the length of the lobby. He skidded to a stop in front of Tuck, who made a snap for it – and missed, closing his jaws on air, as Riggs simply turned his head sideways just enough to avoid the intended robbery. Tuck jumped up and charged Riggs, who made a feint in one direction and then simply stepped aside, chewie still protruding from his mouth, watching Tuck spin out of control as he attempted a fast course reversal. A piercing whistle sounded; both dogs stopped in their tracks and looked at Tom, who was standing with his forearm raised and his palm outwards. Riggs dropped to the floor, Tuck looked at Bruce who made the same hand signal – and Tuck lay down next to Riggs, watching Bruce. A murmur of approval echoed through the group.

"Okay, folks, it looks like the dog show's over," said Sam. "Pretty impressive, isn't it? Let's hope that was the toughest thing they have to do today. Let's get our comm and weapons checks behind us – it's about a quarter of eleven – forty-five minutes to station time."

Tom and Bruce waited until the group all gathered in the Murrow Room, then they followed them inside.

Hank was waiting for them; he said, "Mom and I are ready with the TV setup. She's in the ladies' room, putting on her face. I've laid out your conduction headsets and your radios. Channels are set up same as we had at the rehearsal. As soon as you're ready, we'll have our comm check. Our call signs are the same as Wednesday morning – we are Sniffer One through Sniffer Five, by age. Internally, we'll use our own names, as always."

"Thanks, Hank," said Bruce. "Looks like it might be time to get them outdoors for a few minutes."

"You go first, Bruce," offered Rob, "but let's check out your headset first."

Bruce inserted the lead from the single earpiece under his belt, fed it under his shirt, led it out at the collar and placed it carefully in his left ear. He tucked his shirt back in and clipped the radio to his belt in the small of his back. "I'll be right back," he said, "and I'll get my shoulder holster and Taser then. We've got time yet."

Hank said, "Bruce, copy?" Then he went over to Bruce, lifted the tail of his coat and turned on the radio. Again he said, "Bruce, copy?"

Bruce cleared his throat and coughed.

"Workin' fine," said Hank. "Five square."

Bruce looked at the dog at his feet and said, "Tuck, SPOT." The dog got up and went to the heel position. They headed for the door. In the earpiece, Bruce heard a quiet "Got baggies?" from Hank. Bruce said "yup" quietly. He turned to look at Hank, who nodded. Hank watched Bruce leave the room and turned his attention to Robert. "How can I help, Dad?" Bruce heard him say as he pushed the elevator call button. The door opened immediately; a man stood inside.

"Hi, Larry, how's it going?"

"Up and down, Bruce, up and down," said the agent assigned to ride shotgun on the elevator. They both laughed.

"Need to take this pup for a little run," explained Bruce. "He already has a favorite spot in the little park at the side of the building." The elevator hummed quietly as it descended. Bruce noted that he heard nothing in his earpiece. *Must be the elevator cage is blocking the signal,*" he thought to himself. *"I'll make a check from the park."*

"Have a nice run, you guys," said the agent, as the doors opened. He and Tuck walked straight out through the ground floor lobby. Bruce noted that the initial screening stations were in place and technicians were testing the sensitivity of the metal detector frames.

"Back in a minute," he said to the agent at the check-in station. Leaving the building, he turned to the left and walked to the end of the building, Tuck staying precisely on station. He turned left into the park and said "Tuck, STICK." The dog trotted over to a struggling patch of grass and relieved himself against a flowering crab-apple tree. He then wandered around, looking here and there.

Suddenly, he stiffened and looked at Bruce. He came over to Bruce and whined. He walked back in a different direction and went up to a man seated on a bench, reading a newspaper.

Roger Damon

The bench was behind a chest-high bush.

Tuck stood in front of the man and wagged his tail and looked over at Bruce. *"Oh my God,"* thought Bruce, *"Not now. Not this early. But I have to try."* He gave a quiet whistle and Tuck bounded over to him and sat, even as he slapped his thigh. He bent over and said softly but clearly, "Tuck, SNIFF." As the dog bounded back to the man, Bruce heard Hank say in his earpiece, "What's up, Bruce? Say your twenty."

"Stand by, Hank," Bruce muttered. Tuck was dancing at the man's feet, yipping and whimpering.

"I'm sorry, sir," Bruce called as he walked casually over to the man. "He does this with everyone he likes. Tuck, DONT, DONT." The man, sweating heavily, seemed to cower behind his newspaper. "Tuck, SPOT. Goood Boooy, Tuck, Goood Boooy."

He said, "I'm sorry, sir. He means no harm. He thought you might like to play with him, that's all." He walked away, Tuck muttering at heel.

Reaching a safe distance, he said quietly, "Get the picture, Hank? I have a positive perp sitting on a bench behind a bush in the little park just north of the building. He's holding his newspaper with both hands. I saw no wiring but he's got a big gut. He's really scared. Need backup for takedown, I am solo. Get Robbie as part of the team NOW and I don't care if he does look like a waiter."

"On the way, Bruce," said Robert in his ear. "We'll work up our plan in the elevator. Gurney to follow. You stay out of it but maintain visual. Switch to floor. Rob out."

Bruce reached behind his back and gave his frequency selector one click. "Sam, Bruce. Code."

"Go, Bruce," replied Sam. Bruce repeated the essence of his previous transmission to Robert, adding, "Rob responding with other agents, gurney to follow."

"Saw them run out of here, been waiting for status. Keep it quiet down there if you can."

Bruce walked slowly, Tuck at heel, staying about seventy-five feet back from the sidewalk, where he could see the suspect's head. The man sat as still as stone, newspaper open to a large single-page advertisement. Bruce felt frozen in time.

238

It seemed to him as if ten minutes had passed, it was perhaps three, before he heard Rob say, "That'll work. Bruce, your twenty?"

"I'm in the southwest corner of the park, out of the perp's range of vision. He's the only person sitting on a bench holding a newspaper in front of him."

"Rog, I see you both. We are four; one will pass in back of the perp and circle around his left side, another will appear to cross in front of him. They'll turn simultaneously and go for his arms and hands. The third will get his feet and I'll open up his clothes and disarm his weapon. Team ready? GO."

From the corner of his eyes, Bruce saw the suspect twist his head and neck to look his way. Tuck, a bundle of nerves, was following Bruce's hand signals, going from RUG to PLATZ and back again. Tuck looked at him curiously, as if to say, *"Hey, Bruce, I'm a Three and I learned this in One. I know how to sit and lie down."* Bruce tried to ignore the smooth motions of the team's deployment; the first member headed in his direction, then circled to his right while another, apparently absorbed in a *Time* magazine, sauntered slowly towards the first. He saw the third agent and Rob, in his waiter's get-up, standing together, looking across the street, apparently oblivious.

As the first two drew closer to the suspect, they turned and began walking towards the man on the bench, who had resumed his frozen stare, head and eyes straight ahead. Then, Hank appeared around the corner of the building, carrying his camera, followed by Sam.

The timing of the two agents was perfect. The suspect lowered his newspaper as he heard their footsteps. Just as he raised his eyes, they whirled and launched themselves, each grasping a forearm and bending it back against the bench. The third agent, who had broken into a run, tackled the man's feet, while Rob slapped the newspaper aside, ripped the man's coat open and yanked his shirt out of his pants, popping buttons as he did so.

"No problem," said Robert; "Pull-wire igniter. I have it secured in my left hand." He pulled a pair of pliers from his pocket and cut the fuse. As the man heaved and struggled ineffectively, Robert dropped the pliers and popped open a switchblade knife that had appeared in his hand.

"Gotta get to the cap," he said. "There. Ground him, but gently. Don't care about him, but don't want to bump the explosive." Robert stepped back, out of the way; the two agents on the perpetrator's arms heaved him up and forward; held at the feet by the third, he was rotated forward and lowered face down on the pavement. Instantly, his wrists were handcuffed behind his back and his ankles were shackled. Two more agents appeared, dressed as ambulance attendants, pulling a lowered gurney with a blanket. They rolled the suspect onto it. Robert stepped in and cut away the man's shirt. They saw a double row of dynamite sticks, held tightly to the man's chest and abdomen by duct tape and what appeared to be elastic bandages.

Rob handed the blasting cap and its two inches of fuse to one of the agents. "Don't pull that little wooden handle, guys." He reached in with the knife and cut the tape securing the blasting cap. Using his fingers, he gently pried it loose from the dynamite stick in which it was embedded. He handed to another agent, saying, "Don't drop this, either. It's sensitive. You might try for a print from it, though, so handle it by the fuse."

Bruce said, "Want a baggie for those? Looks like Tuck won't need all I have."

"You guys think of everything," said the agent carrying the blasting cap, rather gingerly. He took the baggie from Bruce and placed the cap – a brass cylinder, its diameter a little bigger than a pencil's and about an inch and a half long, into it.

Robert said, "The pull-wire igniter is American – probably stolen from some construction project, along with the dynamite. That's a Chinese cap and Czech fuse, if that means anything," he added, as the other agent placed the igniter in the plastic sandwich bag. "You can get a signature from the crimping of the cap to the fuse and match it up with a specific crimping tool, if you ever find it," Robert continued, "just like you do with spent bullets and suspect weapons. Call us if you need help with it."

"We'll write the source, time and date on these baggies for the evidence trail," one of them said.

While the conversation was transpiring, the "EMT" handling the gurney unrolled the three restraining straps and passed the ends over the man to his partner, who passed them through the matching buckles. They pulled them very tight, totally restraining the man, who was now sobbing and babbling.

"Sounds like Arabic to me, Bob," said the gurney team leader. They had a blanket ready and threw it over the man, covering him completely. The leader picked up the towing handle and said, pointing, "The van is that way. We'll Miranda him inside it." They left the scene.

Robert looked at his dirty knees. "These are the only whites I have with me today. Must think about that next time I play waiter. Let's get back to work."

As they went toward the front entrance, Robert said, "Jack, you on floor?"

"Affirm."

"Need another set of white pants when we get up there."

"They're already on the way. Jack out."

"Rog."

Hank, carrying his camera by the handle, said, "Nice work, guys. I got it all. Timer said a minute and a half, total, from take-down to gone." Bruce looked around and commented, "Looks like we did it without any audience to speak of."

* * *

As the group re-assembled in the Murrow room, there was applause, hand-shakes and back-slapping.

Sam said, "Super job, Bruce. Thanks to you and Rob – and especially to Tuck, here. I just had a call from the van. Luckily, we had an Arabic-speaking agent at the temporary detention facility. After they Miranda'd the perp, they found a Press Club photo ID in his coat pocket. There was also a three by five file card with instructions, written in Arabic. There's a sketch map on the other side showing him where to go when he gets to the thirteenth floor. Looks as if he got on the job a bit early."

Bruce said, "Thanks, Sam – we were lucky. It's a good thing Tuck had to pee. How're we doing on time? I need to get my weapon on – I won't do that again. All I had was my back-up and I didn't dare to use it. Besides, you'd said 'keep it quiet' and I think we did."

Hank handed a TV cassette to Sam. "Here's the entire apprehension. I wish we could have included Tuck's ID – he really carries on."

"That's right, Sam," Bruce said. "I thought I wouldn't be able to shut him up. I think he actually asked me to say SNIFF, because he'd fingered the perp on his own and needed me to let him show me. I bet he was about to take me by the sleeve and lead me over to the bench. How are we on time?"

Ari said, "May we have a copy of that tape, Sam?"

"You certainly can," he replied. "Folks, it's eleven-fifteen – be on station in fifteen minutes. No change in plans."

Tom and Riggs entered the room and came over to Bruce and Robert.

"Nice work, guys, I think we passed each other in the elevators. Riggs is ready to go – I heard the whole thing in my earpiece and waited until you were headed back in. Where's Mom?"

As if to answer his question, Elaine came in the door. She wore a very tight white sweater under a loose red jacket with the 'Nine News' logo embroidered on the left lapel, a red miniskirt over black stockings and black shoes. Her glossy lipstick matched the jacket and her eyes were surrounded with eye shadow. Conversation in the room stopped.

"Mom, is that you?" Hank asked from across the room. Laughter erupted.

"Thank you very much, gentlemen," said Elaine. "I felt I had to do something to keep your roving eyes away from my left armpit." She walked around the table to Hank, picking up her communications equipment on the way.

Sam called out, "Weapons check, gentlemen and lady. Tasers first."

The five Hendersons formed a circle. Each removed a Taser from his or her shoulder holster. Robert opened his briefcase and handed a dart module to each person and watched while each person installed it in the weapon. He did the same.

"Switch to Safe," he said. Each unit showed a small green

diode on the rear of the module.

"Switch to Fire." A small red diode glowed brightly.

"Switch to Safe." Each person said "green."

"Check laser." Bright red dots danced on the ceiling.

"Lasers off." The red dots vanished. A similar litany was being held throughout the room in groups of two and three people. Bruce handed a back-up dart module to the others; they stowed them in the pocket of their holsters and returned the weapons to their carrying position.

Elaine pushed at the bulge it made under her left shoulder. She said to Robert, "This jacket still isn't exactly stylish."

"Don't worry, Laney, you'll pass easily," he said, giving her a hug.

"Hank, we might as well get out there," said Elaine. "We need to get hooked up. We'll do the comm check from the lobby," she said to Sam, as they passed in front of him.

Sam looked at his clipboard and announced, "ID check team, ready?" Six men nodded. Sam raised his arm and said into his sleeve, "Floor freq check, ID team, over."

"Check one."

"Check two."

"Check three."

"Check four."

Check five."

"Check Six"

"Go, guys." They headed out the door and went down the lobby to the end, where Jack had set up queue guide barriers and tables with desk lamps for the ID checks.

"Service check team, ready?" Six more men nodded. These were part of Jack's security team who would eyeball each waiter before they went into – or came from – the banquet hall. "Service one, floor freq check, over." A similar litany followed as before, with each man confirming he could transmit and receive on the floor frequency.

"Gurney One, ready? Oh, no, they should be back up here pretty quickly. The transportation team took the perp to the detention facility as is. They're getting photos of him as he was apprehended, then they'll get the explosives off for more evidence. He's broken about six major Federal laws I can think of. Okay, then Gurney Two, Ready?"

"Gurney Two, loud and clear" was the answer in all the earpieces on the floor frequency. The two agents, wearing the uniforms of ambulance attendants, were in the corner of the room recently vacated by Hank and Elaine. Their gurney stood against the wall, ready for instant use.

"Nine News, radio check," chanted Sam.

Hank's voice came back, "Nine's on station, loud and clear."

"Sniffer One, got your clean pants on yet?"

"Sniffer One, loud and clear, twenty's the men's room, ready in three, will go on station, over," responded Robert.

"Copy, Sniffer One, stand by a minute please. . ." Sam turned to another agent who had entered the Murrow Room, signaling for his attention. They conversed quietly for a moment, then Sam spoke into his coat sleeve again, saying, "Sniffer One, detention wants to know status of perp's load."

"Load is inert, just handle with care. Could be old stock which can be sensitive. The parts I saw were recent, but I didn't see it all. Somebody should note manufacturer and lot numbers, but you'll do that anyway, over."

"Thanks, Rob. Bouncer clear."

Tom said, "I might as well go along, Bruce, and get ourselves comfortable. Riggs isn't used to his new vest – says it needs some breaking in. Just kidding, of course. We'll stroll up and down the hall a bit before we go on station."

"Good luck, Tommy," said Bruce.

Sam said to the agents remaining in the Murrow Room, "I'll be in the library and will make the final release checks from there. Good luck to all of you."

Bruce sat down in the nearest chair and reached down to Tuck and roughed up his head. "You were a gooood boooy today, chum. No telling what kind of mayhem you saved. That guy could have blown this whole floor off the face of the earth – do you know that?" Tuck closed his eyes in pure ecstasy and rolled over on his back. Bruce strapped on his **"SERVICE DOG IN TRAINING"** vest. The big dog stood up and shook.

Bruce's earpiece brought Sam's voice saying, "Floor, Bouncer. It's time, folks. If you're not on station please advise. Yes, that's like saying raise your hand if you're not here, but we just had the comm check so I know you're listening." There was a pause and Sam continued, "I was just advised that the first elevators are now loading. Shotguns on elevators are verifying most faces against photo ID's. Weapons are released; I say again, weapons are released. Bouncer out."

Bruce reached for the radio clipped to his waist and clicked to the team frequency, just in time to hear Tom say, "Riggs, SNIFF."

About a minute passed and he heard Tom whistle – then he heard Tom say "Goood Boooy, Riggs, SPOT. That went pretty quickly, family."

"Nobody unusual in the first batch, folks," said Hank. "Mom's getting the once-over, though."

"Be still, Hank, if you can't be nice, just be still." Bruce stifled a chuckle at the tone of Elaine's voice.

Hank continued, "Sorry, Mom. I have five photos I'm scanning through on the secondary cassette. They'll be pretty obvious."

Robert cut in, "The first batch has cleared the final ID check. It went pretty fast."

"Door opening on next elevator, Riggs, SNIFF."

The checking of each incoming elevator went smoothly. Riggs seemed to understand that he didn't have to recheck people; on the "SNIFF" command, he went directly into the new group of people, circulated and stopped, looking back at Tom. As soon as the ten or twelve people moved along down the hall, Tom would pat his left thigh and Riggs would trot back to the SPOT position, facing the elevators. Occasionally, Tom would nudge Riggs with his knee while he was at the SPOT position – at heel – and the big dog would sit, staying alert for the next command. They handled several elevator loads of journalists with no delay.

Hank, who was monitoring the floor channel with his second radio, passed along any information that was transmitted on that channel. At 1145 Hank said, "The speaker is rolling," indicating that the decoy limousine and the vehicle carrying the VIP had left the White House. Eight minutes later, Hank transmitted, "Limo is out front."

The final plan was for the VIP to get to the thirteenth floor by way of the service elevator and enter the ballroom via the route used by the waiters – through the west annexes. In that manner, the VIP would be exposed to the open hallways for only three or four seconds and that would be at the far end of the lobby and hallway complex. The elevator traffic appeared to be peaking – each door, when it opened, discharged about fifteen people.

When the quiet gong sounded, announcing its arrival, Riggs would look up at Tom expectantly. At the previous rehearsal, Tom had learned that it was easiest for Riggs to allow about half of the people to exit the elevator before issuing the SNIFF command. Riggs would follow the group and work his way to the front of it, weaving back and forth, head high, mouth closed, breathing deeply through his nose. Then he'd turn back towards Tom. The subject of many pats and comments, he endured them stoically.

At 1153, the left-hand elevator doors opened and a large man led the group out of it. "SNIFF, Riggs," Tom commanded, seemingly for the hundredth time.

The dog took a few steps toward the rear of the group that was following the leader, walking briskly. Riggs suddenly broke into a trot and yipped. Tom removed his Taser from its shoulder holster, saying, "Dad, Tom, got one. He's leading the group. Tall, on your right as you look this way."

"Got him, son, Riggs is trying to lick his hand. He's stopped. He's mine." Tom returned his Taser to the shoulder holster.

Bruce, hearing the brief conversation, switched to the floor frequency and announced, "Sniffer has a perp."

Saying, "Tuck, PLATZ. STAY, STAY," he opened the door, went into the hall, saw Robert by the library entrance in his waiter's whites, holding his tray against his chest, saying to a man near the perp, "How did this dog get in here? Is he yours, sir? Go ahead, folks, somebody hold his collar."

Riggs continued to yip and whimper, tail wagging furiously, dancing next to the tall man, eyes on his face. Tom whistled, the dog whirled around and the tall man moved away quickly, looking at his wristwatch.

Tom said, slapping his thigh, "Sorry, folks, He's my dog.

Riggs, SPOT. SPOT. Goood boooy."

Robert followed the perp for a few steps. Most of the people were congregated around Tom and the dog. Robert switched on his Taser and brought it out from where he had been concealing it behind the tray.

From a distance of about five feet, he watched the laser dot move across the floor and up the man's left leg, past his calf, to the knee and finally reach the thigh. It seemed like slow motion.

He pulled the trigger; heard a loud "pop," and the man fell to the floor as if he had died on the spot.

"Takedown, takedown at library," said Robert on the floor frequency. Four men came out of the library, waving their gold shields and formed a barrier between the perp and the on-coming crowd.

One of them said, "Please keep moving, keep moving and give us room to help this person."

Robert and one of the agents from the library rolled the man on his back. Robert took a quick look inside the man's jacket and said, "Same setup. I'll just cut the fuse for now."

Aware of bright lights, he tucked his Taser under the man's knee, cut off the lowest three shirt buttons with his pliers, reached in, made another cut and held the pull-wire igniter and an inch or so of fuse up to Hank and his camera. Then he sniffed it and said, "It's inert," and put it in his pocket.

"The Taser is safe, the single round has been expended, I put my Taser under his knee for now – the darts are still in his leg."

The two men lifted him and placed him on the gurney that had just rolled up. Robert picked up his Taser and stuffed it between the man's thighs.

"You again?" Robert said to the agent who dragged the gurney.

"Yes," he said, "We just came up the service elevator from the van when we heard the call." They crossed the motionless perp's arms across his chest, covered him completely with a blanket and tucked it in all around, not bothering with the straps. They spun the gurney around and quickly dragged it back into the Murrow Room.

Tom and Riggs followed; Bruce and Robert exchanged an arm punch, grinning.

"Nice work, big brother," Bruce said. "I guess we got lucky," Robert responded. Bruce looked at Tuck and said, "Tuck, SPOT." They went to the station recently vacated by Tom and Riggs. Bruce heard Robert say, "Sniffer one on floor. We have secured an armed subject in the Murrow Room. Time, eleven fifty- eight."

""Family, Hank... Last elevator en route."

A moment later, they heard, "Family, Hank. VIP is in west annex, entering ballroom." Then they heard Bruce say, "Tuck, SNIFF." Not more than thirty seconds later, Bruce was heard to say, "Tuck, DON'T. Goood Boooy, Tuck. Last elevator load is clear. Sniffers standing down. Going to floor frequency."

Robert looked at his watch; eleven fifty-nine. Sam, Ari, Hank and Elaine came into the Murrow Room. Hank turned his camera on the bomber, who appeared to be dead.

Robert knelt, pulled the blanket off the man, felt the carotid pulse and announced, "Fast but firm. He's probably vaguely aware of what's happening. He'll be coming around in about ten minutes. Sam, I'd like to divest him of his explosives, but first we'll get the Taser darts out, if they aren't already."

He retrieved his Taser, ejected the dart module shell and returned the unloaded Taser to his shoulder holster. He cut the wires from the dart shell and handed it to Sam. "This has data on the time of discharge, Sam. There's also a little pile of confetti that was released when I activated it, if you need proof that the darts came from this specific weapon. Now, roll him on his side so I can get at the darts."

With his knife in his hand, he followed the bundle of hair-thin wires to where they disappeared into the man's thigh and quickly slit open the man's pants.

"Baggie?" he asked; an agent reached down, holding one open.

Using the pliers, Robert cut off the wires, pulled out the little darts and dropped them into the baggie.

Hank said, "I taped the takedown as well, Sam."

"You folks are incredible," said Sam. "Go ahead and

undress him as far as you need to."

"Thanks, Sam. Let's slide him onto the floor." With Robert holding the feet, they dragged the gurney out from under the unresisting man, who remained dazed and incapable of movement or communication.

Robert pulled open the man's jacket, cut off the remaining shirt buttons and opened it fully. They saw a similar arrangement as earlier; a double row of conventional dynamite in stick form, held in place with duct tape and elastic bandage.

"Old fashioned, but simple and dependable," observed Robert. "The middle stick in the bottom row has a blasting cap inserted and stabilized with duct tape. There was about an inch and a half of fuse is protruding from the cap. The rest is straight gelatin dynamite."

Knife in hand, Robert carefully cut the tape around the cap and worked it free, holding it by the fuse. Tom held a baggie open and Robert dropped it in and handed it to Sam.

"Fingerprints and crimp characteristics, Sam. Maybe the same crimping tool – wouldn't surprise me. We are dealing with the same sources for fuse, igniters, caps and explosive as earlier today."

He continued to work with the knife, cutting through duct tape and elastic bandage. When it all lay freely on the floor, he said, "Go ahead and cuff him – he's all yours, Sam. His legs are beginning to twitch a little, so you can tape him up all you want." An agent produced a long self-locking plastic tie and a pair of handcuffs. He put the tie around the man's ankles and crossed the man's hands on his waist. Cuffing the man's wrists, he used another plastic tie to secure the cuffs through the man's belt.

The agent looked at the dynamite, counting. "Two rows of twelve sticks – what did you have on the other guy?"

The gurney-handler replied, "It was the same. The other guy had a Press Club photo ID and a card, in his inside jacket pocket."

The nearest agent removed the NPC ID from the bomber's lapel and handling it by the edges, placed it in a baggie. He then searched the coat pockets and pulled out a card, handling it carefully also, as he put it in another baggie. He handed both to Sam.

"Thanks, Ben – I'm glad you wore your latex gloves. Anybody here read Arabic?" Sam asked.

"I can read the numbers," said Hank, from behind the camera. Laughter erupted and the tension in the room was broken. When it died down, Sam said, "The last entry in the last line on this card is underlined – it says 'one two zero,' so this perp was on schedule." Everyone looked at their wristwatches. It was 12:04.

Ari came over to Tom and Robert and shook their hands. "That was a totally professional intervention, gentlemen. Congratulations. I must get back to my boss. That last bunch of journalists was pretty curious as to why a bunch of shield-carrying agents was taking care of a person that had a stroke or something. Glad you folks didn't allow cell phones upstairs." He turned to Elaine and Hank, who were still filming events in the Murrow Room as they transpired. "And I'm glad that you two didn't find any unwelcome guests. Mrs. Henderson, I've been groping for a word to describe how you look today. I think the word is 'saucy' – would that be correct?"

"Thank you, Ari. That's the nicest thing anyone has said to me today," Elaine answered. "Hank, don't say a word."

"I don't have to, Mom. I've got it on tape." He turned off the camera, swung it off his shoulder and put it down. "That sucker seems as if it weighs about thirty pounds by now. I'm glad I don't do that for a living."

"You sort of do, Hank," Elaine said. They chuckled.

"Nice safe job, huh, Mom?" They began divesting themselves of their interconnections.

Robert strolled over to Elaine. "Have I told you today how much I love you, sweetie?"

"Thanks, Rob," she answered. "If that had been anyone but you out there, I would have been really scared when I saw all that dynamite."

"Yep," he said, "that was enough to blow out all the windows on this floor and many people with them."

Sam joined them and they all moved to the nearest chairs at the table. He said, "I have a second secure van standing by for this one. The first perp is talking a blue streak. I don't want them to even see each other, let alone talk. If there's a conspiracy here, I want to nail it. We'll take more than the usual precautions against a suicide attempt. Rob, you said the setups were the same?"

"That's correct. Same sources for the fuse and the caps. You could probably match the duct tape as coming from the same roll. Might even find matching fingerprints on the caps."

"Then, if they didn't set each other up, there has to be a third person involved. Just by listening to NPR, he already knows that they've either failed or delayed. Perhaps one of our perps could be convinced to take us to the person who sent them on their way. Wait a minute – I just thought of something." Sam took his radio off his belt and changed the frequency. He brought his hand to his mouth and said, "Van One – Bouncer." There was a pause and he continued, "Say the name on your passenger's NPC ID." He reached in his jacket pocket and extracted the NPC photo ID from the bomber and looked at it while he waited for the answer.

"Your copy the other day was better than this one," he said to Robert. He motioned for silence, pressing his speaker more tightly to his ear. "Copy, Van One. Bouncer out." He looked around the group and said, "Our perps made two copies of somebody's NPC ID. It's the same name on each. We'll check with Jack to see if it matches with the person who reported losing one. And, Mrs. Henderson, what sixth sense told you to look for two suicide bombers?"

"I don't know, Sam. I wish I did. When I saw those little twin girls the other day, it came to me in a flash as something we should prepare for. Bruce and Rob always talk about redundancy. I thought that it would apply to anyone who wanted to insure his success."

Jack appeared in the doorway and said, "I've arranged for a couple of waiters to bring lunch in to you folks. They'll be here momentarily. You'll be having the same as the Prime Minister, if that's OK." He held the door open for the two agents to maneuver the gurney with its motionless and totally blanketed cargo into the hall and in the direction of the service elevator.

"Also," Jack continued, "I have a message from Ari. The VIP has been informed about what has taken place here and he wants to meet you, so plan to be in the basement at 1:50

PM. I'd invite you inside for his speech, but we think that all those journalists would have more questions for the Hendersons than they'll have for the VIP. As far as we can tell, the first incident was not seen by anyone. However, the second incident was witnessed by an elevator full of reporters, all of whom are skilled at observation. They were not close enough to see what you were doing, Robert; they saw nothing to indicate that you weren't a waiter helping the EMT's with some 'first aid.' However, they are very curious about who it was that had the heart attack, or stroke, or whatever. They haven't tumbled to the fact that there are no empty seats in the ballroom, or that there was a gurney with a couple of ambulance attendants standing by."

"It's also fortunate that the last elevator contained people who were pressed for time to get into their seats," said Sam. "If it had happened a few minutes earlier, we wouldn't have been able to get the perp onto the gurney for all the reporters in the way. Let's keep it that way, Jack – nobody on the hotel staff knows anything."

"As a matter of fact, Sam, they don't. There might be a little talk, of course, but there were no staff members in the lobby. I'm the only staff member with a radio on the floor channel. Enjoy your lunch, folks – it's here." He left with a wave of his hand.

Three waiters rolled multi-deck carriers into the Morrow room and quickly set up six places at an adjacent table. One of them, obviously a supervisor, said, "please come and enjoy your luncheon, folks. You'll find that you're not on the 'rubber chicken' circuit today. Mr. Jack told us that you were to be treated like royalty and he doesn't say that very often. He also said that if we offered drinks on the house, you'd thank us but probably not accept our offer. Is that right?"

"That's right, sir," said Bruce, "But we do appreciate the thought. Can you tell me how long the question period will be today, after the speech?"

"Yes, sir. The speaker is scheduled for forty minutes, with fifteen minutes following for questions. If you wish, I'll have a portable radio brought in so you can listen to what he has to say. It's broadcast, as you know, on Maryland Public Radio. I'm sorry, ma'am," turning to Elaine, "that our speaker's policies precluded TV coverage of today's luncheon. But somehow I think that you're aware of this."

"Yes," she said, "journalists consider us TV folks as somehow not quite up to their level of professionalism. I think they are jealous of our abilities to get on a scene quickly with full visual coverage as a situation unfolds, without needing to sit down and write about it and have it published some hours later."

Hank appeared to choke. He put a handkerchief to his mouth and his face turned as red as his mother's jacket.

"Aha," said the waiter, "Thank you for explaining that to me. I understand. Are you all right, sir?"

Hank nodded vigorously, most of his face in his handkerchief.

"Again, please enjoy your lunch. André will be standing by to serve you, should you need anything." He bowed slightly, walked around Riggs and Tuck, looked back at them curiously, shook his head and left the room.

Elaine said, "Hank, what happened? Did you choke on a chicken bone?"

Sam chuckled. "I think I just learned how Henry Henderson came by his sense of quick humor. He got it from his mother. Mrs. Henderson, I congratulate you. That was the most heartfelt, spontaneous explanation of your scam that I could possibly imagine. How did you say that with such an earnest, straight face?"

Hank wiped his eyes and looked at his mother. "Mom, sometimes you break me up. How long have you been waiting to deliver that line?"

"It just came to me, son. I would have stammered out something else if I'd have known it would set you off."

They all moved to the table that had been prepared for them. The team of waiters had spread a crisp linen tablecloth and laid out beautifully presented napkins and silverware. At one end, a platter of steaming roast beef, topped with bright green parsley, waited for André to serve slices ranging from dark brown end cuts to rare. Separate serving dishes contained mashed potatoes, gravy, peas and carrots. A garden salad with halved cherry tomatoes, mushrooms, raisins and thin-cut cucumber slices waited on the left of each place. Crystal water glasses were at each place, with a dew-dropped silver pitcher holding a further supply. A cloth-covered basket held a supply of warm, fresh-baked rolls. Plates of butter and cruets of oil and vinegar and dishes of assorted salad dressings were distributed in the center of the table. A fancy frosted cake, decorated with two four-inch German shepherds occupying opposite corners – one standing, one sitting, occupied the other end of the table. Its message, in bright red frosting letters, read "TO THE HENDERSON TEAM – WITH OUR THANKS."

André stood ready at the beef platter. He said, "We apologize for serving everything family style, but we were told that you wouldn't be upset very much. Ma'am, how would you like your roast beef?"

* * *

Setting aside her empty coffee-cup, Elaine looked at her watch. "I've got time to get out of these duds before we go downstairs to meet the VIP." She pushed her chair back from the table. "That and wash my face. I feel like I did in college drama productions."

Sam said, "Before you leave, Elaine, I want you all to know that the personnel of Henderson Enterprises will each be receiving a substantial bonus for today's work. It won't be going to the company; it'll be going to each of you as individuals. The end of the fiscal year is coming up pretty soon and if I don't spend what's in my budget for honorariums, I'll lose it. Under the circumstances, there's not enough money in any Government account to reward you people for what each of you has contributed today."

"Totally unnecessary, but also totally appreciated, Sam," said Bruce. "We did our best to do the job you asked us to and Lady Luck came down on our side."

"You're all more than welcome. I must run along. Please be sure to bring the dogs to the little reception in the basement. The Prime Minister wants you to demonstrate their capabilities. He also wants to see a Taser – he's highly experienced with most weapons."

"If there's going to be a live demo," said Hank, "I request permission to skip the ceremony."

"Understandable, Hank," chuckled Sam. "But so sorry,

permission denied – stand by one." Sam pressed his earpiece closer to his ear, as the group chuckled at the riposte.

"Well," said Sam, after acknowledging a rather lengthy message, "our boys have had a busy lunch. The first perp sang a beautiful song in Arabic – He speaks almost no English at all.

"He has decided that he does not want to go to Paradise yet; he told our Arabic-speaking agent in Detent where to find his leader, in a motel near Jefferson Circle. Four agents went there immediately, found he hadn't checked out and got the ID for his rental car from the hotel registration. One agent went into the garage, found the car and stood by it. Meanwhile, the Detention supervisor described events to a judge on the phone, got an immediate verbal OK for a search, papers to follow. The warrant arrived by courier at the motel within twenty minutes, so they got a key, went to the suspect's room and listened outside the door.

"They heard the question-and-answer part of the NPC lunch program on a radio inside the room. They unlocked the door quietly – no chain – and burst in. Suspect was sitting on the bed, listening to the radio. They secured him just as the question period was ending. They looked around and in a wastebasket, they found short pieces of fuse, duct tape and three or four Ace bandages.

"In his suitcase – he was packed, ready to leave out of Dulles this evening – there were two passports that belong to our two bombers. They Miranda'd and charged him and took him to Detent and they are arranging a line-up for positive ID by our singing perpetrator. So – we definitely have a conspiracy here and I think the principals involved are in custody."

21

1405 Saturday, May 18, 1998
Basement, National Press Club

Ari came over to Bruce and Tom. He said, "Sam just brought me up to date. Looks as if you folks have cracked a big one. The ringleader is one that we know and have been looking for. I need to talk to Sam – I have an idea. He should be here in a few minutes – he's coming down with our VIP in the service elevator."

Bruce replied, "Tom and I need to take our pups outside. We won't be long. We'll be ready in a couple of minutes." They walked around the un-marked car that sat in the entrance and went down the alley a short distance. Several agents and Metro police were stationed in the alley; they watched the proceedings. Bruce and Tom said "STICK" to their respective dogs. Riggs headed for a hydrant, while Tuck preferred a telephone pole. They then looked at their masters, who had returned to a spot across the street from the door.

Robert joined them, having changed back to his street clothes. "We need a quick conference, guys," he said. "All the explosives are off-site and, hopefully, secured as evidence. We don't have anything to use for them to find, except my hands. I've been handling the dynamite and the fuses and I haven't washed them. I'll be the perp."

"That should work, Rob," Bruce said. "We'll explain the circumstances to the VIP; we'll keep the dogs here in the shade, then call them in, one at a time and see how they do."

"That'll work," Robert answered. He turned to go inside. Bruce gave a shrill whistle; both dogs stopped their tussling over a piece of broken pallet and looked up. The men slapped their left thighs and the dogs came to them at a trot. Bruce and Tom had the dogs lie down, passed their hands in front of the dogs' eyes and walked back to the entrance to the basement.

Elaine and Hank came out of the elevator, which was

stacked with equipment cases, the TV equipment and Elaine's suitcase. She had changed into normal attire and had replaced the glaring red lipstick and overdone eye shadow with more conservative makeup. Hank and Tom moved the load out of the elevator; Bruce said, "Might as well leave our gear right here. It'll give the dogs something more to sniff at."

They had just completed placing the gear cases near the door when the elevator doors opened again and Sam and Richard came out, followed by a distinguished-appearing man with a shock of white hair.

Richard said, "Mr. Prime Minister, I want you to meet the team of people that truly saved our lives today. Their planning and execution was absolutely perfect. These are the Hendersons" – indicating each of them – "Robert, Bruce, Mrs. Elaine, Tom and Henry."

The Prime Minister shook their hands. He said, "I understand that you people saved many lives today – including my own. I am deeply grateful – and I'll find a way to express my appreciation in a more formal manner at an appropriate time. In the meantime, as Ari has told you, I would like to meet your dogs and, if possible, watch them work. Can you do that for me? My plane won't leave until I get there, I hope."

Robert responded, "Yes, Mr. Prime Minister. These dogs are trained to find explosives that are hidden, or pinpoint a person who is either wearing them or has been handling them recently. All of the explosives that were involved today are in safekeeping elsewhere, but since I handled them extensively, we are hoping that enough scent remains on my hands that they'll focus on me. We'll do this one dog at a time. I'll just sort of work myself into our group here. Go ahead, Tom, put Riggs to work."

Tom stepped forward and said, "Mr. Prime Minister, we'd like to introduce Riggs. He's four years old and specializes in explosives. If you look across the street, you'll him and another dog, Tuck, lying in the shade of our van. Riggs is looking at me, waiting for a signal. I'll slap my thigh and he'll come and sit. I'll tell him to 'sniff' and he'll begin by either searching the room, gear, or by checking out each one of us – except myself." Riggs lay with his head between his paws, watching the group. Tom slapped his thigh and Riggs came at a gallop and sat, eyes riveted on Tom, tongue lolling.

"Riggs, SNIFF," said Tom and the big dog went directly to Ari, then the PM, took a side trip to the equipment cases and dismissed them with a contemptuous snort. Suddenly, he turned, trotted to Robert, sniffed at his hands, sat and yipped once, tail wagging.

"That's the signal, Mr. Prime Minister. When we see this reaction, we know without a doubt that the individual is either carrying, or has been handling, any one of many known explosives. This is what he did upstairs in the lobby, only somewhat more aggressively, because there was so much dynamite that he perceived a much larger odor source." Tom went over to Riggs, said "Goood boooy, Riggs," and stroked his head. "This, sir, is his reward for finding a perpetrator. Your turn, Bruce."

Bruce said, "We'll do essentially the same as Tom did with Riggs, Mr. Prime Minister. This fellow's name is Tuck. He and Riggs are trained to work together – covering situations where one dog may not be enough. We used some of the techniques used in training sheep dogs, where multiple dogs are utilized in many cases. You may have noticed that he was content to lie there and watch Riggs do his work." Bruce stepped into Tuck's line of vision and slapped his left thigh. Tuck trotted to Bruce and sat, mouth open. "Mr. Prime Minister, if you don't believe that dogs can grin, look at this one." The group chuckled in agreement. "OK, Tuck, SNIFF."

Tuck whirled around, nose high, mouth closed, his eyes half open. He walked slowly in front of the group, his head twisting and turning, his nose wrinkling with the effort of savoring the unbelievable assortment of scents that are not detectable to humans. He pushed his way between the Prime Minister and Riggs, turned towards Robert, took a step or two closer and pushed his nose into Robert's left hand. He sat, looked back over his shoulder at Bruce and barked once. It was a vibrant, resonating pulse that seemed to shake the building. Riggs wagged his tail in appreciation and the Prime Minister applauded. Bruce stepped in and said "Goood boooy, Tuck," as he reached down and scratched Tuck's chest and throat, while Tuck managed to get in a face-lick.

"Very, very impressive, Mr. Henderson," said the Prime Minister. "Ari tells me that his recruiting efforts haven't met with success – is that right?"

"That's correct, sir," responded Bruce. "However, some of us might like to come for a visit someday, if our work schedule ever allows it to happen."

"You'll be welcome, I'm sure. Ari would like for Mrs. Henderson to advise some of our *sabra* groups in his organization about unarmed combat; I understand that you're an expert in this field, madam."

"I manage to hold my own, thank you," Elaine replied.

"Speaking of weapons," continued the prime Minister, "I would like to examine this electrical weapon that you employed today. Is this something that you can do? Mr. Robert, I believe you're the weapons expert in the organization?"

Robert opened his jacket slowly and extracted his Taser. He held it by the barrel and extended the handle to the Israeli head of state. "It's unarmed and inert, sir," he explained. "Sam," he asked, "Do you have the expended darts in your pocket?" Sam withdrew the baggie from his coat pocket and handed it to the Prime Minister, as Robert extracted his spare dart module from the shoulder holster.

"These are the darts that the unit fired," Robert continued. "Please excuse the blood on them. Sam will be saving these as evidence. You'll note that each dart has a fine wire attached. I trimmed off the excess, just for convenience. Each dart is ejected from its own barrel, but remains connected to the weapon in your hand. At the moment of penetration into a suspect's body, no matter how slight, the darts, charged with many thousands of volts at very low amperage, discharge this voltage into the target's body. The very high voltage immediately scrambles the central nervous system so that muscle control is totally and instantly lost. The darts will penetrate several layers of ordinary clothing. If a person is wearing body armor, a hit anywhere else will disable the target, as it's equally effective on any part of the body – hands, legs, feet, arms, neck – whatever is exposed and relatively unprotected. Incapacitation lasts for at least five minutes, which is plenty of time to disarm and secure the target by conventional means. Please allow me to activate the unit for you, sir, so that you can see how the laser designator makes it easy to select the impact area."

Bruce took the unit by the barrel, turned it on and handed it back. "Note the small red light – it's blinking, telling you that the power is on, but there is no dart module in place. If I were to install the module -" he held up his spare module – "you would have a green light, telling you that the unit was ready to fire. However, your laser designator will come on when you depress the trigger to the first stop. You may wish to select a target – perhaps that waste barrel over there – and see how easy it is to aim by looking at the target. You can easily discharge the weapon while holding it in a concealed position, or from near your hip. That means you do not have to assume the position of a conventional shooter, aiming a pistol."

The Israeli aimed at the floor directly in front of his feet, applied an ounce or two of pressure to the trigger with his index finger and twitched his eyebrows as a brilliant red spot appeared on the concrete surface.

"Is it all right to pull the trigger?" he asked.

"Certainly, sir," Robert responded. "You'll feel a release of finger pressure and the unit'll reset when you let it go. Perhaps you'd like to select, as your target, the first letter of the word '**REMOVAL**' on the barrel I mentioned." The laser spot skittered across the floor and crawled up the barrel and danced erratically around the letter "**R**." There was a slight "click" and the spot disappeared.

"What kind of range and accuracy can you achieve, Mr. Henderson?"

"About 5 meters, but I recommend getting as close as you can. This morning, I followed our suspect for a few paces until I was almost alongside him and then I nailed him in the left thigh from about a meter. He was very nervous and alert, but he never suspected that he had been targeted. From where you are to the barrel is about six meters."

"What is your reload time?"

"About five seconds," Robert answered. "For example, this unit has no module in place. You can turn it off" – he demonstrated – "open the chamber, remove the module shell, insert the new dart module" – he went through the motions, but did not insert the dart module – "close the receiver and you're back in business."

Sam offered, "We people in law enforcement like these very much. We have a few and will be procuring more. The dart module stores time and date of firing data; also, each firing releases a small batch of confetti bearing the unit's serial number. It can be used for tracking and recording who fired a weapon and when. Just to be totally sure I picked up a few pieces of the confetti and it's in the baggie along with the module. There were enough witnesses for today's action that we don't need to get the confirmation of the shooter, the time and the date to make the apprehension stand up in court. If the shooter has made a mistake, the subject will recover completely without damage within a half hour and will have little memory of what transpired, with no pain of significance. Also, the traces of blood on the darts, when recovered, will establish the DNA characteristics of the target. This will also prove to be of significant legal value."

Ari looked at this watch. He said, "Mr. Prime Minister, may I propose a possible alternative to the long court process that our perpetrators will face here in America? Since their leader had their passports in his possession, there is ample evidence of a conspiracy. I propose that we sedate the three gentlemen adequately for our flight home and take them along with us. That way, the incident never happened here in the USA and perhaps we'll be able to persuade their leader to tell us who his controller might be and where we might find him."

Silence followed Ari's proposal.

The Prime Minister looked at Sam and said, "Your decision, sir. This episode was executed on your soil and, while I think that Ari's suggestion would lead to quick justice and a possible further development of our intelligence, all at a great cost savings to the American judicial system, that you, Sam, might have some insight that we lack."

Sam was silent for a moment, collecting his thoughts. "Ari," he said slowly, "I'd really hate to be up against you. You're aggressive and you focus carefully on a situation in order to extract maximum advantage. Admirable characteristics, Ari, admirable. I wish certain of my agents –

none here, by the way – would display your tenacity and determination. But – as you said, Mr. Prime Minister, this is the United States of America. Our basic philosophy is that every person is presumed innocent until proven guilty in a legal court of law. Some of our laws were broken today by our perpetrators. Federal laws.

"Laws against attempted murder of high officials of a foreign government. Possessing weapons of mass destruction. Concealing weapons without a license in a public building in the District of Columbia. Possessing explosives without a license – seems trivial, but it'll add to the years they'll face in a Federal prison. Secreting explosive devices on their person with the intent to commit murder.

"Our analysis of the number of people that definitely would have been killed will multiply the charges against them significantly, even though our estimates will be conservative. Falsification of official documents in order to commit a high crime. Direct involvement in a conspiracy, where each person is equally guilty of the crimes committed by any member of the conspiracy. That's just a start, from the top of my head.

"The evidence against these people is overwhelmingly complete and convincing. They were apprehended in the action of completing their intentions – 'in flagrante delicto'- with only minutes remaining. The least charge against them will be attempted suicide.

"Now," continued Sam, "a few years in one of our fine Federal facilities might change their minds about their political persuasion – with deportation to their native lands facing them if they choose to misbehave in prison. We might just call on you to provide secure transportation, but only following their conviction and sentencing."

Ari said, "I can see why law enforcement people in America are frustrated. Why do your criminals have more rights than the victims?"

"Because, Ari, our laws are designed to protect everyone – even the criminals. We have a sad history here in certain parts of our country of vigilante justice – targeting people of differing ethnic origins and accusing them of violent crimes of the worst sort – of which they were frequently totally ignorant and equally innocent. Our blacks suffered, our Asians suffered and certainly our Native Americans suffered. We cannot repeat that part of our history. So, when a person is found guilty of a crime, there is a very high probability that he or she's indeed guilty. In fact, we leave it to our individual States to decide whether or not they'll employ the death penalty – the ultimate sanction – from which there is no recall – as when new evidence is brought to light. DNA identification has already released people from Death Row, as it's called. That's why our laws are what they are, Ari."

Richard looked at his wristwatch again.

He said, "Mr. Prime Minister, if we are done here. . . .."

The VIP said, "He's hinting that we have another appointment this afternoon, for which we are probably late already. Words cannot express my appreciation and admiration for what you people have accomplished here today. Believe me, we shall be in touch and very soon."

Ari added, "I'll be staying for a few days – I hope to get out to your training area and yes, I'll bring a toy that perhaps you'd like to keep for me. It has a voracious appetite for standard nine millimeter rounds and you can almost conceal it in the palm of your hand."

Robert grinned as they shook hands. The Prime Minister got into the rear seat, Ari rode in the front passenger seat and Richard sat behind the wheel. An agent appeared in the doorway, looked both ways and signaled for Richard to depart with a left turn. With a subtle toot on the horn, they were gone.

Bruce said, "Wow. What a day – let's get things loaded up."

"No problem if each one takes two," said Hank as he picked up the TV case and the camera and carried them over to the station wagon. Elaine followed with the tripod and her large shoulder bag. Opening the lift gate, she placed them behind the rear passenger seat. Tom carried Elaine's and Robert's small suitcases and put them in with the equipment. Robert went to the Blazer, opened the lift gate and said, "Riggs. Tuck." The yawning opening was all the invitation the dogs needed. Shoulder-to-shoulder, they trotted to the Blazer and leaped in. As the dogs watched, everyone gathered at the rear of the station wagon and helped each other remove their coats and shoulder holsters. Robert took each Taser, checked it, removed the dart modules from the weapons that had not been discharged and placed them side-by-side in a foam-padded aluminum case.

"Mine is in my suitcase, Rob, right on top," said Elaine, "Do you want it now?"

"Might as well," he said. "One less trip to the armory that way." He pulled her suitcase closer, opened it and removed the unit and placed it with the others. "Five Tasers, all off, nine dart modules. Check," he muttered. "Laney, you're the only one that doesn't have to go to the armory this afternoon to unload and put away your back-up weapon."

Bruce pulled his cell phone from his shirt pocket. "I think I'd better call the ranch."

Automatically, he dialed the number of the office line. *"Stupid,"* he muttered to himself, *"Elaine is right here."* He was about to re-dial when Lisa answered the phone on the third ring.

"Henderson Enterprises," she said.

"I see you have found your true vocation, sweetheart," said Bruce.

"BRUCE!" she said excitedly, "Are you all right? We listened to the broadcast and there was nothing unusual. Lattie said it started on time and ended a little early."

"I'm fine, sweetheart and so is everyone else. We had a very exciting time, however, but I can't tell you about it now. We did get to meet the speaker, just a few moments ago. Lisa, Tuck and Riggs both earned their cookies today. The extra training paid off."

There was silence, as Lisa digested the significance of Bruce's innocent-sounding remark.

"Oh, Bruce," she finally said, are you sure that you're all right? And everyone else also?"

"We're all fine," he answered, "and we'll be ready for a walk or a run, followed by a light supper. We'll be there in an hour, traffic permitting. I can't wait to see you."

22

1000 Saturday, May 19, 1998
The Ranch

The Jet Ranger's rotor blades pounded the air as it made a tight base-to-final right turn, flared and set down gently on the lawn in back of the house. The subdued roar of the idling turbine engines stopped abruptly and the gearboxes moaned in a descending whine as the pilot turned off the fuel boost pumps, the igniters, the comm master and the switch that energized the master electrical bus. The spinning rotor blades continued to hiss through the air as the aircraft commander emerged from the left side of the craft and slid open the passenger door. He assisted the two passengers as they got out. One was a very elderly gentleman; the other a man perhaps in his early sixties. The older man was dressed impeccably in a black suit, a white shirt and a black tie, while the other wore more casual clothes – a light yellow jersey, open at the neck, tan slacks and open sandals without socks – sure signs of a seasoned Washingtonian anticipating a muggy May day.

As there was no windsock to indicate wind velocity and direction, Robert had moved to the lawn to indicate the desired landing direction with a pair of bright yellow paddles. He said to the aircraft commander, "No chart on your lap, Tommy?"

"Who needs one? You said look for the bright red roof on the barn, nine point one nautical miles out on the Casanova 281 degree radial, LZ eleven hundred sixty MSL, look for the 'H' cut in the grass on the west side of the house. I put it in the GPS as a user waypoint the first time we came out here. That's close enough for a let-down on instruments."

"Just like the old days, Tommy," Robert chuckled. "I'll take a Marine helo driver any day. Gentlemen, I'm Robert Henderson. I hope that Tommy's pilot didn't scare you too badly today."

"It was a nice smooth ride, although Tommy told us it would be bumpier going home," answered the younger of the two passengers. "I'm Everett, by the way; I don't believe we've met, although I've heard many good things about you. This gentleman is George."

"I'm very glad to be here and safe on the ground again," said George, shaking hands with Robert.

"A cool, dry, hand," thought Robert. *"The ride didn't rattle him at all."*

"Ah," said George, "there's Stephen, over on the deck; Halloo, Stephen!"

The trio made their way across the grass to the deck as the pilot began his post-flight checks. Tommy produced canvas socks to be placed over the ends of the rotor blades and threaded their ropes loosely through little rings that popped out from the fuselage.

Stephen, Lattie, Rudi, Bruce and Lisa lined the deck rail. The awning had been extended since early morning, keeping things cool. A large glass pitcher of iced tea, streaming with condensation, was on the table, along with an assortment of Danish pastry.

"Stephen, old friend, will you please do us the honor of making the introductions?" George asked. "There are a couple of folks here that I'm very anxious to meet – starting with this lovely lady," he said, striding briskly to Lisa.

Stephen said, "Lisa, dear, this is my old friend George Stantial. He has been with the State Department for many years and has now lapsed into the status of Whatever Emeritus. George, you're holding the hand of my next daughter-in-law, Lisa Holder, from Austria. Don't hold that hand too long, now, or she might change her mind about who she'll be marrying."

Lisa smiled into the bluest eyes she had ever seen. They were framed by bushy white eyebrows that seemed to wave with fierce independence. The deep lines channeled in the tanned face seemed to say, *"I am a man of maturity, with infinite patience and wisdom."* She raised her left hand and held both his hands in a firm grip and said, "I am so glad you wanted to come and meet with us. Mr. Stantial, this is my father, Rudi Holder, from the little town of St. Wolfgang, near Salzburg,

Austria."

George turned to Rudi and the two men looked at each other, eyes locked. Their right hands met in a firm grip and made one slow oscillation – up, down and apart.

"Mr. Holder," said George, "Please call me George, so that I may call you Rudi. I have heard much of your story from Stephen and I truly admire your courage and restraint."

Rudi answered, "It is myself who is honored, Herr George. When a man knows how and when to shake hands like an old Austrian farmer, I know I can trust him."

George turned to the group. He said, "I am so happy that Everett canceled at least three appointments to come today. Many years ago Everett was one of those 'bright young men' that we took on in State, thinking that in time, they'd be our replacements. Everett and I have worked together most of that time and he has rewarded our hopes many times over. Everett has already been in contact with the Austrian and Swiss ambassadors and with certain other people and what he has to tell us will be very interesting – and, Rudi, I hope very satisfactory from your standpoint."

The introductions continued around the table. "But where are your boys, Robert?" George asked. "I heard through the grapevine that this whole tribe was involved in bringing down some macabre effort to bollix things up at the National Press Club last Friday."

"The boys are working the dogs, Mr. Stantial. We have some routines here that have to continue, pretty much on schedule. We'd planned a little demonstration for later today, if you're willing. It won't take much time and is actually part of their regular training."

Elaine offered iced tea to everyone as they sat down and made sure that the snacks were within reach.

Lisa began by saying, "Gentlemen, you all know why we Holders are here. We come to discuss a matter of great concern to us, because it'll be of even greater concern to many other people when – or perhaps I should say if – it becomes common knowledge. I think that this morning's time will best be served if my father tells you the substance of his story – where the gold came from, how it came to be in his possession, what he has done to keep it out of the minds –

and hands – of other men and why he has taken so long to come to this point. Father?"

Rudi's story-telling was masterfully accomplished. The entire group sat motionless. Rudi described, using simple, clear sentences, when he was a young man of sixteen: "There was I, working – totally in terror about what would happen to us, hating these Nazis. Then, when we have put all the gold into ingots, I was hearing the machine-gun fire that killed my parents, my cousins and my friends. I had to control my face and my feelings while I drove through three horrible nights. There was no sleeping for me the daytime like they did, half drunk, half crazy.

"Finally, while they watched and made notes, carefully I dropped one hundred and eighty gold bars – one at a time – into the water of St. Wolfgangsee."

Rudi paused, cleared his throat and took a swallow of iced tea.

"Then, for the first time, the devil of a Major drove the truck. In a little bit, he stopped and told the Herr Oberst to 'do it here and hurry.' Herr Oberst took me a few meters into the woods and shot me, but he was not good enough with his fancy pistol. It was Lisa's grandmother, a kind *Frau*, who found me and cared for me. When I was well enough to walk, I told them that I would return one day. I walked home to Zohor. In some years, I began working as a forester.

"Even when I started working for Nikolai I didn't tell him about the gold. I just send him the coded messages that answered his questions."

At that point, Stephen interrupted him. "Yesterday, I had a friend bring out the files on the Third Man. That was what we called Rudi in those days. What he did for America is incredible. We were able to successfully – and correctly – deduce that Russia could not initiate a ground attack, either through Austria or through East Germany, simply because they didn't have the means to do it – not enough artillery, not enough tanks, not enough ammunition and certainly not enough soldiers in all of Czechoslovakia. Even their show of firing exercises at the artillery range across the river from Linz in the early fifties severely depleted their ammunition stockpiles east of Vienna. We are deeply in debt to him for the marvelous job he did, under extremely trying circumstances. Rudi, excuse the interruption – please continue."

Rudi continued with his story, explaining how they converted the one gold ingot that had been hidden in the glass shop into smaller, easily concealed bars and how Andrew Henderson, whom he knew only as Nikolai, smuggled them into Austria during four separate trips.

Lattie raised her hand. She said, "Excuse me, Rudi." She reached into her pocket and withdrew the little bar and unwrapped its covering of white tissue paper. She said, "This is the last one of the one hundred and sixty little ingots that my husband smuggled into Austria for Rudi. I want you gentlemen to hold it in your hands and think about where it came from."

There were several moments of silence, broken only by the trill of a meadowlark off in the taller grass nearby. The little ingot passed from hand to hand around the table until it was returned to Lattie. She re-wrapped it in the tissue paper and returned it to her pocket.

"Please go on, Rudi," she said.

Rudi described how he didn't learn Nikolai's real identity until the morning of their attempted departure from Czechoslovakia and how he suffered an untimely death while riding a bicycle. He made the group understand his feelings of total helplessness for the next two days, while he did all he could for the man he had come to know as the only friend he had in the world outside his own family. And they heard how Andrew learned the story of the gold only the night before he died. The group sat spellbound as Rudi described how he entered Austria, evaded interception and reached St. Wolfgang. He briefly described his reunion with his brother and the rest of the group after they were able to cross into Austria from Hungary and their start of a new life in a free democracy. They shared his dismay recalling how the political situation in Czechoslovakia continued its decline as Russia continued to guide and assist its development of repressive totalitarianism.

Rudi went on to tell them how the machine shop prospered and how he finally shared his knowledge of the gold with his own family. He described how some of the money from the little gold bars was used to pay for deep diving lessons and for the equipment they'd need when the time came to verify the gold's location and subsequently remove it to a safe hiding place.

"Then," said Rudy, "My really big worries began. As time passed, I became increasingly concerned that the gold would somehow fall into the wrong hands and be used to start yet another Reich, or create a new drug empire, or even both. When this Saddam devil began killing his own people, I thought now is the time, but there was nobody I could turn to. It was easy to keep track of Andrew Henderson's family. I thought then, as I do today, that somehow they'll hold the key to the proper disposition of the gold. We must try to correct some of the wrongs that have been done to so many people."

"And so," concluded Rudi, "We got out all the gold. It is safe in the little chalet on the northeast shore of St. Wolfgangsee and will be safe there even if the house burns to the ground. Now, here we are together and we must decide what to do with it."

George cleared his throat and said, "Everett, I think perhaps it's time for you to tell your side of the story and what you have been doing for the past seven days."

Everett said, "The past week has provided absolutely the most fascinating – yet terrifying – days of my life. On a very secure line, I was able to have a conference call with the Ambassadors of Switzerland and Austria and with a man who represents a consortium of Jewish organizations that is located in Austria. I said to them, 'Gentlemen, we must play a game of what if.'

"'What if I could produce, in Austria, seven thousand, five hundred and thirty pounds, or one hundred nine thousand eight hundred Troy ounces, of nearly pure gold? Its worth would be on the order of thirty-two million US dollars. It came from the Holocaust. It'll fit in one small truck. What should be done with it?' And they said, as I expected, 'We'll get back to you.' And then, with the others listening, I reminded the Swiss ambassador that more than one government and an Austrian consortium of Jewish organizations, has been pushing the Swiss banks to hand over many millions of dollars of blood money. I used that very impolite term, blood money, because it was the harshest description I could imagine. And I added, 'Your Swiss bankers have been dragging their feet on this issue, sir. Dragging feet that are stuck in the mud of their own avarice and the mud of the perfidy that Switzerland has inherited.' I made myself sound very angry when I said it and I guess I really was. And he said again, 'Sir, I really will get back to you. By Thursday next.' And, he did."

Everett stopped and slowly took a swallow of his iced tea, which no longer had dewdrops coating the glass. He blotted his lips carefully with his napkin; his listeners were holding their breath. Rudi could stand it no longer; his face reddened, he took a deep breath and – just in time – Lisa placed her index finger gently across his mouth.

She asked, "And what did the Swiss ambassador say, Everett?"

Even Rudi joined in the laughter that rocked the table. Rudi said, "What a jewel is this daughter of mine, *ja?*"

"I'm sorry, everyone," said Everett. "I'm afraid I was enjoying the moment just a bit too much. Rudi, the three major Swiss banks that are involved are willing to accept the gold in your possession at ninety-nine point nine percent of its open-market value on the transfer date and, within a year from that date, will provide additional funds that are double that amount and make the first of several payments to the Jewish consortium that will total over one billion dollars."

A murmur of awe and appreciation swept around the table. Rudi rose from his chair, hugged Lisa, turned to Everett and hugged him unrestrainedly.

"That is wonderful, wonderful," he said. "When I was young and much more foolish than I am now, I had these dreams of preventing such a thing from ever happening again. What you'll be doing is making an apology to the world and to the people whose grandmothers and grandfathers died in the Holocaust. Never can the world allow such a thing to take place again."

"I understand, Rudi," Everett said, "but there must be no publicity of your part in it. The details of the actual transfer of the gold are still being worked out. They'll be looking for one of the quiet roads crossing from Austria into Liechtenstein."

Epilogue

1100 Sunday, June 21, 1998

Zohor, Republic of Slovakia

E_{pilogue}

Ten people clustered at the side of a narrow dirt road and looked at an ancient family cemetery, shaded on three sides by a forest of mature oak trees. It was roughly fenced with granite posts about a meter high. A wooden cross, nearly black with age, a protective roof sheltering a crucifix, bore the name "Jezocova" carved into a white ivory scroll. Several limestone grave markers, recently cleaned, stood in a cluster at the rear of the graveyard. Behind them stood a larger rectangular monument, about a meter tall.

Rudi Holder removed small bouquets of flowers, one by one, from the trunk of the first of two cars parked in the shade. He muttered a name to himself as he handed each bouquet to Lisa or Elaine. He closed the trunk.

He went over to Lattie and Stephen and said, "We'll go to Andrew's grave first." She took his arm as he led the way into the cemetery. The short grass was dotted with wild flowers, vibrant with color. The monument was a simple granite slab without a name. It had only a date – 15 February 1955. Latin words, incised deeply into the stone, spelled *E VERITAS PRELIATOR LIBERTAS*.

Lisa handed a small bouquet of red roses to Lattie; she smiled her thanks and placed the flowers at the base of the smooth granite slab. Wordlessly, she turned to Rudi and hugged him. He placed his arms on her shoulders.

"Lattie, he was a true fighter for freedom and I hope he

approves of what we have done for him and for all those other people."

She nodded, her face streaked with tears. Rudi released her and she turned to Stephen. He said, "Rudi, there are no words to thank you for your loyalty to this man and for your dedication to your principles." They shook hands.

Rudi cleared his throat. "Please, dear friends, let me tell you just a little something about these others here." He moved to the markers at the rear of the two rows and said, "In this row of five people, all are my family. Here is my grandfather, August Jezocova. He died in nineteen fifty-three and never knew that I was working for America, Stephen. Next to him is his wife, my grandmother. She died in the early summer of nineteen forty-five. She was very sick with tuberculosis, but really died from a broken heart, because of what happened at the glassworks."

Elaine placed a small bouquet at each of the markers.

Rudi moved to the next pair of markers. He said, "Beginning here, you'll see that each marker has the same date of death – May eighteen, nineteen forty-five. That's the day that the Major machine-gunned everyone in the glassworks while I was out in the courtyard hearing it happen. Here are my father and mother, Lukas and Sarah Jezocova. My mother was a wonderful artist in glass and my father made the business prosper before the war. He could do anything with his hands. He was strong, but not strong enough to turn away the bullets that killed him and the rest of the people in these two rows. The last marker in this row, here on the left, is my dear cousin Anne-Marie. She was such a pretty girl; her sweetheart died in the war but she never knew it. She made the most beautiful little animals from glass when it was red with heat. We always said she could stop gravity from pulling her little creatures out of shape. Actually, she made the pull of the earth do the last of the forming. She'd just watch as the heads of her little animals would come to just the right position as the color went out of the glass."

"Do you have any of her work, Rudi?" Elaine asked.

"Yes," answered Rudi. "Some of the villagers gave me several of her beautiful pieces. They are all back in our house – there are two for you, Elaine and a pair also for you, Lisa. I thought you might like them as one of your wedding presents from your old *Vati* who made you study so hard the English."

Moving to the front row, Rudi explained, "This first marker is the last of the direct family that died in the glassworks. Here is my cousin Silvie Jezocova. She was an artist with the diamond wheel and taught the others who went to Austria in nineteen fifty-five. It's her technique you see in the wineglasses I left with you. Silvie was several years older than I was and was the sister to Anne-Marie. Her husband was also killed in the war, but, like Anne-Marie, she never knew it. At least they are together now.

"And here -" pointing at the next three graves - "are the other people who died in the glassworks. They are not related, but we were all 'family,' so here they still lie together. The first is Sergé Hegrova, a genius with the blowing pipes and with the furnaces. He had a brilliant future ahead of him. He and my father talked about starting a new part of the business after the war – blowing special orders for chemical laboratories. He brought this next person, Mêlnik Tczebeki with him when my father hired some new help in nineteen thirty-nine. Mêlnik had a – *Klumpfuss* – umm. . ..Lisa?"

"It's called a clubfoot in English, *Vati*," offered Lisa.

"Yes, a clubfoot. It's why he wasn't taken in the army."

Rudi paused, looking into the past.

"And this last grave is Mêlnik's sweetheart, Gustina Hûsak, also a wonderful talent and imagination with the diamond wheels. She'd put a beautiful floral design on stemmed glasses so perfectly that you couldn't tell where she started and where she ended. But now he and Gustina are together, he's running like the wind through the flowers in Heaven, holding Gustina's hand and in the afternoons they are making beautiful stemware for God's tables."

As Rudi had explained each person's uniqueness and skills, Lisa and Elaine alternated placing one of the small bouquets at the foot of each marker.

"So, dear friends, that is the story of some of the people in this special little place. The last work they did on this earth was not to their liking, but we have now seen the end of it. I hope that they approve. Everything I have told you is written down and I have copies for you to take when you leave.

"Now, we have done much driving today and we have just one more stop to make to carry out a tradition that began hundreds of years ago. We'll continue down this old road, we'll pass our old family farm and we'll stop in another a couple of kilometers from here."

"Is there anything left in the old farmhouse, Rudi?" Bruce asked.

"Nothing at all. Only the house. I came back here again in nineteen fifty-seven and met the people who had purchased the house from the Gypsies who took it over after we abandoned it. The table my great-great-grandfather made was still there. The owners had heard the stories about the glassworks and when I offered to buy the table, they gave it to me, so I had it trucked to St. Wolfgang. We'll have breakfast on it tomorrow. They are nice people – they are the ones who keep the graveyard looking nice. After they lost their baby, they called and asked if they could bury her here. Of course I said 'yes' so now it's their family cemetery also."

The group split apart and got into the two cars. Bruce drove the first car, with Lisa at his side, while Robert followed with Rudi in the passenger seat. The driver/passenger positions had remained unchanged since they had left the chalet early that morning, while the others – Elsa, Georgi, Peter, Elaine, Stephen and Lattie played mix-and-match in the rear. It had turned into a wonderful time for the Holder and Henderson families to share their many overlapping memories; the Hendersons learned details of the gold recovery and the planning and trials that went into it, while the Holders heard how Robert and Bruce had developed their business and some of the adventures that they had encountered.

The Henderson entourage, with Lisa, had arrived in Munich two days earlier. Operations at the ranch had been left in the able hands of Tom and Hank. Rudi and Elsa had met them at the airport, each with a comfortable Mercedes. Lisa's reunion with her mother had been emotional and joyful; Elsa, petite and vivacious at sixty-three, had taken Bruce under her wing immediately, along with Lattie and Stephen. Peter, Georgi's son, had been waiting for them at the baggage carousels and had collected all the luggage tickets, saying,

"You'll please go on ahead. I'll follow you to the chalet as soon as I have collected all the bags. My son, Andreas, is just outside with our car and will help me."

Since their arrival time was rather early in the morning, like most east-bound trans-Atlantic flights, the first day had been spent mostly resting and enjoying the afternoon sun on the lawn in front of the chalet. For dinner, Rudi had arranged for a small banquet-room at the Hotel "Im Weissen Rössel" in St. Wolfgang. It had been a special occasion for Lisa. She leaned close to Bruce and said, "When I was sixteen, I worked here in the summer as a waitress. *Vati* said it was a good place to hear and speak English. It's such a pretty place; I always dreamed of coming here with you on our wedding night. Surprise, sweetheart, that's what we're going to do in three more days! I know in America, it's the man's job to take care of these arrangements, but I didn't think you'd mind doing it the Holder way."

Bruce had responded, "You made all the arrangements for the wedding so far, why should I object? It looks like a great place. Do they have room service? We may not want to get out of bed for a day or so. . .."

She had grinned and patted his thigh, saying, "Maybe longer."

Smiling to himself at the memory of that moment, Bruce heard Lisa say to Lattie in the back seat, "This little hilltop is where Andrew had his last few moments. We'll stop down the road in just little bit. Bruce, pull over to the left side of the road and stop where you see the little white cross on the right side." Bruce spotted the cross about a hundred meters ahead, activated his left turn signal, pulled to the left side of the road and parked. The second car stopped just behind him. Rudy came up and opened the rear door for Lattie as Stephen emerged from the other side of the car.

The rest of the party gathered around Rudi. Lattie, between Rudi and Stephen, held each by an arm. Rudi said, "The morning sun was just above the trees and was shining right in our eyes. Nikolai – sorry, Andrew – crested the little rise there, saw this little downhill, pedaled hard, turned to me and was laughing and didn't see a pothole just about where we are standing. The front wheel collapsed; he went over very fast and very hard. It was immediate. He and I spent our last nights together in the woods over there, about fifty meters behind the little cross. You know the rest. After the Slovakian Republic was formed and travel across borders was no longer a problem, I made the little cross. The people back at the farm keep it painted and also the name – just 'Nikolai' – and the date – 15 February 1955. Not many people come this way and nobody here knows the story."

Lisa, who had been holding the last little bouquet, handed it to Rudi. He started towards the little cross, but Lattie held him back. "Let me do it," she half-whispered. "You've already done so much."

She walked across the road; Rudi and Stephen followed closely. She bent over, smoothed away the wisps of grass that crept up the cross and placed the bouquet there at its foot. She stood erect and gazed into the woods behind the cross. "I can't imagine how you were able to get through the nights here, Rudi," she said. "Thank you for everything."

"I did all I could, Lattie," said Rudi. "There is nothing to see now, back there in the woods; *Mutter Natur* has taken over, because we moved Andrew to his final resting place in nineteen ninety-two and everything was filled and smoothed over."

"And now," continued Rudi, "Elsa and I'll do the driving, as we'll go directly to Vienna for a late mid-day meal. Then, we return to St. Wolfgang and the chalet, where we'll watch the young men prepare for tomorrow morning's adventures."

* * * * *

St. Wolfgang, Austria
0715 Monday, June 22, 1998

The chalet hummed with activity. Earlier in the morning, while the Holders and Hendersons were having an Austrian breakfast – crusty rolls called *Semel*, cheese, butter, sliced cold meats, fresh fruit and coffee, noises came from the ground floor. It was a continual clanking, hammering and imprecations directed towards a certain father and grandfather who had "placed "too much concrete in the hole." As they finished their breakfast, Peter and young Andreas, his son, came upstairs.

They announced, "the concrete was difficult to break up,

but we have done it. The cover plate is exposed and we have screwed in the lifting eyes. We are ready to hoist it out."

Georgi asked, "Is the truck ready, all cleaned, full of petrol, the oil OK, the pallet ready and the truck ready to park at the door?"

"Ja, Grossvater, alles in Ordnung", replied Andreas. "Excuse me;" he continued in English, "I forgot to be speaking your language. That was impolite of me. Yes, Grandfather, everything's OK, just as you asked."

"The army escort will be here in an hour," added Peter, "and I checked with the Swiss bank representatives; they stayed in town last night. I gave them a map and asked that they be here at seven-thirty, or even a little before."

Rudi said, "we'll wait until the Swiss are here also, so they can see that nothing has been disturbed when we pull up the cover plate. We might as well go downstairs."

Single file, everyone followed Rudi down to the ground floor and over to the corner, where there were signs of recent clean-up of concrete chunks and dust. A large rug, rolled up, lay against one wall. A small sump pump, still dripping water on the bared concrete floor, lay off to one side.

Because the ground under the chalet sloped from the front to the rear, there were two entrances at "ground level" – one at the front of the building and one at the rear, facing the lake. The only windows on the ground floor were on the rear of the building, so nobody happened to notice the arrival of a dark blue BMW until it came down the driveway and parked on the grass next to the truck. It bore Swiss "ZH" license tags, indicating Zurich registry.

Elsa was the first to see them. She said, "Look – here are your Swiss friends."

Georgi produced a revolver, concealed it behind his back and leaned against the inside wall. Rudi stood in the doorway. Three strangers were just closing the doors of their car.

"Good morning, gentlemen; if you're who I believe you should be, you have come to the right place. Please, come into our little cottage."

The three men, dressed in conservative black suits, white shirts and plain black neckties, looked a bit out of place. Andreas, speaking in Czech, said softly, "It looks like the penguins got out of the zoo." Stifled chuckles resounded,

Robert, responding in Czech, said, "Andreas, you and my son Hank will get along famously."

The oldest of the three visitors was the first to enter the cellar. Elsa stepped forward and introduced herself and asked, "Would you gentlemen like some coffee this morning?"

"Thank you, no, but perhaps a bit later. Good morning to all of you. We should introduce ourselves and perhaps, under the circumstances, also offer positive identification. Here are our passports and letters of introduction from our employers in Zurich."

Rudi took the passports and without looking at them, handed them to Lisa, who opened them and compared the photos with the solemn faces of the visitors.

Robert stepped forward and, speaking in German, said, "Gentlemen, also under the circumstances, I must ask you if you object to our examining each of you for weapons."

The visitors looked at each other and smiled; "Naturally. One cannot be too cautious."

Elaine stepped forward as all three men spread their arms obligingly. She went behind the first man, quickly felt his ankles with one foot and patted his armpits, reached around and felt his waist and the small of his back. She circled to his front and felt each forearm. The process was completed in seconds. She repeated the process on the other two men.

"Well done, young lady; you have done that before," said the youngest man. Elaine merely smiled.

"And now," directed Rudi, "please place your briefcases on the floor and push them out of reach with your feet." They complied, eyes darting at each other. Lisa picked up two briefcases and carried them to a table. Elaine picked up the third and followed Lisa. None were locked. A quick look confirmed that all three men were unarmed. Peter, who had stepped outside during Elaine's body search, returned quietly.

"The car is also clean," he announced.

Rudi's keen eyes watched the procedure closely. He relaxed visibly as Elaine stepped away from the table and Lisa returned the passports to the visitors. Turning to the table, he picked up three documents and handed one to each of the Swiss.

He said, "Gentlemen, we can now proceed. This is a listing of the gold ingots we are about to retrieve. Their weight and serial numbers appear. They'll be removed in numerical sequence, because that's how we placed them – in storage, as it were, in nineteen seventy-three. It'll take us a few minutes to open the vault, which has been sealed all this time. What is your pleasure?"

The older gentleman responded, "I believe it'll be adequate for us to confirm the serial numbers and to verify the total quantity. An examination will be conducted, of course, by our bank's assessors, but that should be a formality. We have seen this configuration before."

"I'm sure you have, gentlemen," said Rudi, unable to suppress just a hint of sarcasm.

"Let me suggest the following. We have prepared a shallow wooden crate that will receive three layers of sixty bars. The crate is on a wooden pallet that, in turn, is placed on a roller conveyor. Steel strapping will keep the crate from shifting during the trip. We also have partitioning material to separate each ingot and each layer. This is all in readiness in the cargo compartment of the truck that you saw outside. We'll back the truck close to the door. One of us will be outside at all times to insure that there'll be no interruption to our work. It might be easiest if two of you stay with the truck to supervise the packing. When it's complete, you may place your own lock – you brought one?" Both men nodded, the youngest man pointed at his briefcase in answer.

"This will be hard work, but also will not last very long. Each bar weighs about twenty kilos. We'll form a line and pass them along. We'll now open the last barrier, which is a water seal. The vault was opened only this morning after we pumped out the water that was above the gold. Feel free to take off your coats, gentlemen."

Rudi nodded at Andreas, who picked up a pry bar and placed it in a ring with a hook. Eye-bolts had been turned into threaded holes in the aluminum plate; short bolts, which had protected those threads from concrete, having been removed as part of the earlier preparations. A chain, with carabiners at each end, connected the eye bolts. Andreas placed his pry bar under the chain and used the opposite wall of the sump as a fulcrum. One heave and the rubber water seal was broken and Andreas lifted out the plate, then a piece of cardboard. His eyes widened.

"It's really here," he said.

Rudi chuckled. "My grand-nephew is such a person for jokes. I really expected him to say, 'There's nothing there, Uncle Rudi.' You can all take a look, then we'll go to work."

Everyone laughed, the tension broken. The youngest of the visitors took a small camera from his briefcase. He said, "We would like to document the process."

"Fine," responded Rudi, "but please do not show any part of any person, or any part of this building except the hole in the floor. I'd rather just give you a picture that I took before we closed it up." The visitor put his camera back in his briefcase and said, "There's really no need for pictures, I suppose."

The sound of the truck's engine starting up came to their ears. Georgi had propped the door open and backed the truck to it, leaving just enough space for people to get in and out of the ground floor. He called in to Bruce, "Perhaps you could take a look in the hole, then come and enjoy the view of the lake. We'll change the outside duty from time to time."

Bruce came to the door; Georgi handed the revolver to him.

"Please, just keep your eyes open. We do not expect any difficulty."

Bruce looked at the revolver; it was a Smith and Wesson .38 Special. He spun the cylinder; six bright copper eyes gleamed out at him. He slid it under his belt.

In the basement room, there had been a steady procession of sight-seers; the bright flash of the gold held them in thrall and they turned away, one at a time, obviously subdued. The older visitor climbed up the wooden step Georgi had placed behind the truck; Elsa handed a clipboard to him with the documents and he sat on a stool by the open box.

Lattie said, "I think this work will be a bit heavy for me, so I believe I'll sit down and watch." Stephen nodded assent and joined her.

"The rest of us, we should spread out between the hole and the truck and one of you should get in the truck to do the final placement," Rudi directed. "You'll stack the gold in the box making ten rows across, three rows in the long direction, thirty per layer, 6 layers deep. We'll nail the top on the box after all the gold is in place and then we'll band it. Be careful that you don't pinch your fingers. Andreas is the youngest and the strongest, so he'll do the initial lifting."

A second visitor followed the first into the truck body, sat on another stool and took a pen out of his pocket.

Rudi sat in a chair next to Andreas and looked down along the line. He assured himself that everyone was in position to receive, turn and hand off the ingots.

"Begin in the upper left corner, my boy," he said to Andreas. "Always work left to right, just as if you were reading a book. Your father will supervise the same sequence in the box in the truck."

Andreas adjusted a foam pad placed in readiness for the operation, knelt on it and reached down into the hole.

"Oh. How cold it is," he said. "Uh . . . and heavy also."

He handed the bar up to Rudi, who held it aloft. "This is the cold of death, my boy. This is the weight of sadness and grief that a madman and his even madder hirelings inflicted on innocent people who have been persecuted and abused since centuries."

There was absolute stillness – almost reverence – in the room as each bar passed silently from hand to hand. Rudi, eyes half-closed, counted in muttered Czech.

"One, two, three, my dear Major, four, is the Devil laughing at you now, five, six, you putrid Colonel, seven, you were so weak in spirit, seven, that you let – eight – your underling trample your soul also – nine – under his dirty feet – ten – eleven – and you did his job – twelve – so poorly that I am here – thirteen – because you closed your eyes – fourteen – when you shot me – fifteen – you couldn't look me in the eye – sixteen. . .." his voice trailed off and he just counted.

As the thirtieth bar came out of the little vault, Rudi laid a hand on Andreas' shoulder.

"We'll stop for a bit, as they'll have to put the board on the top of that layer. Everyone, let's take a little rest. I told you it would be hard work." Andreas got to his feet and stretched.

Georgi went to the door and called to Bruce, "If it's chilly out there, you can come in for a few minutes and get warmed up." Bruce answered, "Gladly," and handed the revolver to Georgi as they changed places. Georgi spun the cylinder, watching the bright copper bullets resting in their chambers, then put it under his belt and buttoned his light jacket.

Rudi went to the truck to check on how first layer had been set up. "Exactly right," he observed. "Are they coming too fast, or anything?"

"No problem," said the older Swiss. "I saw that I was to start at the bottom of the list and work my way up." He handed the list to Rudi, who observed a neat row of check-marks next to the last thirty numbers. He returned the clipboard. Georgi, standing on the step, reached in and placed a piece of plywood over the layer of ingots.

"Four minutes of work, then three minutes of rest," announced Rudi. "Six times. Everybody ready? They'll start coming slower because it'll be harder for Andreas – ready, Andreas?"

And so the operation continued; the outside assignment rotating between Bruce, Peter and Robert. The passage of forty minutes seemed to occur in far less time; as the last ingot left each person's hands, they followed it to its companions in the box.

Georgi went into the truck, hammer in hand. One last layer of heavy cardboard concealed the contents and he nailed the cover in place. He picked up a piece of pre-cut steel strapping and laced it under the conveyor rollers closest to the box and, using a strapping tool, cinched it tightly and crimped a steel splicer around the bands where they overlapped on the box top. After repeating the process on the other side of the box, he collected his tools, jumped down from the truck, closed the rear doors, lifted the tailgate and latched it.

He nodded to the younger visitor. "It's all yours."

The visitor opened his briefcase, took out a padlock, passed its shackle through the hasp of the rear doors and snapped it closed. "My associate in Liechtenstein has the only key," he said.

"Now," offered Elsa, "You have your choice of either coffee or a cold drink. The sun is well up and we've all been working hard. Let's enjoy this morning. We all have a fairly long drive ahead of us."

The group dispersed and seated themselves at one of the three round tables between the chalet and the lake. Elsa and Lisa brought trays with coffee cups and an assortment of pastry. Andreas, now in swim trunks, jogged past the group and plunged into the water. He swam briskly out for a hundred meters, dove and emerged after swimming underwater towards shore for forty or fifty meters.

"Andreas has quite a set of lungs," observed Bruce.

"Yes, he does," answered Peter. "He swims like a fish and has received his certification as a deep diver. He and I have a diving school operation that will be quite an asset for him as time goes on. Uncle Rudi and my father haven't dived since the gold was recovered, but I've stayed with it. Andreas has an idea of being a marine biologist – he knows every fish by its Latin name. He's only twenty-one and will be in his third year of college this September."

Two Austrian Army personnel carriers stopped in front of the chalet, then backed into the driveway. Each carried four people – an officer, a driver and two grenadiers. All wore body armor and side arms and the gunners carried Oerlikon 10.5 mm assault weapons. Bruce noted the time: 0800.

The senior officer, a Major, came up to Rudi and shook his hand. "I trust our paint job on your remarkable vehicle is satisfactory, Herr Holder?"

"Absolutely, Major Baumann. I'd think it was one of yours, with the antenna and those letters and numbers on the bumpers. Would you and your men enjoy some coffee and snacks before we start our journey?"

"I'm sure we would. Are all these people to be in our convoy?"

"No, it'll just be myself driving the truck and my brother, Georgi. We'll alternate driving. Most of these people will meet us at the border as observers."

The younger Swiss said, "The blue BMW here will follow the convoy, Herr Major. Not closely, but we'll have you in sight."

"Fine, sir. Herr Holder. I have camouflage jackets and pants for you both to wear – that way, you'll be invisible to any observers – just another couple of Reservists out spending our tax dollars." The driver of the second vehicle handed two combat uniforms, neatly pressed, to Rudi. A second man handed over two rather bulky vests.

The Major explained, "This is body armor, Herr Holder. We very much prefer that you and your brother wear them, both for appearances' sake and for practical reasons. They are hot and not very comfortable, but there'll be a nice breeze with the windshield partly open. When we drove your vehicle, we saw that it's well maintained and capable of highway speeds. We have three preplanned fuel and rest stops between here and . . .our objective. As soon as you change your clothes, we'll be on our way. At this point, I am the only one who knows our destination. My men are prepared to be away for two days. We don't want to know what the nature of your cargo is, but you should know that we are prepared to protect it – and you – with our own lives."

Rudi and Georgi took the garments and disappeared into the chalet.

"Very impressive, Herr Major," said the older Swiss. What time do you expect to be at our destination?"

"We'll drive approximately five hundred and forty kilometers. It's almost totally autobahn travel. If we depart from here in the next fifteen minutes, we should arrive at the transfer point not earlier than 1545 – it's six straight hours of driving, we'll have three stops of a quarter hour each and a change of drivers and guards at the second stop. Should it concern you, each of these men is under my direct command and I have known each of them personally for years. The other officer – Lieutenant Hapsburg – and I'll be with you for the entire trip. Also, we'll be in radio contact with the other drivers as soon as we are close to Innsbruck. Also, at any time, we can be in discreet communications via cell phones."

"As can we. I suggest that we exchange cell phone numbers now," said the Swiss. He brought out a small note-pad; the Major did the same; each scribbled a number on their pad, ripped out the page and exchanged it with his opposite. The Swiss took a cell phone from his breast pocket, looked at the number he had just been given, tapped in those numbers and waited. Shortly, the ringing of a cell phone was heard. The major and the lieutenant each retrieved their cell phones, which continued to ring.

The major said, "I'll answer, Lieutenant," flipped open the mouthpiece and said, "Good morning."

The Swiss responded, "Call me right back," terminated the connection and waited. The Major repeated the sequence his Swiss counterpart had initiated; the Swiss cell phone rang, the Swiss said "Thank you" into the mouthpiece and put his phone away.

"Thank you for doing that, sir'" said the Major; "I would have done that in any event, but I'm glad you did it first. I am reassured that the Swiss are as thorough as their reputation proclaims." They laughed together – politely.

Bruce said to Elaine, "You know, Sis, that's done easier here than it would be for me to do in New Jersey. All Europe has one standard for cell communications – no roaming, no hidden fees that surprise you. We didn't have the sense to do that from the outset and now we are headed for quagmire. It's also why we rent cell phones in Europe – ours won't function here."

Rudi and Georgi appeared, looking very military. "Very nice, except for the boots, gentlemen. They could do with a touch – no, more than a touch, I'm afraid, of black polish. Are we ready?"

Rudi swung into the driver's seat of the truck that was so familiar to him and started the engine; Georgi got into the passenger seat; Elsa came over and kissed Rudi. "I know that you and your cargo are in good hands. Drive carefully, old man."

The major got into his vehicle, both military vehicles purred into life and the little convoy left the chalet, wisps of dust hanging in the air as they swung left towards St. Wolfgang and the autobahn entrance. The Swiss BMW followed shortly.

"Well, people," said Lisa, "while they have a six hour drive, it'll be about four hours for us. I have the directions to the transfer point and we'll have time for a lunch stop at the top of the Alburg Pass. We'll leave the Autobahn in St. Anton so you can see the mountains. My mother has already packed the lunch and we should leave within a half hour. You'll all want a warm jacket, as it can be cool at the summit of the pass. I'll drive the first car; Robert, you can follow in the second – all right?"

* * * * *

1450 Monday, June 22, 1998
Southeast of Feldkirch, Austria

A Mercedes sedan, bearing Swiss ZH plates, pulled off the narrow dirt road into a field where a dark blue BMW waited. The field was packed firmly from many vehicles – apparently, it was used as a temporary parking spot for drivers waiting for the obscure border crossing to be operational. A sign, fastened to the red and white gate extending across the roadway, read *"Nur für Militarische Lastwagen"* – indicating that the border crossing was accessible only for either Swiss or Austrian army vehicles. The gate marking the border was locked in the "down" position, symbolically blocking the road.

A uniformed Swiss colonel and a civilian got out of the Mercedes and came over to the BMW, which contained three men. They appeared not to know each other, as there was hand-shaking and introductions to the civilians who were waiting.

The officer said, "Our vehicles are due here in a few minutes. I'll get our side of the gate unlocked." He walked a few steps over to the gate and produced a key attached to a large aluminum tag. He looked at two padlocks that secured the gate; selecting one, he inserted the key, unlocked it and placed the padlock on a hook welded to the gate. As he returned to the civilian vehicles, two more Mercedes sedans pulled into the field. "It's beginning to look like a high-end used car lot," observed the Swiss officer to his companion.

The sound of engines signaled the arrival of two three-vehicle military convoys, from opposite directions – one Austrian, one Swiss. The Swiss vehicles stopped at the gate; the lead vehicle of the Austrian contingent pulled in to the field. The Austrian major got out of the personnel carrier, went to the barrier, unlocked the remaining padlock and raised the gate. He pointed at Rudy, who was driving his truck and directed him to turn in and park. The Swiss officer signaled to the first Swiss vehicle in line to come forward into

288

"I have only one wish, Everett," said Rudi. "It's a very simple one. Let's use my truck – it's excellent condition. Georgi and I designed and built it for one thing only – to help us get the gold out of the lake. And I'm not so old that I can't drive it for the last time. Two times I have counted those bars – the first when I dropped them into that cold, dark water and again after we took them out. I must watch them pass through my hands for the third – and last – time."

Austria and back his vehicle towards Rudi's truck.

Rudi and Georgi got out of the truck; they waved at the two Mercedes, signaling the occupants to join him. It was quite a contingent – Bruce, who had been driving the first vehicle; Lisa, Elsa and Lattie. From the second Mercedes came Robert, with Elaine, Peter and Stephen. In the meantime, the three civilians from the BMW and the Swiss officer and his companion came over to the group.

The officer said, "We are the strangers here, as I understand you people were all together earlier today. I hope you all had a pleasant trip; it has been a beautiful day to travel."

The civilian, who had arrived with the Swiss officer, looked at the new arrivals. He said, "I know these three gentlemen from Zurich; it's very nice to see you again." They shook hands. The civilian turned to the Austrian group and asked, "Now, which one of you would be Herr Rudi Holder?"

"I am," replied Rudi and you're. . . ?"

"I am Walther Brand, sir and I am humbled to be the representative of the consortium of the organizations who are about to benefit from what you have successfully brought here today." Rudi saw that the man was wearing a beautifully embroidered yarmulke – the small skullcap worn by orthodox Jews. "Now," continued Brand, "I would like to meet your companions, Herr Holder, all who have contributed in some way to the reason we are here." The Austrians and Americans came forward and introduced themselves to Brand.

The oldest of the trio of bankers said, "I believe we can dispense with the formalities of positive identification. Should anyone desire to see them, we each have our passports and letters from our respective financial houses. You and I talked on the telephone yesterday, Mr. Brand and I said that if I said the word 'reparations,' that you would respond with. . .."

"Are long overdue," Mr. Brand said.

"Thank you, Mr. Brand. Everything is in order and as soon as the vehicles from both sides are prepared, the transaction will proceed. With us, we have twenty-eight bonds, in various amounts, to hand over to you. Each is made out in the name of the organization that you transmitted to us by fax a few days ago. Each is complete except for the signature of each institution's final approving authority. Giving these to you now is symbolic of the commitment of Switzerland's banking community and they'll become legal documents upon qualification of the collateral, which we'll expedite. We expect to have a quiet signing ceremony for you to attend within four working days."

The group walked over to the two trucks, parked back-to-back, about four meters separating them. Rudi noticed that there was a height difference in of the bed of the two trucks – his was several inches lower than the Swiss.

To the driver – a Swiss sergeant – he said, "You have the roller conveyor sections inside? And a place to attach a pulley?"

"Yes, everything should work out. What should I call you? You have no rank insignia."

"That's because I'm not in the Austrian military, sergeant. Call me Rudi, please. The major here wanted me to look like a soldier just for today. Anybody who took a close look would see that I'm a bit overage."

The sergeant smiled and said, "It looks like he wanted to keep you alive, anyway." He prodded Rudi's chest lightly with his fingers. "We had to wear the same stinky suits today also. I didn't think this was an Austrian military vehicle, but it would fool most people. Looks like quite a machine."

"Thank you. It has served us well over the years. It was an American army three-quarter ton truck originally and we did some modifications," answered Rudi.

Mr. Brand, standing next to Rudi, said, "Rudi, I am so pleased to meet you. I have the utmost admiration for you and for what you have accomplished." They shook hands again.
"Thank you, Herr Brand," answered Rudi, "I'll be very glad to have this 'accomplishment' out of my hands. You do know its history?"

"Most certainly, Herr Holder, most certainly. I was told that you were involved in its . . umm – conversion. And that you lost several family members at the end of the process. I am so sorry, Herr Holder."

"Yes, it was that loss that set me on this course. But look at what I have gained – these American friends and that pretty girl there – my daughter – will marry him" – pointing at Bruce

– "tomorrow."

The older banker called out, "Ladies, gentlemen, are we ready to proceed?"

Rudi looked around; he saw that the Austrian soldiers and their Swiss counterparts had deployed into a circle, facing outwards. About fifteen meters separated each man; they held their weapons in an attitude of readiness. Bruce, Robert, Elaine, Lattie and Stephen, with Elsa, Georgi and Peter Holder, were clustered on one side of the opening between the trucks. On the other side, the Swiss bankers stood expectantly as the youngest took a key from Mr. Brand and unlocked the rear door of Rudi's truck. Rudi and Georgi stepped forward, lowered the tailgate, opened the doors and motioned the Swiss sergeant to bring his vehicle closer. When about eight feet separated the vehicles, Rudi signaled the driver to stop.

The sergeant turned the engine off, came to the rear and lowered the tailgate. He said to Rudi, "How can I help?"

Rudi reached in his truck and removed a pulley with a hook and said, "Hang this up front somewhere. It'll see a thousand kilos of pull because the package has to go uphill."

Climbing nimbly into the rear of his truck, Rudi picked up a coil of nylon rope and handed one end to Georgi, who handed it to the sergeant as he said, "Thread the rope through the pulley and give me back the end."

While the sergeant was doing this, Georgi pulled three roller conveyor sections from the Swiss truck and placed them against the similar sections under the pallet in the Austrian vehicle. He laid their other ends on the Swiss truck's bed, leaving about a meter angling upwards inside. The sergeant needed no further instruction; he placed the remaining conveyor section in line with the sections which ramped up from the Austrian truck. In the meantime, Rudi had cut the steel banding that secured the box and its pallet, to the rollers. The box and pallet showed no inclination to move, even when Rudi pushed it a little. As Georgi pulled the rope, Rudi fed slack from the coil. Rudi took the rope, passed it around the rear of the box, while Georgi tied a loop in the rope. He handed a carabiner to Georgi, who hooked it into the loop he had just tied. Then Georgi took out all the slack in the rope end coming from the box and tied it to the carabiner.

The sergeant observed the procedure closely from the other side of the conveyors. He commented, "I see that you gentlemen know how to tie mountaineers' knots that can be untied easily – even after they've been heavily loaded."

Georgi smiled back and said, "We've done this before, but the rope was wet."

Rudi adjusted the position of the rope around the box, placing it a few inches above the pallet's top surface. He then passed a turn around the winch's capstan and pulled out all the slack, then passed two more turns around the capstan. Holding the coiled rope in one hand, he sat on the bed of the truck and eased himself onto the ground.

"Everybody ready?" he asked. He put on a pair of heavy gloves, switched on the winch and took up the strain. Immediately, the box quivered and began to move ponderously. It moved easily along the rollers until the pallet came to the Swiss roller section, where it had to transition to the uphill slope – about ten degrees of angle. The winch groaned in protest; Rudi took off the strain he was holding, as Georgi reached in to the truck and took out two pry bars. He handed one across to the sergeant.

"It needs a little help here," he said the sergeant.

As Rudi again took up the strain, the two men lifted the leading end of the pallet with their bars, using the rails of the conveyors as a fulcrum. The load lurched up onto the first set of rolls and stopped at the next. They repeated the process until the leading edge of the pallet was supported on the third rollers in the sloping sections. Georgi placed a short board behind the pallet and Rudi let off the tension and turned off the winch.

"Now," said Georgi, "we'll brace the bridging conveyor sections." From his truck, Rudi handed down three sturdy sawhorses about a meter tall, three long planks, three short square lengths of wood and three hydraulic jacks. Each sawhorse, resting on the long planks, was placed at the mid-point of the bridging conveyors. A hydraulic jack was placed on the center of each sawhorse's heavy crossbar and Georgi pumped up the piston of the center jack until it approached the underside of the conveyor. Then he inserted one of the square pieces between the piston and the underside of the conveyor rails and pumped the jack until it began to lift the far end of the bridging conveyor. Seeing the process, the sergeant imitated it on his side, while Georgi repeated the sequence on the near side.

Georgi nodded at Rudi again; Rudi switched on the winch and again took a strain on the rope. The two men on the ground continued to assist the transition from the level to sloped conveyor sections until the load was fully supported on the bridging conveyors. Then, the load moved easily. There was some slight settling of the saw-horses as the load crossed the mid-point of the opening and the Austrian truck began to lift itself as the load slowly transferred to the Swiss vehicle. As Rudi continued to take in the rope, the leading edge of the pallet passed the end of the Swiss truck. Georgi picked up the short piece of wood from the rear of Rudi's truck and placed it behind the pallet; Rudi slowly released tension and the loaded pallet stopped on the grade with the rope hanging slack. The Swiss truck settled as the load transferred to it.

Georgi said to the sergeant, "When the center of the box passes over the end of your truck, these bridging conveyors are going to go down onto your floor. Please make sure that there is room for them and that your other sections aren't in the way. You and I'll hold the bridging conveyors under control. Be sure to hold them from underneath, so that if Rudi decides to let go of the rope, the box won't roll back downhill and crush your hands."

The sergeant climbed into his truck and adjusted the conveyor sections on the floor. *"Ist Spiel genug,"* he said – "There's enough room. What does this load weigh, anyhow?"

"About three thousand four hundred kilos," responded Georgi casually.

"Mein Gott!" the sergeant exploded. "In such a little box…" His voice trailed off and he hopped down and stood across from Georgi, who nodded to Rudi. The box… moved upward slowly; Georgi removed the wood stop from the rollers and tossed it into the Austrian truck as he said to the sergeant, "You shouldn't need this at your end, if you unload the pallet with a fork truck."

The ramp conveyors gave a lurch and began to swing to

the horizontal position; Georgi and the sergeant steadied them with their hands. Now level, the box moved easily again; as it cleared the sloping conveyors, Georgi picked them up and slid them into the Swiss truck. Rudi brought the pallet and its load to a stop in the center of the Swiss truck. The sergeant climbed back into his truck, removed the pulley, unclipped the carabiner from the loop and easily removed the rope from around the box. He handed it to Georgi, who said, "We'll untie everything later" as he passed it to Rudi, who placed the rope coil in his vehicle. Georgi then took the strapping binder and two pieces of steel strapping and climbed into the Swiss truck; he and the sergeant secured the box to the conveyor sections.

"There," said Rudi, "as long as you don't try to beat a Porsche getting away from a stop light, you'll have no problem." They chuckled and shook hands.

Rudi and Georgi placed the jacks, sawhorses and wood pieces into their truck, shut and latched the rear doors and raised the tailgate and chained it closed.

The sergeant looked out at the perimeter guards and looked at his colonel, who nodded. He whistled, jabbed a pointed finger at the two nearest soldiers, who came at a run. They climbed into the Swiss truck; the colonel came up to them and said quietly, "Load your weapons after the radioman is aboard." The soldiers nodded. The sergeant lifted the tailgate and secured it, while the soldiers unrolled the canvas end curtain and tied it in place. "We made an alteration to the rear flap – we cut a couple of windows in it and sewed clear plastic in the openings," explained the sergeant. "We were told to be able to observe to our rear by our platoon officer and our colonel told us to make sure the back flap was kept closed – so we can do both."

"Good thinking, sergeant," the Swiss officer chuckled. "I suspect we'll see more modifications like this. Gentlemen, we are ready to move out," he added turning to the group of civilians.

Handing his briefcase to the younger banker, the Swiss spokesman said, "Mr. Holder, would you and your family please step forward?" Rudi, Georgi, Hilda, Peter and Lisa complied.

"Mr. and Mrs. Oakes, we would like for you to join the Holders." Stephen and Lattie did as requested, looking at each other, eyebrows raised in wonder.

"It's just a small gesture, but we thought that it would be meaningful to each of you if we made a little ceremony out of this moment. In exchange for what has just transpired, I have here" – he turned to the younger man who was holding the briefcase open – "the bundle of certificates that I mentioned a few moments ago. In deference to our American observers – and I am pleased to note that there are no government employees among them – nor any American politicians – I will state that these bonds, when formalized in a few days – will have an aggregate total value of roughly thirty-two million, four hundred and fifty-seven thousand United States dollars, the expected value of the contents of this Swiss vehicle as of the close of business in Zurich today. Perhaps you'll accept these documents, Herr Holder and let them pass through each of the hands that have allowed this event to transpire and deliver them to Mr. Brand.

"Feel free to look at them, as perhaps they'll allow you some comprehension of what you have accomplished. I must also comment on the inexcusable attitude of our banking system with respect to honoring those individuals who, in good faith, made deposits in our banks in the period of nineteen forty through nineteen forty five and were subsequently denied access to their money. Most of those fortunate people – I say fortunate because they survived the war – were subsequently impoverished by our actions and only recently have we begun to extensively search to find any survivors. Mr. Brand's organizations have been and will continue to be extremely helpful to us as we try to make amends."

He handed the bundle to Rudi, who by now was weeping openly. He handed them to Georgi, who simply handed them to Elsa and put his arms around his younger brother. Elsa just handed the bundle to Lisa. With Peter looking on, she slowly leafed through the pile and passed each document to Peter, who collected them and handed them to Lattie. She looked at the topmost document, shook her head and handed them to Stephen, who turned to Mr. Brand.

Mr. Brand said, "It's my turn for a short speech. I must say that I'll never, never comprehend the sequence of events that have allowed this transaction to become reality. To the Holder family, we owe a debt of gratitude for your ability to carry out your ideals. Only your honesty and diligence in achieving a worthy goal is the reason that today's events have transpired. I understand that you had no way of assisting in the development of freedom in your native Czechoslovakia and that history overtook you when Communism quietly subsided and the Czechs and Slovaks found that they could go peacefully, each in its own way and suddenly, you had no use for the gold. Now, it has become the catalyst that has resulted in the Swiss banking system realizing that its previous actions were not in the best interests of its customers, regardless of their racial or ethnic origins.

"Mr. Oakes, here is a list of the Jewish organizations that have allowed me to be their representative and the amounts they'll receive. We respectfully appreciate your part in this situation. As a retired member of one of America's oft-reviled security agencies, your contacts in the American government and their subsequent ability to keep this development out of the media's grasp, are nothing short of fantastic. Thank you. There are copies for each person having an interest in this transaction. Now, I am going to bow my head in silence for a few moments and reflect on the source of this treasure."

After a few moments of quiet; Mr. Brand said, "Thank you, everyone." Handshakes, wishes for safe journeys, for good luck and expressions of admiration followed. Bruce hugged Lisa and said, "Your father and uncle make a great team; they know how to get a job done quickly and easily, don't they?"

The Swiss colonel said, "We'll be on our way shortly. Sergeant, bring in your detail." The sergeant gave a short whistle, waved his hand above his head in a circular motion and the Swiss in the security detail jogged to their trucks. The sergeant saluted his colonel and said, "The lead vehicle will wait for you, sir." He saluted the Austrian major and shook the hands of Rudi and Georgi.

He said, "I'd like to do this again sometime. Maybe I'd learn what happened today. Drive safely!" And, with a wave, he was into his truck, started the engine and moved through the barrier. The other Swiss vehicles came into Austria just far enough to circle around; one went to the head of the convoy, while the other positioned itself behind the vehicle with the gold. The Swiss soldiers climbed aboard, the colonel closed the barrier and locked it with both padlocks. He tossed a salute at the Austrian major, held up two fingers, ducked under the barrier and jogged to the lead vehicle. Then, with a muffled roar and the smell of diesel exhaust, they were gone.

Elsa went to Rudi and handed him a bundle of clothes. "Why don't you and your brother get into the back of the truck and put these on? You can't go to supper with us while you're playing soldier, you know."

The Austrian major said, "Thank you, Frau Holder. Rudi, we'll drive your vehicle back to *Riedenburger Kaserne* in Salzburg. We'll give it a new paint job and bring it back to you in St. Wolfgang when it's done." He called in his men, pointed at two of them and said, "You two will drive the little truck. As soon as Herr Holder returns his flak vests and fatigues, we'll head for the *Kaserne* in Feldkirch for supper and overnight."

He turned to Lisa and Bruce and said, "I understand that you two will be joined in marriage tomorrow. It'll be at the chalet on the lake shore?"

"Yes," answered Lisa, holding Bruce's arm. "This has not been the usual day before a wedding. Nor will tomorrow be; we are driving part way to Salzburg now, we have reservations at the *Alte Posthotel* in St. Anton tonight. We'll go the rest of the way tomorrow morning."

Herr Brand asked, "Will it be a formal wedding with many people?"

"Not at all formal, Herr Brand," answered Elsa. "As mother of the bride, I have had very little to do. The wedding will be at four in the afternoon, in our chalet of the lake shore; light refreshments will be served after the ceremony. If, for any reason, you'd like to come, we would be delighted to have you."

He smiled and answered, "I'll be there. Weddings are happy times; I am returning to Salzburg tonight and I would dearly love to see where the gold was placed and where it was subsequently hidden."

Rudi, now wearing comfortable civilian clothes, said, "What are we waiting for? I would really like to sit in the back seat of something."

"So would I, Rudi," added Georgi, handing the army clothing and the body armor to the Major.

The spokesman for the bankers said, "Herr Brand, you'll be coming with us for the moment; we understand your car is in Feldkirch and we'll take you to it. If you wish, you may return the bonds to us for safekeeping. We assure you that they'll be available this coming Friday in Zurich, when we'll have a quiet signing ceremony and presentation. We'll be responsible for their safety until then and you can travel unencumbered."

Brand replied, "Gladly. Thank you very much. That would be very nice."

He turned to the Holders. "I'll see you tomorrow, then, in St. Wolfgang. I will have a wineglass and a napkin and I'll ask you, sir, "looking at Bruce, "to crush it under your heel in memory of the many marriages that never took place between the young people of my faith." He shook the men's hands and hugged the three ladies and departed with the bankers.

Lisa said, "Bruce, you drive one car and Robert, will you follow in the other? We'll go straight through the Alburg tunnel and then turn left and follow the way we came this morning. You'll recognize the *Alte Posthotel* – the old brown one next to the main road on the right-hand side, near the railroad station."

The major saluted the group and said, "This mission has been very enjoyable. I believe I have figured out what is in the box and I'll scoff at the rumors about the Nazi gold and tell the rumor-mongers that there is no such thing. We'll let you people depart first, as we'll be a bit slower."

Rudi shook his hand. "Don't scoff, Major. Who knows – there might be more somewhere."

* * * * *

1500 Tuesday, June 23, 1998
The lawn of the chalet on the shore of St. Wolfgangsee

The weather continued to cooperate for Bruce and Lisa's wedding. Warm and balmy; the guests could clearly see the details of the Zwölferhorn across the lake; light winds rippled the surface of the water. In the early part of the afternoon, Herr Brand had arrived for the festivities. Rudi, Peter and Georgi took him about a hundred meters offshore in a rowboat, where they sat and drifted for a long time. Nobody heard what they discussed; Elsa had noted that Rudi had his face in his hands some of the time. Knowing how emotional Rudi could be, she had suspected – correctly – that Rudi was re-living his entire life, beginning with the telling of the horror of the glassworks.

When they finally had come ashore, Elsa prodded Rudi.

"It's time for you to put on some decent clothes. Your only daughter is being married in an hour and you're dressed like a fisherman."

"I was dressed like a fisherman when I fell in love with you, *Liebste.*"

"Well, then, I fell in love with you before that – before you even knew I existed, silly man."

"*Ja,* sure, probably when you helped your mother give me my first bath," he had responded with a leer. She punched his arm, but couldn't suppress a grin.

"Maybe it was then; maybe it was when we were fishing." They'd hugged and he'd gone off to change his clothes.

Lattie had decided that since American convention couldn't be observed – there was no way that the bride and groom could avoid seeing each other before the wedding – that at least they wouldn't be in the same car together during the drive from St. Anton to St. Wolfgang. There was some objection to this.

"What if there's an accident and one of us dies?" Lisa pouted.

"So drive carefully, darlings," she'd advised. But she had prevailed and the couple had been separated for the uneventful three hour drive. Elsa had hustled Lisa into her bedroom and left her to begin her own preparations for the ceremony, assisted by Elaine.

In like manner, Robert had taken his younger brother by his arm and said, "Since I'm your best man, what I say goes for the next hour or so." Bruce hung his head and dutifully followed Robert's instructions.

At 2:45, there had been flurry of activity. Flowers were delivered; the caterer set up the tables for a buffet and laid out an impressive array of cheeses, meats, sweet rolls and an American-style wedding cake, complete with a little bride and groom with their feet in the frosting – this last, courtesy of Elaine, who had brought it from home. The caterer looked at it, shaking his head.

Guests began to arrive. There were not many; and most shared a common experience – they had come to Austria with Georgi. Otto and his wife Zelda, a glass-blower and cutter, respectively, from Lambach, now retired; Jenna, a glass blower and her husband Janosh, who brought a dozen beautiful wine glasses; Oskar, now a retired glass blower from Lambach and his son Thomas, with his wife; Anatole, now the owner of a jewelry shop in St. Wolfgang and his wife Sarah, who designed the gold wedding rings for Anatole to make for the couple. Bruce's ring incorporated his father's ring, which Lattie had given to Lisa. Last of the guests to arrive was Jamon, also a retired glass blower living in Lambach. The women all wore beautiful dirndls in the patterns of their adopted native towns; the bright colors rivaled that of the flowers in the gardens and the window boxes of the chalet.

Among the guests was the cleric from the St. Wolfgang church, who Rudi had promised to take fishing when the post-wedding party had more or less ended. The man had refused his usual fee if Rudi would show him one or two of his special places on the lake.

The mother and father of the groom walked slowly together to the front row of chairs and sat on the right-hand side. They were followed by Rudi and Elsa, who wore a beautiful dirndl, which had been her own mother's – and her grandmother's before that. The pattern and the style was that of the formal attire of the Salzkammergut in the early part of the 1900's.

There was no music except for a single melodious cuckoo

calling to his mate in the afternoon; it was the first thing Lisa heard as she came out the rear door onto the lawn and followed Elaine down the lawn, towards Bruce and Robert. She was dressed in a simple white frock – no hat, no veil to cover her radiance; a bouquet of wild flowers in her hands. Rudi turned to meet her, took her hand and the three of them stood before the cleric. At the proper time in the ceremony, he took Lisa's right hand and placed it in Bruce's left, shook Bruce's right hand and returned to Elsa.

The cleric opened his Bible, asked the questions, heard the answers and vows, all spoken softly but clearly; and made the pronouncement that joined the pair. He turned to Herr Brand.

"This gentleman has something unusual to add to this beautiful ceremony."

Brand stepped forward and withdrew a white napkin from his pocket.

He said, "This family has been especially kind to the people of my faith. In their honor and in the honor of those of my faith who have gone before us, I have asked the bride and groom to drink a toast to each other and then give me their glass. They'll perform an ancient Hebrew custom, always done with great joy at our weddings.

"I am told that the glass was made by two of the guests that are with us today – in honor of the Holder family. Every guest at this beautiful ceremony will receive one, as a special gift from the bride and her family. "

Lisa leaned towards Bruce. She whispered, "Surprise!"

Robert handed Brand a stemmed crystal glass; the white wine quivered as he lifted it so that the sun's rays fractured in its facets.

"Such exquisite work," he said.
He handed it to Lisa.

She said, "Bruce, I pledge to you that I will love you forever." She took a sip and handed the glass to Bruce, her eyes glowing.

He said, "Lisa, I pledge to you that I'll love you forever."

He drained the glass.
Brand took the glass from Bruce. Again, he held it to the

light. "So beautiful," he murmured. Carefully, he wrapped it in the napkin and placed it on the ground in front of Bruce..

Bruce slowly stepped on it with the heel of his right shoe. The crackling sound triggered a round of applause and shouts of acclamation as Bruce took Lisa in his arms and kissed her soundly.

The End

Acknowledgements

Why did I write this first novel?

First, we must accept the facts of the Holocaust.

From http://nazigold.greyfalcon.us/ we can learn the following – which is just a small portion of the information readily available about the "Nazi Gold:"
"It is no idle statement that when the Third Reich began to crumble in 1945, many German fanatics went about their task as advised by Hitler in December of 1944: the hiding of vast Nazi riches for future use by Fourth Reich posterity. The statement that the bulk of this huge treasure hoard came from concentration camp inmates seems to be a safe bet...that billions of dollars worth of jewelry, gold, and money was taken from the hapless Nazi victims is a gruesome, but true, fact of history.
"During the final days of World War II, German SS officers crammed trains, cars, and trucks full of gold, currency, and jewels, and headed for the mountains of Austria. Fearful of arrest and determined to keep the stolen loot out of Allied hands, they concealed their treasures and fled. Most of these men were eventually apprehended, but many managed to evade capture. The intensive postwar Allied investigation that followed recovered only a sliver of this mountain of gold. What happened to the rest of it, and what fate befell these men?"

Living in Austria, courtesy of the US Army in 1952 – 1954, and being reasonably fluent in German, one could hear many stories – sitting at a corner table in the evening, especially if you kept the beer coming. "My grandmother watched them wading chest deep, where one of them stood to mark the spot. They made many trips back and forth from the truck, carrying something heavy."
I was thinking about writing this story when a telephone conversation with an Austrian friend, who happens to be

quite active scuba diving in the local lakes, asked me to send a particular American item to him. "It's the new model of the Leatherman; it has an attachment loop for a lanyard. You know, if I drop it when I'm diving, it's gone forever." Impulsively, I asked him, "What are you doing? Looking for the Nazi gold?"

His excited response and un-characteristic forced laughter brought Shakespeare to mind: " . . . she protests too much, methinks."

Subsequent reflection made me wonder: "what would a person become if they found it? How would their life – and personality – change? It would not be like winning Megabucks, simply because of its origin . . ."

So – I invented Rudi, and I invented the story that follows. It is a work of fiction; its characters, their agendas, and their motivations are nothing more than the products of my over-active imagination. I've tried only to set them in environments that some of you may recognize.

My thanks to the Honorable Madeleine M. Kunin, Vermont's 77th Governor (1985 – 1991) and United States Ambassador to Switzerland from 1996 to 1999. Answering my questions about Switzerland's response to the World Jewish Congress and its negotiations with Swiss banks and the Swiss government which began in 1995 on behalf of various Jewish organizations concerning dormant Jewish World War II bank accounts, she gave me the insight on how to conclude the story.

And to editors Kay Garrett in Dallas: thank you for releasing me from the entrapment of adjectives, as well as to Gina Logan of Norwich University for stifling my verbosity. Steve Tuttle of TASER International advised me on the relative safety of the high voltages of Taser projectiles vs. explosive vests worn by people we encounter in the story . . .

Last, but by no means least, my thanks to my wife, Doris, for her for her enduring and long-suffering support, encouragement and understanding of my long hours at the keyboard.

Roger Damon   St. Johnsbury, Vermont
5/6/2014

www.ingramcontent.com/pod-product-compliance
Lightning Source LLC
Chambersburg PA
CBHW051519260626
47170CB00003B/691